FAREWELL ALEXANDRIA

*Forthcoming titles by the same author
published by Pharos Publications:*

Fiction

BEYOND THE WHITE WALLS a thriller set in modern day Egypt
  but harking back to the esoteric times of the Pyramid Age

OPERATION COPPER a suspense novel about kidnapping in
  France

The TIPPETI-TOO series, a fable in three parts for 'children' aged
  eight to eighty

MAURAG and THE SMOKEYS, two short stories

Non fiction

The SHORES OF WISDOM the story of the Ancient Library of
  Alexandria, the world's first great international culture centre.
  To be published in English and French.

Derek Adie Flower

FAREWELL
ALEXANDRIA

PHAROS PUBLICATIONS LTD
1997

Published by Pharos Publications Ltd
Kissack Court
29 Parliament Street
Ramsey
Isle of Man

ISBN 0-9530942-0-0

A catalogue record for this book is available from
the British Library

Typeset in New Century 11/13pt by
Scriptmate Editions
Manufacture coordinated in UK by
Book-in-Hand Ltd 20 Shepherds Hill
London N6 5AH

All the world's a stage,
and all the men and women merely players:
they have their exits and their entrances;
and one man in his time plays many parts,
his acts being seven ages.

William Shakespeare: As You Like It, Act II Scene VII

To
Frédérique and Merial
without whom this book would not have existed

Alexandria, August 1st, 1990

The yacht glided through the gentle swell, its engines throbbing in the silence like a powerful murmur.

On the top deck a man sat in a canvas chair and gazed towards Alexandria. A warm breeze caressed his skin, a breeze coming from the hot deserts to the West, from those immensities of sand which reached from the white beaches to the stifling heart of the Sahara.

It was 6.20 a.m., and the sun rising over the horizon framed the silhouette of a mosque in gold, while through the early morning haze appeared buildings which stretched for as far as the eye could see, grey against the brilliant pallor of the Egyptian dawn.

Like a gull sweeping across his vision, his mind winged back to the day he had first viewed the waterfront from afar. Over fifty years had passed, yet its magic still bewitched as it had ever since Alexander the Great had created the city port destined to eclipse all others.

He closed his eyes to fix in his mind the fleeting wonder of the moment, conscious that a brutal reality would shortly rend the spell. Alexandria was now a backwater, a forgotten city despite its four million inhabitants, a mongrel agglomeration of edifices which ill reflected the glory of its past.

He got up and went over to the railings, peering at the approaching mainland. He reached for his binoculars and suddenly the outlines of Mohammed Ali's palace at Ras el Tin bounced into focus. His gaze swept eastwards, past Quoit Bey fort, dominating the Pleasure Harbour, and along the thirty kilometres of apartment blocks, villas and hotels which crowded the Corniche, to the distant Montaza palace once the King's summer residence. How the coastline had changed since the famous motorway along the sea had been built, skirting the bays which had been the playgrounds of the rich Alexandrians for nearly a century. Stanley Bay, the Spouting Rock, Glymonopoulos Beach, Sidi Bishr, Mandara ...

He looked westwards, beyond the main harbour and docks, past the shabby suburbs of Mex and Dakhaila sheltering in the sweep of the great bay, to the old fort at Agami where the white sands began. Agami. What a flood of memories that name conjured, making his heart beat a shade faster. Agami had signified Marguerite, for it was there that their bodies had first touched, evoking the passion which had fashioned his destiny.

He drew a deep breath. Could six decades have passed since the thrill of those happy days? Happy? Yes, they had been the moments of his life not tinged with loneliness; bright moments of hope, of awakening passion and exchanged love.

He focused again on the uninterrupted clutter of bricks and concrete now smothering the former holiday homes which had nestled in the dunes amongst the fig trees and palm groves. He shook his head. Elegance had long disappeared from Alexandria; half a century and an extra three million inhabitants had seen to that.

The yacht changed direction, turning due south, and Julius glanced at his watch. They would be there in ten minutes, he reckoned as the smell of the city wafted over the waters, bringing memories of his early childhood in the Arab quarter where the acrid stench of sweat and donkey dung mixed with the pungent odours from itinerant kitchens cooking *kefta*, fried fish and *foul medammis*, the spiced brown beans. It was the Alexandria of his youth which was beckoning him, where he had grown-up then abandoned once Marguerite had gone.

The engines' throbs became a purr as the yacht crept past the massive fort, squatting like a toad at the entrance to the Eastern Harbour, right where the great Lighthouse had once stood, and he could hear clearly the background bustle and the metallic cry of a muezzin calling the faithful to prayer through a faulty loudspeaker. And a moment of nostalgia made him aware that a part of him had remained chained to Alexandria.

Yet why had he come back, he asked himself?

Three weeks earlier, closeted with the secretary of State, the reason had seemed clear. He knew Egypt and the Middle East better than anyone in the political and business worlds of his adoptive country. His experience of the zone's complicated affairs was invaluable, and his friendship with the leaders of certain countries, and especially with Egypt's

Presidents, had made him an unofficial mediator in the multiple problems and conflicts which had beset the area over the past twenty years. The fratricidal fighting in the Lebanon, the plight of the Palestinian refugees, the safeguarding and recognition of Israel, the war between Iraq and Iran, the genocide of the Kurds, and now the threat from the ruthless Baathist junta in Baghdad bent on grabbing the oil rich but vulnerable states of the Persian Gulf.

He had warned Washington that Saddam Hussein was ready to pounce on Kuwait in a matter of days, even hours, and ostensibly that was why he was back, to be on the spot when the simmering cauldron boiled over. To see how the worst could be avoided, to lend his influence and energies to finding an improbable yet essential solution to the never ending conflicts in an area which was one of the world's epicentres of religious, economic and ethnic contentions.

But now that he was here in Alexandria, on his eightieth birthday, could he honestly say that the visit had been dictated solely by a desire to serve his country and further the efforts made for a lasting peace? Wasn't there a more personal reason? To measure himself with the ghosts of the city and prove that he was bigger?

A steward appeared with a cup of strong, sweetened tea.

"Will you be needing anything, sir?" he asked before retiring.

Julius sipped the tea. "Yes. Find Major Salvini and tell him I would like to see him in the study in ten minutes."

He watched a sailing boat tacking in the harbour centre until his thoughts were interrupted by the rumble of anchor chains, and he looked at the eastern causeway leading to the Corniche. A couple of kilometres from where they joined, in an area which once had been a haven of gardens and select mansions, was his house. He had not visited it in thirty years but he knew it would be as he had last seen it, an oasis of elegance in a crumbling slum.

He smiled as he thought back to the first time he had gone there, a presumptuous bank clerk with the nerve to imagine he could love and marry the owner's daughter. The smile faded. How empty his life had been without Marguerite. Why had he allowed her father and mother to eradicate love from his system? He had never got over the injustice of their action. It had cost him not only Marguerite, but a son he could have loved and cared for as his parents had for him. He pursed

9

his lips. What would Marguerite have said if she could have seen George now?

Yet fate had not always been unkind to him. It had hoisted him to a position in the world far above average men and those seemingly powerful beings who had trampled his happiness into this city's dust. And if he had no son, he had a grandson. Yes, a youngster who bore his name and in whose veins ran his blood, even if not Marguerite's.

He frowned. There was something about young A.J. which still worried him, a streak in his make-up he could not understand. Had it been a mistake to take him aboard the yacht and hide him from both the international terrorists and Interpol? He had been a revolutionary, a terrorist even, with a price on his head, but he had repented. Yet had he really, or did he believe he had because he was Maryanne's son, because he wanted to be able to love and protect a grandson, he who had not been able to cherish his own son?

He would have a word with Laurrie and make sure a close watch was kept on A.J. Today especially.

He walked down to the lower deck and along to his study where a man was waiting for him. He was medium sized, robust but with a romantic face, delicate features which belied the strength of the body, and eyes which were dark blue and penetrating.

He clicked his heels and saluted militarily. "Morning sir."

Julius went over to him and put a hand on his arm. "Good morning Laurrie. Please sit down. I presume everything is under control for today?"

He gazed at him with affection. If only his son or grandson could have been like him. Lorenzo Salvini was true to his name and bloodline, honest to the core, loyal and dependable. Don Francesco, his uncle and Julius' lifetime friend, had been like that, as was Pietro, his father, and Clara his aunt, 'little Clara' as they used to call her, whom Julius had always considered a sister.

"Yes, *Padrino*." Major Salvini smiled. Julius was indeed his godfather and in private he used the term with a touch of humour, as Julius was well aware. Through respect he stubbornly refused to call him by his christian name, and to address him as Mr Caspar was something he knew Julius would not tolerate from a member of the family he judged more his than the son he had sired and the grandson his daughter had given him.

"I'd like you to send two of your men to meet Maryanne and the others at the airport."

"I've arranged for Mercier and Reynolds to go. And the Governor of Alexandria will be there personally to welcome them. Of course I'm having the yacht searched from top to bottom even before the Egyptian Security men do their job. So you needn't worry, by the time we've finished it should the safest place in Egypt for the President."

Julius nodded slowly. "As for A.J., I would like him off duty from midday onwards so that he can be with his mother and feel that he's part of the family ... "

"Sure, I've detailed him to look after George, he's good at that."

"What do you think about him?"

"Well, there's been nothing suspicious in his behaviour, and it's possible he's going straight for the moment. But to tell you the truth, I don't trust him, whatever the appearances."

"I know what you mean, even if I'm beginning to give him the benefit of the doubt. But maybe that's because I'm becoming stupidly sentimental ... keep an eye on him, this evening especially."

He stood up and walked over to the window, and for a moment gazed silently out at the waterfront. Then he asked, "ever been to Alexandria?"

"No, but my father has described it in such detail I guess I could make my way around blindfolded."

Julius smiled. "You wouldn't be missing much if you did. Looking at it now it's hard to believe that it was once a city of beauty and elegance, and for five hundred years the most enlightened centre of Hellenic, Jewish and Christian thought in the world. But after its destruction by Arab conquerors in the 7th. century, it slithered into oblivion till Mohammed Ali put it back on the map. However in the last two or three decades laziness, mediocrity and dust seem to be the destructive forces ... you should have seen it when I was a lad, a great flourishing port renown for the sparkle and style of it's fashionable clique, millionaires of every nationality leading lives of princes. Then after world War II Alexandria fell asleep and never woke up again. Yet curiously, dozing away, shabby and forgotten it still manages to cast a spell on one."

"Enough to make you want to come back to it?"

"No, though I'm glad to be here for this occasion. You see, unlike your father, I was born here; born an Alexandrian, and that is a fact which nothing can change. A little part of me has stayed rooted here even if I feel American from head to toe. And possibly when I die I'll be buried here in the little cemetery where my father and mother rest ... "

He broke off as a fleeting apprehension gripped him, and instinctively his fingers went to the silver cross beneath his shirt. Why this sudden anguish, he wondered, why the presentiment of impending peril? Was this city where he had experienced humiliation, despair and near death responsible? Was it like the siren Circe bewitchingly calling him to rest?

No, his time had not come yet. He still had so much to offer and accomplish. Today might mark the fact that he was an old man, but he felt as robust and determined as the brawny youth who had plunged into these very waters and swum in the August heat of sixty summers ago.

"I'm going for a swim," he said turning abruptly. "Tell A.J. to join me at the pool. I want to speak to him."

"Yessir!" The major jumped to his feet and strode to open the door.

Julius nodded him his thanks and added, "if you like, tomorrow I'll take you to see the place where your father, your uncle and your aunt lived. We'll all go. They were hard times but happy ones. It was there that our great adventure began. And if it's still standing I'll show you the building where I was born ... "

In a cabin two decks below his grandson lay on a bunk and stared at the ceiling. If only Najla had been there to share this day with him, he thought. Then he frowned. Najla had paid with her life because of some fucking slip-up. Or had there been a tip-off?

He sat up abruptly. There would be no mistakes this time, and no chance of any double-dealing. The evening's events depended on him and no one else. He stretched, yawned, then glanced at his watch. 6.15 a.m. That gave him another 25 minutes before he had to be in the canteen for breakfast. His lips drew into a grin. It would be his last breakfast there and the last time he'd have to take any goddam orders from anyone. This time tomorrow he'd be free. The excitement surged in him spurring him off the bunk.

Christ! Life was going to be great without those bastards buggering it up for him. Specially that sonofabitch Laurrie, who reckoned he stood on the right hand of God Almighty.

The cabin door was thrown open and a face peered in.

"Get a move on, if you want breakfast. The major wants us ready at 6.45."

He gripped the edge of the basin to control a sudden rage and choked back a 'fuck the major' on the tip of his tongue. "O.K.," he muttered through clenched teeth. Just a few hours more, he thought savagely, just one more bloody day ...

As he dried his face he looked out of the porthole. So this was Alexandria! This crappy mass of shitty old buildings no different to other Middle Eastern towns, and God knew he'd seen enough of them. Tripoli, Tunis, Beirut, Algiers, Amman, Baghdad ... arseholes with only one redeeming feature, their lurking violence. Controlled in some and open in others, but there all right; simmering and ready to explode the moment the ring leaders decided.

He grabbed his electric razor and began passing it over his jowl. What the hell, he thought staring at his reflection, tomorrow he'd grow a beard again and throw the damned thing away. And one thing was certain, he wouldn't stay this side of the Med. Not even this side of the Atlantic. Sure, he'd go first to New York and deal with that Zionist swine who'd married his mother ... pity he wasn't going to be on the yacht this evening ... no, just as well he wasn't, or his mother would be too, and that was the last thing he wanted.

He reached for a photo of her. "Don't worry, Mom," he muttered, "when it's all over I'll look after you. I'll make sure no one ever harms you. You'll see, I'll make up for all these years I've had to be away ... you'll understand Mom ... "

Then he pulled on a pair of jeans and a T-shirt and flattened his hair with his palms. He let himself out of the cabin, sprinted up a companionway to the principal cabin deck and ran silently to a door at the end.

It was ajar so he could see inside. George was sitting in the wheelchair staring straight at him. He slid out of view. Everything was going according to plan. Tom would wheel George along to the massage pool, and for a couple of hours the chair would be safely out of the cabin while security searches were being made. To think that that innocuous looking contraption hid the centrepiece of the operation!

He smirked. Not one of the stupid bastards had the vaguest suspicion that their fate was hinged under George's fat bum.

He turned and made his way down to the crew's canteen. He was hungry. He always was when something exciting and dangerous was about to happen.

ANTOR

Alexandria, August, 1910

Joseph Caspardian climbed the stairs to the fifth floor landing
and paused to get his breath back. He was a heavy man in
his early forties with a bird-like head perched on massive
shoulders. His black hair was sparse and streaked with grey,
and the face furrowed with lines of fatigue. He leant his crutch
against the wall and fished in his trouser pocket for a
handkerchief which he passed around his neck and over his
forehead. Then he fanned himself with it until a moan had
him hobble hurriedly to a door on his right. As he fumbled
with the key the moan ceased and an airless silence enveloped
the building again; a silence punctuated with an occasional
creak or distant cough, muted and contained in the afternoon's
swelter.

He stood for a moment on the threshold, staring blankly
at the familiar room. The air moved slightly as he closed the
door then wrapped him in its clammy heat. He could hear
the murmur of voices in the bedroom, a low and uninterrupted
chant. Suddenly came the scream, cutting at his nerves like
a scalpel. He bit his lower lip and shut his eyes as the scream
turned into a groan then into a gut gripping moan. There
was another brief shriek followed by an interminable silence.
Clasping his hands together he prayed to the Virgin Mary,
beseeching Her to help Anna. Tears formed in his eyes,
blurring his vision, till the baby's cry, plaintive and
demanding, eased the muscles in his body. He crossed himself
twice, whispering his gratitude to the Madonna, then wiped
his brow with his sleeve.

His child was born! Finally, after all those years of hoping,
the miracle had happened. He stared at the bedroom door,
wishing he could wrench it open to see and touch this baby
of his. See, touch and kiss his beloved Anna too, but he knew

he must not. He must wait till Hosina the midwife, called him. What was happening there was women's business and he must not interfere.

He limped over to the window and glanced down at the empty street. Later he would go to the shop where he had seen the small silver cross, the one he had promised Anna. He wished he could have bought it that morning and been able to give it to her now, but she would understand. She would know he had not forgotten, only that he had not had time.

There was a movement behind him and he turned. Hosina was in the doorway, smiling and beckoning him.

"It's a boy, *howager*, come. You have a big fat baby son."

The christening took place in the church where Joseph and Anna had been married twelve years earlier and Antor Giulio cried throughout the ceremony, a healthy omen, Joseph declared proudly at the little celebration afterwards.

"Mark my words," he said to Leo Stavrapoulos, his neighbour on the fourth floor landing, "my boy will go places. Further than any of us here can imagine. He'll be clever and he'll be rich. I can see it in his eyes. Isn't he the finest baby you've ever seen?"

Leo nodded enthusiastically and clinked his glass with Joseph's. Sure he was a fine baby; sure he'd go places. One only had to look at him to know that.

That night, with Anna nestling in his arms and baby Antor in his crib at the end of the bed, Joseph spoke of his hopes.

Antor would have a different life. He would work with his brain and not his hands as he, Joseph, had been forced to. He would not be a manual labourer, not a carpenter working the flesh off his fingers for fifteen hours a day. He would be a gentleman as his grandfather had been, and generations of Caspardians before him, until the Turks had forced the family to flee their lands and possessions and become penniless immigrants. Once the name of Caspardian had meant something. Once the men had been held in esteem and their wives waited upon. Not like he and Anna. Poor Anna! If only he could make more money and afford the help of a servant, even for a few hours a day. How would she cope now that there was the baby to look after also?

Anna pressed his hand in the dark. She didn't need a

servant; they were more trouble than they were worth. And as for Antor, he would become what the Lord wanted. They would make sure he grew into a good and dutiful son, and the Lord in Heaven would decide whether he would be rich and clever.

She fingered the little cross Joseph had given her. What was the use of planning, she thought, when God only knew what the future held for them all. But of one thing she was certain, her boy would take care of her when she would be old and tired. He would be there to look after his father too, for in twenty years Joseph would be an old man. She shivered slightly. Poor Joseph, how the accident had aged him. Yet he never complained, trailing his truncated foot as if it were a temporary disablement which time would remedy. She kissed him gently and laid a finger on his lips.

"Shhh, you must sleep," she whispered. "We will pray God that He will look after our son and make him into the man you want."

Yes, he'd be strong, that son of hers, and love his parents and fear God. What more could a mother ask?

He was a sturdy baby with calm brown eyes and a happy gurgle. He ate and slept well and Anna marvelled at the ease with which he was growing. Then one evening when he was six months old he began to cry, and that night he started coughing, a pathetic, heart-rending whooping cough which convulsed his little body.

For seventy-two interminable hours she watched him weaken and thin with the fever as she sponged his tiny forehead and changed his bedclothes, only leaving his side to catch snippets of sleep in a nearby chair. And throughout she prayed, never giving up hope, strong in her faith in the Virgin and Her compassion.

Four days after it had started, the fever abated and the ordeal was over. That night she brought the cot back into their bedroom and slipped into the sheets next to Joseph.

"Oh Joseph," she murmured, "the Virgin took pity on us. She heard our prayers and now our baby is out of danger. We must forever be grateful as we are the most fortunate of parents. Now we must pray that he gets well quickly."

Anna had not needed a doctor to tell her that Antor required all the care a mother could give to nurse him back to health.

And though he never regained the chubbiness of his early months, he grew into a healthy little boy with his mother's big eyes and his father's nose.

He was a quiet child, happy to play on his own while Anna did the household chores, or sit on Joseph's knees listening to his parent's chatter. Yet, despite his docility Anna thought she detected flashes of fire in his brown eyes. Not of rebellion, but of a smouldering inner intensity. Perhaps Joseph had been right when he had said that the boy would be intelligent. Maybe he would 'go places' and lead a life very different from theirs.

Not that there was anything dishonourable about the way they lived. They were poor even if Joseph was earning more now and had moved them into a bigger apartment near the harbour. But they owed no money and had to account to no one save God for what they did. What more could one want of life, she asked herself? Yes, a little more leisure for Joseph. He worked so hard. And perhaps a new dress for herself to replace the brown one which had worn thin with the years. And, of course, a good school for Antor who was now five.

It was a matter to which Joseph had given a lot of thought.

"I'll send him to the Lycée Français," he confided to Leo, "he's clever and will learn fast."

Yet how would he pay for the school books, and the special French lessons Antor would need to get accepted? Over the past four years he had been able to put a little money aside but it would need a lot more to educate his son the way he wanted. Also, the new apartment had meant new furniture, some of which he still had to buy, and he didn't want to indebt himself with money lenders. He thought too of sending him to the Liceo Francesco Crespi which cost very little, but Anna would not hear of it.

"It's run by a whole lot of unbelievers. Antor must go to a Catholic school and be brought up as a good Christian, just as you were. And the liceo is too far away, at least half an hour by tram ... "

So Antor went to Don Bosco's where his father had gone. It was run by Salesian priests whose order was founded by St John Bosco, and whose mission was to provide a pragmatic education for children of the Italian working classes. They did also cater for those of middle class backgrounds, the sons of former pupils who had been successful in their trades, but these got their schooling in separate classrooms, and a social distinction had developed between these 'scholars' and the 'artisans' as they were called. Joseph was conscious of this and, as he accompanied his son into the bleak looking building in Rue Khedive el Awal, he swore to himself that as soon as he could afford to, he would transfer Antor to the 'scholars' section.

That first year at school was tough for Antor. The 'artisans' were a rough lot and, though no sissy, he was put out by their crudeness. There was not one he wanted as a friend and several of the older were downright aggressive with him. Perhaps because he was not Italian they singled him out for the hardest throws at *'palla avvelenata'* a favourite game where teams flung wooden balls at each other, whoever was hit being penalized. But the cuts and bruises did not stop him learning, and a year later he was fluent in Italian and already a proficient little carpenter.

At Christmas he brought home a bookshelf fashioned and put together all on his own and without nails or screws. Joseph proudly showed it to his friends saying that he could not have made it better himself.

It was a happy family Christmas that one of 1918. The war was over and an atmosphere of extravagance had gripped the city. And luck, for once, had come Joseph's way.

A Frenchman for whom he had made a desk commissioned 16 window frames and 12 doors for a house he was having built. It was the first order of its kind and marked Joseph's transformation from simple carpenter to mini-industrialist. It also meant that Antor put away his artisan's' black overall and went to a classroom instead of a workshop.

Until he was sixteen, Don Bosco became his second home for eight months a year. His quick intelligence and eagerness to learn made him a favourite with teachers, and with one especially who was to have a particular influence on him.

He was a man in his late forties with twinkling deepset eyes and a smile never far from his lips. During recreation he would gather a few boys around him and talk about subjects which were not on the school curriculums, recounting the wonders of ancient Egypt and the origins of Alexandria. He told too of the exploits of men like Stanley and Livingstone and explained the greatness of Abraham Lincoln and of Benjamin Franklin.

"They were men of courage and determination. But more, they had a heart. Always put your heart into what you're doing, *ragazzi miei,* and with faith in God you will stride along the path He has set you. Remember, no man is great unless he lives with his heart. History is peopled with powerful men but few were great. Strength without love is like a giant with feet of clay. Inevitably it will wither and perish."

Don Michele would tap his chest with his index finger. "Your hearts, you must feel them beating and put them behind everything you do."

The Alexandria of the early nineteen twenties did not consider itself an integral part of Egypt, at least not the people who made it 'tick'. They were the French, the Greeks, the Italians, the Turks, the Jews, the Armenians, the Swiss and the British who owned the rich trading houses responsible for the wealth and sparkle of the great city-port. They, along with a handful of powerful landed Egyptians, effectively governed Alexandria, just as the British, through the *Khedive* and a sympathetic cabinet, ruled Egypt. Yet an underlying Egyptian nationalist sentiment did exist there as in the rest of the country, and was the cause of sporadic outbursts of mob violence. One such exploded on March 9th. 1919, the day after the popular nationalist leader, Saad Zagloul, was packed off to prison in Malta. Starting in the provinces, the rioting rapidly spread to Cairo and Alexandria, where crowds of *fellaheen,* the usually docile peasants, stormed through the cities screaming and pillaging, urged on by terrorist agitators.

Antor was returning from school by tram when a frenzied mob suddenly surged down the street, smashing out at cars, carriages, carts and shop windows, and beating up anyone who looked European. It swept over the tram, knocking the conductor from his seat, and shouting at the occupants. All happened so fast that Antor had not even the time to jump off and run to the safety of a side street.

Trapped in the tram, he witnessed the savage brutality of which a maddened mob was capable, and he was not to forget it for the rest of his life.

Two seats away, an elderly Jew, conspicuous by his side curls and broad rimmed hat, shook his fist at a rioter. The next moment five men went for him, pushed him through an open window and hurled invectives at him as he fell, bleeding, to the road, to be further kicked and beaten by those outside.

With the rioters now bent on finding Europeans to attack, a large woman seated next to Antor stood up suddenly and shoved her baby at him. Her voluminous black dress billowed out as she gesticulated at the men, luckily concealing him and the baby. That was what saved him.

Shots were then heard and the mob dispersed, chased by a lorryload of soldiers who were hitting them with truncheons while firing over their heads. Antor scrambled out of the tram and was about to run off, when he saw the old man lying in the gutter. His clothes were torn and covered with blood and his head was smeared with donkey dung. He was groaning feebly.

Antor rushed over to a doorman who had regained his seat outside the entrance to a block of apartments.

"Quick," he shouted, pulling at his *gallabeya* sleeve, "that man, he's badly hurt. You must help him."

The boab freed himself with a curse, then glanced at the prostrate form. "Howa yehudi," *(He's a Jew)* he growled and, shrugging his shoulders, spat and looked the other way. Then the groaning stopped.

Antor had never seen a dead man but instinctively knew he had one in front of him now. For a moment he crouched by him wondering what he should do, then remembered that his mother would be waiting for him, terrified probably that he too might have been attacked. He stood up, turned slowly away, shaken by the sudden knowledge that a friendly people could do such an appalling thing to an old man simply because he wasn't one of them. Why, he kept asking himself as he ran home, why?

A few days later when he walked with his mother by the spot where it had happened, he cried, "he was there, just behind that cart."

Anna crossed herself and took his hand.

"It's the will of the Lord, Antor. We must pray that his soul will rest in peace, poor man."

He had not been frightened by what he had seen, just as he was not scared when the rioters rushed at the tram. He was bewildered, stunned because neither his father nor his mother had been able to explain why the man had been killed.

They accepted it as an inevitable part of life. He, not yet in his teens, could not.

The experience troubled him for a long time, but it also taught him a fundamental lesson; that men could be very different from what they appeared, especially when a crowd. That, he was not to forget.

One summer, when he was thirteen, hair began to sprout on his chest and his voice broke. By the autumn it was low pitched and raspish.

He had grown into a strapping youth with his father's broad shoulders and measured a metre and eighty five centimetres, a good head taller than any previous Caspardian. The dark haired Armenians from whom he descended had been muscular but short and Joseph wondered who could have been responsible for the unusual height. Anna with her Maltese father and Sicilian mother could not claim the credit and simply saw it as a mark of God's favour. He had wanted him as big and strong physically as he was morally, and every day she sank to her knees and thanked Him for the son He had given her. Yet she too had her part in his being so fit and healthy, she would mutter to herself.

Had she not prepared for him the wholesome meals on which his body had thrived? Had she not walked every morning to the vegetable market for fresh tomatoes and beans, *courgettes* and *bamya* stopping at the fruit stalls to choose the ripest apricots and figs, then calling on the way back at Mustapha's for an earthenware pot of yoghurt? And who had made the twice weekly tram trips to Dakheila for fish from the fishermen's nets rather than from the market near the harbour where, by noon, the stench gripped one's stomach? She had kept chickens on the roof for fresh eggs and even rabbits grown fat for the Sunday stew in winter. She had spared no effort to ensure that her son had the best food their meagre resources would allow. So, if he was big and healthy some of the merit was hers, and if he was serious minded and obliging, again she was partly responsible, as was Joseph.

Yes, he had been a good father to the boy, teaching him to look after himself and to respect others without being submissive, coaching him the rudiments of boxing so that he could assert his rights if the occasion presented itself. And despite his mangled foot, he had taught him to swim on the

Sunday afternoons when they went for a picnic at Stanley Bay after mass, and watched the smart crowds sunbathing by their terraced cabins while the three of them sat on the rocks by the water's edge and were cooled by the spray from the waves.

For a while she had feared that the physical change in Antor would affect his character as it did in so many boys. But her worries were without foundation.

The months became years and Antor did not change, at least not in the way she had apprehended. He was not influenced by youngsters of his age and showed no resentment to parental authority as so many did. He was curiously detached from his school companions and never went off with any of them for games or, when he grew older, to the cinema. He had only one friend, Francesco, who was two years older and lived a quarter of an hour away.

Anna liked Francesco and often suggested that Antor ask him round on Thursday afternoons, but he rarely came and she never understood whether it was because her son did not ask him or because he had some reason for not wanting to.

"He has to catch up on his homework," Antor would explain. "Maybe he'll come during the holidays, Mother."

It was only later that she discovered the reason. Francesco's father was an invalid and his mother was dead. An elderly aunt came to cook the evening meal and put his young brother and sister to bed, but everything else he did. While other boys were playing or relaxing with their parents, he cleaned their three rooms, did the shopping and washed his father before getting down to his homework.

Francesco was strongly religious, as Anna gathered the few times she saw him, and as such his friendship for Antor could only be beneficial, she decided. She was right, but only partly. His difficulties, accepted with unshakable religious faith, had a curious effect on his young friend. They developed in Antor a determination never to know poverty like Francesco's and a considerable doubt as to God's bounties to His more faithful servants.

Why were good and deserving people punished the way Francesco's family was? Why did he have a happy home and not his friend? Why were some born rich and others fettered to tragic poverty? These were questions which troubled him but which he did not discuss with Francesco for fear of

23

offending him, nor with his parents as he knew it would shock them. Also because he was developing an inner certainty that only those who helped themselves could survive. How could he discuss this with a mother who was steeped to the roots of her greying hair in religion, and considered God a far off relation who somehow would help if one threw oneself humbly on His mercy? His father couldn't answer him, nor could Don Michele for all his wisdom and understanding. Only time and experience would solve the disturbing questions, he decided.

So he kept his thoughts to himself and worked as hard as he could, pleasing his parents and his teachers and giving the image of a responsible, God fearing adolescent. But inside him burned a rebellious fire. Not against his father or mother or the masters at Don Bosco's, but against a so-called Divine Justice.

At the early age of 14 Antor knew that justice was not of this world. God was not interested in it. It was man created and man dispensed and if one wanted to survive, one had to be equal to those who dealt it. Somehow, he swore to himself, he would be one of them.

He left school in 1927. He was not yet 17 but his intellectual capacities were such that the headmaster, Don Mazzoni, considered him ripe for an academic career in the framework of the great Don Bosco organization at Turin.

"It is not often one comes across a boy as gifted and dedicated to work as your son," he confided to Joseph. "Let me send him to Italy where our Institution will take care of him. There he can continue his studies and get the degrees which will open to him the rich and rewarding world of the soul and the intellect. Antor possesses unusual qualities which would be wasted in some mediocre occupation. He is destined for a special calling."

To Don Mazzoni's disappointment Antor had no wish to go to Turin. He wanted to stay in Alexandria and get a job. Joseph and Anna were secretly delighted. He was their only son and the idea that he might leave them had filled his mother with dismay.

"He is wise, our son," she cried when he told them of his decision. "This is his home and this is where he belongs. He was never meant for an academic career whatever Don Mazzoni may think. Believe me, he will surprise not a few people in the years to come." Anna, with her mother's instinct, had sensed the ambition in him.

Don Mazzoni had a certain authority among the city's merchants. For over 20 years he had been headmaster of Don Bosco and there were quite a few prosperous businessmen who had been pupils of his. One of these, Luciano Bogdadli, was manager of the Ford motor car agency and had friends in all the leading cotton and shipping companies owned by rich Greeks from Smyrna, influential members of the Jewish community or old established British families, like the Choremis, the Christofides, the Toriels, Barkers and Finneys. Don Mazzoni talked to Bogdadli who had a word with Leon Behara, manager of the Christofides Shipping Agency where, on July 3rd, just two weeks after leaving school, Antor began his job as assistant to the accountant.

For three months he received no salary but learnt what he was expected to do, checking bills of lading, preparing customs documents and making interminable entries in huge ledger books. He also found himself being dogsbody to the Christofides women and to Roger, the Chairman's 17 year old son.

To begin with he got instructions from Leon Behara. "Madame Christofides' dressmaker needs paying. Check the bill she brings and make sure it's initialled by Madame, then come to me for the money." Or, "go through these accounts from the Nile Cold Storage Co. and check that the totals are correct."

As the family got to know him, though, the requests came direct. Madame Christofides phrased hers graciously, always thanking him for what he did. Her daughter Helen was polite but thoughtless, disturbing him for a whim, while Roger was downright unpleasant, ordering him about as if he were one of the servants. "Hey, you over there," he would shout, "go to the Rialto cinema and get me a box for the 6.30 show. And I want a centre one." Or again, "get me a bottle of beer." Antor would pick up the piastres thrown at him and answer with an inevitable "Yes, Mr Roger," and, controlling his anger, go off to do what he was bid.

His trial period over he began receiving a salary. Three pounds and twenty piastres a month. It was not much, even for the standards of the time, but it was a beginning. And when Leon Behara called him into his office and handed him the money, Antor felt a tickle of excitement along his spine. At last he too was a breadwinner.

Back at home he went straight to the drawer where his mother kept her housekeeping cash and placed three pounds in it. One day, he swore to himself, he would put ten times that amount and he would see to it that neither his mother nor his father would ever have to worry about money again.

He stayed for three years at the Shipping Agency, acting as assistant not only to the accountant but also to the freight manager and to the man in charge of the insurance department. He learnt a lot and fast, getting familiar with the intricacies of the shipping business and marine insurance. Then came an offer to work as a shipping clerk at Picciotti's, one of the leading cotton exporters.

He enjoyed his work there. The hours were long but the pay good. Fourteen pounds a month and no one gave him orders; they asked him to do things. Even the manager was quietly polite sensing perhaps the strength of character behind his youthful looks.

He was 20 now and his personality had affirmed itself, giving him an air of purposeful competence. He was liked even though no one could get close to him, as if friendship was a luxury for which he had no time. Indeed, he had few leisure hours to himself. Work commenced at 7.30, which meant leaving the apartment not later than 7 o'clock since he walked to the office. There was a break from 1 to 3 p.m. but he never went home for lunch, preferring to spend an hour at a nearby gymnasium or practising his boxing. In the summer months, when the offices worked through to 3.30, closing for the afternoon, he would take a tram to the Eastern Harbour, walk out along the sea wall and let himself down onto the concrete boulders. He would have a swim then settle in the shade and study until it was time to go home.

If Antor had no time or inclination to cultivate friendships, this applied to women as well as men. He was still a virgin and had not dated a girl in his life. Dating meant courting, and courting was a very definite prelude to marriage. There were plenty of cheap brothels at an easy distance from where he worked, but not once had the thought crossed his mind to venture into one. Though normally constituted and with a strong vitality, the sexual urge in him had been harnessed and transformed into a dynamism which found outlet in his swimming and boxing, as well as in the concentration he applied to his work. He was perfectly aware that he was an exception where sex was concerned, and that most men of his age had a good five or six years of experience behind them. But it didn't preoccupy him; the time would come when the right partner would present herself and until then it was a matter he purposely put from his mind.

His first year of work at Picciotti's coincided with the financial chaos which shook the American and subsequently the European markets as a result of the Wall Street crash during the bleak week of October in 1929.

The company felt the repercussion, involved as it was in the export of cotton to industries hit by strikes and liquidity problems, but its clients were far flung enough for it not to be seriously affected.

The situation, though, was one which preoccupied all the responsible staff, and Antor was constantly being drawn into coffee time discussions as to the reasons of the crisis and the flaws in the American and European capitalist systems which had led to it. Umberto Picciotti, the youngest of the four brothers who owned the company, and its financial director, often dropped into the general office where Antor and six department managers worked. He would perch on a desk and, clutching a newspaper, would begin:

"Have you read this? It's crazy! How could grown-up, sensible men have allowed it to happen."

Umberto had spent two years in San Francisco at the Bank of America and a further seven months in New York with a shipping firm. His opinions were listened to with respect for he was the only man there who had visited the USA and had first hand experience of banks and finance houses.

Antor listened and asked the odd question. Umberto was talking about a world totally foreign to him, a vast and fascinating realm where money ruled absolute, creating and destroying empires. More than the wherewithal to buy life's necessities and luxuries, it was a power in itself with little in common with the money which circulated in and out of pockets, shop tills and bank accounts, and he wanted to learn more about it.

He set about reading all he could on the principles which

governed world economics. One of the books, Keyne's 'Monetary Reform' had been translated into Italian a few years earlier by Piero Straffa, and it became his favourite. He also studied the works of Ricardo, Smith and Marx, but soon realized that without practical experience their theories were likely to remain abstract notions for him, subjects about which to argue and debate, but not of any pragmatic use. So he decided to get a job with a bank.

He knew that it would not be difficult to be taken on at the Ottoman Bank where his father had an account. With his references and knowledge of languages — apart from Arabic and Italian he now had a smattering of English enough to make himself understood, and could converse fairly fluently in French — they would employ him any time. But from what Umberto Picciotti said, he would be better at a private bank, like the one owned by the Zekla family. The Picciottis were understanding about his wanting to leave, and gave him an introduction to Raymond Zekla with whom Umberto played golf.

The Zeklas were Turkish Jews from Smyrna, who had settled in Egypt in 1878. They had been money lenders for generations, until Moses and Nahum Zekla had founded the family bank in Egypt in 1885. Forty years later, their sons, Raymond and Emile were bankers to the leading firms and cosmopolitan rich of Alexandria. They were respected and sought after socially, Raymond especially, a man of culture and charm whose home was the weekly meeting place of intellectuals, and especially of bibliophiles, as books were his passion.

Forming part of this coterie were George and Helen Wirsa, who lived in a vast house near Rond Point, the elegant residential area to the south of Route d'Aboukir known as Moharrem Bey. George was a millionaire landowner and one of the leaders of the Alexandrian Coptic community. His hobby was collecting rare books and manuscripts, and the library at his home housed a remarkable collection.

He was also an important client of the Banque Zekla, and one morning his signature was required for a transaction. Rather than drive out personally to his friend's house, browse for an hour amongst his books and discuss his latest acquisitions, Raymond, who was busy, decided to send Antor.

He had been in on the negotiations and would be able to answer any queries.

When Antor stepped into the marble floored vestibule and followed the servant in his embroidered short coat and billowing Turkish trousers through the series of richly furnished sitting rooms, he was amazed. He had never imagined that people lived surrounded by such opulence, not ordinary men and women. He had been to the apartments of one or two reasonably well-off businessmen and presumed that the homes of others would be similar; comfortable, bourgeois residences, clean and spacious, with either solid and dark, carved furniture, or the modern chrome and leather type like in Umberto Picciotti's sitting room. Yet walking across the intricate parquet floors, over Persian rugs and past silk and damask lined walls hung with paintings, he felt curiously elated, as if he were moving through a dimension which, though unfamiliar, was not foreign to him.

George Wirsa received him in the library, a long room with French windows opening onto a terrace and with books reaching from floor to ceiling. He was a man in his late fifties with crinkly grey hair, an aquiline nose and thickish lips. His eyes were light brown and moved lazily. He was dressed for the yacht club — blue blazer, open neck silk shirt and scarf, white trousers and white crocodile shoes. He looked round as Antor entered the room.

"Ah, you must be Caspardian. Good of you to come. Take a seat by the desk. Bassiumi, bring coffee. How do you take yours? *Mazbout* or *ziada*?"

"If you don't mind, I'd prefer tea, sir," he answered, settling into a high-backed leather chair.

The servant nodded and withdrew. Wirsa went on studying a book, then replaced it carefully on a shelf and came and sat opposite Antor, who handed him a folder he had taken from his briefcase.

"These are the documents for signature, Mr Wirsa. The last three are copies for you. Mr Zekla suggests you look carefully at the fourth paragraph on page two; it has been altered as you requested."

The man nodded, reached for his spectacles and began reading.

Antor studied him, trying to fathom what made him

different from others. Did anything really, apart from his wealth? He didn't radiate an inner force or give an impression of great wisdom, only an attitude of ingrained superiority cemented by years of getting his own way. He was suave and polite, as he could well afford to be. Penning his signature to those three sheets of paper would make him richer by some £25,000, nearly three times the capital of J. Caspardian and Son, and Antor knew he had done nothing to earn them. Neither used his brains nor worked in any way; simply wielded the power his wealth gave him. As easy as that. He smiled to himself. One day he too would sit behind a desk in a room like this, with a young man bringing him documents to sign, with lawyers, bankers and businessmen making him richer by the hour. One of the immutable laws of nature was that men liked to serve, to sweat their guts out to make the powerful even more so. If they did it for George Wirsa, they would do it for Antor Caspardian!

His thoughts were interrupted by the reappearance of Bassiumi carrying a tray with tea and coffee and pastries. He took his cup in silence while Wirsa went on reading. He sipped it; strong and sweet, just as he liked it. Then he looked through the French windows to the terrace beyond and saw her, a slip of a girl in a pale yellow dress. She was walking up the steps and, as she passed the window, she glanced in. Was she a daughter, he wondered? Yet she didn't look like the man, with her sleek auburn hair, white skin and delicate features.

"Fine," Wirsa said, "I presume I'm to initial the pages as well?"

Antor watched him reach for a gold pen, rapidly scratch his initials, then sign the documents. Seven seconds of scribbling and a 2 kilometre stretch of land along the beach at Agami, bought six years earlier for a few hundred pounds, was sold to another of the bank's clients for just under £26,000. And this money, Antor knew, would be invested in two apartment blocks going up on the Route d'Aboukir, right opposite the Alexandria Sporting Club; smart apartments in a fashionable area which would fetch high prices and bring George Wirsa yet more money ...

He gathered the papers, put them back in the briefcase, and stood up.

"Thank you, Mr Wirsa. If you'll excuse me, I must get back to the bank."

The man looked up at him.

"How did you come, by car?"

"No sir, by taxi."

"Then if you don't mind waiting a minute, the car is taking my daughter to Rue Fuad, and can drop you off. Make your way back to the hall and Bassiumi will take you to the car. Marguerite shouldn't be long." He smiled, nodded a dismissal, and reached for the phone.

Antor walked back the way he had come, his senses now attuned to the surrounding luxury. He paused to look at a tapestry, to finger a polished table top, to examine a jade statuette. He felt at ease, as if he had grown up and lived in a house like this, as if his place were with the Wirsas of this world.

He reached the hall as the girl was coming down the sweep of marble stairs. In a single glance he took in the slim ankles and long legs, the tiny waist and firm little breasts, the pallor of her skin and the grey of her eyes; trusting eyes which held his for a moment then seemed to lengthen like her lips into a smile.

"Good morning," she said in a voice which was not yet a woman's. She spoke in French with the lilt peculiar to the Eastern Mediterranean basin.

"Good morning, Mademoiselle," he answered, smiling back at her. "Your father suggested that the car could deposit me at the bank, which is near where you are going; that is, if you don't mind."

"Of course not, only we'll have to wait a moment or two for Nourna; she's getting my things ready." She paused, looked down at her hands, then: "I saw you with Papa in the library just now."

"Yes, I saw you too. I'm Antor Caspardian. I work at the Banque Zekla and brought some papers for your father to sign."

She came towards him and held out her hand.

"How do you do. I'm Marguerite."

He took it in his, a warm, vibrant little hand, but before he had time to press it slightly, it was gone.

"Nourna, do hurry," she cried, turning and looking up the

stairs, "we'll be late. Ouf, how slow she is! Come on, we'll go to the car."

She walked quickly across the hall, through the vestibule to the front door, held open by a servant. Antor followed her, watching the movement of her hips, the way the pleated skirt swished around her knees, aware that something very new was happening to him. It was not only a question of love, but a sudden certainty that she was the person with whom he wanted to spend his life, an unquestionable fact which he now saw as clearly as the big Chrysler parked at the bottom of the steps.

The chauffeur opened the door and Marguerite slid in. Antor hesitated. Normally he would have walked round to the other side and climbed into the seat next to the driver's. A bank employee was supposed to know his place, and not occupy one which wasn't his.

"Aren't you going to get in?" she asked, indicating with a nod of her head the expanse of black leather beside her.

Though he had a remarkable memory, Antor could never remember what they spoke about during the fifteen minute drive to the city centre. Certainly she did most of the talking, chatting away, probably, about a film she had seen or the dancing lesson she was going to, or even the pony her father had given her; things of her everyday life, while he nodded and listened, drinking in her presence, only vaguely aware of the words floating from her lips. Later, she admitted that she had prattled away because she feared that a silence would be more eloquent than words, revealing sentiments she knew she must hide. How could a girl of her upbringing have such sudden and strong feelings about a man she had never seen before, and only met a few minutes earlier?

When the car drew up at the bank, Antor held his hand out for hers.

"Au revoir, Mademoiselle, and thank you."

He did not attempt to hold her hand or give it the slightest squeeze; for a long moment he gazed searchingly into her eyes, then climbed out of the car. He did not look back. He heard the chauffeur close the door and a few seconds later the engine rev up again.

As he was stepping through the bank's entrance, she called his name. He turned and saw her at the car's window, her hands resting on the lowered glass, and her face leaning out slightly.

"I'm having a few friend's for lunch at our cabin at Sidi Bishr, Sunday. Would you like to come?"

He turned and crossed the pavement again.

"I'd love to. Where shall we meet?"

"At the house, around twelve. And bring a bathing costume..."

He nodded and watched the car disappear into the traffic. The picture of Marguerite calling him from the car was one he would remember all his life.

Antor did not talk to his mother about Marguerite for several months, yet Anna sensed that something had changed in him, and her mother's instinct told her that a girl was responsible. She didn't tax him on the subject, as she confided to Joseph, for she knew he would tell them when the time was right.

He spoke about her one Sunday as they were returning home from Mass.

"I met her for the first time two months ago, Mother; you'll love her. She's beautiful in every way. But she's still only a child, so we won't be getting married immediately ... "

"Who is she, Antor, do we know her family?"

"No. She's called Marguerite Wirsa, only I'd rather you didn't mention it to anyone for the moment, not even to Madame Hitawi."

"And her parents, do they know you want to marry?"

He shook his head. "I don't think so. No one knows. It'll be time enough to tell them when I'm in a position to ask them the hand of their daughter."

Anna looked sharply at her son. What could that mean? And why all the secrecy? What was wrong about people knowing that he wanted to marry this Marguerite Wirsa even if they had to wait a few years? Hadn't she and Joseph been engaged for three years? It was normal, even wise. Wirsa? She had heard that name mentioned by Madame Hitawi. Yes, they were rich Copts who lived in a huge house. Snobs of the first order, her friend had said. Could it be their daughter her son had fallen in love with? Dear God, but how would they ever accept as a son-in-law a young man like Antor. He could have all the qualities in the world but all they would see was that he didn't come from the same background. And for that, they would do everything to prevent such a marriage.

What Antor did not add was that not even Marguerite knew that she was the girl he wanted as his wife. He had expressed his love for her through his eyes and on the rare occasions that his skin had touched hers; occasions when he too had felt the blossoming emotion in her, but never in words. That would come later when he was sure of her love and certain that she wanted him as husband as much as he wanted her as wife. When that happened, their love would be strong enough to overcome all obstacles, even the disapproval of her parents.

Antor was clear-headed enough to realize that he was not the husband they would want for their daughter. They expected her to marry within their own circle, that hermetic group of two dozen or so families who lived, thought and acted in a style to which their fortunes had accustomed them. In the three months that he had frequented Marguerite and her friends, he had become conscious of how deep an abyss existed between them and him. And if they were polite, even friendly, it was because of Marguerite. Not one of them would have dreamed of asking him to their homes alone.

But it was not her friends who mattered; it was George Wirsa and his wife, Helen. They too were charming and polite with him, just as they were to every guest in their house. Helen had never been heard to sharpen her voice or known to look annoyed, and a permanent smile tilted upwards the corners of her mouth, as if to show there was nothing in her life which could possibly irritate her. Antor knew, though, that her graciousness masked a will to dominate, and that when she set her mind against something or someone, there was little anyone could do to shake her convictions. Marguerite's father might be persuaded to accept an outsider for his daughter if the man were clever and ambitious, and if he reckoned he wasn't marrying her for her money; perhaps if he felt her happiness were at stake. But not her mother; she wanted Marguerite to marry as she had, not the man but the position.

Antor was aware that if she smiled at him, it was because he represented nothing more than a stray dog her daughter might have brought home out of the kindness of her heart; the sort one feeds and pats but sends to sleep outside. The idea that he might want to marry her daughter would have

34

changed the smile into a hollow little laugh; the very thought was too absurd not to be funny, she would have murmured to her husband, and the door of her house would have been firmly shut in his face.

Yet he knew that Marguerite would be his. The feeling had become a certainty one Sunday when he had gone swimming with her and the others at Agami.

The Wirsas owned one of the first villas on the beautiful beach to the west of the city which was becoming the favourite weekend resort of many wealthy Alexandrians. Kilometre after kilometre of white sands stretched for as far as the eye could see, while fig trees and date palms sprouted here and there on the high sand dunes.

Running across the beach, Marguerite shouted that they should all swim to an island some three hundred metres out at sea. But only Antor followed her, the others happily fooling around at the water's edge, throwing seaweed at each other.

Marguerite was a good swimmer and within ten minutes they were twenty metres from the island. But suddenly she turned and cried, "Antor, help. I've got a pain in my side."

He swam quickly to her and put his arm round her waist.

"Just hold on to me and don't worry, we'll be there in a moment," he said. "Don't try to swim, relax and let me carry you."

She put an arm across his shoulders and held tightly to him as he got her to the shallow waters. Then, disengaging herself, she kissed him on the cheek.

"Thank God you were there, Antor. Without you I might have drowned."

A hand to her side, she climbed onto a flat rock, sat down and drew her knees up under her chin. Antor remained in the water, his body now prey to a violent desire. He wanted her so badly that he started trembling.

She glanced at him sideways, a soft questioning look in her eyes.

"You're shivering. What's wrong?"

"Nothing," he murmured and dived into the clear waters. When he surfaced it was with a shell.

"It's for you, if you'd like it," he said, shaking the water from his hair and swimming close to the rock. "Feeling better now?"

"Yes ... it's beautiful." She took the shell and turned it over in her hands, her fingers touching it delicately, almost caressing it. "I'll keep it always … as a souvenir." She put it to her ear. "It's wonderful. It has the sound of the sea in it. Here, listen."

She leant over and held it for him to hear, the tips of her fingers touching his cheek. Antor heard only the thumping of his blood careering through his arteries.

A little later they swam back to the mainland and joined the others. A servant had put up a parasol and Nourna had come with sandwiches and lemonade. Marguerite said nothing of what had happened and no one seemed to notice the shell Antor was carrying. But both of them knew that their bodies had touched and that something had awakened in them. The shell was their talisman.

The following months were difficult for Antor. The physical side of his love was a torment, at night especially when there was no way of banishing her body from his thoughts except in sleep, and even then she seemed ever present. But if in his dreams he could make love to her and give vent to the desire which gripped him like a fever, in the morning he would wake, dissatisfied and tired, counting the hours till he would see her again, though afraid of what her presence would do to him.

There was no way, of course, for them to be alone together for any length of time. Wherever she went, either the devoted Nourna or her mother's maid would accompany her. No respectable Alexandrian girl was allowed to leave home without a chaperon.

And if Nourna were not there, one of the other girls' elderly governesses would be discretely in the background. Only at Agami, or on the beach at Sidi Bishr, was it possible to slip away from the supervision by diving into the sea and swimming far enough out to be lost from sight in the gently rolling swell.

But Marguerite was not the type to want to sneak away and flirt surreptitiously, just as he was not the kind to be happy with that. Others, like Christofides and Mottram, who used a brothel behind Ramleh Station might be content with stealing a kiss from these well bred girls, but not he. He wanted her fully, to share his life and children; to be both spiritually and physically part of his every day existence.

On a hot afternoon in May he went to tea at her home. Marguerite was waiting for him in a small drawing room, off the main sitting room, where she and her friends gathered if they were not numerous. Despite it's high ceiling and rich furnishings, it had an air of intimacy absent elsewhere in the house.

She was standing by the window, gazing out into the garden through the partially closed shutters, and cooling herself with a Japanese paper fan. She was alone. She turned and smiled at him, and Antor knew that if he did not act then he might have to wait a long time for another opportunity. He strode across the room took her hand and brought it to his lips.

"I love you, Marguerite. I want to marry you," he said hoarsely.

He saw the expression in her eyes change, the look of girlish welcome turning to wonder and excitement, yet tinged with a flash of fear as she glanced over his shoulder at the open doorway. Then they closed, and he felt her body touch his as her face tilted upwards.

"Oh Antor ... " she sighed.

He kissed her gently, brushing his lips against hers, fearful lest the strength of his passion frighten her. He caressed her hair and pressed her head against his chest, gritting his teeth, while he arched the rest of his body away from her so that she would not feel his stiffness. An eternity passed as he kissed her forehead and eyelids, cupping her face in his hands.

"Do you love me darling?" he asked. He knew now for certain that she did, but he wanted to hear her say so.

"Yes, Antor. I love you. I love you terribly." There was almost a desperation in the way she said it.

"Then you'll marry me," he stated.

She nodded and opened her eyes wide. "But not yet ... we need a little time ... Mummy and Daddy ... you know, I must prepare them. They wouldn't understand ... "

Antor rested his hands on her shoulders, his fingers pressing softly into her skin. "I know, my love. But I ... we can't wait long. We need each other too much. I'll talk to them ... I know they'll agree when they see how much ... "

Her fingers were on his lips, trembling.

"Please. Antor, not yet," she whispered anxiously, "we must wait a little ... they mustn't suspect anything for the ... they'd..."

She drew away from him suddenly as he heard the clicking of high heels on the parquet flooring, and he realized someone was walking towards them. "You promise?" she added before running to the other side of the room, and putting a record on the gramophone.

Helen Wirsa appeared in the doorway.

"Ah, there you are, Marguerite. Good afternoon Antor. Haven't the others arrived yet? Where's Nourna?" The eternal smile was on her lips, but her eyebrows were raised, and there was no mistaking the subtle rebuke in her voice. Her daughter should not have been alone with a man.

"She's preparing tea, Mummy. Antor has just arrived ... and the others will be here any moment. Do you mind if we put on some music?"

"No, of course not. But not too loud. Daddy's in the study and mustn't be disturbed. I'll stay and listen to it with you till the others come. Do sit down, Antor. What do you all plan to do this afternoon?"

He watched Helen Wirsa carefully. Had she suspected anything? He wished in a way that she had arrived a minute or two earlier. The cat would have been out of the bag, and he would have known how they stood. Basically, he was certain of her disapproval; she would do everything she could to stop her daughter marrying him. And until she came of age, Marguerite would have to bow to her parents' wishes, which meant nearly four years. Neither of them could wait that long. He bit his lip as an impotent fury gripped him. Somehow he would have to persuade George and Helen Wirsa, for he sensed that Marguerite would with difficulty marry a man her parents didn't approve of, let alone run away with him, however much she loved him.

Yet he realized there was no way by which he could convince the Wirsas that he would be able to look after her on a salary of £20 a month. And Helen's prejudices apart, George Wirsa would only begin to consider him as a possible son-in-law if he had a solid financial background, and excellent prospects, the sort which would allow him to offer Marguerite a style of life similar to the one to which she was accustomed.

That night he lay awake trying to decide what action to take. The possibilities open to him were few, so few that they were rapidly reduced to two. Either to go on at the bank and hope that in a year or two his position and salary would permit him to ask for Marguerite's hand, or try his luck as a businessman right away, and attempt to make a lot of money rapidly. By the morning his mind was made up.

"Father, would you like me to come and work with you?" he asked at breakfast, "if so I'll quit the bank immediately."

Joseph put down his cup of coffee and stared at him. Then he got up slowly and walked round to him. He grasped him by the shoulders and crouched over him.

"My son, it's five years I've been waiting to hear you say that, and you ask me if I want you to?" There were tears in his eyes as he hugged him. Then he straightened up. "Anna," he called, "I have great news for you. Antor will come to the factory. He is leaving the bank to come and work with me. May the Lord be thanked ... Ah, now I feel there has been a purpose to all these years. You'll see, Antor, it's not a bad little business. It's not big, as you know, but it's like a second family for me. The men, they're good men. They work well, and I am well respected by our clients. You are clever and you will learn fast. At the beginning you will find it a little difficult, perhaps; everything must be checked so carefully before it goes out. The men are capable, but they make mistakes sometimes. I see those mistakes and I put them right. One year with me and you'll know all the secrets of the trade."

For two hours, until it was time to go to Mass, Joseph talked on excitedly about the business he had created, and how he had always hoped Antor would join him in it, forgetting that his son already had a pretty good idea of it from the Sunday afternoon sessions when he helped with the accounts. Antor smiled and listened, judging that it was not the moment to tell him that, if he were giving up his job at the bank, it was not to slip into overalls and transform himself into a manual labourer. He decided he would humour him for a week or two and then explain what he had in mind. Joseph Caspardian and Son would not remain an unknown woodworking concern on the edge of the Mahmoudiah canal, nor its owners *petit bourgeois* Armenians whom no one in Alexandria had ever heard of. Antor was determined that he and his father would become rich, and he reckoned that with the banking experience he had gained, he knew how.

Monday morning he was in Raymond Zekla's office explaining why he had to leave.

"My father needs me, Mr Zekla. He's no longer young, and his business has expanded so rapidly that it would be unfair of me to let him cope on his own. He wants me to look after the financial side of the concern, to deal with banks and so on. I'm sorry in a way, as I liked it here. Banking fascinates me. But the fifteen months I've spent with you will come in very useful now."

The banker hid his disappointment.

"I'm sorry to lose you, Caspardian. Keep in touch; who knows, perhaps we can be of use to your father. Who does he bank with, if it is not being indiscreet?"

"The Ottoman Bank, sir, but I see no reason why he shouldn't come here for the sort of finance I think he will be wanting. I'll certainly suggest it to him."

When he got up to leave, Raymond Zekla did so too. He accompanied him to the door and shook his hand, an act of politeness not lost on Antor. Bankers, he knew, had a sixth sense where money was concerned, and the clever ones could sniff it long before anyone else.

For the first ten days he followed his father about in the three sheds, watching the men at work, assessing the machinery and examining the stock in hand. He listened to Joseph as he chatted away about wood grains, varnishes, and the right humidity content necessary to avoid cracking, or while he explained the best way to bend wood without splitting it, and how to make joints almost invisible to the naked eye. The expertise of a life's work were in his words and his hand movements, but Antor's mind was elsewhere.

The Sunday afternoon visits had given him an idea of the workshop's financial situation. He knew that it was making money, and that the order books were full for months ahead. But he had not realized the potentials or the value of the stock piled in the long shed at the back of the premises. Precious heaps of wood might lie there for years, his father told him, waiting for a suitable order to make use of them.

"See this oak? Had it for over three years, straight from Rumania. Now an Englishman wants me to panel an entire room like the inside of an old sailing boat. What better? And that mahogany over there, it'll be used to line the library of some Pasha's home, or maybe an office. I've had it for five years, ready for whoever wants it."

Hundreds, no thousands of pounds of merchandise were lying dormant, tying up capital that could be used to buy new machinery and enable the men to turn out three times as much finished products. He took a careful look at the order books and discovered that while 30 per cent concerned municipal tenders, and 25 per cent work for building firms, the balance were for what Joseph called proudly his prestige clients, the time wasters who demanded a high degree of quality yet invariably kept him waiting years for payment.

"But they're the ones who are responsible for my being a businessman and not just a humble carpenter," Joseph protested when Antor taxed him about them, "and I make good profits with my private clientele. You've seen the books. In some cases as much as 70 per cent. All right, they take a little time to pay, but you can't make that with the building firms or the Municipality. In any case, what's the worry? Aren't we making a good £2000 a year? Why d'you want to change things?"

"Because we can do much better, Father."

It had taken him only three weeks to work out a plan to transform the artisan type workshop into a fully fledged industry, coaxing his father into telling him what innovations could be made to increase production at little cost while, at the same time, cutting down on stock and getting rid of the clients who were difficult payers and whose orders could not be processed through the production line. In his projection he also did away with six of the staff, and showed a company with a high profit ratio to its capital and plenty of liquidity to structure further developments.

Joseph was impressed, but not sufficiently to want to change from the old system.

"Why not leave it all as it is, Antor. We're happy this way. What's the point of doing all this? We have the money we need, the Lord be thanked, so what would we do with more? The day will come when it will all be yours ... then, yes, you can try out these clever ideas."

But Antor could not wait. The changes, he argued, should take place immediately, and in his calm yet forceful way he talked his father into them. Just as he persuaded him to rent a modern office in Rue Cherif where to receive customers

41

instead of getting them out to the dusty premises at the factory, and to buy a second hand Ford, employ a chauffeur, and move into a bougainvillaea covered house with a tennis court in the fashionable Bulkeley district.

"Why the tennis court?" Anna had asked, "who will ever use it?" She was not quite sure what her two men were up to, but she was certain that girl of Antor's was behind it all. She was pleased, though. She had always dreamed of having her own garden, and it was pleasant to be driven to town instead of having to take the tram. She put her foot down when Antor suggested they take on a cook.

"I've prepared your food all your life, and no one is going to change that. And what do you want me to do with my time? Play pinnacle and gossip with a whole lot of silly hens who've got nothing better to do? You do what you like outside, but the running of the house is my affair, and the kitchen especially."

That summer Antor worked overtime. He would be out at the workshops by 6.30 a.m. to check that the workmen were there, and that the day's work was proceeding as programmed. Around 10 he would drive back to the office, shower and change, then begin the rounds of the municipal offices and construction companies to secure new orders. When these closed at 2.30, he would go to collect his father from the factory, drive home for a light lunch, before going on to a beach to cool in the sea for an hour. At six he would be at the office for two hours desk work, dealing with letters and invoices, and making the necessary entries in the company's books. He worked Saturdays, and often Sunday evenings, while Marguerite and her friends were in Europe, away from the sticky heat of Alexandria.

Early in September he had a meeting with his former employer, Raymond Zekla.

"My father and I are now in a position to discuss the possibility of your Bank financing the extension of our factory, which we have planned for next year," he said, coming straight to the point. "As you know, the company banks with the Ottoman Bank, but I have convinced him to put the proposal to you first. I felt I owed that to you, Mr Zekla."

The banker smiled. Already there was a noticeable change in the young man, which did not limit itself to the way he talked. The cut of his lightweight suit was good, the crease in the trousers impeccable. His hair was carefully brushed and his fingernails manicured. There was a touch of elegance in the way he sat, but beneath it all a toughness which he had not noted in the youth who had left them only three months previously.

"Thank you, I appreciate that. Perhaps you would like to sketch the broad outlines of your requirements and Mr Oppenheim could then have a look at the company's accounts, when they are ready."

"I have them with me, together with a financial study based on next year's market potential, full costings of the new plant with expected earnings over three years and, of course, the guarantees we can offer. I know the way Mr Oppenheim likes a project presented." This time it was Antor who smiled. "Might it not be an idea if he joined us? It could save time for everyone," he added.

Raymond Zekla nodded. It was the first time a customer had suggested how he should run his bank's business, but he was not irritated. Antor Caspardian did not irritate. Somehow, there was a freshness in his approach and a capacity to make people see things the way he did, which dissolved any tension his directness might provoke. He pressed a bell on his desk and a secretary appeared.

"Ask Mr Oppenheim to come here, if he is not busy, and arrange for some coffee. Also no telephone calls till I say so."

"Would you mind making it tea for me," Antor said, smiling at the young woman, "strong and sweet, if possible?"

Two hours later he left the bank satisfied. He had got what he had come for, a loan of £12,000 with interest at 4 per cent and repayable at the rate of £3000 per annum. But more important to him, Raymond Zekla now knew the financial position of J. Caspardian and Son and its potential, and he was a close friend of George Wirsa.

Antor felt he had killed quite a few birds with one stone. All he had to do now was convince his father to go ahead with the project!

That, however, was something he was never fated to do. The same evening, shortly after dinner, Joseph slumped suddenly in his chair. His hand went to his heart as a low moan escaped from his lips. Then, before either Anna or Antor could reach him, he reeled over and fell to the floor, dead.

His father's sudden disappearance stunned Antor. It had not occurred to him that death could snatch without warning what he had always considered an integral and vital part of his existence. He had never known life without the comforting presence of a father he not only respected but loved. Whenever he had got home, from school or from work, the two bastions of his childhood and adolescence had always been there, immutable and apparently indestructible. Yet one had now vanished, inexplicably and without warning. Apart from a gut gripping grief which was physical in its intensity, he experienced a curious sensation of unreality, as if nothing around him really existed, not even his mother, old overnight, and numbly whispering prayers by the side of her husband's body, until they dragged her gently away to dress her for the funeral.

"It can't be," he kept repeating to himself as he followed the coffin onto the draped catafalque with its horses and plumes of the deepest black, then supported his mother behind the slow moving cortège to the cemetery.

When it was all over, when the last acquaintance had shaken his hand and murmured polite words of condolence, when Anna had been put to bed and the house was muffled in the silence of sorrow, he got in the car and drove along the Corniche, the new highway built on the city's 30 kilometre waterfront.

He parked at Mandara, jumped over the parapet onto the sand, took off his shoes and socks, and waded into the sea. And as he stared out towards the horizon and inhaled deep breaths of algae smelling air, reality came slowly back to him. He squared his shoulders. He was a man of substance now, and whether the Wirsas liked it or not, overnight he had turned into a person they could no longer dismiss as a nobody, not financially. Socially, maybe, but the next few years would change that. Alexandrians lived and breathed money. They went to bed with it, fondled it and got orgasms from it. Being rich was not just an asset for them, it was a virtue which eclipsed all others. A man without money was not only a nonentity, he simply didn't exist. And if a rich man lost his, he too was dead, since the superstitious Alexandrians had no wish to keep the company of a ghost.

But when those who arrived at their offices at 10 a.m. and lunched at the Union Bar or the Sporting Club, who talked shop in their boxes at the cinema, and then went on to a buffet dinner at a friend's house, when those, the so-called elite of Alexandria's society began to take notice of him, Helen Wirsa also would have to.

Marguerite arrived back from Europe on October 10th. He phoned her immediately he heard she was home, and when her soft voice came on the line the pain, which had been with him since his father's death, eased.

"Antor, is it really you?" she cried, "how wonderful. How did you know I was here? I was going to try and ring you this evening. Oh, Antor, I'm so sorry about your father. Magda told me. It must have been awful for you. But when can I see you? ... not this evening, I must stay with Maman and Papa. What about this afternoon? We're going to the Sporting Club to watch the tennis. Why don't you come too, or do you have to be back at the bank?"

"No darling, I'll be there. I missed you, you know."

"So did I you, Antor. Did you get my postcards?"

"Yes, and I keep them in my wallet."

"There's one other I forgot to post, so I'll give it to you ... must run now. See you at the Club."

Had she really missed him, he wondered as he replaced the phone? Marguerite was still such a child in certain ways and could be easily influenced. Who knew whether or not those months away had altered her feelings for him.

The weeks passed and he saw her almost every day, just as Roger Christofides, now down from Oxford, Robert Menasche, Eduardo Stagni and three or four others of her group did. At first she had been taken aback by the change in him; in a curious way it seemed to frighten her a little. The fact that he now dressed and acted like the other young men she knew disorientated her. Before he had been different, somehow dependent on her. Now it was he who dominated the group putting up with her friends because they were hers, as if he had suddenly outgrown them and had more in common with the older generation than with their playboy sons.

Rapidly, though, she accepted his new stature and became

proud when she saw him having a word with her father on the activities of the Bourse, or leaving their table at the Sporting Club to talk with Eduardo's uncle about an order for timber. Her eyes would flash as if to say, 'look what a man my Antor has turned into'. She loved him, yet was still frightened to let anyone suspect it. On the trip back from Europe, her mother had hinted that in due course Roger Christofides would make an ideal husband for her, and she knew that sooner or later, after her eighteenth birthday, pressure would be brought to bear on her to marry him. If it were suspected that there was anything between her and Antor, that pressure would become immediate and overwhelming, and would force her to make a choice for which she was not yet ready. They or him.

"We must be patient," she whispered every time she and Antor managed to snatch a moment together, "please don't spoil things by letting anyone know about us. Mummy and Daddy aren't ready for it. In a while, you'll see, they'll understand." She half believed this, now that she had seen the change in her father's manner towards him. Perhaps with time and success in his business they might let her marry him.

For her sake, Antor acquiesced. The subterfuge was childish, and completely against his nature, but he saw no alternative. If he wanted to marry her he had to win her parents' consent, and to do that he needed a lot of money, fast.

He threw himself into his work with a frenzy which began to worry his mother. Some days she would not see him at all. He never lunched or dined at home, stopping by only for a change of clothes before joining the group at a cinema or after, at a party in one of the houses. Sometimes he would go back to his office at midnight to prepare work for the next day, leaving notes for his secretary pinned on the wall. And he did not stop at getting profitable orders for doors and windows, or bargaining down the price of wood from the importers; he began diversifying. His six years spent with the shipping firm, the cotton brokers and the bank had taught him a lot. If they could do it, he said to himself, so could he.

While at Picciotti's he had met a manager of a Lancashire mill, a certain Basil Wilding. He had helped him with his shopping, and looked after him through customs when he had left. "If you ever come to England, look me up," the man had said, handing him his card. So he wrote to Wilding asking to be put in touch with an English firm interested in importing cotton and not yet tied up with the established exporters. At the same time he made an arrangement to buy cotton through a clerk at Serpakis's and, contenting himself with a small profit margin, started a steady flow of business.

He took on, too, the agency for a new brand of refrigerators made in Italy, and this was followed up by bathroom fittings, radios and sewing machines. Never losing an opportunity to make money, he also began dabbling on the Alexandrian stock Exchange. Every day, from 11.30 to 12.30 he would go to the Exchange, watch for a while, then place his order. His months at the bank had given him inside information on some of the quoted companies and his new relationship with the Zeklas enabled him to check, by a phone call, whether his hunches were valid. In the space of nine weeks he made himself £3400. The £3000 he reinvested in his company, while the £400 were set aside for a special purpose.

As the mild Alexandrian winter gave way to the breezy spring, he found time to take part in weekend parties and excursions organized by Marguerite and her friends. There would be picnics at Aboukir, an hour's drive from the city, and sometimes trips to Rosetta and Damietta. Or they would go to an *ezba* in the heart of the Delta, not far from Damanhour, where he saw for the first time the vast tracts of rich, green *birseem*, the Egyptian clover, the blossoming cotton plants, the rice paddies and the endless fields of cauliflowers and water melons. It was the Egypt of the *fellah* and the water mill, of the oxen with the ibis perched on their backs, of a civilization which harked back to the times of the Pharaohs, parallel to yet so different from the one he had been brought up in. Or they would drive out into the desert, beyond Lake Mariut with its wild duck and still marshes, to a house built like a castle, unexpected and austere outside, yet, curiously peaceful within the high garden walls which screened a profusion of hibiscus, honeysuckle and mimosa. And when the swimming season started, there was Agami, the favourite beach of everyone, or Sidi Bishr, at the other end of the city, where one or other of them owned a large, double cabin big enough for all to rest in after lunch, listening to records or playing cards.

If the *hamseen* were blowing the sand from the desert and the dust from the fields, as often happened in March, they would crowd into a cinema or go to a tea dance at the Beau Rivage Hotel or San Stefano, and Antor would be close to Marguerite, holding her hand as they watched a film, or her waist as they danced a fox trot. And for those few moments of pleasure, he would spend hours late at night catching up on work, poring over documents, figures and plans.

On Easter Monday he invited the group for lunch at his home. The six months of total mourning in which Anna had isolated herself were over, and she agreed to meet and receive his friends. It was to be the first time she set eyes on Marguerite too, and Antor was eager that the encounter should be informal with other people about.

It turned out to be a sunny day, and the buffet was laid out on the veranda which ran the whole length of the house. The garden, with its beds of poinsettias and marigolds, carefully tended for two weeks by a gardener from Nouza Gardens, was full of colour and charm. Anna prepared the dishes herself — green *melohia* soup, rice with *kufta*, spears of *kebab*, stuffed vine leaves, giant prawns, *tahina*, and sweetmeats of various kinds. It was the wholesome food of the Egyptians, not that found in the smart international homes, where elaborate French cuisine was the rule of the day.

"But it's delicious," Marguerite exclaimed, tasting the well spiced *melohia*, "what is it? I've never had it before."

When she had arrived, she had gone straight up to Anna and taken her hand. "I'm so glad to meet you at last, Madame, I'm Marguerite. How lovely it is here. We have a garden at home too, but it's not as friendly as this one."

She had prattled on, and Antor had watched the two of them sitting side by side, happy to see that his mother had begun to smile again.

She wore an ankle length dress of grey wool crocheted by young girls at a nearby convent, with no ornaments, not even the necklace of seed pearls offered to her by Joseph the Christmas before he died, and her hair was pinned in a small bun on the back of her head. Yet despite her simple, almost drab appearance, she emanated a quiet dignity. Each of the men took her work-scarred hand and kissed it on arrival, and the girls bobbed a curtsy. And Antor knew it was not through habit or good upbringing; there was more than politeness in their manner.

Marguerite stayed with her until Anna retired indoors before coffee.

"How sweet she is and sad, but in such a beautiful and gentle way," she said.

Antor nodded slowly. Gentle? Yes, the fight had gone out of Anna. Bereft of her life's partner, she had given up all struggle, waiting patiently to be reunited with the man she had loved, and praying it would not be too long a wait. Her sadness was beautiful for there was no bitterness in it, only serenity.

Two months later Helen and George Wirsa threw a ball for Marguerite's 18th birthday.

Antor had grown accustomed to the opulence of the rich Alexandrians, but he had never experienced anything like the extravagance of that evening. When he arrived at the mansion, most of the three hundred guests were already there, crowding the buffets and the dance floor built specially in the garden under a huge marquee. Helen was living up to her reputation of being one of the city's leading hostesses, by no means a sinecure. It was not enough to hire the San Stefano orchestra for the evening and hand the catering over to Pastroudis or Baudrot, as many a less enterprising hostess might; a touch of artistic originality was also necessary. This she had achieved by asking her friend, J.G. Domergue to dream up something suitable for the occasion.

Domergue was a French painter much in vogue in Parisian salons, where women raved about him and his portraits. He had come to Alexandria at Helen's invitation and was busy sketching a handful of her friends. The agreement between them was tacit yet definite. The ones he did of women introduced by her would be pastel sketches, head and shoulders only, while those of her and Marguerite would be full length and in oil.

The decor he designed for the ball consisted of long white panels of material hung to the sides of the marquee, on which he had depicted views of Alexandria in the days of Cleopatra.

Palaces, temples, the harbour with Roman and Grecian galleys, even the great lighthouse were sketched in charcoal on the sheets, which undulated gently in the evening breeze. The effect was dramatic yet ephemeral, but the focal point of the decor was a full length portrait of Marguerite which was unveiled suddenly, showing her as a smiling, guileless Cleopatra.

There was little doubt as to the allegory. Helen wanted to mark the point that her daughter was queen of Alexandria that evening, an heiress who, through her heritage, could aspire to a top position in the city.

She herself was dressed in a Vionnet ball gown of shimmering silver, ordered specially from Paris, and around her long neck sparkled 32 perfectly matched diamonds. With her hair cut short, and her classical features accentuated by careful make-up, she epitomized the self-assured elegance of the ambience in which she moved.

Antor was standing not far from her when the portrait was revealed and he noted the look of triumph on her face. As the guests clapped their appreciation the smile widened and for once the eyes glowed too. How, he wondered with a certain heaviness of heart, would a woman with a vanity and pride such as hers, accept to let her daughter marry a parvenu. But with Marguerite's look of joy when she saw him, and the pressure of her fingers as he took her to the dance floor, the determination to succeed came back to him. She and no one else would be his wife. It might take months, even years, but she would be his, whatever Helen Wirsa might think.

With Marguerite in his arms he glanced up at the portrait. It didn't represent the girl he knew and loved; it was a brittle caricature, more like her mother than her. The painter had caught the features but not the soul and, wanting to please Helen, had portrayed her daughter as he reckoned she wanted him to; the heiress of her Hellenic pedigree and her father's Alexandrian money. Those, Antor knew, were the forces with which he would have to contend.

Marguerite and her friends left for Europe and the clammy heat enveloped the city once more. July gave way to August and Antor went on working.

There was no question of taking a holiday, even for a few days. Only during Ramadan, the Moslem month of abstinence from any form of nourishment during daylight hours, which that year fell in August, did he relax his rhythm a little. The factory closed at one-thirty and did not reopen until 6.30 the following morning, and government offices packed up just after noon, as did the contracting companies.

Antor would get back home for a late lunch, rest for half an hour, then go to his mother's room and keep her company for a while. At around 4.30 he would go to the Sporting Club for a tennis or golf lesson, after which he would dive into the pool before relaxing on the terrace. Three evenings a week he would return home around seven for an English lesson with a young employee from the British Institute who, as often as not, he kept to dinner to improve his conversation and learn about the ways and habits of a people whose empire was the greatest among the western nations. By the end of the summer he was almost fluent in English, and his tennis had improved enough for him to play in the club tournament. Only his golf was not getting on as well as he would have wished. Somehow his concentration waned as he trod the greens now yellowing from the heat, retracing steps he had so often taken with Marguerite.

September passed and the welcome autumn coolness returned, tempered by the warm breezes which caress Alexandria well into November.

Then Marguerite arrived back and the gentle routine of weekend parties at Agami, afternoons at the Club watching tennis and golf matches, evenings at the cinema or listening to records started again. As usual, Antor kept pace by working late at night and getting up at dawn. He willingly sacrificed a few hours sleep to be at Marguerite's side.

Around December 15th, everyone began making plans for Christmas and New Year. Antor would have liked to give a big party at his house but he knew he couldn't ask that of his mother. It was only the second Christmas without Joseph, and she wanted to pass it quietly with the one or two people she had always known.

She had grown frail. The once chubby cheeks were lined, and her eyes had lost all sparkle. Antor had got a doctor to visit her who found nothing organically wrong, and simply prescribed a meat diet with plenty of spinach and lentils.

"Give her a glass of wine with meals. She needs building

up, that's all. Of course the best would be a change of air. Why not send her to Helouan, the spa south of Cairo? I know of a very pleasant pension there where she would be well looked after."

Anna would not hear of it.

"What would I do there on my own?" she protested. "I see little enough of you here in our home. I don't want to go away. This house is the only link I have with those I love. I'll get better, I promise you Antor. All I ask is that you be a little more with me."

He had tried spending at least two evenings a week with her but it changed nothing. Within half an hour she would say she was tired and go off to bed.

It was Marguerite who suggested he go to spend New Year's Eve at Luxor.

"We're all going there, so why don't you come too? Oh, please Antor, do try. It won't be the same without you. We'll be staying at the Winter Palace Hotel, and they're doing a gala on New Year's Eve. It'll be wonderful. You will come, promise me that?"

Antor thought fast. To stay under the same roof as her was an opportunity he would not miss. In a hotel there would be a multitude of ways to be together without anyone knowing. But his mother, could he leave her? Supposing she fell ill while he was away.

"There's nothing I'd like better, darling. Only my mother, you know, she's not well, and I wouldn't like to leave her alone in the house just then."

"Couldn't a friend stay with her? I'm sure she would be all right if there were someone to keep her company."

Marguerite was right, he decided. It might even do his mother good to have someone in the house. It would change her ideas and keep her busy preparing the odd meal. He brought the subject up with her the same evening as he accompanied her up to her room. When he explained that he wanted to go to Luxor for two or three days, she laid her hand on his and looked him searchingly in the eyes.

"It's Marguerite who wants you there, isn't it? Go, my boy, and don't worry about me. I'll be all right. Maybe I'll ask Madame Hitawi if she would like to come and stay as she's alone too now. Be careful, though, Antor. Marguerite is a lovely

girl, but she's terribly young. Don't expect too much from her
... I wouldn't want you to be unhappy. Oh, she's in love with
you, you don't have to convince me about that, I saw it the
moment you brought her here at Easter with those other
friends. But being in love isn't loving. One is a weakness and
the other a strength. I know which applies to you, but I'm
not certain for her. Only time will tell ... "

"I know, Mother. But she'll be mine. I've wanted that from
the moment I first set eyes on her. And if she's a little weak,
it doesn't matter as I have strength for both of us, believe
me. And we'll have children, a son certainly, just as you and
Father had, who you will spoil, or try to, as all grandmothers
do. Don't worry about Marguerite and me; very soon the time
will be right for me to speak to her parents, and we'll get
married. It will be a wonderful wedding, and you must promise
you'll get strong again for it. You wouldn't want to be ill when
you're only son is getting married ... "

Anna had settled back in her bed.

"Don't fret about me," she repeated, "only don't do anything
rash."

He left Alexandria in the afternoon of the 29th and drove
leisurely along the new desert road, arriving at Gizeh a little
before sunset. Acting on a sudden impulse, instead of going
left after Mena House Hotel and along the Pyramid's Road
to Cairo, he branched to the right and up onto the sandy
plateau where the great pyramid of Cheops surged massive
yet romantic. The setting sun projected its shadow across the
sands, the village below, and over the golf course to the distant
fields of *birseem* undulating amongst the date palms.

He got out of the car and stared up at the tier upon tier
of granite blocks, marvelling suddenly at the ingenuity of the
ancient peoples of Egypt who had conceived and actually built
such a monument. Was it really true, he wondered, that it
was more than a grandiose tomb, and that its shape and
measurements represented arcane mysteries of the universe?

How little he knew of the wonders of ancient Egypt, he
realized. In Alexandria he had not even visited Pompey's pillar
nor was he certain where the famed lighthouse had once stood.
And the Pyramids, the Sphinx, Saqqara and Memphis had
meant little more to him than postcards stuck on a rack. They
belonged to a world which had nothing to do with the one he

had struggled up in, where bustle and business stretched time to its limit and left no space for conjecture about the past. Now, though, he found himself suddenly caught up with this other Egypt, esoteric, yet marching hand in hand with the blatant civilization of the 20th century.

He turned and faced East, his eyes scanning the oasis of green, and over to the distant Mokhattem Hills, with Cairo beneath blinking its first lights through the dusk. How magic and removed from its turbulent actuality it seemed. And for a moment, as the Pyramid's shadow stretched into the misty distance to the golden silhouette of the Citadel, he became part of a historical duality, where time hovered between a pulsating present and an imperturbable past.

He walked back to his car and drove down to the hotel. He would not go on to the city, he decided, but would spend the night there. He booked in, changed, and ordered a drink on the terrace. The first stars were appearing, and the towering monument had shed its cloak of granite opacity to reveal itself in eternal black. Involuntarily he shivered, gulped down his cocktail, and gained the warmth of the hotel's foyer.

The next day he drove into Cairo, visited three potential clients, and at 7 p.m. hailed a taxi to the station

Fourteen hours later his train drew into Luxor. He got into the hotel just before midday and found a message from Marguerite. 'We're off to Karnak but will be back for a late lunch. I miss you.' He smiled. It was the first time she had written words which expressed more than a feeling of camaraderie. Obviously she felt herself freer from supervision here.

Once up in his room he unpacked, changed into lightweight clothes and opened a packet he had kept in his jacket. It contained a small leather box with, in it, a 4 carat diamond bought from Alexandria's leading jeweller.

It had cost nearly twice what he had expected, but no one could fail to be impressed by it. Marguerite would wear it that same evening; he would slip it on her finger as they danced their way into the New Year, and the next morning he would speak to her father.

He breathed in deeply. They would have to agree. Wouldn't the ring and his known capacity for making money convince them that he could take care of their daughter in a manner befitting a girl of her background? He snapped shut the little box. If love did not count for Helen Wirsa, the ring might.

He went to the window and threw open the shutters. Shading his eyes from the glare, he gazed out across the Nile and the strip of rich vegetation to the arid hills of the Western Desert. Then he watched a group of tourists in wide brimmed hats slip off donkeys which had trudged them back from their sightseeing, and wondered if he shouldn't jump in a *garry* and join Marguerite at Karnak. But as likely as not he wouldn't find her, he decided, so he went out and wandered around the Temple of Luxor, a little way along the waterfront, glancing impatiently at his watch every five minutes.

He got back to see two horse drawn carriages stop at the steps to the hotel's entrance and Marguerite skip off one, slim and cool-looking in a blue cotton ensemble. He was about to run after her when he heard his name called.

"Ah, Caspardian, you missed something just now. You'll have to visit Karnak. No one can come to Luxor and not go there. Don't you agree, my dear?"

Helen nodded to her husband and then smiled at Antor.

"So you managed to make it after all, Antor. You'll join us for lunch, won't you? Shall we say in half an hour?"

Antor bowed over her outstretched hand, then followed her and George Wirsa into the hotel. While he did so, he wondered whether Helen had purposely blocked his way to join Marguerite and the others. He clenched his fist and controlled his impatience as George suggested they go to the bar for an aperitif. Every minute he could be with Marguerite was precious, but he was wise enough to know that a show of courtesy to her parents was probably time well spent.

It was when he was beginning to wonder whether he would ever be allowed to have her to himself that what he had hoped and dreamed of happened suddenly.

That afternoon he and Marguerite unexpectedly found themselves on their own. After lunch the older generation had retired to their rooms for a siesta, as had Roger, Eduardo and Robert. Helen had suggested the girls do the same but Magda Lambrakis had said, "we aren't at all tired, Mrs Wirsa. Do you mind if we stay here with Antor and tell him all about Karnak?"

There had been a moment of hesitation, then Helen had nodded.

"All right, but as long as you two girls stay quietly out of the sun here, and Antor promises not to take you into the town. You've had enough sightseeing for today, and tomorrow will be tiring."

Ten minutes after she had left, Magda put a hand to her mouth. "After all, I think I will have a rest; you don't mind do you?"

When she had gone Antor took Marguerite's hand in his. He stared at it for a long moment, then brought it to his lips and kissed each one of the fingers.

"Come," he said quietly, "I must talk to you. But not here; where we can be just the two of us for once. We'll go to my room."

"But Antor ... " It was not a protest, simply a flutter of uncertainty.

"Don't worry, darling, I only want to talk. I need to, and maybe we won't have another opportunity to be together for a long time. Come," and he led her gently to the staircase, up the one flight and along to his room. His hand trembled as he put the key in the lock. Before going in, she glanced cautiously up and down the corridor to make sure no one saw her and, once inside, ran over to the window.

"I shouldn't be here, Antor," she whispered as he came close to her.

He put his arms around her and murmured, "this is where you belong, my love."

For a moment she nestled against him, then disengaged herself. "You said we would talk, and I believed you; that's why I came in here. But you mustn't try to kiss me, please Antor, you know it's wrong."

"Wrong?" His eyes were blazing. "Don't you realize I love you, and that you love me too? I want to marry you! There's nothing wrong about my wanting to kiss you, to hold you in my arms, or even to make love with you. But I don't ask that, not yet. I simply want you to realize that we must tell your parents that we love each other and want to get married. I can't go on waiting like this, playing a childish game of deceit, just because we're afraid of what they might think. I'm a man and you're no longer a little girl, you're a woman. We're entitled to live the life we want to. Look, to show you how I feel, I've got you something."

He went quickly to his suitcase, unlocked it, and took out the leather box.

"I was going to give it to you tonight, but you'll have it now." The anger had gone from his voice. "Give me your hand, darling," he said softly, as he reached out for her. "I've never loved another woman, I've never even kissed one before and, if you'll marry me, I never will."

He slipped the ring on her finger and drew her to him. Marguerite gave a little gasp but did not try to draw away. He saw her eyes fill with tears as she gazed at the stone, moving her hand slightly so that it sparkled in the afternoon light. Her face lifted towards his and her lips began to tremble. "I ... I ... "

His mouth closed on hers and he felt her arms tighten around his neck. As the kiss prolonged itself, her body pressed against his. The blood was racing through his veins and he could feel her heart beating almost in rhythm with his. She was clinging to him now, her fingers in his hair and her thighs glued to his. He kissed her eyes, her neck, her ears and hair, whispering his love for her while little gasps fluttered from her lips.

"Oh God," she murmured as he picked, her up and laid her on the bed, "Antor ... no ... no ... "

He put himself upon her and pressed her body into the mattress. His lips silenced her as, with one hand, he cupped her breast inside her blouse, and with the other undid his shirt buttons. When he felt her fingers gently stroke his bare back, he knew that nothing would stop him. The excitement was such that he longed to rip the clothes off and plunge himself into her, but instinctively he controlled himself. He swung his feet off the bed and drew her into a sitting position. Still kissing and caressing her, he took off her blouse, then her bra. Flinging off his shirt, he brought their naked torsos together. The effect on him was electric; a first orgasm burst through him, sending shudders over his whole body. He gasped and grasped her tightly to him, feeling her taut nipples through the thick hair on his chest. He slipped out of his trousers and was conscious of a moment's shyness as his throbbing virility strained up in front of him. He bent down again, undid the button of her belt, and slid her skirt from her. Her eyes were closed but her lips were mouthing words he could not hear, words of love and yearning. He began kissing that body which he had caressed so often in his dreams; the shoulders, the breasts and tummy, the thighs and hips. And as his tongue discovered one part, his fingers explored another, until neither of them could wait any more.

He lifted her slightly and removed the pants which hid her total nakedness, then lay on her again. Her words turned into a groan as he began to feel between her legs. Then she opened wide her eyes and said, "now Antor, now ... " Her thighs went up around his hips and very slowly he began to press himself into her. There was a slight cry, then he was deep inside.

For an hour they remained as one, while waves of orgasms swept their bodies into an ocean of love and fulfilment.

There was a knock on the bedroom door. With a shock Antor realized that it was not locked.

"Just a minute," he cried, "who is it?"

"A message for you, *howager*."

"Keep it, I'll collect it when I come down."

"Yes, *howager*."

The servant moved away. Antor got up, went over to the door and locked it. When he came back to the bed, Marguerite smiled up at him and whispered, "you're so handsome. I never realized how beautiful your body was. I love you so much, I'm frightened. And this ring ... I don't know what to say." She rested her hand on his hip and gazed at the diamond.

"Just 'I will'. Nothing more. You're my wife now, my darling; nothing can change that." He began kissing and caressing her again.

"I don't think we should. They'll begin to wonder where we are," she murmured as he moved on top of her. But she knew she could not stop him, nor did she want to. She had never expected she would love a man the way she did that afternoon.

Later, it was he who decided they should stop. He helped her dress and watched her comb her hair and put on a touch of lipstick.

"Every time I look at you, you're more beautiful," he said. "I don't know how I'll be able to be separated from you again. You're mine, Marguerite, mine for ever. Tonight, you must come to me. Promise me you'll be back in my arms tonight."

She promised, and when he had held her tightly again, he told her to go and find Magda first to know whether her mother had asked where she was.

"Avoid her as much as possible," he warned, "a mother has

an uncanny way of guessing about these things where her daughter is concerned. Meet me downstairs with the others in about an hour ... "

He felt her tremble a little as he led her to the door. "Don't worry, darling, trust me and love me, that's all I ask."

She smiled and rested her head for a moment on his shoulder.

"If only we could stay here for ever, Antor. I don't want it to finish."

He kissed her temples. "It has only just begun. Now that I have you, I'll never let you go. In a few hours we'll be together again, remember?"

As she was leaving she slipped the ring off her finger and handed it to him.

"You keep it, and give it to me at midnight..."

Half an hour later he went downstairs to the hall porter's desk.

"There's a message for me, I was told."

"Yes, Mr Caspardian, a call from Alexandria. You are requested to phone your home as soon as possible."

Antor frowned. His home? That could only mean one thing; his mother must be ill. Why else would they call him?

"Get me this number as fast as you can."

"Yes sir. I'm afraid there is a delay for Alexandria, but I'll do my best."

He glanced around the hall and over to the main sitting room. None of the group seemed to be there; probably they were out on the terrace. But he had no wish to join them and make idle conversation after the intensity of the passion he had just experienced, pretending that nothing had happened, that nothing had changed in the last two hours.

Two hours! In that brief period his world had become another, and he felt as if some uncontrollable process had altered both his physical and psychological make-up. He was not just a man now, he was a giant. He lit himself a cigarette and clapped his hands. A waiter came running.

"Get me an iced beer and bring it to me in the garden."

"Yes, *gnab el howager*."

But it was still too warm to sit outside, so he installed himself by a table under a slow moving fan, and waited. He could see both the stairs and the lift exit, and would watch

Marguerite appear from down one or the other. He would observe the way she moved, the tilt of her head, the curve of her breasts, savouring the knowledge that he, and he only, knew the secrets of that body.

Twenty minutes later a messenger boy hurried over and told him that Alexandria was on the line.

An anguished Madame Hitawi broke him the news.

"You must come back, Antor. Your mother is very ill. They wanted to take her to the hospital, but she refuses to go there."

"But what is it?" he cried, "she was all right two days ago."

"It's her heart, it's much worse than anyone suspected. She hid it from you, not wanting to spoil your plans. She hid it from all of us. When can you come back? She's asking for you all the time."

"Tell her I'm coming, and I'll be there tomorrow. I'll catch the train straight back and will be there in the early afternoon."

"Bless you, Antor, but hurry. We don't know how long she can last."

Oh, God, he thought, he should never have left; he should have guessed. He would never forgive himself if she died while he was away. Yet coming to Luxor had marked an essential moment in his life. Would Marguerite's and his love have exploded into that all-consuming passion, that unbreakable bond, had he not been there?

He stepped out of the telephone booth and called the hall porter.

"Get me a sleeper on tonight's train to Cairo and prepare me my bill. What time does the train leave?"

"At ten past six, *howager*. If you wish to catch it, may I suggest your luggage is brought down immediately."

Antor nodded and went up to his room. He threw his clothes into the suitcase, then rushed off a note to Marguerite.

"My darling,
I have just heard that my mother is terribly ill, so must get back to Alex as fast as possible. You can imagine what I feel about not being with you again today, tonight, tomorrow and all the time you'll be here. But my thoughts will be with you constantly. Come to me soon, Marguerite my love, I miss you already. This afternoon will remain the most wonderful moment of my life, and even though we are not married yet, you are my wife now and the very reason of my existence. As soon as you get

back to Alexandria I will speak to your Father and Mother, and then you'll wear the ring with joy. Keep it somewhere safe, but look at it often so that you will think of me. I love you terribly. Forgive me for not being here to kiss you into the New Year,

your Antor

He took a large envelope and placed the letter and the ring in it. He went downstairs, paid his bill and handed the envelope to the hall porter with 20 piastres and the instructions to give it to Marguerite personally. He turned and stared up the stairs to the landing, praying that she might come down them before he had to leave. There was a sudden constriction in his chest. Oh Lord, he thought, why had his mother been taken ill just then? Why could it not have happened forty-eight hours later?

The porter called to him that his taxi was waiting, and at the same time Magda appeared from the lift.

"I have to leave," he said hurriedly, "My mother's ill. Tell the others ... tell Marguerite I had to catch the train back ... I can't help it."

Two minutes later he was in the taxi heading towards the station.

Antor got home in the early afternoon, and when he tiptoed into his mother's bedroom a smile trembled on her lips.

"I knew you wouldn't leave me to go on my own. You look tired, my son. Sit near to me on the bed and hold my hand ... what a nuisance I've been to you ... I would have left you in peace, but there was something I wanted to say to you before I go to join your father ... He'll be there to welcome me, I know, and I'm happy I'll be with him again shortly. But that wasn't what I wanted to tell you ... let me look at you ... yes, it's as I feared. You've been rash. I shouldn't have let you go off to Luxor ... I should have been stronger and a real mother to you when you needed one. Now it's too late."

"Mother ... " he began.

"No, don't say anything yet, listen to me. Whatever happens, don't be foolish. Don't be bitter, either. The ways of the Lord are mysterious, but they are His ways and we must not question them. Don't try to understand them, accept them. Put your faith in Him, Antor, and you will know peace. You have wandered away from God; you feel yourself strong, and you are strong. Without Him, though, you are nothing." She coughed, and after a moment's silence she put her fingers to her bosom and touched the cross which rested on her nightdress.

"Your father gave me this little cross when you were born. When I have gone I want you to take it and wear it. It will remind you that the Lord is ever present, and that He can do with us what He wishes. And in times of trouble and difficulty He can give us the strength to carry on. You will be alone soon and you will need His succour. It will be a difficult time for you, I know ... but don't be sad. Now let me kiss you."

At ten o'clock last rites were administered, and Antor sat by her side for the next three hours, until the breathing ceased. For a long moment he gazed at her, tears swelling in his eyes as an acute sense of forlornness gripped him. The giant of the previous day had become a babe, bewildered and curiously frightened. He was alone now, without even Marguerite to comfort him. He wiped his tears and lifted his mother's head gently to remove the chain and cross from around her neck. He slipped it over his head and tucked it under his shirt. Then he closed her eyes, kissed her, and left the room.

The day after the funeral Antor phoned the Wirsa's home. It was January 4th and Marguerite should have returned.

"Could I speak to Miss Marguerite?"

"Sorry, *howager*, she's not here."

"When are she and her parents expected back?"

"We don't know *howager*."

"I see. Tell her that Mr Antor rang and would like her to phone him when she arrives."

"Yes, *howager*."

Curious, he thought. They had only booked at the hotel till the 3rd, she'd told him. They must have stopped over in Cairo for a day or two. Yet if they had, surely she would have phoned him, especially knowing why he had had to rush back to Alexandria.

For three days he rang the house morning and evening, but with the same result. No, the family had not returned, and the servants had no idea when they would. He tried the Christofides home, but there too got the same answer. The family was away and no one knew when they were getting back. No luck either at Eduardo's home or Magda Lambrakis', they were in Cairo and not due back for a week. No one could tell him what had happened to Marguerite.

Then, on January 10th, a messenger arrived at his office with a small package marked 'Antor Caspardian. Private and Confidential.'

He stared at it as the muscles in his tummy contracted. The writing was George Wirsa's. Slowly he opened the packet; it contained a written sheet of letter paper and the small jeweller's box with the ring.

Caspardian,

You are a despicable man. We have discovered how you shamelessly abused our daughter, an innocent, trusting girl. If I could, I would have you horsewhipped, but I am a law abiding citizen. I can only hope that you have a spark of remorse which will make you regret for the rest of your life what you have done to Marguerite.

By the time you receive this she will be at a safe distance from you, and I forbid you ever to try and see her again in the future.

The ring with which you deceived her is returned. I curse the day you first came to my house.

George Wirsa

He felt the blood drain from his temples and he gripped the edge of his desk to stop himself from reeling. It couldn't be! That letter wasn't addressed to him! It was some terrible trick of his imagination, a waking nightmare which he must somehow shake off. He read the neatly written words over and over, trying to understand what could have happened. What horrible mistake was responsible for this?

He jumped up, raced out of the office and down to his car. He had to see Marguerite, to touch her and hold her in his arms. He must shout his love for her to the world at large, to her father and mother especially. They had to understand; they couldn't mean what was said in the letter.

Twenty minutes later he skidded up in front of the Wirsa mansion with a screech of brakes. He scrambled out of his new red MG and rang the gate bell furiously. No one answered. He began shaking the gates and shouting Marguerite's name, and a woman came scurrying from the back garden. It was Nourna, her old nanny.

"Please, Mr Antor, please don't shout like that."

"Where is she ... what has happened? Why won't anyone tell me?"

"Oh, Mr Antor," she wailed, "what have you done to my little mistress? Madame and Monsieur were so angry, they said you were never to be allowed in the house again ... that you must never see her again ... that none of us must even speak to you. Please, Mr Antor, go away ... my poor Miss Marguerite, she just cried and cried while the cases were packed ... They've taken her away ... "

"Where to, for God's sake, where to, Nourna?"

"I don't know ... to Europe somewhere ... "

"It can't be! Tell me where ... I've got to know ... please Nourna ... "

"Oh Mr Antor I don't know ... please go, I mustn't speak to you or they'll send me away ... "

She was sobbing, but before he could ask her anything else she scuttled back to the house.

Slowly he turned away, overwhelmed by a numbing despair. What could he do? Even if he had been told where in Europe they had gone, he could not have followed them. An immense loneliness shrouded him as he drove back to the town centre. There was nothing for it but wait until they returned.

Three weeks later the Journal d'Egypte announced the marriage of Marguerite Wirsa with Roger Christofides. Under the heading of 'Sudden Romance', it described how these scions of Alexandria's society had been married in Paris after a whirlwind romance at St Moritz where the two families had been winter sporting. The couple, it went on to say, would be returning to Egypt only in April after a two month honeymoon.

Marguerite's disappearance and her father's letter had shattered Antor, but not altered his determination to marry her as soon as possible. When he had recovered from the initial shock he persuaded himself that the terrible misunderstanding could be cleared the moment he had a chance to see and speak to George Wirsa. He cursed himself for not having asked him Marguerite's hand long before. Once her parents were convinced that he really loved her, and that what had taken place in Luxor was the physical expression of a beautiful sentiment and not a sordid satisfaction of his libido, they would surely change their attitude.

If only he knew what had happened after he had left the hotel. How had her father and mother discovered they had become lovers? Why had not Marguerite told them that she loved him and that he wanted to marry her, that he had not 'abused' her? True, he should not have taken her to his room; he should not have kissed and caressed her and done what only a husband was entitled to do with her. By the norms of the society in which they lived, that was wrong, but in the eyes of God he was her husband, and in the eyes of society he asked for nothing better. Rather, he demanded they should be married. At least, he would, when he could speak to George Wirsa.

The announcement in the newspaper killed a part of him. He read it by chance as he was eating a hurried lunch sent up to him in his office. He vomited violently then dragged himself to the window. As he leant across the 5th floor sill, there was a moment when the road below beckoned him. A small movement of his leg muscles and his misery would be over. He felt his heart pounding and instinctively his fingers reached for the cross beneath his vest.

The agony eased and he was able to breathe again. Hardly aware of what he was doing, he turned slowly back to his desk and threw the newspaper over the mess on the floor. Then he rang for his secretary.

"I've been sick," he said simply.

The young man looked at him and nodded. "Shall I call a doctor?"

Antor pushed passed him without answering, trying to hide the tears which were now streaming down his cheeks.

Antor never saw Marguerite again. He made a point of avoiding places where he knew he might come across her, and cut all relationship with the friends they had in common. He gave up the lease on the house in Bulkeley and went to stay at a pension in Rue Adib. His work routine did not change, but instead of going to the Sporting Club for tennis or golf, he began frequenting a gymnasium for an hour every afternoon.

On Sundays, when he was in Alexandria, he would collect his friend Francesco's young brother and sister, and take them for a picnic on Lake Mariut, or to a remote spot on the rocks at Abukir.

Francesco had been ordained and was away in Turin, training to be a missionary priest. His brother Pietro was a boarder at Don Bosco while Clara, his little sister, was at a convent. Ever since he had been in a position to, Antor had made a point of helping his friend financially, and it was largely thanks to this that Francesco had been able to leave for Italy, knowing that he was there to take care of his family. At first it had been difficult to get Francesco to accept his help, but when Antor pointed out that by doing so his ailing father would at last know a little comfort, he acquiesced.

Antor gave the love which should have gone to Marguerite and a family of his own to the one he adopted. The two youngsters became the brother and sister he had never had, and their father, whom he placed in the care of a capable nurse, a putative uncle. And in those desolate days when he found himself suddenly bereft of the two women he had loved, Francesco's family became a lifebuoy in an ocean of emotional distress.

He began going more often to Cairo and staying there for a few days at a time. He established business relations with building contractors, and appointed agents for his refrigerators, radios and bathroom fittings. And a few months later, at the suggestion of Raymond Zekla's cousin Emile, he invested in development land at Heliopolis adjoining some owned by the powerful Empain Group.

"That's the way the city will expand," the banker counselled, "if you want to invest, it's where you should buy. It may be a strip of desert today at the edge of a suburb, but in a few years it'll mushroom with buildings."

Emile Zekla was responsible for Antor's meeting Renée Naggiar at a party given in his Garden City villa. It was his first social outing in the year, and he had gone to it only because he felt that not to would have seemed rude, and Emile Zekla was not a man one slighted if one was green on the Cairo business scene and needing contacts.

Renée had noted him immediately.

Most of the men present were in their middle forties, with a premature heaviness around their jowls and waists. Their attraction lay purely in a capacity to dominate by the inordinate amount of money they had either inherited or amassed. They were neither elegant nor witty, like their Alexandrian counterparts, and the women, bar Renée, were not as beautiful or sophisticated as those who had made the city of Cleopatra the most fashionable of the Mediterranean. Antor was a good fifteen years younger than any of the men, and streets ahead for sheer animal attractiveness. Yet curiously, despite his swarthy good looks, there was an aura of innocence about him which contrasted with the jaded sensuality of the others, and this Renée found irresistible.

She went over to Emile Zekla and asked him who he was.

"Antor Caspardian ... comes from Alexandria. Very bright businesswise."

"That's why he's here, of course. Tell me, Emile, do you know anyone who isn't either rich or clever?"

"Come, my dear, is it my fault that the people I know just happen to be ... anyway, for a banker there is no such a creature as a clever pauper. Do you want to meet him?"

"Certainly. An attractive man with brains, here in Cairo, is a rarity not to be missed..."

Renée was not beautiful in the classical sense. Her eyebrows were straight and her mouth too wide, but the eyes were a luminous honey brown, sparkling with sensuality, and her body undulated like waters buoyed by strong undercurrents. She was the most physically attractive woman of Cairo's moneyed society.

At first Antor had been embarrassed when she had slipped her arm through his and led him to the dining room where a buffet supper was being served. He felt out of context, aware that several pairs of eyes were watching him and that lips had begun to whisper as heads nodded in his direction. While sure of himself in the company of men, he was awkward with women, and totally out of his depth with Renée Naggiar. He wanted to leave, to get back to the familiar solitude of his hotel room and prepare himself for the business talks he would have the next morning. But somehow he could not. He was trapped by this woman whose hand would fleetingly rest on his, whose knee touched his thigh while they sat at one of the small dining room tables, whose eyes were scrutinizing, at times laughingly at others intently, every part of his face.

He had not thought about women or sex since that afternoon in Luxor. His losing Marguerite so abruptly after his mother's death had badly shocked his nervous system and stifled his sexuality. Now, however, he was aware of a novel sensation; of an animal consciousness of this woman's presence, as if the pores of his skin were identifying themselves with hers. It was not a question of liking her or of being flattered by her interest in him; it was to do specifically with his body. After dinner there was music and they danced. The sensation accentuated itself and became localized. With the curve of her stomach pressing his crotch, the desire which had lain dormant for months awoke suddenly. Renée smiled and pressed her fingers into his back. Half an hour later she asked him to accompany her home.

She taught him a lot. Nearly all about the sexuality of a woman's body and quite a bit about his own, throwing his adolescent concept that love and sex marched hand in hand to the winds.

"It's the body that counts, and with one like yours you can achieve miracles. Leave love to those who need an excuse to bed a woman."

Antor began enjoying the power of his sex appeal and, at Renée's prompting, tried seducing other women. "I want them to taste you just once, so that they know what they're missing," she confided mischievously, and he was astonished at the rapidity with which some of them stripped pride and clothes to have him take them. He was also surprised by the effect his rampant virility had on the men. They became curiously eager to do business with him, even to be seen in his company.

"You're a kind of fetish," Renée explained, "subcon- sciously they associate themselves with you and hope it'll do the trick with women — the fools! Did you know that half of them are impotent? They can only make it if they've diddled someone on a grand scale, or hit the jackpot on the Bourse. Otherwise they go plop and remain plop. My husband's like that," she added as she lay in bed with him and licked his nipples, "but you mustn't ever be, promise me. Never castrate yourself for the sake of money ... and don't smirk, it happens more easily than you can imagine."

Antor rolled on top of her and went on grinning. His business was one thing and his sex another. His mind took care of the one and his body of the other. The two would neither meet nor mix.

If his body was active, in demand, and obtaining excellent

results, so was his business. Cairo became an even better market for his imports and factory products than Alexandria. Since he found himself spending several weeks at a time in the capital, he rented an apartment in a modern block overlooking the Sporting Club at Gezira which Renée chose for him and decorated in the latest trends; smooth textures, pale woods and modern paintings. It was the successful bachelor's pad, impersonal yet convenient for entertaining and womanizing, activities he did not indulge in at Alexandria, where he continued to stay in a pension and worked from morning to night. There he saw no one outside business contacts and Francesco's family, and spent as little time as possible in the city which held too many ghosts for him.

On September 1st he was sitting in his office, when a letter was brought round by hand for him. It was marked "Private and Confidential" and the handwriting was not one he recognized. He slit open the envelope and looked at the signature. Magda. Why on earth should she write to him?

Dear Antor

I would have liked to see you and tell you the sad news, only I did not have the courage. Please forgive me. Marguerite died yesterday after giving birth to a baby son. It is an awful shock for all of us and I know it will be very painful for you especially.

Two weeks ago Marguerite gave me this letter, which I was to let you have if anything happened to her. Somehow she must have sensed she might die.

She was such a wonderful person, we will all miss her terribly. Ring me if I can help in any way,

Magda

He stared at the letter for a long while, reading it over and over. Marguerite dead? He mouthed the words as if to give them substance. It couldn't be. Yet Magda would not have written it if it were not true. She had died while he was a few kilometres away, at the factory or in the office, giving mundane instructions or checking orders and accounts. The one woman he had ever loved, and who should have been his wife, had gone from this world without his even knowing it!

He felt no sensation of shock, no desperate grief, as when he had learnt of her marriage. Just incredulity.

He put down Magda's note and reached for the pale blue envelope with his name written in Marguerite's girlish handwriting. He opened it slowly, leant back in his chair, and began reading.

My dearest Antor

If you ever receive this it will mean that I am no more, and I don't want to die without sharing my secret with you. It is our secret and should have been our joy had our destinies been different. Why did you leave me Antor? Had you stayed by me I could have been strong and my life would not be what it is. But it is too late to try to turn back the clock. Believe me, Antor my love, there are no reproaches on my part, only infinite sadness. Life would have been so wonderful together.

In a few days time our baby will be born. Yes, it is the fruit of our great love. It is your child, thank God, and it has been this certainty which has kept me from going mad these last months.

If I live, I will tell you the truth one day, if I die, you will learn it now. I don't know whether you will thank me for this, but I feel I owe it to you and to our child.

I have never stopped loving you. Nothing that has happened has changed my feelings for you, nor ever will.

If only you had left me a note or a message that afternoon.

I learnt that your Mother had died; I'm so sorry for I know how close you were to her and her going must have made you very lonely. I have been lonely too, so I know what it means. But if all goes well I won't be any more for a part of you will be ever present in our child.

Goodbye my beloved, father of my little one, and may God bless you.

Marguerite

The funeral took place the following day. Antor sat in a back pew of the Coptic basilica amongst a congregation of men and women who dominated Alexandria's social sets. Greeks, English, French, Italians, Jews, Copts and Egyptians, the cosmopolitans of different nationalities and different religions but of one creed. His eyes travelled down the aisle to the altar and the flower covered coffin in front of it. Immediately behind were George and Helen Wirsa, immobile like black draped statues, not a flicker of expression on their drawn features. Next to them was Roger Christofides whispering to his mother and a little further down he saw Magda, staring at Roger.

He closed his eyes, wanting to shut them and their world from him, wanting to pray as he used to with his mother and father in the early days of his childhood. The prayers came to him mechanically but empty of significance. His lips moved yet his mind was elsewhere, harking back to Marguerite's letter. 'If only you had left a note or a message that afternoon ...' Her parents, those two effigies of righteous sorrow, must have lied to her, fabricating God knew what story to impede a marriage they deemed unsuitable. He tried not to hate them, there in the church where all should be forgiveness and compassion. It was not their fault if she were dead, but it was if she had died unhappy and alone, if his capacity to love had been killed, and if that baby would never be his son.

He stood up and made the sign of the cross as he took a final look at the coffin. For Marguerite's sake he would try not to hate them, but he would never forget or forgive.

London, 1938

Antor Caspardian stood at the hotel window and gazed down at the grey waters of the Thames. It was his second visit to London, but the first had been no more than an overnight stop on his way to the Midlands, and a curtain of drizzle had clouded his vision of the city. This time was different. He was planning to stay ten days, and the weather was sunny. Renée had been supposed to meet him there, but at the last minute had changed plans.

"Enjoy it all the same," she had urged, "and don't treat it like Manchester — a place to do business in and get out of as fast as possible. Forget about work, and make the most of what London can give you, and which you won't find anywhere else. The theatres, the museums, Wimbledon, the changing of the Guard at Buckingham Palace, Madame Tussaud's ... I could go on all night with the things to do and places to visit. Ten days will be only enough to scratch the surface, but at least it'll be a beginning."

She had told him where to stay, what restaurants to eat at, and given him three introductions to friends of hers, one of which had resulted in that evening's invitation to a play and dinner.

He glanced at his watch. 6.15. It was time to get changed. The Redferns had said they would meet him in the hotel foyer about' seven o'clock, to have a drink before walking across to the theatre, which was apparently right next door. He wondered what sort of a woman Joan Redfern would turn out to be.

Not your type, Renée had said, but that was nothing to go by. What was his type, anyway? Had he a preference for a certain type of woman? In the past five years he must have made love to dozens, and they had meant nothing more than a moment's physical pleasure. Not intense pleasure, not the piercing almost painful explosion of the senses which his first experience had given him. That would never come his way again. Not even Renée, sexually stimulating above all else, had brought that about in him. No woman would, he knew, for he would never love one as he had Marguerite.

The Redferns turned out to be punctual and pleasant, he American and she Irish, both of them in their early forties, Antor guessed. The conversation flowed easily as they drank their cocktails.

"I hope you'll enjoy the play. We chose it for two reasons; one, because the theatre is so convenient and two, because Cecily Bentley has the leading role. She's fabulous and a friend of ours. After the show we'll go backstage and see her. Maybe we'll get her to join us for supper; she wasn't sure when I spoke to her this morning as she has had some prior engagement she may not be able to get out of. Have you seen her act? She's made one or two films and I thought they might have been shown in Egypt. You'll love her, she's a marvellous actress ... "

Antor had never been to a play, and he was not at all sure what to expect. Actresses and film stars were celluloid unrealities for him who had little in common with life, his life at any rate. He had somehow imagined that a play would be even less credible than a film, and was prepared to be bored silly with the whole performance. But he had not catered for Cecily Bentley.

From the moment the curtain had gone up and revealed her there, no more than five metres away from him, he felt he was alone with her on the stage, sharing her joys and griefs, her angers and passions. He was totally captivated by her, not only by her acting, but by her extraordinary presence. She gave him the impression that he had always known her; that her laugh, the tilt of her head and the curious, fluttering movement of her hand in her hair, were as familiar to him as his mother's way of pursing her lips, or his father's passing his index finger up and down his nose. The applause at the end of each act had irked him, as if it had been an intrusion into a privacy which had enveloped them. What were the others doing there, watching a performance which was meant for him and no one else?

Cecily was a revelation to him. She was like no other woman he had ever met. Slender to a point of frailness, with a mass of auburn hair and dark blue touching-on-violet eyes, she exuded a vibrant charm which, linked to a considerable talent, had made her very rapidly a box office draw. The public loved her and made no secret of it. When the curtain came down on the last act, the audience got to their feet and gave her a standing ovation.

"It's like this every night", Joan Redfern shouted in his ear. "Isn't she fabulous!"

Twenty minutes later he was introduced to her. She had wiped the paint from her face and hidden her magnificent hair beneath a towel.

"I shouldn't let a stranger see me like this" she'd said laughing softly. "You're no true friend, Joan, but I'll forgive you. Did you enjoy the play Mr ... ? I'm sorry, that name's a bit of a mouthful."

"Antor Caspardian. I thought you were marvellous," he said simply.

"Well that's praise for you, Cecily. A completely unbiased and fresh opinion. It's his first evening in London and his first play."

"And he's right. You were superb, darling, as you always are. You'll be dining with us I hope?" Mark Redfern added.

There had been a flicker of hesitation as her lips opened, perhaps to mouth some excuse; then her eye had caught Antor's.

"I'd love to," she said, "but you'll have to give me half an hour. Let's meet at the hotel; I'll be over as soon as I'm dressed."

"May I come to escort you there?" Antor asked.

"That's very sweet of you, but please don't bother. It's right next door, and I won't be long." She smiled at him, and Antor felt a tingle around his solar plexus.

Over dinner he learnt that she was married, with two children, and that her husband was abroad for two weeks. Laughingly she had added, "I'm an abandoned woman for a short while. If I weren't, I couldn't be dining with you as James isn't a great one for night life. He's right, probably. Says I must get to bed before midnight when I'm working, and usually I do."

"Then we must celebrate the exception to the rule," Mark Redfern said, "and go on to a spot of dancing."

Later she admitted to Antor that she hated nightclubs and had only agreed as it was a way to stay with him. To touch him and feel the pressure of his fingers on her back as they danced, and to watch the movement of his lips and the blinking of his eyelashes.

"They're much too long for a man," she said on the Sunday morning when she had woken in his bed.

Three days had passed since that first dinner. Days which, for Antor, had meant twelve hours of inconsequential waiting till the theatre curtain rose and she was there again.

She was not able to meet him except after the show, and he couldn't remember later how he had filled in the hours. Probably he had followed Renée's suggestions and done some sightseeing, but his mind had been so totally taken up with Cecily that he was conscious of little else.

After the show he would wait for her at the Savoy, then take her to a restaurant for dinner. They talked of their lives and habits, she of the theatre, principally, and he of Egypt, innocuous topics which were cover-ups for the feelings and words they would have liked to express. And the following mornings and afternoons became blanks of longing for him, meaningless intervals in a play of passion. But he was careful not to brusque her, sensing that she was not a woman who would lightly give herself to a man, however attracted she might be. Also his own feelings towards her were different to those he usually felt. Mixed with a strong physical desire was a sentiment very near that which he had experienced for Marguerite.

On the Saturday evening they dined and danced at the hotel. As her cheek rested against his and her slim body moved with his to a romantic melody, he was overwhelmed by a profound tenderness and almost without realizing it he whispered three words into her ear he had not uttered for more than five years. She pressed his hand and looked up, her eyes sparkling.

"Oh Antor," she sighed, surrendering, "I think I love you too. But ... "

That night and for the eight which were to follow they forgot that 'but', banishing past and future as they gave themselves to each other in a total abandon of senses and sentiments. Yet deep and consuming as it was, their passion flared like a fireworks display, brilliant but transient.

On the Sunday they had driven out in her car to the country and lunched at a country hotel outside Canterbury.

"London's not England," she said as they left the city's

sprawling and murky suburbs and motored through the orchards and gardens of Kent, "and I'm not letting you go back to those desert dunes of yours without having an idea of our countryside. Isn't it absolutely lovely!"

He nodded, taking in the tailored beauty of the surrounding landscape with its wheat fields neatly delimited by hedges, its dark leaved woods framing an occasional grey stone mansion, and the flower covered villages where cottages seemed to emanate from treasured snapshots. It was all so totally different from anything he had seen or experienced before that it bewildered him, and instinctively he threw an arm around her shoulders as if to reassure himself by touching and caressing part of the reality about him.

After lunch she asked him if he would like to visit her home. "It's not far from here and it's rather beautiful."

It had been a mistake. The Jacobean manor house which had been the seat of the Viscounts Brentwick for over two hundred and fifty years represented the part of Cecily which could never be his. As they strolled through the terraced gardens, across the lawns and down to a gazebo by the shaded waters of a lake, he had the uncomfortable sensation of being an intruder, tolerated only because his visit was a fleeting one. Chilton Hall, with its black and white floored entrance hung with family portraits and its reception rooms filled with tradition, disorientated him. As did the two fair haired and well-behaved children who were called to say hello to him. It all made him feel alien, and Cecily a stranger. That night, as if to avenge himself, he made love to her fiercely, desperately almost. That night Maryanne was conceived.

He left as programmed at the end of ten days. Had Cecily's husband not returned, he might have stayed on, but he was not prepared to share her with anyone, least of all with the courteous aristocrat who was the father of her two children. Compromise was not in his nature, and even had Cecily been willing to give up everything for him, he would not have accepted. He had been brought up to regard the family as sacrosanct, and he was wise enough to know that too much bound her to a way of life which he could never offer her or form part of. Perhaps because of this he was able to put her from his mind when he got back to Egypt. The ten days of wonder which meeting and loving her had meant for him were part of a dream, of a world which had been his by some miraculous accident. And as such he chose to remember her. He did not write nor try to communicate with her and was thankful that she too acted in the same way.

Only on New Year's day did he phone her from Cairo and learn about the baby.

"Don't worry, Antor," she said "everything will be all right ... yes of course I shall keep it. I may never see you again but I will have someone to remember you by forever. I've already chosen the names; Matthew or Maryanne ... I hope she'll be a girl ... "

On June 5th, as he was in his office discussing the purchase of a warehouse next to his wood-working factory, his secretary handed him a telegram. It consisted of a single sentence.

'Maryanne arrived yesterday. She's lovely, just like her father.'

Antor made a lot of money during the next three years.

Convinced that war would break out before the end of 1939 he made a rapid trip to Europe that summer. His aim was to stock his warehouses with as much merchandise and raw materials as he could afford to buy. His reasoning was simple. If Germany were to declare war on England and France, and Italy were drawn into it, the battles would stretch to the Mediterranean. That would disrupt shipping. Egyptian economy was based on cotton, its main export, and the needs of the country were dependent on the smooth functioning of cargo ships depositing a vast range of imported goods in its ports and carrying away the famous bales of cotton. A lengthy interruption of sailings would hit business badly. But adroitly planned for, this could be turned to an advantage. For the shrewd opportunist he had become, it presented the kind of challenge he enjoyed.

His steamer docked at Genoa on a warm July morning and three hours later he was in a train heading for Turin. He gazed at the gray stone villages clustering like grapes around the hill-top churches, at the terraced vineyards with their trellised vines, down to the long flat plains of the Po river, green with pastures and gently rustling poplar trees. Then he looked at the black shirted fascist sitting opposite him and wondered whether it were true what was said about the Party which had ruled Italy for over 15 years; a clique who trampled on the notions of freedom with the excuse that the means justified the ends, means which included violence towards anyone who voiced a doubt as to the Duce's way of governing the country. Those 'ends' were apparent everywhere, from the magnificent autostradas to the grandiose public buildings and the civic pride reflected in a surprising national efficiency. Yet was the price for this order after chaos too high, as it had turned out to be in Germany, he wondered? But more important, would Mussolini join forces with Hitler in a European conflict in accordance with the Axis pact? If so, a war would stretch to North Africa, and Egypt would become of immense strategic importance. In that eventuality, the letters of credit he had with him would buy him the wherewithal to make a real fortune.

The train began to slow as the outskirts of Turin came into sight. Another quarter of an hour and he would be at the station where Francesco would be meeting him. He leant back in his seat and closed his eyes. It was five years since they had seen each other and he wondered whether he would find his friend very changed. Probably not, he thought, a smile playing on his lips. Francesco was the kind of man who somehow was not affected by the passing of the years.

He caught sight of him immediately as he stepped onto the platform, and wasn't surprised to see him dressed in the habit of a priest. The long black robe fitted him like a second skin.

They strode towards each other, embraced, then walked arm in arm to the 'Topolino' parked in a side street.

"It's not your MG but it goes like a bomb. We'll go to the hotel first and get rid of the luggage. I'd have put you up at my place only we have a visiting bishop and he has monopolized the two guest bedrooms. But I've arranged for us to dine on our own in my study, like that we've got all evening to catch up on our news. You're looking fit, Antor, and there's a halo of prosperity around your head. Things must be going well for you."

Antor laughed. "Which means that Pietro has been writing to you. It's true, business is good and your brother is turning out to be an excellent element at the factory. He's quick and has the knack of talking people into doing things the way he wants. I'm thinking of moving him over to the import-export company ... "

He broke off as the car drew up in front of the hotel and

only later, in the seclusion of Francesco's study, eating the *pasta alla carbonara* prepared by the priest's *perpetua* and savouring a Barbera d'Asti wine, did they settle back and talk. The hours sped by as they recalled the times spent together and recounted what had happened to each other since. Inevitably they discussed the future too, and the dangers which were besetting Europe and the world in general.

"There are forces at work which no one will be able to stop," Francesco said, "forces of evil generated by what is negative in man. Hitler is not just a tyrant, he is the expression of the malaise in our society, of an illness which, alas, has to manifest itself if it is to be got rid of. Mussolini too incarnates a sick nation. He is the giant with feet of clay which Don Michele used to talk about at school, remember? The two will plunge us into an era of disaster as the black plague did in the 14th. century, wiping out a third of Europe's populations. Now, 600 years later, the same desolation will sweep through these lands, only instead of pestilence the killers will be bullets and bombs. You believe me when I say there will be war?"

"I not only believe you, I am convinced of it. That's one of the reasons I'm making this trip. I want to be ready for the war. There'll be a lot of money to be made and I intend to be one of those who make it. Does that shock you?"

The young priest smiled. "Coming from you, no. Each of us has a role in life and it would appear that yours is making money. All your creative forces are channelled that way, and as I know that you'll use money for positive purposes, I'd be the last person to criticise you."

It was Antor's turn to grin. "Isn't that condoning the means to justify the ends?"

Francesco shook his head. "There's always an element of good which comes out of evil, and I would rather it be you who makes the money than some war profiteer with no scruples. Only if you transgress your own moral code would I be shocked. But there is little fear of that. It is a code based on the staunch Christian principles you inherited from your mother and father. It will take more than a bomb to shake those."

Cairo, June, 1942

The swimming pool at the Gezira Sporting Club was packed and Antor wondered whether he would have a quick dip before lunch in the restaurant over the way, or simply come back later when the crowd would have thinned. His eyes scanned the tables filled with members sipping iced drinks. More than half were in army uniform, young officers up on leave from the western desert, with a few days to forget the horrors and hardships of the war in North Africa.

Cairo had changed in two years; the war had seen to that. It now out-rivalled Alexandria for sparkle and fun. It had become an oasis of pleasure and the nerve centre of the Allied High Command in the Middle East.

The elegant Semiramis Hotel on the banks of the Nile had been requisitioned as Army headquarters, and the Long Bar and terrace at Shepherd's was the favourite haunt of officers of all grades. Unlike Alexandria, whose port was a prime target for Axis bombing, Cairo gave the image of a haven out of reach of the destructive turmoil raging at the country's borders. But it was a facade, as Antor and many others were aware. The British were unpopular and a number of Egyptians, from the King and his pro-Italian clique to the students chanting German slogans, would have welcomed a change of sides, especially with Rommel and his troops advancing resolutely across Libya to Egypt's frontiers. The war had brought privations to the ordinary people. Shortages and soaring prices were kindling resentment and the oasis of peace and luxury was a mirage which could vanish overnight if for one moment the British relaxed their grip on the country.

A woman brushed past him. She moved gracefully between the tables and joined a group sitting near the edge of the pool. Who could she be, he wondered? She was new there, certainly.

He went to the changing rooms and slipped on his bathing trunks; from the pool he would get a better look at her. Five minutes later he was up on the high diving board waiting for the swimmers to clear the water below. He glanced across at the table. Three faces were turned expectantly towards him. He went up on his toes, stretched his arms, and dived. When he surfaced, he swam the length of the pool, then back to near the table.

She was talking to a man on her left and Antor had time to study her. She has dark haired with a long, strong face and eyes which flashed with intelligence. An aquiline nose gave her a haughty look which was softened at moments by a captivating smile. She stopped speaking and looked in his direction. He smiled but received no response. She was staring at the water just beyond his elbow, he realized, completely oblivious of his presence. Seen face on there was something tragic in her features, as if generations of suffering had helped to chisel them. He heaved himself onto the pool's edge, walked back to the diving boards and jumped onto one of the lower ones. Again, as he poised to dive, he glanced towards her table. This time she was standing with her back to him, preparing to leave. He dived, swam a length under water and surfaced to see her disappearing down the steps which led to the polo grounds. He looked across at the two men she had left. One of them he had seen before, whereas the other, who bore a vague resemblance to her, was a newcomer. A brother or cousin, perhaps?

As he was towelling himself in the changing rooms, he thought it would be interesting to discover who she was; one of his acquaintances was bound to know. A new face at the Club never went unnoticed.

He found out about her ten days later from Emile Zekla. The banker mentioned her by chance as they were discussing an army supply contract for which Antor had tendered, and the implications for business men if the Germans took over the country.

"The position is very serious. The Afrika Korps could be soon on Egyptian soil; if Tobruk falls, there will be little to stop them, short of a miracle. And what will your position be under German occupation? There are rumours that the British are to evacuate their nationals, and many of the leading Jewish families are already packing their bags. I'm not, though I hate to think what might happen if the Gestapo gets a say in the running of the country."

"I'm not Jewish, I'm an Egyptian national ... "

"I know, Antor, but you could be a marked man. You've done a lot of business with the British and you've made yourself quite a few enemies amongst your competitors. If the Germans get here ... "

"They won't," Antor stated categorically. "The Allies will be fighting with their backs to the wall and they'll stop them somehow. They'll just have to."

Even as he was saying it, he was evaluating the damage to his businesses should Rommel march into Cairo. What Emile Zekla had just said was perfectly true. He wasn't British and he wasn't a Jew, but he had snaffled important contracts from under the noses of other Egyptians and it was well known that he was on good terms with the British officers who dealt with the tenders.

"I wish I could share your optimism, Antor. I was talking the other evening to a lady who had managed to escape from Tunis. Her family lost everything because of their Free French sympathies. She and her brother are thinking of going to South Africa as they don't want to find themselves in the same fix here. Fascinating woman, half Turkish and half French, not exactly beautiful, but striking. Looks as if she has stepped out of a Babylonian frieze."

A vision of the woman by the club pool flashed before Antor's eyes.

"I'd like to meet her sometime," he said, then returned to the subject of finance for his contract with the Army.

He met her at a party given on a houseboat moored off Gezira, the smart residential island on the Nile. There were some thirty guests and she was standing by herself on the deck, staring out across the river at the setting sun. He went up to her and, after a moment's silence, said, "I hope I'm not disturbing you, but I'd like to talk with you. I'm Antor Caspardian."

The magnificent profile turned towards him and two brown eyes stared coldly into his.

"And what would you wish to speak about, Mr Caspardian?"

The voice was low and melodious, and he wondered how old she might be. It was not the voice of a young woman yet, close to, her face had a fragility he had not expected. There was hardly a wrinkle on it.

"Anything. You preferably. I'm told ... "

"Then our conversation won't be long. I'm not a subject I'm fond of discussing, especially with a stranger, but I would like a drink. Whisky and soda, preferably weak with plenty of ice." The words were spoken softly, not as a rebuke but as a statement of fact by a woman who was obviously accustomed to speaking her mind.

He smiled. "I'll be back with it immediately, if you'll excuse me."

When he returned, a man was standing with her, listening head bent to what she was saying. He was the man he had seen with her at the Sporting Club. Antor paused, then went up to her and handed her the glass.

"I hope it's as you like it," he said.

A faint smile wavered on her lips. "Thank you, Mr Caspardian. I'd like you to meet my brother, Prince Yussuf Zelficar. And Yussuf, as this gentleman has not yet been introduced to me, perhaps you would do so now."

The man raised an eyebrow. "Of course, Maza. Mr ... eh ... Caspardian?" He hesitated a moment over the name and Antor wondered if he did so purposely, "I would like to present you to the Comtesse de la Marlière."

Antor took her outstretched hand and kissed the fingers.

"Tell me, Mr Caspardian," she said as he straightened, "what else do you do apart from diving proficiently from the high board?"

So she had noticed him.

"Nothing of much interest. Like most of us here I scrape a living. A full time occupation, I'm afraid."

He allowed the hand to slip from his and asked, "are you planning to stay in Cairo, or is this just a passing visit? Half the people here will be off to Kenya or South Africa before the end of the month."

She glanced at her brother who had turned to another guest.

"Yussuf is leaving for Johannesburg on Wednesday and is trying to persuade me to go with him."

"And will you?"

She leant against the boat's railings and flicked the ash from her cigarette into the Nile.

"I don't know yet. My husband is in prison in Tunis and Johannesburg is an awfully long way away ... " She let the sentence trail off and then looked him in the eyes. "Do you think the Germans really will reach Cairo?"

The aloofness had gone and with it the bantering condescension of the previous minutes. He could see she was worried, and her lips curved to reveal the sadness he had glimpsed at the Sporting Club.

"No, I don't, even if everything points that way. Most people here, bar the English, would say the opposite. They'd advise you to get out as fast as you can. Even the British army is evacuating its families. There are all kinds of wildcat rumours and if you took them seriously you'd be under the impression that Rommel's only half an hour from Alex. But he'll never get there, believe me, and if you want to stay in Cairo, do so without fear."

"What makes you so certain? Inside information or just wishful thinking?" A touch of diffidence had crept into her voice.

"Neither. Call it intuition, backed by what I know of the British army. In fact, whether the Germans and Italians get here or not makes very little difference to me. I'm an Egyptian national but my grandmother was Italian, and I have a lot of friends who are. Some are in prisoner of war camps and if the Axis forces get here they'll be freed, which would make me very happy. I have no vested interest in keeping the British in the saddle even if I make quite a bit of money through them. Wishful thinking doesn't come into it; its just an opinion and one I'm prepared to stick by."

He didn't tell her that his office was in the Immobilière building and that leading war correspondents forgathered at the Ermitage restaurant on the ground floor, or round the corner at Maxim's in Adli Pasha street, and that he had made the point of cultivating the friendship of such top newsmen as Vernon Bartlett, Stephen Barber and Alan Moorehead.

She threw her head back and looked at him through half closed eyes, a vaguely mocking smile on her lips.

"It's pleasant to hear an optimist ... "

"I'm not an optimist. I'm a realist. If I weren't, I would not be here tonight. This is a gathering of the rich; of those who either inherited money or acquired it. I belong to the second species. My father began life as a carpenter and ended up as a small entrepreneur. Nine years ago I inherited what was no more than a carpentry shop and turned it into an industry. From a raw and inexperienced youth I have become a successful businessman. And I'm not saying it to try and impress you but to convince you that I'm a realist and not an optimist."

He smiled and offered her another cigarette. Her lips parted and she gave a short laugh.

"Not now. Thank you Mr. Caspardian, you've made me feel better."

He talked to her for half an hour and when she was about to leave she asked him if he would care to join her at lunch the next day.

"There'll be a few friends ... a kind of farewell party for Yussuf."

Maza was staying with an aunt in Garden City, in a house which reminded Antor of the Wirsa's home in Alexandria. Only the furnishings were old fashioned and the setting less sumptuous. There were a series of intercommunicating sitting rooms with sofas and chairs upholstered in various shades of pink damask, and innumerable small tables crammed with silver objects. In the main drawing room the parquet was covered with an Aubusson carpet, and a full length grand piano, submerged with silver framed photographs of women in tiaras and men in morning coats or uniforms, took up one corner. A group of guests were standing by it when Maza came over to greet him.

"Ah, Mr Caspardian, come and meet some friends of mine," she said guiding him towards the group. They were all young, he noted, in their early twenties. She went up to a fair haired, good looking woman and said:

"May I present to you Mr Caspardian from Alex- andria? Mr. Caspardian I'd like you to meet the Queen of Albania."

As he bowed over the hand of exiled Queen Geraldine, and was then introduced to the others in what sounded like a recital of a page from the international Gotha — two princes Romanoff, one Hesse, one of Greece, and the daughter of the ruling house of Italy — he was conscious of a feeling of elation, bordering on disbelief when she presented him to the next guests. More princes, this time the Egyptian ones, Mohammed Ali, Abdel Moneim, Abbas Halim, men he knew by sight and from newspaper photographs, but had never expected to meet. Who was this woman, he began to wonder, who could casually gather around a lunch table a dozen or so members of the European and Egyptian royal families? True, Cairo was rapidly becoming flooded with ex-monarchs and their relations, but one did not automatically meet them for that.

Antor was not a social climber, but he was still sufficiently insecure, despite his wealth, to be impressed by names and titles. It was not the social element they represented which dazzled him, but the thought of the power which their positions must have given them. Queen Geraldine might be a woman like any other, but until a short while before her wishes would have been commands. A Romanoff had ruled over the largest empire in the world even while he Antor, had been working in the Don Bosco carpentry shop, and of the Egyptian princes, who could tell whether one might not become King of Egypt if anything happened to Farouk? As he sat between the Italian princess and the daughter of the South African ambassador at the long marble topped dining table, he could not stifle a bubbling sensation of euphoria that he should be rubbing shoulders with royalty; with history, he said to himself. For each one of them represented, if only distantly, an episode of power in the history of man. It was not his yet, but he had now touched and tasted it, and his appetite had been whetted.

Maza de la Marlière did not leave for South Africa with her brother. She stayed in Cairo and became Antor's mistress. Curiously, though, their relationship was more intellectual than physical. Renée Maggiar had taught him how to dominate women; Maza showed him how to manipulate men.

"You can't just go through life making money for the sake of having a whole heap of it. You must make it work for you, and I don't mean making it produce more money. It must be a spring-board for you from which to jump, or dive if you prefer, into other spheres. It's all a question of contacts. For the moment you've got some good ones, I presume, in the Egyptian business world. But that won't get you very far. Not to where a man of your calibre should be going. Once this stupid war is over, get out of Egypt. Go to America, North or South, but go there well prepared. The other day at that lunch you met a few of the people who count ... no, don't interrupt me, darling, please ... you may think that they're shadows now, sort of effigies of a power that once existed but, believe me, they can be very useful to you. You'd be surprised how influential they can still be in certain circles. Why do you think I go on seeing and entertaining them? For the kudos of having a bunch of highfalutin names with which to impress the other guests? Because I live in a world of make believe which must forcibly be peopled with princes? No, my dear Antor I'm not that childish. These people have connections which you could never have; which even I, the daughter of a once reasonably influential prince, could never have. That's why I cultivate them. One day my husband will need them. With their connections he and I may be able to recuperate a little of what we have lost. We will need a lot of friends in a lot of high places, and they have them. That's why you're going to cultivate them too, and I'm going to help you."

"What makes you think they'll want to be 'cultivated' as you put it by a man they've never heard of? It's different for you, you're one of them. I wouldn't know where to start and I'm not particularly social in any case."

"Leave it to me, darling, and just do what I tell you."

He did. He gave up his flat in Gezira and moved to a twelve roomed house in Garden City, rented for a song as the owners, Anglo-Greeks, had fled the country when Tobruk had fallen and the Afrika Korps was entering the Egyptian desert. He engaged a chef and two Sudanese menservants and began receiving the people Maza invited. He found himself enjoying the role of host which he fell into with ease. But his social life in no way impaired his business activities. To the contrary, through new acquaintances he learnt of opportunities which otherwise would have been lost to him, and Maza too turned out to be a clear-headed counsellor.

Egypt was living the critical days of El Alamein. From Alexandria one could hear faint echoes of the raging battle, and those who feared most a German takeover of the country had packed their bags and were frantically selling furniture, pictures, cars and real estate. Someone with cash and the guts to invest at that crucial moment could acquire incredible bargains.

One evening Maza phoned him.

"I have just heard that an entire office block near the Cecil Hotel can be had for £15,000, but the deal has to be concluded tomorrow. It's an opportunity not to be missed, whatever the outcome of the battle between Montgomery and Rommel."

They drove down to Alexandria at dawn, taking the village road. Antor had got himself a military pass through a friend at G.H.Q. just in case they were stopped. A wise precaution for both on the outskirts of Cairo and near Tanta there were military road blocks. It was a beautiful day and sitting at the wheel of the second hand sports saloon Alvis he had just bought, Antor felt a thrill of well being. His thoughts, during the four hour drive, were far from the holocaust two hundred kilometres away. It was as if he and Maza were gliding through a no man's land where time had been turned back, and the horror of a world war absurd figments of a collective imagination. The ageless peace of the Delta was the only reality.

By midday, he had signed a cheque and the five storey building had become his property.

He and Maza decided to spend the rest of the week in Alexandria.

The town was full of wild rumours and clandestine preparations by certain of the community to welcome the Axis troops. Absent were the familiar khaki and white uniforms of the British soldiers and sailors now recalled from leave. Yet a curious stillness pervaded the city despite bursts of anti-aircraft fire from the harbour and the swoop of Luftwaffe planes at night, followed by the sinister blasts of exploding bombs. Nerves were taut and at times tempers flared, yet the elegant life of parties, dinners and cocktails by the Sporting Club pool continued with Alexandrian insouciance.

At one such party Antor learnt that the Moharrem Bey home of the Wirsas was for sale. George Wirsa had died three months previously and Helen was moving to Cairo for health reasons.

"May I use your phone?" he asked his host, and a few minutes later he was speaking to Raymond Zekla.

"Antor Caspardian here. Sorry to bother you at home, but I have just been told that Mrs Wirsa is selling her house. Is it true? ... do you know what price she's asking? £20,000? She's out of her mind! No one will pay that sort of money today. I'm prepared to give £12,000 but not a piastre more, and my offer stands for 48 hours. Will you speak to her?"

"Of course, Mr Caspardian," the banker replied, "I will get onto her lawyer first thing in the morning and I will also speak to her personally. Ring me at the bank around 12.30 and I will try to have an answer by then."

"Thank you. And may I ask you not to reveal that I am the buyer?"

"Why do you want it?" Maza asked him when they drove past the mansion the following morning, "you're not going to live there and you know the sort of rent you could get if you let it."

"Remember you said that money must be made to do things for one? Well, by buying that house it will be doing something very important. How can I explain? You see, a part of my life began there, and another part died there. It's a place I both hate and cherish. Does that make any sense to you? I don't know what I'll do with it; all I know is that I want it. I've wanted it since I first walked into its marble floored entrance ten years ago, and I'm going to buy it cost what it may. The owner is asking a ridiculous price and I've offered more than it's worth, if one values it as a business proposition. But if necessary I'll pay what's she's asking; that's how important it is to me."

Maza smiled. "You won't have to. You'll get it at your price. You're a businessman first and a sentimentalist second, and you have an uncanny knack of setting your sights at exactly the right figure where a transaction is concerned."

She was proved right. When he phoned Raymond Zekla he was told that Helen had agreed to accept his offer.

"She has no idea that it is I who am buying it?"

"None, Mr Caspardian. She didn't even ask. I told her that I could vouchsafe for the purchaser and urged her to accept."

"Fine. I'd like to remain out of the picture till the property is legally mine. I would be glad if the bank could act as my nominee for the formalities of the purchase. Is that all right?"

"Certainly. Could you call round at five o'clock this afternoon to sign the necessary documents?"

That evening he felt an urge to go to the house and allow himself the luxury of telling Helen Wirsa to whom she had sold her home. He would have liked to watch the ever present smile fade and her eyes widen with incredulity. She would be shocked, humiliated, enraged, and he would have savoured a brief moment of revenge. Yet he had not bought the place for that reason. Helen was a creature of the past, a ghost he would rather let lie. He had ceased actively hating her a long time before. No, the buying of that house had been an act of faith towards himself. It was a tangible proof that what he had set himself to get, he could obtain. It was a trophy, a mascot and a talisman rolled into one. He would never live in it, but nor would anyone else.

Leaving Maza with friends, he drove to Rond Point and parked in front of the mansion. He stared at it for a long while as if photographing it in his memory, taking in details of the stone work, counting the number of windows, examining the gargoyle atop the arches of the entrance and garden doors each end of the house. Curious how he had never noticed them before, he thought. But then the structure of the place had not interested him when Marguerite had been there. Only she had counted. She with her silky dark hair, her laughing gray eyes, her grace and sensuality. A knot began to form in his throat. Abruptly he switched on the engine and drove away into the enveloping dusk.

Air raid sirens started to wail but he took no notice, speeding east along the Route d'Aboukir, then branching off towards the sea and onto the Corniche. He stepped on the accelerator until the Alvis was racing at 150 kilometres an hour, screeching round corners and past the odd car creeping to the shelter of a garage. At Mandara he slowed, turned around and parked by the edge of the beach, facing west towards the long sweep of bays leading to the distant city centre.

The sky was dark now and pinpointed with brilliant stars. He lit a cigarette and inhaled deeply. Once before, he remembered, he had come to this same point, the day he had buried his father. The poignancy of that moment came back vividly, gripping him like an icy hand on his chest. He remained immobile while the sky suddenly blazed with flares, tracer bullets and flashes of anti-aircraft fire. It was curiously unreal, as if happening in a world with which he had no tangible link. The minutes ticked by.

Then he heard the rumble of a fighter plane not far ahead. The engine spluttered and he looked up to see a dark shape spouting fire and diving towards him like an avenging Nemesis. He ducked in his seat and was conscious of a terrifying blast almost on top of him. There was a moment of lucidity as something hit him, ripping into the core of his being, then all went black.

"You're a very lucky man, Mr Caspardian." The voice was low pitched and comforting. "It's a miracle you're alive. But the danger isn't over yet, and we need your full co-operation if we're to pull you through. Do you understand me?"

Antor nodded imperceptibly. Where was he, he wondered, and why was he unable to move? He tried to raise his head but immediately a hand was laid on his forehead, pushing him back in the pillows.

"Don't try to move," the voice continued, "you must stay absolutely still for the moment. In a day or two we'll take the bandages off your face and you'll be able to see. Then, with patience and a good dose of luck, we'll get you on your feet again. But you must do exactly what we tell you if you want to be more or less the man you were before the accident. I say more or less as you can't expect to live through an experience like yours without paying a slight price ... "

What could that mean? What experience? Suddenly it came back to him; the air raid, the port lit by flares and, against the artificial incandescence of the sky, the black mass swooping down at him. But the price?

As if reading his thoughts, the doctor put a hand on his arm.

"If all goes well you'll be able to lead a normal life. But never forget that you were on and off the operating table for nearly twelve hours having bits of metal removed from your chest and abdomen, and your left leg stitched together again. It was touch and go as to whether we would have to amputate it. Fortunately a British army surgeon — the best in this field — agreed to operate, so you'll have him to thank if you walk normally again."

He was kept in hospital for four months and convalesced at his house in Cairo for another two. The ordeal left him with a series of small scars on his chest and stomach and a leg which, shorter by two centimetres, gave him a slight limp. Also, across his cheek, stretching from ear to nose, was a thin red line which altered the expression on his face, lifting very slightly the upper lip.

"It's rather attractive," Maza commented, "makes you look Machiavellian."

She was now more than his companion; she was his adviser and his one contact with the outside world.

It was a world which had changed in the weeks that he was cut off from it. The summer had passed and with it the threat of German troops invading Egypt. Italians packed away their flags and forgot the celebrations they had prepared for their battle weary compatriots, fifth columnists were thrown into prison and the moments of anxiety and tension faded like a mirage in the Western desert. Cairo and Alexandria became hot spots of pleasure and insouciance again, while the wealthy became richer by the hour through black marketeering, army contracts, or by the simple fact of being in the swim in the most important country in the Middle East.

Isolated in his fourth floor hospital room, Antor was cut out of this post El Alamein boom. Worse, his businesses lost money and credibility. Without him on the spot to take decisions and grasp opportunities, they stagnated and got into financial difficulties. Maza did her best to help but she had difficulty in getting anyone to carry out the instructions she relayed.

The problem was that the men with whom he had developed his businesses, the ones he could rely on and trust, his intelligent 'collaborators', as he called them, had gone; the Italians to prison of war camps in 1940, and the Jews to Palestine two years later. He had had to replace them with what he could find, with men who had neither experience nor integrity.

Left to their own devices, they managed to bring two of the companies to the verge of bankruptcy, and lost the wood-working factory a series of follow-up orders. The greatest damage was to his reputation with the British army, when they failed to honour contracts, involving him also in hefty penalty clauses. It was a worrying situation for Maza who took the brunt of it, not wanting to tell Antor what was happening for fear that it might jeopardize his recovery. The doctors had emphasized the need for absolute rest and she reckoned that was more important than the success of his businesses.

Curiously, when he was fit enough to project himself back into a world of responsibility and challenge, his reaction to what had happened was not the explosion of wrath she had expected.

"The stupid bastards," he had muttered after she had explained the situation.

Then he had looked at her and shrugged his shoulders. "It's not the end of the world. It means a little more hard work and a little less play. I'm not going to let three incompetent crooks wreck my business life. What infuriates me is that it would have been so easy for them to have made money instead of losing it, and yet they managed to go against the current and sink when everyone else is literally wallowing in wealth. It's not their dishonesty which is criminal, but their incompetence!"

They had grown close in those five months, getting to know each other in a much subtler way than before. He discovered a frailty in her which he had never suspected, and she a spirituality which was in curious contrast to his pragmatic opportunism.

"I'm not sure I'll ever really understand you, Antor," she said one afternoon as they were walking slowly to the polo ground at the Gezira Sporting Club, exercising his game leg, "one moment you are totally caught up with the material sides of our existence, and the next you calmly tell me that money, power, success, are of no particular interest to you. Which I don't believe, incidentally."

"You're wrong not to. Money, for its own sake, honestly doesn't mean very much to me. It's what one can do within it that does. The same applies to power."

"That's what they all say. Then when they've got it, somehow the tune changes."

"Maybe, but as I have little of the one for the moment and virtually none of the other, what are we arguing about? When I'm disgustingly rich and powerful to a degree that no one can imagine, then we'll discuss the subject in question. Of course, I'm interested in making money and being successful in my businesses; I always have been and there is no reason why I should change suddenly. You once told me that one must be careful to use money the right way; not to let it dominate one. You were right. I intend to dominate it. In itself, it doesn't mean much to me, but used for what my friend Francesco terms as 'positiveness' it's a fascinating and admirable instrument of power."

Though they did not actually live together, she went to his villa every day, which was only a few streets away from her aunt's house, and their friends and acquaintances took it as a matter of fact that they would get married sooner or later, no one dreaming of inviting one of them to a dinner or a party without the other.

Just after New Year's day, 1943, Maza suggested they drive up to the Mokhattem Hills, the sandstone heights which stretched behind the old city of Cairo and the famous Citadel.

When he had parked, they got out and stood gazing westwards across the vast agglomeration of ramshackle houses, modern apartment blocks, mosques and palaces, parks, rubbish dumps, warehouses and cemeteries, over the Nile and the flowering island of Gezira, past Dokki with its museums and University, to the distant Pyramids, outlined against the orange spreading dusk. Maza shivered in the evening breeze and Antor put his arm around her.

"The first time I came here was with my father," she said, snuggling against him, "seven years ago almost to the day. It was when he told me that he had chosen a husband for me." She paused and glanced up at the evening star beginning to glitter above the spot where the sun had set. Then she laughed.

"I was an obedient, affectionate girl in those days, and very insecure and shy. The marriage wasn't forced on me ... I just did what was customary, and found it absolutely natural that I should marry Jean although he was 26 years older than me. My Father wanted it, and that was sufficient. I think I was quite excited about the whole thing even if I knew that the marriage was in reality a financial transaction between two middle aged men. Jean was very wealthy and he bought me as he might have a thoroughbred mare. It's not the happiest of marriages ... apart from anything else, he's an inveterate gambler and has cirrhosis of the liver due to his heavy drinking. But when he's sober he's courteous at least, and for that I'm grateful to him."

"Why are you telling me this, Maza?" Antor asked.

"Because I want you to know that as soon as the war is over, I will ask for a divorce. And when I'm free, I would like to be with you always. We could get married then ... "

She felt the pressure of his fingers on her arm lessen a fraction, and after a moment of silence his lips brushed her temple.

"Maza," he began, but she interrupted him.

"No, darling, don't answer immediately. Just think about it ... both of us know what we feel for each other. I'm not ashamed to tell the world that you're the only man I'll ever love, but that's not why I'd like to be your wife. It's that I believe we belong to each other and are good for each other ... that we could do great and beautiful things together. That's what marriage is supposed to be all about. I know, I shouldn't be the one saying all this but if I'm to share my life with a man, I prefer to be honest and tell him that I want to be married to him. Also ... " She didn't finish her sentence but turned and gazed at him with that semi-tragic yet calm look which had captivated him the first time he had set eyes on her.

"Maza ... "

She put a finger on his lips. "Just think about it, darling."

Five days later Antor had to go to Alexandria for the wedding of Clara Salvini.

Francesco's little sister was marrying a young Greek she had met at the Liceo Verdi, whose family owned a prominent pharmacy. Theo Strapakis was a pianist, and music had drawn the two youngsters together. Clara had long looked upon Antor as an elder brother and the one person she could turn to for advice and guidance while her brother, Pietro, was away in a prisoner of war camp near Suez. She had written to Antor and spoken to him about her growing attachment for her future husband, and one day she had telephoned him in Cairo and said, "he has asked me to marry him, what should I do Antor?"

As he led her up the aisle now and glanced down at her pretty face veiled with lace he wondered suddenly why he had taken on the responsibility of pushing her gently into marriage. To her query he had not answered, "do you love him?" but "let me find out a little more about him". And when he had, it was not she who had decided, but he.

"Go ahead and marry him, from what I hear he's a nice man and the two of you have a great bond together, and that's terribly important." Was he really being honest when he said that? If he had been, then shouldn't he marry Maza?

With 'little' Clara gone — young Theo had said that as soon as it was possible he would take her away to America where cousins of his father had interests — the last ties with the past would disappear. Nobody would remain to remind him of his youth, of his parents and friends, of Marguerite. He would be alone, free maybe, but desolately alone.

Maza was right. They were made for each other. She loved him and probably he did her. Not the way he had when he was twenty, but with a maturity which would replace the body and soul passion of his first love. Marguerite was a spirit of the past and one couldn't live with spirits. Maza was a beautiful actuality, a woman who could share his life fully, a companion suitable for the great adventure he and she would embark on.

When he got back to Cairo he immediately phoned her home. There was no answer, but a few hours later a servant came with a message from her aunt. Maza had left Egypt.

At first he refused to believe that she had gone like that, without a word, walking out of his life as unexpectedly as she had stepped into it. She was probably hiding, for some reason, at a friend's house, or in one of the hotels. He spent three hours desperately phoning around Cairo but finally had to come to terms with reality. The only woman who could have been his love, his companion, his wife one day had gone.

Why, he cried to himself, had he not told her what she really meant to him when she had spoken to him up in the hills only eight days before? He, the opportunist, the grabber of whatever could be useful to his career, the supreme egotist, had let the last chance to happiness slip between his fingers. Was he cursed, where love was concerned to remain a loner all his life?

He plunged into a furious sadness, and that evening got drunk for the last time ever.

Cairo, 1950

Antor stood at the top of the sweeping staircase in the Royal Automobile Club of Egypt, gazing at the crowd of people in the room below. It was New Year's Eve and the hall was full with men and women in evening dress. The club, situated in Kasr el Nil street, was one of the most exclusive in the Middle East, admitting as members only those who had the right connections and, especially, the right sort of money.

Antor had proved his worthiness after loosing heavily at poker to the King, and his savoir faire had earned him not only the royal friendship but also that of Felix Misrahi, a textile millionaire, who was one of the club's most influential members. It was rumoured that Misrahi made a point of losing a good £200,000 a year to Farouk, and that he reckoned the money was well spent to keep in the monarch's good graces. A word from the Palace kept the tax inspectors' eyes partially closed to the enormous profits of the Misrahi Cotton and Trading Company, and ensured that a hefty part of them made their way out of the country to accounts in Switzerland and the Lebanon.

Emile Zekla had suggested to Antor that he join the coterie of those who gambled with the King when discussing what to do with the 'excess profits' of his companies. These profits could escape the fiscal authorities if ploughed back in improvements such as new machinery, new premises or general expenses. Alternatively, some 80 per cent disappeared in tax. In Antor's case they amounted to a considerable amount of money, which he had no intention of reinvesting since he had decided to sell his businesses.

Trade in 1950 was booming and the stock exchange ebullient; the right moment to go liquid, he reckoned. Also, contrary to most industrialists' advice, he was contemplating investing heavily in Italy in an oil refinery, and needed as much cash in Europe as he could lay his hands on.

He had spent 1944 and 1945 getting his companies on their feet again, and immediately after the war had started dealing in scrap metal, a market which was wide open, and in which a few clever men made rapid fortunes. He was one of them. And his subsequent dealings in army surplus stocks, with visits to battered Italy and France, had opened his eyes to the enormous construction potential in these countries.

One of the sectors which was rapidly expanding, and in which lay an extremely profitable future, was the refining of crude oil. Most of the pre-war refineries had been destroyed or badly damaged and, with the shortage of Europe's traditional fuel, coal, and the increased demand for petroleum, the reconstruction of the refineries had become an immediate necessity. Antor had invested most of his gains from his 'war surplus' activities in a relatively small refinery near Genoa. He held 50 per cent of the shareholding but was eager to gain complete control of it, and that meant exercising his option on another £750,000 worth of stock. So had matured the idea of selling a good part of his assets in Egypt, and of exporting both the capital and the profits accumulated in the past two years. To get that sort of money out — a strictly illegal activity — needed a lot of back-scratching in high places, and Felix Misrahi knew exactly whose and where.

As a start, the two men did business together, bartering machinery for textiles. Then came the social involvement with dinners at Antor's house and duck shooting parties on lake Qarun at the Faiyum, 80 kilometres south of Cairo, and finally the poker sessions with the King at the Misrahi mansion off the Pyramids' Road. Antor was not a gambler and had never played a card game, but with his customary single-mindedness he now learnt poker and bridge, and became recklessly proficient at both, playing for high stakes with inveterate old hands like Emile Ades, Mohammed Sultan, Nabil Ismail and, of course, Misrahi.

During the first few games with the King, Antor played cautiously making sure neither to win nor lose. Then came the moment to 'pay homage' to his sovereign, and he did so with a mastery which surprised everyone. £52,000 in one evening was something of a record and it gained him exactly what he had set out to achieve. By 1950 more than a million pounds had made their way to a numbered account in Switzerland. It went without saying that when his name had been put up for membership at the Royal Automobile Club, there was not a single vote against it.

On December 31st 1950, he invited 12 persons to dinner there.

Two of them were businessmen with whom he intended to conclude a nine million dollar deal, the first of its kind for him. The men were accompanied by their wives and he had decided to give them a taste of Cairo's glittering social life.

The New Year's Eve ball at the Club was one of the highlights of the season. Along with the Bal des Petits Lits Blancs in May, it was considered the smartest social event of the year. Echoing the extravagance of pre-war Alexandrian festivities, the dinner was entirely flown in from Paris, as were the women's gowns, mostly from Dior, Balmain and Jacques Fath. And since the rich Cairots loved to parade their money around the necks and wrists of their wives, a breathtaking glitter of emeralds, diamonds and rubies glowed like fluorescence above the undulating waves of tulle, satin and silk.

Antor smiled to himself as he stood at the top of the sweeping staircase leading from the hall to the first floor reception area and watched the guests move slowly past him, some giving him a sideways glance, obviously wondering who he was, while one or two stopping to shake his hand and exchange a greeting. He sauntered down, a hand in his dinner jacket pocket, knowing that later, when they had assessed his guests, they would recognize him as one of them, call him by his christian name and invite him to their homes. He smiled because he didn't need them any more. He had made the grade financially a long time ago, and now his determination to get socially even with the Wirsas of this world could be fulfilled. The humiliations of his early life would be vindicated.

His face clouded as he reached the last step. A woman with her grey hair swept into an immaculate chignon had entered the hall. He couldn't see her features, yet there was something in the tilt of the head and in the movement of her fingers, as she touched the clasp of her black pearl necklace, which plunged him back twenty years. She of all people! Yes, he was sure it was Helen Wirsa.

He felt a hand on his arm.

"Antor, for heaven's sake, you look as if you've seen a ghost. What's the matter?" It was Joyce Misrahi. "Your guests have arrived, come and greet them."

He only vaguely heard her. Helen, with her haughty smile

and implacable disdain! Why, after all these years, had she still the power to stir such a feeling of resentment in him?

He had chosen a round table to get over the tricky formality of social precedence. When guests included Prince Ali Khan and his new wife Rita Hayworth, a cousin of King Farouk's, an Irish peeress, a former British Ambassador, and one of the richest men in Central America with their wives, the question of who to sit next to whom was not easy. The problem was immediately resolved by Dorinda Walker, the unconventional Englishwoman with whom the British diplomat was staying.

"Poor Mr Caspardian, how on earth are you going to seat us without turning half your friends into enemies. I know, we women will sit where we like and the men will move places after each course. It will also make for more amusing conversation."

She was right. It not only made the dinner more relaxed but also attracted the attention of other tables where people began doing the same. At the third course Antor found himself next to Mrs Walker.

"Ah," she said, "now I'll have the chance to get to know our host and to find out whether my hunch was right."

Antor smiled and raised an eyebrow. "Your what, Madame?"

"Mon intuition," she went on in French. "Something has ruffled your inner feathers and, despite your insouciant appearance, you're agitated. I wonder why? Don't answer if you don't want to." There was a twinkle in her eye as she reached for a glass of wine. "Joyce told me you were born in Alexandria ... I lived there before the war. Which may explain the feeling I have that we've met before. Have we, Mr Caspardian?"

"I don't think so, Madame, or I would certainly have remembered it."

"Hmmm. I think it was something or someone related to Alex which upset you. I wonder what? A man or a woman? A woman, I'm certain. You're not the sort to be put out by a man ... "

He decided suddenly to confide in her.

"Did you by any chance know the Wirsas in Alexandria ...?"

When he had finished she said, "is there any way I can help? I remember Marguerite well. She was a lovely girl." The laughter had gone from her eyes.

"You're very kind. Help?" He stared across the dining room. "Yes, perhaps you could. Do you think you could get Madame Wirsa to come to this table later?"

"I'll try, if that's what you really want."

The following day Antor sent six dozen roses to Dorinda Walker's home. They were to thank her for having helped him confound the only person he had ever hated. It had not been a revenge, for that he could never have. Nothing would atone for what Helen had done to him, for the aching within him which would never be soothed. But it had been a long awaited moment of satisfaction, a transient triumph and a balm to his mutilated pride when the Englishwoman returned to the table accompanied by Helen and her escort.

"Helen, ma chère," she said, "I would like you to meet my friends ... probably you know most of them, Lady Massereene, Sir Giles and Lady Colt, Prince and Princess Ali Khan ... "

The men had stood up and bowed over Helen's fingers as the famous smile hovered on her lips.

The round of introductions reached Antor.

"And last, but far from least, our charming host, Monsieur Antor Caspardian, who I think you knew in Alexandria."

Antor watched the smile fade and the eyebrows collapse into an incredulous frown. Her hand flew to her throat as she shook her head in bewilderment.

"Oh no ... no! How could you do this to me," she threw at Dorinda.

Then, turning to the man who had accompanied her she gasped, "I need air ... help me get away."

When they had gone Antor turned to Mrs Walker and took her hand in his. Raising it to his lips he said simply, "merci Madame."

GEORGE

Alexandria, August 1st, 1990

Sir George Christofides opened his eyes and stared up at Tom,
the male nurse, who grinned and said, "you had a good night,
Sir George. You slept like a babe."

George groaned. A helpless, bloody little baby; yes, that's
what I am, he thought. Back to square one, and Alexandria.

Tom threw off the bedclothes, picked him up, and carried
him to the bathroom.

"See, we're in the harbour. Got in half an hour ago. Can't
say it looks much of a place. Was it always like this?"

He held George in front of the porthole before sitting him
on the lavatory. "A.J. says you were born here, like Mr
Caspar," he prattled on, "must bring you back memories ... "

George closed his eyes. Memories! God, that was all he had
left. Scattered fragments of life's illusions which were now
lugging him back into that big house with its creaky parquet
floors; to Nanny in her blue uniform; to children playing on
the beach at Sidi Bishr, while he sat on the steps of the Wirsa's
cabin fully dressed with socks, shoes and a hat, watching
them; to Helen — 'grand-mère' — with her unwavering frosty
smile, and her eyebrows arched in permanent reprimand ...

Helen! He had not given her a thought in years, yet
suddenly her presence was almost physical, forcing him back
to those days when Nanny would take him to her for lunch
every Saturday.

How he had dreaded those lunches in the huge, Renaissance
style dining room, alone with her, while she checked his table
manners, ready to pounce if he took too large a mouthful or
pushed peas onto his fork with a finger. It was worse, though,
when there were her friends, those terrible Alexandrian
women who would pinch his cheek and murmur, " qu'il est
mignon, but who has he taken from, Helen, chérie? The

Wirsa's or the Christofideses? He doesn't really look like any of you."

The bitchy old hens. They must have known that Roger Christofides was not his father.

Tom was back ready to clean, wash, dress and feed him. Like when he had had his appendix out at the Anglo-American Hospital at Gezira a month after they had moved to Cairo.

"They say Cairo's more fun these days. I suppose you've been there too, Sir George? I'd like to have a look at the Pyramids and the Museum. Major Salvini has said I could go up for the day when the guests fly back there."

George was not listening. He was in the sitting room of Helen's house in Maadi, the fashionable suburb south of Cairo, full of well kept gardens and veranda fronted villas reeking of bourgeois genteelness. She was at her desk reading his school report, and he was watching her eyebrows rise and the perpetual smile contract.

She removed her spectacles and looked at him with her grey green eyes which squinted very slightly when she was angry.

"Your report is again very unsatisfactory. I warned you last time that if you didn't work better I would have to take severe measures. You leave me no alternative. I'm going to send you to a school where discipline is strict and where you'll be a boarder without the distractions of home life to keep you from studying." She sighed. "I suppose I'm to blame in a way. I haven't been severe enough and you've been spoilt."

The bloody woman. She'd kept her word all right. The English School at Heliopolis, considered the best in the Middle East, and run like a British public school. He smiled to himself. A public school, yes, but with a difference. It had girls as well as boys.

He had fallen in love within two weeks. She was slim, fair haired with classical features and dark blue eyes. An amalgam of Betty Grable and Greer Garson. Sensuality mixed with good breeding, like Georgina ...

What he had not done to win Anne's love! Learnt to rumba for the boarders' Saturday dances, got himself into the hockey 2nd eleven, and memorised parts of Hamlet.

'To be or not to be' ... God!, how appallingly apt those well worn words were now. He had to be or not be till he died, till someone or something decided his fate. Fuck it! Why had it happened to him of all people? Why not to Julius?

He had got nowhere with Anne, not even a spot of light petting. She was the only girl to resist him, remaining faithful to some insignificant senior prefect.

Then his voice broke and with it had come a desire for more than occasionally holding Anne's hand and taking her for walks round the school grounds. But when he'd tried to press his groin against her leg while dancing a tango, she had wrenched away from him with a "try that sort of stuff with Anthea, not me!"

He had. Anthea, plump, with tits the size of water melons had taken him backstage in the Assembly Hall during a break, undone his belt as he kissed her, and felt inside his trousers.

"Wow," she had giggled, "who'd have thought you had it that big." She had let him fondle her breasts and rub himself against her but not go the whole hog. Yet the shattering explosion of pleasure had come all the same...

A spoon was being pressed against his lips, hard and cold, and his mouth was filled with mushy cornflakes. He spat them out furiously. The stupid bugger, couldn't he see he was dreaming of Anthea's nipples, large and taught, the first he had ever kissed. But had he really experienced those moments of intense sexual stimulation with which his memory was baiting him?

"Please, Sir George, don't be like that. You have to eat. Would you prefer porridge again? I thought you'd like a change..."

Tom sponged his dressing gown and presented him with another spoonful. George opened his mouth. What the hell, porridge or cornflakes, it was all baby food, the same he was relentlessly fed, soggy and tasteless, every bloody morning of his bloody life.

Anthea and her fleshy body dragged him back to those nights in the sixth-form classroom. Five sessions of forty minutes or so when she had put him through the tricks learnt from dirty postcards. And on the sixth, a furious Matron staring aghast at their locked, naked bodies.

He had got caned by both the housemaster and the

headmaster, with the threat that if ever he was caught even kissing a girl he'd be thrown out.

"I've got a good mind to expel you, Christofides. But I'm prepared to be lenient because it would cause Madame Wirsa a great deal of vexation, which I don't want. She is a generous patron."

Those fucking four hundred trees she had had planted round the dusty playing fields had kept him in that prison for another ten weeks, made him sleep in the housemaster's room, do an hour's special PT every afternoon, and stopped him going to the boarders' dances.

The worst had been not to be able to fornicate any more.

But he had got his own back on the lot of them. A half holiday with the Ambassador's wife giving away the end of term prizes and he on the way to the 3rd floor lavatories for a quiet smoke, when he had heard his name called:

"Christofides, where d'you think you're going and why aren't you in your gym clothes?"

"I thought today was different, sir."

"Who asked you to think? Get changed and down to the playing field immediately. Report back when you've done the circuit 15 times. Don't stand there gaping, get moving, boy."

That was when something had clicked in him.

Tom wiped his mouth. The spoon was replaced by a fork with what was presumably scrambled eggs. George wasn't sure, it all tasted so alike but this at least was pleasant. He grunted his satisfaction. Tom wasn't bad as far as male nurses went, and he had had five of them. Bastards every one without the scantiest respect, lugging him about as if he were a sack of potatoes.

Tom was different, he seemed to care. He quite liked him...

He swallowed the mouthful and opened his mouth for the next.

It was the first time he had flaunted authority.

"I'm not running round those bloody fields any more. I'm not taking orders from you or anyone. I'm getting out of here."

As simple as that. He wasn't the one gaping then.

That moment had changed his life. He had realized suddenly that he was born to give orders, not receive them.

He opened his eyes and stared at his reflection in the ceiling to floor mirror. You pathetic, hopeless fool, he flung at himself. Where did it all get you? Who gives orders to whom now? You're back to Alexandria, back to subservient childhood, to helpless babyhood, that's where it's got you. He closed his eyes to blot out the image of his misery. He would not face the humiliation of the present when the past, exciting and dynamic was his whenever he wished.

From that day he had done exactly what he wanted within certain limits, which he had defined himself. He had not gone back to the English School but had accepted to receive private tuition. And when Helen had cut off his pocket money he had gone to a jeweller in the Khan Khalil and sold the gold cufflinks left him by his grandfather. With the money, £42, he had gone off to the Gezira Sporting Club and played poker with a pimply faced Scot who was always game for a gamble. The little brat had beaten the last piastre out of him, but he had booked him for another go the next day. The gold watch went for that, but it was the last piece of personal property he was ever to flog. The game had lasted 4 hours and he had wiped the floor with the little shit. What was his name? Mac Something …

What he wouldn't give now for an evening's poker session. Just one. He'd beat them all, even Julius. His fortune against the Alexandrian's. No. His own life, active and powerful again, if he won, against the right to die if he lost. But he wouldn't lose. He'd been a winner since he'd won those £120 from MacLelland. Yes, that was the boy's name.

"A spot of tea, Sir George. I've made it myself and it's exactly as you like it." Tom's hand was behind his head pushing it gently forward while the beak of his special cup was fitted between his lips. "Slowly does it, there's no rush."

He choked. They were the words Nadia had used that first time in the brothel behind the Ezbekieh Gardens, a stone's throw from Shepherd's Hotel. She was the most expensive, £10 a go, but worth every piastre. "Slow down, petit, you're not a drill. Women like it hard but slow."

She had taught him a lot, and sometimes for nothing when

he got her really excited and brought on an orgasm, which none of the other clients ever did.

He stopped coughing and opened his eyes. Avoiding the mirror; he looked out at Alexandria's waterfront with it's apartment blocks, bays and Corniche stretching way into the early morning glare. Didn't seem to have changed much since back in 1949 when he had sailed away from it for England. Just dirtier and drabber.

He still vaguely remembered that day. Perhaps because Julius had said that it was then he had seen him for the first time, at the Sporting Club with Helen and Raymond Zekla. What he'd never forgotten was the feeling of excitement when the liner had sailed out of the harbour. Somehow he had known he'd never come back; that he was sailing away to success, riches and fame. No schoolboy wishful thinking either.

Flashing through his mind came long forgotten impressions of those first months in England. Oxford. Could any place be more different to Alexandria than the 600 year old university city with it's limestone built colleges, its undergraduates punting on the tree-lined Cherwell, and the rich green surrounding countryside. It had meant freedom for him. Freedom to live as he wanted, freedom from Helen, from the dust and glare of Cairo, from the restricted social perimeter of two sporting clubs, five cinemas and a handful of friends' houses.

Tom was passing the shaving brush over his jowls, so he closed his eyes again. Being shaved was one of the sensual luxuries he had always enjoyed. Now it was a tiresome necessity, but that first time in the High Street it had marked a psychological transit from adolescence to manhood. What was the name of his barber at Oxford? Cecil? No, Cedric. 40 years practice in brushing up a foam, razoring off the shadow of a beard and patting the skin with a special aftershave lotion had made Cedric the most sought after barber for those who could afford him. And two shops down, the coffee-house where he would devour breakfasts of eggs, spam, tomatoes, sausages and bacon after the nights of gambling and drinking.

Drink, gambling and money. Those had been the secret of his success at Oxford. They had permitted him to dominate his clique within a couple of months of settling into digs in a red brick house off the Banbury Road, owned by a doctor's wife with a penchant for good-looking lodgers. Mary Chambers! A box of chocolates, the clothing coupons he didn't need, and an appreciative look at her bottom had got him into her bedroom within a week.

"I must show you the view from this side. Come over and have a look, only shut the door or it will bang ... "

He had banged her just about every afternoon and she'd been the first woman he'd had to muzzle so that the neighbours wouldn't hear. Good sort, Mary, she hadn't even made a scene when he started bringing girls back to his room.

Tom wiped his face and patted Eau de Cologne on his cheeks. Then he lifted him and carried him back to the bed. The half an hour of massaging began.

Money. It hadn't taken him long to realize it was all that counted. Masses of it and the world was yours. Plus an SS1 two-seater named 'Effie' one got for an 18th birthday and for having passed the entrance exams to Christchurch. That flame red sportscar had won him notoriety, even before the champagne and caviar parties. Envy too. And how he had enjoyed that in the eyes of those provincial bums who pretended to disapprove his extravagances while dying to be roared away in 'Effie' to the Bear at Woodstock or Stanton Manor for a drink and a good dinner, not that muck they got in the College halls.

The fun had really began when he moved into two sunny rooms at the 'House'. Below was Mark, also from Alexandria, above, Nicholas, a cousin of the King of Yugoslavia, and round the corner on the same landing Julian, 6th. Viscount Brentwick. All three rich, privileged and determined to enjoy life to the hilt. Work was forgotten except for a frenzied three hours before the weekly tutorial to rustle up five pages usually filched for a fiver from an impecunious undergraduate up on a scholarship. Eight months devoted solely to the pleasures of the senses, and the mind only called into action when a pack of cards was produced. Till some drunken shit — he had never discovered who — had peed out of his window as the Bursar was passing and drenched the sod.

If only he could piss on someone now. No, not just someone, Julius! How he would love to see the arrogant, double-dealing sonofabitch drenched in urine. Not that he cared one way or the other about him any more. He didn't even dislike him now, but it would be a satisfaction, a symbolic revenge ...

What a fuss they had made. And thank God they had or he might have stayed on for the mandatory three years. What would his life have been then?

Called before the Master, flayed for behaviour incompatible with that of a House undergraduate, he had forestalled the announcement that he was being sent down by a curt "if that's the case, sir, I'm leaving. The sanitary arrangements leave too much to be desired." And 24 hours later he had packed four suitcases onto 'Effie' and motored off to London.

Only one thing had troubled him during the hour and a half drive. Money. Not a pressing problem as he'd won a lot and his allowance was sent three months in advance. But London was not Oxford where lodging was free, and the sort of accommodation he intended to get was not boarding house price. The Ritz or nothing. The smallest, pokiest, bathroomless room, maybe, but at the Ritz. It was not given to everyone to take up residence there, and obviously that was what sly old Bill Masters had thought.

Tom rolled him over onto his stomach and began pummelling his thighs. He was chattering away about something, but George was not listening. Gazing blankly at the bedhead, he was thinking of the meeting with the man who had introduced him to business.

He had made an overture the third evening while they were alone in the hotel's bar.

"Care to have a drink with me? My name's Masters, Bill Masters."

His reaction had been one of studied coolness. "Kind of you, Mr. Masters, but I'm already drinking."

"Then mind if I join you? A large dry Martini for me, barman, and whatever this gentleman is drinking for him. No I insist. Fine place London. Are you from these parts? I'm planning to buy an apartment. What d'you reckon's the best area? The hall porter says Mayfair or Knightsbridge."

"I really wouldn't know. I live here at the hotel."

"Do you now! So do I, till I find the right place. I'm over on business ... "

And believing him to be several years older than he was, Masters had gone on to explain what his business was and how he was looking for an eventual partner.

They dined together in the Grill, and over brandy in the lounge George was being offered the franchise for the U.K. and Europe for a cream which was supposed to alleviate the pains of rheumatism and which, Masters claimed, had made him a fortune in the USA.

It was his gambler's instinct which had prompted him to accept the offer but not to put a cent of his own money into the venture. And, somehow, he had convinced Bill that this was in his best interests. The crafty American had stumbled on a man as plausible and persuasive as himself!

Fortune smiled on the daring, he'd learnt that in his gambling. He applied the same poker-face brazenness in business and, by God, it worked miracles that summer. Within two months he was over in Paris signing up a deal with Pierre.

What a city of sparkle and elegance Paris was then. Perhaps wanting to forget the horrors of the Nazi occupation, it had shed the mantle of austerity and hailed luxury back into its boulevards and homes. Within two years after the end of the war it was again the capital of fashion and extravagance.

He had felt immediately at home there. The flamboyant streak in him which, in austere London still smarting from post-war restrictions, had caused more than one raising of an eyebrow, in Paris was accepted and welcomed.

Over a bottle of Bollinger at the Hotel Crillon, he and Pierre Pigaud had toasted their new company. 'Pharmaceutiques Christogaud'. Terrible name but the best they had been able to dream up that day. Offices in Rue Cambon and a suite at the Hotel Loti, and he was ready to take Paris by storm. But first he had gone off to Switzerland for a week at Montreux with his grandmother.

Tom sat him up, put a bathrobe on him, then lifted him onto the wheelchair. How he hated the contraption. At least while lying in bed or floating in the massage pool he could forget what he was; a parody of the famous international businessman, described by Time magazine as 'one of the cleverest young tycoons in Europe.' Young? Yes, he had been once, before he had become this withered, useless hulk, paralysed to the eyeballs, looking older than Julius, his father, dammit, who was 80 today. Christ, when would the agony end? If only he could speak, utter even a word or two ...

Curious how Helen had capitulated so easily.

When he had told her of his decision she hadn't tried to force him back to Oxford, even though she didn't know he had been sent down. Nor had she threatened to cut his allowance. Not that he really needed it, but it was useful for those luxuries he didn't want to give up. Probably Raymond Zekla had been responsible. He was her friend and her banker and must certainly have influenced her. At dinner, after hearing about the sales of Bill Master's creams and the new company set up in France, he had said, "you can't be a student and a businessman at the same time. A choice has to be made."

And the next day he had suggested they go for a walk along lake Leman's waterfront.

"I believe you've made a right decision. You're not cut out for academic life. You're headstrong and a gambler, two so-called defects which personally I qualify as assets in a businessman, as long as they are accompanied by rigid discipline in work and a basic professionalism. Take the Swiss, everything they do is neat and orderly. Look at their countryside too. The mountains over there, the lake with its swans and paddle steamers, everything is harmonious, regulated, dependable and supremely professional. That's why they are the bankers to the world. Be like the Swiss in your business and you'll go a long way."

Typical Levantine banker, that Raymond Zekla. Suave, double-faced, with a sixth sense for sniffing out potential success. He must have recognized the latent tycoon in him, as he had twenty years earlier with Julius. He and his cousin Emile had been thick as thieves with the bastard.

And talking of bastards, what was that delinquent A.J. doing standing at his cabin door? He didn't trust the little sod. He was sure he was up to no good, even if Julius and Laurrie reckoned he'd turned a new leaf. Bad blood didn't.

Why had he changed the wheelchair in that hotel lavatory? No one had noticed, but he had. Hell, what did it matter. Nothing mattered any more.

He closed his eyes and took up his reveries. Emile Zekla? No before that. He must have been only 19, not bad to be an established businessman at that age. Yes, he remembered now. Christ, had that youngster really been him ... ?

Alexandria, 1956

A limousine drew up at the entrance to the house at Rond Point.

Immediately, the front door was thrown open and a servant came hurrying down the steps, bowed to the form in the back of the car, and gave a big smile as he watched Antor Caspardian climb out of it.

"Welcome, *gnab el howager,* welcome back."

Antor looked about him. How the area had changed since he had bought the place. Blocks of apartment buildings, jerry-built and already shabby, crowded round the mansion on what were once the gardens of other luxurious homes. Urchins played in the streets, and refuse piled up at irregular intervals on the broken pavements. But the house and its lawns, rosegarden and bougainvillaea covered trellises were just as they had always been. No one would imagine that it had been vacant for 13 years, at least not from the outside. Only when one walked through the marble floored vestibule and looked the length of the intercommunicating reception rooms, void of their rich furnishings, did one sense the emptiness.

He opened the door of the library. In contrast, here little had changed since that morning a quarter of a century back, when he had first caught sight of a graceful girl through its French windows. Only the books were not there, those rare manuscripts which had been the real passion of George Wirsa. But the heavy mahogany desk, the high-back leather chairs, the grandfather clock and the low coffee table were the very same ones, as were the thick velvet curtains and massive brass chandelier.

He stood for a moment by the window, gazing into the garden, then turned and sat at the desk. There was a knock on the door and the servant came in carrying a tray with a cup and a silver teapot. While he poured the tea, Antor stared at the chair opposite him. It was a ritual enacted the few times he came to the place. He had vowed, while sitting in that chair twenty-five years earlier and sipping a same cup of strong, sweet tea, that he too one day would own a house like this one. But fate had decided that it would not be one like it, where he might have lived a normal life, but this mausoleum, this shrine in which he had never spent a single night.

He wandered back through the halls, his footsteps echoing like heartbeats, and climbed the stairs to the upper floor. During her lifetime he had never visited Marguerite's bedroom, but he had always known which one it was. He went into it and closed the door behind him, leaning against it with his eyes closed.

Suddenly she was there, with her girlish laughter, her large grey eyes fixing his, and her arms stretched towards him. He whispered her name and fought off the surge of overwhelming loneliness. Oh God, he thought desperately, why had they not been allowed to live their love? Why had they, two beings made for each other, been so cruelly separated? Where was the justice of God, of that God Whom his mother had worshipped so devotedly, and Whom his only friend, Francesco, served with the fullness of his heart and soul?

Instinctively, as always in moments of emotional stress, his fingers went to the silver cross on his chest. Slowly the turmoil stilled and the anguish abated. He opened his eyes and looked about the empty room then took a deep breath, and let himself out.

He walked quickly along the passage, down the stairs and out into the heat of the June sun.

Ten minutes later he was being driven along the Route d'Aboukir and into the Alexandria Sporting Club. He had an appointment for lunch there with Raymond Zekla before catching the plane to Cairo in the afternoon.

Curious, he thought, how Alexandria had become a ghost city. It had been his home, the scene of his childhood and youth, of his love and despair, of his early successes, but he had somehow outgrown it. Also, with the passing of the years the once great mercantile centre of the Mediterranean had become a backwater, a drowsy, tatty agglomeration of homes and places of work, its people living in its memories like actors in a disused film set. The clever merchants and bankers, those Greeks, French, Jews, Italians, Turks, Maltese and British, who had made the city the jewel of the Near East, had abandoned it, moving to Beyrouth or Geneva, Buenos Aires, New York, Paris or London. A few had simply gone to Cairo, until the bloodless revolution of 1952 had toppled the monarchy, and given the warning that Egypt could soon be unhealthy for nationals of other countries.

He had not waited for the rot to set in. As soon as the war was over, and it was possible to travel again, he had followed Maza de la Marlière's advice and gone abroad, leaving the faithful and competent Pietro Salvini, then out of concentration camp, to look after his businesses. And, without anyone in Cairo really realizing it, he had become a wheeler-dealer of international stature. He was not yet the legendary 'Alexandrian' of the sixties and seventies, but amongst the banking communities of Geneva, Beirut and New York, and with certain high level officials in London and Washington, his was a name which commanded respect.

As the car approached the Club House, he thought back to the last time he had been there in 1950, just after he had signed a deal with the banker, Marcel Kharami, which had given him a 25 per cent stake in the Crédit Méditerranéen et d'Outremer.

That was when he had seen that boy for the first time, sitting at a table on the club terrace with his grandmother and the Zeklas.

Helen had not recognized him when he had passed and saluted the banker and his wife, but he was certain Raymond would have told her who he was.

He had caught the lad's eye afterwards in the lobby, and had hoped to recognise something of Marguerite in him. But he had found no trace of the woman he had loved in her son; the glance the young George Christofides had thrown him was full of the Wirsa arrogance.

Yet later that afternoon he had called round at the Banque Zekla.

"I want to know more about Mrs Wirsa's grandson," he had said to Raymond, coming straight to the point.

"What in particular?" the banker had asked. "I don't know him well. For the last six years he and his grandmother have been in Cairo, and I have had little opportunity of seeing either. I gather, though, that she considers him a bit of a problem. Very stubborn and undisciplined. They're off to Europe this evening, and she's sending him to a new school, in England."

"Who pays for his education? Did his ... I mean, did the Christofideses leave any money? From what I heard, there wasn't much left when the old man died."

Raymond Zekla nodded. "The shipping agency had been running at a loss during all the war years, and the money you paid for it only covered the debts accumulated by the family. George Wirsa gave his daughter Marguerite a handsome dowry when she married Roger, but he got through a lot of that, and his second wife has control of what remains. Even old Mrs Christofides has very little, just enough to keep her decently till she dies. She lives in a pension now. None of which is a secret to anyone ... "

"So the boy will be completely dependant on Mrs Wirsa?"

"Yes. But why do you ask?"

"Let us say that I had a certain respect for old Mr Christofides, which I don't share for Mrs Wirsa. Also Roger was ... well, he was reasonably friendly, once I didn't work any more in his father's business."

He stood up and walked to the window, then stared down at the traffic in Sharia Fouad and across to the tea shop opposite. How many times as a little boy had his father taken him there on Sunday afternoons. He even remembered going with him to a little café opposite, and watching the carriages and motorcars draw up, and the well-dressed women stepping into Pastroudis. The café had gone, but the famous tea shop was always there, like a cornerstone of his life's edifice. It represented the hopes and illusions of a childhood, the struggle from poverty to ease, an era which had long disappeared, but in which his father and mother had played an ever present role.

George Christofides had never had a mother nor known a true father. Whatever he felt towards him, he had to compensate for that. Also, when the time came, the youngster must be free of Helen Wirsa.

"I'll be going to Geneva next week and I intend to set up a Trust for the boy. I would like the bank to act as co-Trustee with me. Have you any reservations?"

"Of course not. Emile will also be in Switzerland at the beginning of July, so he could meet you for the formalities. Do you want me to inform Mrs Wirsa about it?"

"No. I don't want anyone to know about it till the young man is twenty-one."

With the offices of Pharmaceutiques Christogaud SA barely five minutes walk from the Hotel Loti where he took residence, George set himself into a routine of work which would have astonished anyone who had known the sort of existence he had led only 15 months previously. By 8.30a.m. he was behind his Louis XVI style bureau, and for two hours dedicated himself to administrative matters. Around 11 a.m. he would go to see a bank, or call at the head office of whatever firm he needed to do business with, or drop in on a ministry if some dossier needed pushing for import permits or to get the authority to market a new product. One o'clock would find him at Fouquet's, not so much because he liked the food there, as to be seen. The same applied when he went to Maxim's; it was part of his image boosting.

If he personally got publicity — and he made quite certain in various ways that he did — it was so that he could do business more easily.

Which was why, when he needed a car, he rented a Rolls Royce with liveried chauffeur. The afternoons had him again behind his desk, where he remained until 7p.m. After which he would walk back to his hotel, change and start the evening's main activity.

Gambling had become more than just a pastime and a source of income. It was as essential to his mental well-being as call-girls and prostitutes were to his physical. It didn't matter whether he lost or won, as long as cards were in his hands. Yet there was a well organized system to his gambling. Twice a week it was poker, twice bridge and twice 'chemmy'. Also, he would play for four hours exactly, no more and no less. Sometimes the sessions would start at 9.p.m., on others at 11 p.m.

But whatever his nightly pursuits, he was invariably at the office by 8.30 a.m., and the hard work which he and his partner put into the business soon provided results. They expanded rapidly, taking on the representation and manufacture under licence of a range of different products in the pharmaceutical and slimming food field, he responsible for the financial side and sales promotion, while Pierre for production and distribution.

They were so successful that, within eighteen months, Phamaceutiques Christogaud SA was a name of which banks began to take notice, offering virtually carte blanche finance facilities. But then the established drug companies made their weight felt, and that was when the crunch had come.

Banks, George was to learn, were prepared to help a small company with a good potential, but only as long as it did not tread on the toes of their prime clients. Sources of credit dried up and loans were not renewed.

In October 1965, almost three years to the day after it had come into existence, the company found itself in a critical financial position. There were £60,000 worth of bills of exchange maturing and no immediate resources from which to pay them. So drastic action had to be taken to prevent the company from being declared bankrupt within the month.

After a fruitless trip to London to see whether part of the money could be raised through Bill Master's backers, George decided to approach the one person who could tide them over the predicament. On October 19th. he boarded an Air France plane bound for Cairo.

His relationship with his grandmother had improved. He had seen her during the summer when she had come to Paris for a few days, and had also accompanied her to Deauville for a weekend at the house of friends where she had spoken of him and his business activities with a certain pride. He reckoned that she was certainly rich enough to help, if she wanted to, since the Wirsas had been one of the leading families of Alexandria, and the style of life Helen led could only be based on solid wealth. £50,000, though substantial in itself, was a relatively small amount when measured against a fortune which had to be well over the £1,000,000, mark. True, her money was in Egypt, but a way could always be found to make the funds available in Europe.

He taxed her on the matter within hours of his arrival. He came straight to the point, explaining the situation, why the company found itself in trouble despite its successes, how with a little breathing space the position would be reversed, and any advance repaid, and asked her to make available £50,000.

118

He spoke to her as he would have to a banker, pointing out the advantages which she could expect from the company if she made the loan, and listing the guarantees which he and his partner were prepared to give to secure the money.

Helen listened to him while working at a petit point cover for a cushion. She was silent for a while after he had finished speaking, then removed her spectacles and looked at him. Her face had taken on a hard, almost fierce expression.

"You have been frank with me, George, and I will repay you the courtesy. I think this is as good a moment as any to clear certain ideas which you may have, so I'll ask you to listen to me carefully since what I'm going to say is important, and has a bearing on what you have just told me. Firstly, I'm not the rich woman you believe me to be. Your grandfather had a large fortune, most of which he donated to a foundation which cares for the less privileged of the Coptic community. This was done with my full approval and, I might add, it was I who urged him to give away the maximum. I enjoy a substantial income which assures me freedom from economic worries and the possibility to live in a certain style, but no more. So, even if I had wanted to help, it is not in my power to do so.

"To be perfectly frank I'm glad this is the case as it saves me from appearing heartless or ungenerous. But I feel it is my duty to tell you that I am not surprised that you have found yourself in financial difficulties, and in a way it is a godsend. You are headstrong and rash, without the discipline which is the hallmark of a successful businessman. You will never listen to advice, and because you have had what is known as beginner's luck, you thought you were cleverer than others. It is regrettable that certain persons may suffer from your pride, but at least the situation you find yourself in may now make you see reason. You should give up any idea of dabbling in business, and lead the sort of life suitable to your capacities. You are fortunate to have an income left to you by your grandfather, sufficient to let you live very decently here in Egypt where you have a home at your disposal. What is more, should you settle down and marry a girl I approve of, it is in my power to increase that allowance as I think fit, and to provide a suitable home, though this house is quite large enough for me and any family you might have. And in due course, when I die, it would become yours. But if you want to go on living in Paris, it would be a different matter. I doubt that your income would be sufficient to keep you in the style to which you have accustomed yourself. I think it would be wise to have a talk with Mr Zekla. He has been a friend of the family's as well as my banker for many years, and it is he who deals with your income. I am not even certain what it amounts to, as for the past years I have simply given instructions that the bank look after the matter ... "

He had sat in his chair with his glass of whisky in one hand and a cigarette between the fingers of the other. He had not smoked while she was speaking, but periodically flicked the ash into a crystal ashtray near the decanter. The moment she had looked up at him from her needlework, he had known that she was not going to help, and all the while she was talking his mind was assessing his chances of raising the funds in some other way. There had been a moment when those words of hers, venomous in their whispered intensity, had struck him in his weakest spot, his pride. It had been an instant of dismay, as if someone had crumpled his world like a piece of waste paper. But the rebound was immediate.

"Of course, grand-mère. I quite understand, and I am grateful to you for having given me a clear picture of how matters stand. I will certainly go and see Mr Zekla as you suggest. May I pour you a little more sherry? Would you excuse me if I go to prepare for dinner? If I'm not mistaken you have it served at eight?"

Though he knew him by sight, George had never met Emile Zekla. He was bigger than his cousin Raymond, and exuded a power lacking in the Alexandrian banker. He was not at all sure he liked the man.

He spoke a pedantic French.

"Your grandmother phoned me and explained the reason of your visit. She gave me the gist of your discussion about a business venture for which you wanted money, and requested me to clarify your own financial position." He paused and a slight smile played on his lips. "I will begin by telling you what your present income in Egypt is from the dispositions left by your late grandfather, and implemented by Madame Wirsa."

He perched a pair of reading glasses on the end of his nose and studied a file on the desk. "Yes, here we are ... Three thousand one hundred and seventy pounds this year from which must be deducted the two thousand eight hundred and sixty already advanced, leaving exactly three hundred and ten pounds as balance to your credit. Naturally, should you need a little more, we can arrange to advance it against next year's income, though I shouldn't be suggesting it as I know your grandmother would not approve." Again the slight smile. "And now supposing you tell me about your company and the problems you have, so that I can see if there is anything I could do."

George had the irrational feeling that the man was, for some reason, playing cat and mouse with him. But he stifled his annoyance. Perhaps he had been in contact with his cousin Raymond, who would have urged him to see what he could do to help. And since he was there, he might as well explain the situation. He nodded and reached for his dispatch case.

"I have here last year's balance sheet, a profit and loss account for the first six months of this year, a list of the products we import and those we manufacture, a projected financial forecast for the next three years ... "

The banker held up his hand.

"I'll study them later, if you'll leave them with me. When I suggested you talk to me about the problems I had not realized that you had brought all this documentation. Under the circumstances I think I had better speak to you of another matter, which has become relevant now that you have come of age."

Emile Zekla leant back in his chair and began polishing his spectacles.

"Have you ever heard of a man called Antor Caspardian?"

George shook his head. "I don't think so. Should I have?"

"Perhaps not ... forget I asked you, it was just a thought which crossed my mind ... I presume you are not aware that there exists a Trust in your favour, of which the Banque Zekla acts as Trustee."

"A Trust? No, but why wasn't I informed of it?"

"Because we had instructions not to tell you till you were 21."

"But surely my grandmother ... "

"She had and has no idea. And now, if you will allow me to, I will explain what this Trust is. There is a capital sum, deposited at a bank in Geneva, interest on which becomes yours as from now. The Trust was set up in 1950, so you will have at your disposal the interest accrued over the past 5 years. It is not a vast amount, as the capital was invested in growth stock rather than interest yielding securities. Still, it amounts to somewhere in the region of 180,000 Swiss Francs and is, as I mentioned, available to you immediately. The capital, which was 1 million Swiss Francs when the Trust was formed, could now be valued at twice that amount."

George leant forward, his eyes now wide with excitement.

"But this is fabulous! 180,000 francs ... that's nearly 20,000 pounds. I could ... "

"Please, I have not finished. The capital of the Trust is invested in certain stocks, but can be used to raise loans for the purpose of buying real estate, for instance, or even to finance businesses in which the beneficiary is directly interested, if the Trustees are convinced that such an action is wise and justified."

"In other words it could provide me with the £50,000 in question. Fantastic! But tell me, Mr Zekla, who does this money come from? Who must I thank for this windfall? Not either of my grandfathers, or my father or mother, so who?"

"I'm afraid I can't tell you."

"Why?"

"Because those are the instructions. May I suggest it is not a matter you should concern yourself with, but rather that you now leave me to see whether, as a Trustee, I can recommend the financing of your business to the tune of £50,000."

"Recommend to whom?" George queried.

"To the other Trustee."

"And who is he?"

"Once again, I am not empowered to reveal that."

"But this is absurd! Why all the secrecy? If someone has put a million Swiss francs in my name, I want to know who he or she is. I want to know as there must be a reason behind it. People don't give away that sort of money without a very specific reason. You say the Trust was set up in 1950? That's when I went to England. There must be some connection..."

"I am a banker, George, and I have to follow instructions given to me. Those are quite categorical, and I don't intend to deviate from them. I will give you any information you may wish regarding the financial situation of the Trust and what it may or may not do, but nothing more. In any case,

I would have thought that it was more important at this particular moment to see what can be done to save this company of yours, than trying to find out why a certain person did a certain thing at a certain moment."

A note of irritation had crept into the banker's voice. He was right, George decided, first things first. There would be plenty of time to discover who was behind it all, and why. What mattered, was that the money was there, and he was pretty certain now that Emile Zekla would twist his own arm to have the Trust advance those £50,000.

He was not wrong. Five hours later the banker rang and asked him to call round at his office the following morning.

"I have examined the documents you left me," he said as soon as George was seated, "and after consulting my cousin in Alexandria and certain persons at the bank in Geneva, I was able to recommend that your Trust makes available 50 per cent of the amount you require. We believe that if you go to your bankers with part of the sum, with your own money as it were, you will have little difficulty in persuading them to loan the balance. In this connection, you could do well to call at the Paris branch of the Crédit Méditerranéen et d'Outremer. It's a bank controlled by a friend of ours, Mr Marcel Kharami. You may like to open an account there; it could be of help to you. As to the money from your Trust, this can be available to you immediately you have completed the formalities in Geneva. But first, you will have to sign a certain undertaking. One of the conditions attached to the loan is that the Trust will have an option on 50 per cent of the shares of your Company."

George was immediately on the alert. "What does that mean exactly? I have a partner, and I cannot act without his consent where his shareholding is involved."

"Maybe. Yet I noticed that you have a power of attorney from Mr Pigaud which enables you to act with complete freedom. But there is no cause for alarm. You and he will find the conditions perfectly acceptable, and its unlikely anyone would better them. I'm sure he'll be grateful to you for having found the solution to your problems."

George smiled wryly. The cards were on the table. This mysterious Trust wanted control with him of Pharmaceutiques Christogaud. Fair enough. That meant the bankers who administered the Trust reckoned it was a business with a future, that he was a man to back financially. A winner, in other words.

"You're right, Mr Zekla. And thanks for your help in this matter."

"Don't mention it, it's my duty, and a pleasure. Now let me give you these documents to study. They are facsimiles of the ones you will sign in Switzerland. If there are any queries don't hesitate to contact me. When will you be leaving?"

"Tomorrow I hope. It'll depend on Swissair flights and obtaining the exit visa."

He stood up, shook the banker's hand and walked to the door.

"By the way," he asked suddenly, "what was that name you mentioned yesterday before you started telling me about the Trust?"

"I really don't remember, George. Did I mention one?"

New York, May, 1956

Julius walked into his suite at the Waldorf Astoria, after flying in from Geneva.

He had a quick shower and changed clothes before Jack Leigh, a partner in the law firm of Packard, Leigh and Prestman, arrived for the 4.30 p.m. appointment.

Leigh's firm had as clients 9 of the 30 largest corporations on the East Coast, and 11 of the 96 members of the US Senate. Antor had met him in 1952 through a barter deal in which the powerful American Fruit Corporation was involved. Sniffing success, Leigh had courted Antor, and it was through his string pulling that the Alexandrian was able to obtain American nationality faster than usual.

On March 3rd 1954 he had sworn allegiance to his new country, and had marked his metamorphosis from Egyptian to American by a change of name. Antor Giulio Caspardian became A. Julius Caspar.

A cousin of Leigh's, a certain Bill Wakeman, had inherited a stretch of land in New Mexico which geologists had told him was rich with petroleum. But after four years of luckless wildcat drilling he was on the verge of bankruptcy, and had turned to his lawyer cousin for advice as to which oil company to approach and how.

Leigh knew that to try to deal with one of the 'big boys' was tantamount to throwing Bill into the lion's den, and to link up with a small one might result in a fiasco if it were not strong enough financially. So he decided to approach Julius who had recently sold his refinery in Italy, and had hinted he had a hankering to own an oil well.

Julius was not really interested in getting drawn into a risk venture involving a large outlay of capital. Simpler to buy an existing oil company, he told Leigh when approached. Yet after studying the geologists reports, that adventurous side of his which had propelled him from carpenter's son to international millionaire financier, was intrigued. He studied the matter for a week, then flew to Albuquerque.

He was met at the airport by Wakeman, who drove him in a rattling Chevrolet 150 dusty kms towards Clovis. The arid countryside, with its cacti and occasional desert willow, framed by distant peaks of the Sierra Blanca, produced the familiar sense of timelessness which he had experienced in certain areas of Morocco and Algeria. Despite Wakeman's incessant chatter he was filled with a feeling of peace.

"We're almost there, Mr Caspar. See that ridge? Well, from it you can get a good view of my land. I'm taking you there first, so you can have an idea of how it lies."

Ten minutes later he parked the car by a creosote bush, climbed out and with a sweep of his hand said, "here it is. From that water tower in the distance to the hillock over there. No, not the first, the one beyond. 500 acres of pure gold, Mr Caspar. A giveaway."

"Where does it begin?"

"Right behind you. See that post, that's where it begins."

"So where we're standing is part of the land?"

"It sure is. And if you climb back in the car I'll drive you along that road, and show you every inch of it."

Julius said nothing. He stood still and gazed around him. It looked a godforsaken stretch of land with nothing much to excite one. 300 metres away was a shed with a corrugated tin roof, surrounded by bits of machinery. Further on an abandoned derrick, with near it some thirty oil barrels stacked incongruously into a pyramid.

"O.K. it doesn't look much, but I can tell you there's a fortune bedded under there. You've read the geologists' reports. They don't make mistakes, not the ones my cousin Jack got. They cost, but were worth it. It's a real bargain for someone with the right money, believe me. I'm only selling it because my wife wants to get away. And because to do the job properly, one needs more finance than I've got ... "

Julius pretended not to hear. He kicked some of the earth with his foot, then crouched down and took it in his hand. He let it filter through his fingers, then he shut his eyes.

He sensed he was onto something good, but it was not the geologists' report nor Bill Wakeman's sales palaver which told him so. It was a tickle up his spine. That sunbaked, desolate stretch of land, miles from nowhere, was destined to be his.

He straightened and walked back to the car.

"O.K., Mr Wakeman, I'll phone Mr Leigh with my decision in 48 hours. Perhaps you'd be kind enough to drive me back to the airport."

"Back to the airport! But you haven't seen anything yet. I want to show you the whole place. Where I drilled, the machinery ... Jesus, I put five years of my life into this goddam land. You can't make up your mind in five minutes ... "

"I can and I will ... "

"But Peggy, that's my wife, is expecting you for lunch. She'll be as sore as hell ... "

"Mr Wakeman, I'm a very busy man and there's a plane I want to catch. I'm sure Mrs Wakeman will understand. We can phone her from that gas station we passed on the way."

The following afternoon he rang Jack Leigh.

"I've decided to buy Wakeman's land. I'll pay the price he wants, not because it's worth it — I could beat him down to half he's so desperate to sell — but because if ever there is oil there, I don't want him saying he's been gypped. That's got to be made clear, as I don't want trouble later on."

"Sure, Julius, though I don't see how there could be. Once title to the land is legally yours ... "

"Listen, people have a way of imagining they've been had if someone else makes the killing they expected. They even convince themselves, and others, they've been robbed of a birthright. That's why I want Wakeman to get exactly what he's asking, and to have it spelt out that he's completely happy, and that no one has twisted his arm to sell me the land. It's a condition of sale."

"O.K., if that's the way you want it."

"I'm off to Europe then Egypt tomorrow, so I'll leave you a deposit and will sign the act of purchase when I get back. Can you make it here at my hotel on June 28th say 4.30 p.m.? Fine. Also I want you to set up a company to acquire the land and carry out the prospecting, etc ... A name?"

He thought for moment. The name was important. It must catch the imagination yet stand for power and success. And linked to him in some way.

It came in a flash. "Call it the 'Pharos Oil Company'." The famous lighthouse at Alexandria, one of the seven wonders of the ancient world, would be a fitting symbol for his oil company. It could only bring him luck.

Twenty years later the Pharos Petroleum Corporation was the ninth largest oil producing company in the USA. It was destined to make Julius one of the richest men in the world, but was also to be at the centre of the bitterest takeover battle witnessed in American business history. A battle where more than money and the control of a highly profitable concern was involved.

Kent, 1956

In the summer of 1955 Julius had rented a large chalet on the outskirts of Gstaad, the fashionable Swiss health and skiing resort in the mountains between Montreux and Berne. Whenever he was in Switzerland he would go there for weekends, and sometimes even allow himself the luxury of a few days' total escape from the pressing demands of his business activities.

On the morning of July 20th, 1956, he stood by the French windows of the chalet's drawing room and gazed across the terrace to the sloping fields lush with grass, and the fir covered Bernese Alps beyond. The windows were open, allowing him to breathe deeply the refreshing breeze, a balm after the aridness of the Arabian deserts from which he had returned the day before. He listened to the distant tinkling of cow bells as his nostrils took in the clear and subtle odours of mountain harvesting, so different from those to which he had been accustomed in his youth, then turned and went over to a table where his mail had been placed.

The letters were personal, business ones having been sifted and dealt with at the bank, and were mostly from institutions or individuals requesting charity, or thanking him for gifts received or services rendered. He fingered through them till he fell on an envelope addressed to Mr Antor Caspardian. He raised an eyebrow, intrigued. Whoever had written it could not have been in contact for several years, not since Antor Giulio Caspardian had become A. Julius Caspar.

The envelope contained an invitation card.

The Viscountess Brentwick
requests the pleasure of your company
on Friday, August 1st, 1956
at the reception to be held at Chilton Hall
following the marriage of her daughter
the Hon. Georgina Joan Langton
to
Mr George Roger Christofides

Black Tie   RSVP

8 O'clock onwards   Chilton Hall
                                                         Chilton, Kent.

He was drained suddenly of emotion as if all sentiments had been neutralized by a powerful yet soporific shock. Absently he turned the card round. On the back there were six words. 'Do come if you can, Cecily.'

He realized it was the first time he had seen her handwriting. He had never received a letter or a note from her, only a telegram when Maryanne was born. And when he had written to let her know that he had set up a Trust for their daughter, and where to contact him if necessary, he had not expected nor received a reply.

Why had she asked him, he wondered? She could not possibly know or have guessed of his relationship to George. Had it been Maryanne's wedding it would have been different. That, he would have understood.

His mind skipped back to the last time he had seen Cecily, in 1951, on one of his flying visits through London. Quite by chance he had glanced at a photograph on the front page of the Evening Standard. It was of an elderly lady talking to a beautiful woman and a girl on the steps of a church. He did not need to read who the woman was, he recognized her immediately. Her face and figure were exactly as he remembered them. But the girl? 'HM The Queen Mother talking to Viscountess Brentwick (Miss Cecily Bentley) and her daughter, the Hon Maryanne Langton at the marriage of Her Majesty's goddaughter, Lady Anne Muirson with Captain Sir Rupert Goddard.'

He had picked up the paper and examined the photo more closely. So that was what his daughter looked like. There was no mistaking the broad forehead and the nose. They were the

Caspardian stamp. She was not beautiful like her mother, but there was an attractive purity in her features. What sort of person would she grow into, he wondered? On an impulse he had decided to get in touch with Cecily again.

At one o'clock the next day he was in the Causerie at Claridges, waiting for her. He had arrived early to make sure he saw her before she spotted him. He knew that the years had not tarnished her beauty and that she was as desirable as when he had first loved her. If she aroused again that passion in him, he wanted to know it before she sensed it, and he also wanted to capture the expression in her eyes when she saw him again. As a consummate actress she might hide what she really felt, but not in those first few moments.

She turned out to be exactly as he had expected. She entered the restaurant, paused for a moment as she looked for him, and all eyes were immediately on her. The charisma which had made her one of England's most popular actresses radiated subtly, enhancing the translucency of her skin, the golden glint in her swept up hair, and the blue of her eyes. Eyes which, when they met his, widened an instant before matching the smile on her lips.

He took her gloved hand in his, bent over it slightly and said quietly, "you are lovelier than ever, even more beautiful than when I first saw you on the stage at the Savoy ... "

"Oh Antor, it's so marvellous to see you again. I just can't believe it's actually you. Let me have a good look at you ... no, you haven't really changed; perhaps a line more on the forehead and a determination in the fold of the lip, and that ... " she had slipped off her glove and let a finger rest on his cheek. "The war?" she asked softly, then she had laughed. "Actually you look wonderful ... it's nine years isn't it?"

"Yes, bar a few weeks."

"And with you sitting there it seems like yesterday." She paused and looked down at her hands, "yet so much has changed."

"Really so much, Cecily?"

She nodded slowly and sighed. "Inevitably. The war ... one can never cancel those years. At least I can't. That sort of experience ... "

"I know, it must have been terrible."

"You can't know, Antor," she said gently, almost pleadingly, "but let's not talk about it. Let's talk about us, about you

131

especially. And let's drink to the two of us ... yes, that will be lovely," she said as he filled her glass with champagne.

He watched her sip it and smiled. "I saw a photo of you in the newspaper with your daughter. She seems a cute kid."

She laughed. "She is ... I know what's changed in you. It's the voice. You speak differently!"

"You're being kind. What you really mean is that my English is better. I could hardly be understood in those days. It's because I've been in the States a lot ... "

"And are you married?" She hesitated a fraction as she asked it.

"No ... but tell me about Maryanne."

She put down her glass and settled back in her chair. "All right. She's got dark hair and grey brown eyes and a nose that no Langton ever had. She's clever and very affectionate — especially with me — but shy and rather closed in on herself where others are concerned. I believe she'll grow up to be a very nice person ... "

"Does she know?"

"Of course not."

"And will you ever tell her?"

"I don't know ... it all rather depends ... but certainly not till she's a mature woman."

He nodded, then changed the subject. "What can I order for you? Do you still like potted shrimps?"

For a while they talked about their respective lives, inevitably touching on the war years, on her widowhood and the difficulty of bringing up children without a father. She did most of the speaking in that vibrant husky voice for which she was famous, while he listened, his face immobile, but taking in her every word and expression. Then she said the words he hoped he'd never hear and which made his heart miss a beat.

"I want you to be the first to know it, Antor ... I'm going to get married again."

He knew it was absurd to be jealous, yet he was, almost alarmingly so.

"He's a cousin of James, and he was a wonderful friend to me when I really needed one. And the children love him, especially Maryanne. Curiously it was she who decided me in a way. The other day, at that wedding, she said 'Mummy, why don't you marry Uncle Reggie'. He took me out to dinner and that's when I finally made up my mind. He's been trying to convince me to for years."

She rested her hand on his. "He's part of my world, you understand, of my day to day life. He's kind, dependable and not without a certain charm. He's different from you, Antor, and I am glad he is. You are from another planet, fascinating, irresistible and mysterious. Yet part of me will always remain yours. I'll always love you and wish, as I have all these years, that our lives could have been different. But they can't be. We both know that. Possibly I won't see you again but I'll always thank God that I met you. And I have in Maryanne a living proof that our love was worthwhile, that you really cared for me, and that perhaps a part of you always will ..."

He reached for his agenda. He was due in Frankfurt on the 1st for a meeting with Alfred Munnerman. He rang his secretary.

"Madame Helde, would you get through to the Munnerman Bank and postpone my meeting for a couple of days. When you've arranged that, send a telegram to Viscountess Brentwick at Chilton Hall, Chilton, Kent in England saying, 'My very best wishes to your daughter. I will be delighted to come.' Signed, Antor."

He replaced the receiver and for a while went on staring at the card. A smile began to play on his lips.

What an extraordinary twist of fate, that a son he had only seen once, and a daughter he had never met, would become brother and sister-in-law on his very birthday.

Spring, 1956

At twenty one, Georgina Langton was a beautiful young woman, if somewhat on the plump side, with blue-green eyes and a mass of hair a shade more golden than her mother's.

She held herself well and had a natural flair for clothes. The dress she had chosen for her coming out ball was from Hardy Amies, and it gave her a sophisticated look in contrast to many of the other debs. Swathed in red silk, she stood out from them like a ruby amongst opals, and George noticed her the moment he entered the hall at Chilton.

She was standing a little to the left of the staircase, chatting to a group of guests, but it was only when she came over to greet him that he realized who she was.

"Hello George, do you remember me? I'm Georgina. I'm so glad you could make it. Julian said you probably wouldn't come as you're not the 'debs delight' type ... "

George grinned. "He's right, but from what I see, you're not the typical deb. I had no idea Julian had such a beautiful sister."

"Thanks, but you probably didn't even remember he had a sister, period, as the Americans say. Actually he has two, did he tell you?"

"Possibly, but there's only one who counts this evening. Many happy returns of the day," he said, handing her a small packet.

"Oh, you shouldn't have," she exclaimed, "actually my birthday isn't till next week. So I suppose I should wait to open it till then."

"No, presents must be opened when received. Go on, it won't bite you."

She laughed excitedly and opened the packet. It contained a flat leather box with Cartier stamped on it, and inside a slender bracelet braided with strands of different golds.

She slipped it onto her wrist murmuring "it's absolutely super. I don't know how to thank you George."

She meant it too. She was taken aback, and at a loss for

words. George was a good friend of her brother's from his Oxford days but she hardly knew him. She had only seen him a couple of times, and reckoned there was no earthly reason why he should give her such a present. She placed her hands on his shoulders and gave him a kiss on the cheek. For a moment he put his arm round her waist, then she drew away.

"It's the nicest present I've received ... I won't say 'you shouldn't have', because I love it, and I'm delighted you did ... come with me, I want to show it to Mummy."

Impetuously, she took his hand and drew him into the dining room where she knew her mother was talking to other guests.

"Mummy," she cried, " I want to show you something." And so as not to embarrass him she whispered "look what George has given me. Isn't it divine?"

Then she dragged him through the drawing room to the library where she spotted Julian. She signalled to him to come over to them.

"What d'you think of this?" she said, holding her wrist up to him.

Her brother pursed his lips in admiration. "Fab. Who gave it to you, Mother?"

"No, you stupe. Your friend George, here, who is now my friend George too."

George watched her. She was excited by his present and that pleased him. He found himself attracted to her in a way he had not experienced for a long time, not since his adolescent crush on Anne at the English School in Cairo.

He danced several times with her. She was graceful and unexpectedly expert at the South American rhythms he preferred.

He had to leave early to be in Paris for a meeting the following day, but he was already aware that he wanted to see her again, and with his customary panache said, "will you lunch with me the day after tomorrow ... in Paris? You too, Julian. I'll arrange for a plane to fly you over so all you'll have to do is be at Croydon airport at around eleven o'clock. Oh, and bring an overnight bag so you can stay a day or two if you like."

They spent three days there and they were 72 hours which Georgina was never to forget.

Julian knew that George had money, but certainly no idea how much. Nor had he ever been to his friend's apartment. It was a penthouse, overlooking the Esplanade des Invalides, with views stretching from Montmartre to Montparnasse, and a roof complete with lawn and rose garden, giving the impression of a country house perched on the city's rooftops.

Georgina was entranced, and by the end of the stay was completely in love. George was flattered, but his interest in her might have waned had she not shared with him his passion for horse racing. In the weeks which followed he took her to Ascot, Longchamp and the Derby. And it was while watching her at the racecourse at Chantilly two months later, her cheeks flushed, her blond hair glowing in the afternoon sun, that he decided to marry her.

As they were being driven back to Paris he put a hand on hers and asked, "happy?"

"Marvellously."

"And do you reckon I deserve to be happy too?"

"Of course. Who's stopping you?"

"You, if you don't agree to marry me."

She cuddled against him and whispered, "oh George, darling, of course I will." And a totally new sensation gripped him.

A grabber par excellence, and a basic sexualist who got satisfaction from a form of rape of every woman he possessed, when he put his arms around her and their lips met it was as if he were sinking into a sensuality which involved every pore of his being. For the first time in his life he was experiencing love.

They got married five weeks later in a blaze of publicity.

George was determined to make the wedding reception an event which the 500 guests were unlikely to forget, and took in hand all the preparations. He got Maxim's to provide the buffet, Moyses Stevens to do the floral arrangements, Bollinger to supply the champagne, and Edmundo Ross's band to alternate with Sidney Bechet's in Chilton's redecorated ballroom. He had Dior design Georgina's dress, a sumptuous model in pleated chiffon embroidered with rhinestones, and matching ones for the bridesmaids. He wanted to prove to those bankers and industrialists who formed part of the guests that George Christofides was not a man who did things by half measures.

He had reason to be satisfied. Chilton Hall was an admirable setting for a lavish ball and, what elsewhere might have turned out to be brash extravagance, was transmuted on that mild summer evening into a moment of enchantment.

After receiving the congratulations and good wishes for an hour, he and Georgina went out onto the west terrace where guests were seated at small tables. They strolled around, chatting with friends, till George caught sight of his mother-in-law talking to a man he did not know, but whose face was familiar.

"Who's the man with your mother?" he asked Georgina.

"Haven't a clue. Probably a film producer, the place is swarming with them."

"Let's go and find out," he said, leading her towards them.

"Ah, I'm glad you've come," Cecily exclaimed, "I want you to meet an old and very dear friend who I haven't seen for years, and who's come specially to England to be with us this evening, Mr. Caspar."

So that was who he was! George had heard a lot about him, a financier with interests wherever big money was involved. A name with a reputation but without a face. No one knew much about the man, what his origins were, where he lived, whether or not he had a family. Only that he was born in Alexandria.

"I wish you every happiness," he was saying to Georgina, kissing her hand, "your husband is a fortunate man to have such a lovely bride." He turned, and George had the feeling that he was being scrutinized, as if the man were trying to fathom some mystery. He had seldom felt anyone look at him with such intensity. Then came a half smile and the conventional words of congratulation, but in French.

"*Mes sincères félicitations ... et je suis ravi de faire enfin votre connaissance.*"

"*Je vous remercie, Monsieur, moi aussi,*" George answered, adding in English, "Georgina and I are delighted that you are able to be with us this evening."

"Mr Caspar comes from Alexandria, " Cecily put in, and placing a hand on Julius's arm asked, "maybe you knew George's family?"

Once again the penetrating stare. "Yes, I knew a family

called Christofides. Roger Christofides was a contemporary of mine ... "

"He was my father, but was killed during the war. Perhaps you knew my mother too. She was called Marguerite Wirsa before she married. In fact, I was brought up by my grandmother, Helen Wirsa, as my mother died when I was born. She should have been here this evening," he went on, "only she didn't feel up to all of this after the civil ceremony in Paris. If you lived in Alex before the war I'm sure you must have met her."

The man nodded slowly. "Yes, l knew them all ... or rather, I came across them. But you must forgive me, we are talking about twenty five years ago, perhaps more ... "

"Yet I have the feeling we've met before. Mr Caspar." George was turning on all his charm. He wanted to establish a personal relationship with the man. It was not every day that such an opportunity presented itself.

"Possibly, though I rarely go to Alexandria, even when I happen to be in Egypt."

"No, it wouldn't have been there; more likely in Paris or London. You won't have remembered me, but yours is not the kind of face one forgets."

Julius smiled, then glanced at Cecily. "Your son-in-law is very flattering."

"That wasn't flattery, it's true. And you've hardly changed in all these years, apart from the beard."

She was interrupted by the arrival of Maryanne.

"What is it, Mummy? Julian said you were looking for me. Said it was urgent...he stopped me dancing ... "

"Yes darling. I wanted you to meet a very special person, an old, old friend whom I haven't seen for years, Mr Caspar." And turning to Julius added softly, "Julius, this is my other daughter, Maryanne."

"How do you do, Mr Caspar."

"Hello Maryanne," Julius said, holding her hand in his for a long moment while he gazed at her.

"Mr Caspar once lived in Egypt and knew George's family there," Cecily went on, "isn't it a small world, darling."

"Did you really live there? Gosh, how romantic. I've always wanted to go there, haven't I, Mummy! I'd hoped Uncle Reggie would have taken us, and he had promised to. But then he died and, well, that was that. And George never wants to talk about the place, says he doesn't like it. But ... "

"That's true, and there's little reason to," George said. "It's a Godforsaken, flea ridden dump and you can forget about the so-called antiquities. The Pyramids and the Sphinx are as corny as the Eiffel Tower, not to mention the filth, which is unbelievable ... "

"If you like, Maryanne, I'll tell you about it." Julius interposed. "Yes, parts of it are dirty, and the poverty is horrifying, but it is a country blessed with a touch of magic, and the city in which your brother-in-law and I were born was once unique. But that was a long time ago and I'm afraid it has changed a lot."

"Don't you live there any more?"

"No, and I haven't for many years. But I go back sometimes. I was there a few weeks ago."

"Oh Mr Caspar, do tell me, is it true that if one stands on the top of the Great Pyramid and hits a golf ball as hard as one can, it'll always land on the base?" Maryanne asked.

"That's what they say, but I've never been up to try."

"Have you been inside it? Must be terribly spooky."

"Maryanne, instead of pumping Mr Caspar with questions, why don't you arrange for a waiter to bring some champagne."

"I'm delighted to tell her what I can about Egypt, Cecily. It's just unfortunate that I don't know much about the Pyramids ... let's go together to find a waiter, and I'll tell what I can ... "

George watched the two of them walk off together and turned to his mother-in-law.

"Remarkable man that; I had no idea he was a friend of yours. He's made quite a name for himself in the world of finance. Wonder why he's in England?"

"Because I asked him here, that's why," she answered.

"I'd hate to disillusion you, dear belle-maman, but men like him don't do things just because a woman, however beautiful and charming, ask them to. There must be a good reason and I'd like to know it"

"Then why not ask him?" Cecily parried before turning to another guest.

George pursed his lips. "What d'you make of him, Georgie?"

Georgina did not answer immediately but looked to where her sister and Julius were now standing. "Attractive. I wonder if he's an old flame of Mummy's? Yet I don't remember ever seeing him, and she's never mentioned him before. Funny, as we know all her friends. Maybe he was before our time."

"Did you notice how he took to Maryanne."

"And she to him. She's always getting crushes on older men."

"Then we'll have to keep an eye on her," George said half jokingly, "can't have little sister running after him. He may be stinking rich, but he's a bit old and not quite out of the top drawer, from what I've heard. But I want you to charm him. He could be very useful to me. If he's in New York when we go there, we'll look him up."

The day after the ball Maryanne woke at 11 a.m., and lay in bed thinking about the preceding 24 hours. So much had happened that it felt to her as if months of activities and emotions had been crammed into them. In a way, she realized suddenly, her life had taken on a new dimension. All their lives had, not simply Georgina's. And George had been responsible.

Her thoughts focused on her brother-in-law as she stared at the familiar snout of Tang, her Siamese cat, resting three inches away from her nose.

"You don't like him all that, do you? Between you and me, I don't think I do much either." She picked the cat up and held it above her, then brought it down onto her chest and began caressing it.

No she hadn't really taken to George the first time Julian had brought him home for a weekend, and there was something about him which made her uneasy even now. She had to admit, though, that she was fascinated by him. Not by his good looks and charm so much as by the curious feeling that some tenuous bond existed between them which she couldn't define or explain to herself. On various occasions she had found him observing her with his cold green eyes as if evaluating what he saw. Not unpleasantly, but without the slightest warmth or emotion. She had caught him staring at her mother and at Julian too, but with them it seemed less analytical. Only with Georgina was it different. He didn't stare at her. He looked at her with love. Yes, whatever his defects, it was obvious that he loved her sister. Yet in a strange way he had married the lot of them. He acted as if they were his creatures, a sort of clan of his, to mould and manoeuvre as he wished. Which was what he had done the moment Georgina had agreed to become his wife.

He had taken control of all the wedding arrange- ments, and there had been no question of his doing otherwise. He had fixed the date and the place of the ceremony, and decided what kind of reception was to be held at Chilton afterwards. He had chosen the caterers, the bands, the decorators and the make of champagne. Even the flowers. Her mother, Julian and Georgina had acquiesced and left the whole thing to him. All they had been allowed to do was give a social secretary the names of the guests they wanted. He had even chosen her two dresses. The pale green Dior suit for the Paris ceremony and the pink and blue Givenchy ball gown which was hanging over the back of a chair by her dressing table. 'Mind you, he's got taste,' she murmured. It was a lovely dress and made her look quite thin, which she wasn't. Even Mr. Caspar had said she looked wonderful in it.

She snuggled back in the pillows and turned her thoughts to the fascinating stranger her mother had wanted her to meet. Who was he? Her mother had said 'an old friend of the family', but she had never mentioned him before. Perhaps Julian knew. She'd ask him later.

No, after all, she wouldn't ask her brother as he probably wouldn't tell her anyway. He was like that. For Georgie he'd do anything and the two of them had no secrets for each other. But with her it was different. 'Two's company, three's a crowd' was what they usually said when she wanted to be with them. It had always been like that, but maybe now that Georgie had George, Julian might become closer with her. It wasn't that he didn't like her, after all. In a funny way he was quite fond of her, only she was seven years younger and he still reckoned she was a kid so couldn't be bothered with her.

Perhaps she should ask George when he got back from the honeymoon. From what he had said last night he knew the man, or of him.

It was curious how she had immediately felt at ease with him, as if she had known him for years. He was like Uncle Reggie, only stronger. She liked him. No, it was more than that. She felt that somehow he was on her side, a person she could trust. Which was odd as she had only spoken to him for a few minutes. If only he hadn't had to leave so early! She would have liked to ask him so much more about Egypt, and about a whole lot of things, in fact.

Suddenly, she realized that her heart was beating faster. He was really rather fabulous and not at all like some of her mother's friends. And she was sure he liked her too. Perhaps he would come again. Perhaps she could ask her mother to invite him for a weekend.

No, she decided, she wouldn't discuss him with her. She didn't know why, but she just wouldn't.

There was a knock on the door and her mother poked her head into the room.

"Hello darling, not too tired? I feel a hundred and one."

She came in and after giving Maryanne a kiss, sat on her bed.

"I feel fine, Mummy. I'm not tired. But I'm still sort of excited about everything. What time is it?"

"Ten past eleven. But you can go to sleep again if you like, unless you're hungry. We're having a kind of brunch in about an hour."

Maryanne pushed the cat away from her and sat up. "Do you think Georgie and George are already at Capri?"

"No, not yet. I believe they're stopping the night in Rome."

"Gosh she's lucky, Georgie. l wish I could travel like her."

"You will, darling, one day and probably sooner than you think. I wouldn't be surprised if one of those bright young men who were hanging around you last night didn't whisk you away too."

"Oh, Mummy, how can you say such a silly thing. And anyway there's no one I like enough to even think about as a boyfriend."

"Not even John de Courcey? He's good looking, charming and very well brought up."

"And solid concrete from the neck upwards. All he can say is 'well actually'."

"Then what about Clifford Hamilton. I like him, and from the way he was making gooey eyes at you ... "

"Mummy, do stop it. I'm not interested in any of them. And anyway why do you want to marry me off at all costs? Heavens, it'll be years before anything like that will happen."

In fact, only fourteen months were to pass before she met

the man who was to become her husband, and George was responsible for that.

Three days later Julius was back at Gstaad. Out in the garden a woman was resting in a chaise-longue. He walked over, took her hand and kissed it.

"Feeling better?" he asked, as he sat down next to her.

Maza de la Marlière smiled wanly.

He looked tenderly at the proud face aged by illness, and thought back to the day he had found her again, quite by chance, in a restaurant at Chanterella above St Moritz.

He had sat at a table on the terrace and gazed at the breathtaking panorama. Then he had glanced around casually and noticed a woman on her own in the opposite corner. He could not see her face, but there was something familiar in the poise of her head and the way her fingers toyed with the stem of her wineglass. She had turned to call the waiter, and her profile had come into play.

Almost without realizing it, he had got up and walked over to her. Despite a hat which concealed part of her face and dark glasses, he was certain she was Maza.

"Bonjour ma chérie," he had said softly.

She had looked up and given a little gasp. Neither of them had spoken for a moment.

"Hello Antor," she had then whispered, cancelling a decade of absence.

She didn't explain why she had left him without warning, and he didn't ask her. All she said was that she had been ill, and had spent several years in and out of sanatoriums.

"I'm all right now, or so the doctors say. But I have to be careful and stay in the mountains where the air is clean and dry. That's why I'm here."

"Do you live there?" he had asked nodding down at St Moritz.

"No. I'm at a pension in a village not far from here. It's run by a man who was once my chauffeur, and he and his wife are very kind to me. I don't know what I'd do without them. Jean — my husband — died at the end of the war. We'd lost nearly everything but luckily my father left me some means here in Switzerland, so I was able to have treatment and live quietly. Which is all I want ... But don't let's talk about me; tell me all about you."

Having found her, he didn't want to lose her again. At first, though, she had resisted him.

"Forget about me, Antor. The Maza you once knew and perhaps loved has gone forever. I'm a semi-invalid. I could get ill any moment."

"All the more reason why you should let me look after you. I can't leave you here, all alone, in a remote Swiss village. I can't and I refuse to. Come to somewhere nearer me; I'll take a place in the mountain above Geneva, or at Chamonix. You can stay there and we can be together again as we were in Cairo."

"No Antor, but your asking me has made me happier than I have been in a very long time. Come and see me here every now and then when you can spare the time. Come and hold my hand, and talk to me as you are doing now. That's all I ask."

It took him three weeks of phone calls and telegrams before she finally agreed to move to a house he rented at Gstaad. And there, her health restored, she turned the sprawling chalet into a rendez-vous for a cosmopolitan elite formed of writers, politicians, bankers, musicians and members of the international aristocracy. Also, for nearly five years, into a welcome home to which he could retreat from the pressure of his growing financial and commercial interests.

A frequent visitor was the ageing pianist Alfred Cortot, once a personal friend of Jean de la Marlière, who Maza could sometimes persuade to sit at the Steinway grand and play to such dinner guests as Charlie Chaplin, André Malraux, Marlene Dietrich, Nelson Rockefeller, Queen Federica of Greece. It was he who, on a warm May evening in 1962 accompanied 'little' Clara Strapakis as she sang for Julius a week before her début in Paris.

They were moments which Julius was to count amongst the happiest of his life. He was rich, respected and successful, with a companion he admired and loved, perhaps not with the passion of his youth, yet enough to want to marry her. But it was she who gently brushed aside his proposal.

"What's the point, Antor? Ten years ago it made sense, at least I thought so at the time. Then I believed the world was before us, and that we would make a wonderful team to go out and conquer it. As your wife, I felt I could have helped you get to the top. But you managed without me, and I haven't the strength any more for worldly ambitions. Mine are now limited to seeing you smile, to knowing that here, with me, you can find peace and understanding. The moments we have here together are all I ask for. Marriage is for those who have the future before them; I can only count on the present."

Then the illness had claimed her again, surreptitiously like a thief, stealing what was most precious. And the telltale cough had returned.

She leant back in the chair and murmured, "how was it, the wedding?"

"Magnificent, and Cecily's daughter made a lovely bride." He paused. "Yet it all seemed a little unreal, maybe because of the curious situation l found myself in. Meeting for the first time two complete strangers who were my own flesh and blood. Can't happen that often."

"Tell me about them. What are they like?"

He thought for a moment. "George is about my size, good-looking with something of my father's eyes. The same colouring but not the expression. My father's were the kindest a man could have, and honest. I'm not sure that George is basically honest. Mind you, I only exchanged a few words with him, so I could be wrong. But my impression was that he is totally self-centred and an opportunist of the first order."

"Aren't most successful businessmen?"

"You're right. I'm an opportunist too, but I wouldn't sell my soul to the devil to get what I want. George might. He knows how to put on the charm, though, even if he has inherited his grandmother's ingrained scorn."

Maza chuckled. "In other words you didn't take to him. Then what about the girl?"

He smiled. "Ah, she's rather special ... for a moment she made me regret not having a daughter in the true sense of the word. She's not beautiful like her sister; she's got the Caspardian nose and a mouth a little too wide, but the beauty comes from inside her. She has a purity which is disarming."

"Did you manage to talk to her?"

"A little. Mostly about Egypt. She wanted to know all about the Pyramids and Tutankhamen, not my speciality. But I danced with her. Do you realize, ma chérie, I was dancing at my son's wedding with my 17 year old daughter, who had just become his sister-in-law. It's a curious world we live in where such things can happen. Neither my father nor my mother could have imagined it."

"Does she know about you?" Maza asked softly.

"Only what Cecily told her, that I'm an old family friend."

"Will she ever?"

"I don't know, but I suppose so sometime. I'm not sure I want her to."

She began coughing. He reached for his handkerchief and pressed it gently into her hand. Then he stood up and walked slowly back to the house. He didn't like to leave her in such moments, but he had to. Maza hated him seeing her in that state.

London, 1959

Nelson James Christofides was born in the London Clinic on March 14th. 1957. He arrived earlier than expected, while his father was in Lyon concluding the purchase of the Laboratoires Dinard SA, one of France's oldest and most reputable pharmaceutical companies.

The deal was the indirect result of a meeting George had had with Julius Caspar in New York, three months after his marriage. He and Georgina had booked into the Waldorf Astoria where the Alexandrian stayed, and two days after their arrival were dining with him in his suite in the Tower.

George had not broached the subject of business until late in the evening, after Georgina had gone to bed.

"I'm afraid she gets tired easily these days, and has to be careful," he explained after he had accompanied her to their room. "The doctor warned that these early months could be a bit tricky, so she has to take it easy."

"You mean? ... one would never have realized it," Julius said. "If it's not being indiscrete, when's the happy event to be?"

"Towards the end of March."

"Then we must drink to the occasion. A brandy? And how about a cigar?"

"With pleasure," George answered, taking one from the box offered to him.

Julius walked over to a drinks cabinet. "Which would you prefer, Remy Martin or Hennessy? You're a lucky man; fortune seems to smile on you. A beautiful wife, a child on the way, good health and no financial problems, what more can a man ask from life?"

"Quite a lot. Outstanding success in business, like yours."

"Maybe that's tempting fate. I've never had a beautiful young wife, nor a child which I could call mine." He paused and stared at George. "And as to health, I have a leg which gives me a certain amount of trouble and pain ... I've been fortunate in business perhaps as a kind of compensation."

George shook his head. "Your success is entirely due to business acumen and flair, backed by experience. Luck, in my opinion, has very little to do with it."

"That's where you're wrong. An element of luck is in the build up of any successful businessman, and I'm no exception. I just happen to know when it's around, sitting on my shoulder, as it were. I can see it perched on yours now."

"Then do you mind if I take this chance to ask you a spot of advice?" George said, accepting the drink held out to him.

"By all means if you reckon it can be of any use to you."

George lost no time in following up on that advice. Julius had suggested that, if he wanted seriously to capture part of the English pharmaceutical market, the best way was to get control of a well established and respected firm in the U.K or France and manoeuvre from a position of strength. So, following a tip off from his bankers, the Crédit Méditerranéen et d'Outremer in Geneva, he bought up the Laboratoires Dinard SA, a Lyon based company which produced the French equivalent of Beecham's Little Liver Pills and a popular line of painkilling suppositories. It had the name and goodwill which Pharmaceutiques Christogaud lacked, and with it he had the vehicle by which to launch a succession of takeover bids.

Before the close of 1957 he had gained control of Newton and Forsyth, the British group which produced the well known Aurora face creams and owned 32 chemist shops in the Midlands, as well as the £3 million Maxwell and Palmer Biscuit Company which, a decade later, was to become the Amalgamated Food Corporation, a 40 million pound giant with a turnover of £250 million. Its acquisition marked the beginning of a 20 year scramble to riches destined to make George one of the most notorious young business wizards of his age.

Every now and then, in those early years, he would secretly raise a glass to Julius Caspar, not to toast or thank him, but to acknowledge the triumph of man over money. It was a triumph he intended not only to equal, but to better.

He and Georgina became one of the most talked about young couples of the emerging international jet set.

Hardly a week passed without a photo of them in the Tatler or a mention in William Hickey's column in the Daily Express. They were to be seen at the Royal Enclosure at Ascot, at the Bal des Petits Lits Blancs in Monte Carlo, skiing at St Moritz, grouse shooting in Argyllshire and swimming at Capri. They entertained lavishly and were invited everywhere. On the Onassis yacht, in the Patino villa and the Rothschilds Château de Ferrières, to Blenheim, Chatsworth and Longleat, to mention only a few.

And wherever they went, a photographer was there to make sure that George and Georgina Christofides's faces, clothes and social frequentations were suitably publicised. They appeared to epitomise the idle rich, but the Financial Times periodically corrected the impression, and a write up in the Sunday Express told that at 27, with only eight years of business activity, George controlled a commercial empire valued at £150,000,000, and that his personal assets made him a multi-millionaire.

Rumour had it that he was backed by a Middle East bank with headquarters in Geneva and owned by an international financier who had also started life in Egypt, and George did nothing to stifle it. Julius Caspar was regarded with respect in the money centres of Europe. Some might criticise his methods of doing business, but his prestige was such as to lend kudos to anyone associated with him.

He had made a point of learning all he could about the almost legendary Alexandrian, of the way he operated, his companies, his wealth, and even of the woman he was supposed to live with in Switzerland and who shunned the limelight like him. A. Julius Caspar, now in his 49th. year, held few secrets for George, or so he believed. He knew of his early business successes, of his accident, of his indomitable ambition and ruthlessness coupled to a prodigious generosity, also of his change of name and nationality, from the Egyptian Antor Giulio Caspardian to the American A. Julius Caspar. That original name intrigued George. Somehow it was not unfamiliar.

Everyone agreed that marriage had changed George. He was still arrogant with strangers and domineering with those close to him, but with Georgina he was gentle and unabashedly tender, even in public. They were inseparable, and rare were the occasions when he spent more than 24 hours away from her.

Twenty months after their first child, a second baby was born, this time a girl. George was overjoyed and covered Georgina with presents, amongst which was a two year old mare called Diadem.

Six weeks after the birth he had to go to France to sort out a labour problem at the Laboratoires Dinard.

"I don't suggest you come, darling. Lyon's as boring as hell and it'll only be a matter of 48 hours. Why don't you drive down to Chilton, and spend a few days in the country. You could give Diadem a bit of exercising. It'll do you good to get on a horse again ... you don't want your muscles to get flabby."

The Chilton church clock was chiming 4 o'clock when Georgina halted her car at the entrance to the stables. A groom stopped brushing down a horse, doffed his cap, and ran towards her.

"Hello, Graham," she called, "get me Diadem ready will you. I'd like her up at the Hall in about 20 minutes."

"Yes, Ma'am, nice to see you back again. She needs exercising as her Ladyship didn't take her out today, so you may find her a bit frisky. I'll saddle her and bring her along immediately."

She smiled then drove on up to the house. As she ran indoors the butler appeared.

"Is Mummy around?" she asked.

"Good afternoon, Mrs Georgina. No, her Ladyship has gone to Tunbridge Wells and will be back in about an hour. Shall I have tea prepared?"

"No thanks Briggs ... I'm off for a ride. There's a case in the car ... "

The groom brought the mare round to the gunroom entrance and a few minutes later held the bridle while Georgina mounted it.

"I'll be back in an hour," she threw over her shoulder and cantered off along a lane which led past the vegetable garden and up to the high rising field behind.

The groom caught a glimpse of her silhouetted against the skyline as she galloped into the open countryside, and smiled with admiration. A skilled horsewoman, Mrs Georgina, even if she hadn't been riding for some time. She had always been a 'natural' with horses, kind of in her element with them, he thought.

After half an hour the mare trotted back riderless.

Alarmed, Graham got through to the Hall on the house phone. No, Briggs informed him, Mrs Georgina had not returned. He jumped onto Diadem and raced off in the direction he had seen her go.

He found her sprawled, face downwards by a hedge on the boundary of the estate. She was breathing but unconscious. Knowing he mustn't move her, he placed his jacket under her head and galloped back to the Hall. Within half an hour an ambulance was rushing her to a hospital.

George, who had flown back and found her in a coma, reacted in a curious and brutal way. Perhaps because he had never experienced an emotional shock of the kind, he refused to accept the tragic situation or let it interfere with his business life. To his mother-in-law he said bluntly, "there's no point in my moping around at her bedside. There's nothing I can do while she's like this."

"But you can't just leave her ... she could come to any moment," Cecily had cried, shocked at his apparent indifference.

"When she does, call me. Anyway she's got you and Maryanne."

Georgina remained in the coma for three weeks, and when she regained consciousness she was paralysed from the waist down.

George made sure she got the best medical treatment, and surrounded her with outward manifestations of his affection, but they were those of a stranger, not of a loving husband. Flowers and costly presents were delivered regularly to their house in Cumberland Terrace but as often as not, he was away. For the passion which had kept his love glowing was forcibly gone. Secretly he blamed her, and not fate, for the accident, and for no longer being the woman he had chosen as his wife; for denying him her body which was his by right.

One evening in September she complained of a headache

and fell asleep, never to wake again. The post mortem showed that she had died of massive cerebral haemorrhage.

George showed no grief. When her body was taken away he locked the bedroom door and never went back to the house. He disposed of the lease, sent the children with their nanny to Chilton and moved into the Ritz.

With her were buried his lovable sides. Georgina had evoked in him sentiments which had lain latent, such as love and respect. They fell from him to her grave, and he went back to being the calculating hedonist he had been before he met her. Power and pleasure became his life's ambition, and he threw himself into their pursuit with ruthless determination.

MARYANNE

Alexandria, August 1st, 1990

A white executive jet with the monogram AJC in black on its tail landed at Alexandria's Nouza airport. As it taxied to a halt, two limousines escorted by motorcycle outriders drove up to it, and a man in a white linen suit followed by an officer in full uniform stepped out of one and waited for the plane's door to lift open.

Inside the seven passengers undid their seat belts and prepared to disembark. One of them, a woman in a pale cotton dress, slipped on her low healed sandals and stood up.

She had a good figure kept firm by disciplined dieting and looked younger than her 51 years despite streaks of grey in the dark hair swept back from the forehead and ears. She wore little make up, a touch of mascara around the hazel eyes, and a dab of pale lipstick on the firm yet ample lips. She had a handsome rather than beautiful face, with well marked eyebrows, a prominent nose and a firm, almost masculine jawline. It was a face which attracted by its dignity and captivating sincerity.

She smiled at the others and, glancing out of a window, cried "oh Lord, there seems to be a welcome committee."

A young man in jeans and a T-shirt, under which was bulging the butt of a revolver, lifted the cabin door lever then pushed it open. A blast of hot air surged into the plane.

"Yes, Mrs Lauber. Major Salvini told us the Governor of Alexandria would be here to welcome you."

"Then we'd better not keep him waiting in this heat, poor man," Maryanne said, putting on dark glasses.

She walked down the steps to the shimmering tarmac, and the Governor bowed and took her hand.

"In the name of the President and of the Egyptian people I welcome you to Alexandria, Madame."

"How very kind of you. I'm really delighted to be here. I've heard so much about Alexandria. Though I've been to Cairo, this is my first visit to your city."

"Then may I have the honour of showing you round it personally?"

She gave him a broad smile. "That would be lovely. I also hope to go to El Alamein. Is it very far? My father died there, you know ... "

She found herself wondering why she had said that. She had not thought about that nebulous father figure of her childhood for years. She had almost forgotten that James Brentwick, the 'daddy' she had hardly known, had been killed at the battle of Alamein. Yet as her foot touched the Egyptian soil, she had suddenly been projected back 47 years, to a summer afternoon when she had been playing with a doll on the south terrace at Chilton. The postman had brought a telegram and muttered to Nanny "I hope it's not bad news about his Lordship."

Nanny had gone tight-lipped and had hurried over to her mother, who was down by the herbaceous borders with the gardener.

They had not told her immediately that 'daddy' had been killed. She learnt that a lot later. But a few days before, her mother had said; "daddy's in Alexandria now. Do you know where that is, darling? It's in Egypt."

Maybe the officer in his khaki uniform and the soldiers sweating in the heat had been responsible. They had conjured the vision of desert warfare. She shuddered. They also reminded her that her own son was somewhere here in the Middle East, fighting, killing, perhaps. Julius had said that he was in safe hands now, but how could he be? If only she could see him ...

An apprehension gripped her as she was driven to a helicopter at the other end of the airport. Where was A.J.? He was in some sort of danger, she was certain. Her heart began to pound ferociously, and beads of perspiration formed on her forehead. The Governor was saying something which she did not hear. She was fighting an uncontrollable urge to throw the car door open, and flee.

She gripped her husband's hand and did not let go of it till she was in her seat and heard the muffled roar of the engines.

"Feeling O.K.?" Michael asked.

"Just a little tired ... it's nothing ... must be the heat."

She took a deep breath and closed her eyes. When she opened them again they were being whisked over the city's rooftops. She gazed down at the slums stretching back to lake Mariut, then northwards over the apartment blocks, hotels and open spaces to the sweeping bays and glistening blue of the Mediterranean.

She caught sight of the huge yacht anchored by the harbour's fort, and the feeling of anxiety vanished. For her, Alexandria was not this sunbaked, provincial city; it was Julius and his memories. Pietro and Clara too, but essentially the man who had described it to her in its heyday, and who had become, not only for her, the living embodiment of it; in some way its spirit.

She thought back to that first time she had seen him, at the wedding ball at Chilton. No wonder she had instinctively felt he was her friend, someone she could turn to in moments of difficulty. If only she had known then that he was her father. With him to guide her during those critical adolescent years, how different her life might have been. She would not have married Edouard and would never have given herself to George.

Poor George. She felt only pity for him now, yet how she had loved and hated him once. No, she had never loved him; she had been helplessly infatuated. Strictly a physical passion through which he had dominated her. In a certain way he was responsible for the woman she had grown to be. To give him his due, he had well judged her capacities.

"Georgie's got the looks but you the grey matter, and by that I don't mean you're an ugly duckling. Simply that you've got a man's type of mind, which can be a hell of an advantage in life if properly trained."

Her mother, who was present, had asked what he meant.

"That she's cut out to be more than just someone's wife. She's got the makings of a businesswoman, or a banker. She should go to a university and study economics, or follow a course in business."

And he had organized her marriage to Edouard, the young

Lebanese she had met at a party he gave for her 18th. birthday.

"You two should get to know each other," he had said, "you'll be rubbing shoulders at the London School of Economics. Eddie appreciates girls with brains."

Edouard had laughed shyly and slipped onto the chair next to her.

That was how it began. She took to him immediately, as he was gentle and courteous and very different to the boys and young men she had come across. He was intelligent but modest, and there was a vulnerability in him which appealed to her. Very rapidly they became inseparable, lunching together at the University canteen and dining either at the Christofides house in Regent's Park, or at a restaurant in Chelsea near where he lived. They went to concerts and ballets and occasionally to a nightclub. He became a regular visitor at Chilton on weekends, and she began to miss him when he was not there.

They got engaged in March. She was in her bedroom staring out at an oak tree struggling against a gale, when the subject was broached. Not by Edouard; George did the proposing for him. As she was brushing her hair just before lunch, he had knocked on her door and let himself in.

"Hope I'm not disturbing you, Manne (it was his nickname for her), but I wanted a word with you before we get tangled up with the guests for the rest of the week end." He stood behind her and looked at her in the dressing table mirror. "You're turning into a real good looker, did you know that? Eddie thinks so." Then he had come straight to the point. "Why don't you and he get married?"

The blood had rushed to her cheeks.

"And why don't you mind your own business," was all she'd managed to reply.

"It is my business. You're my sister now, and whatever concerns you, concerns me. I know he wants to pop the question, but he's too shy. He's more or less told me so. And you could do a lot worse. His father's one of the richest men in the Lebanon. But apart from that he's intelligent, good looking, and probably quite sexy, if given the chance."

"Shut up, George."

"Don't tell me the thought hasn't crossed your mind! Only

don't go rushing into bed with him, it might scare him off. The Lebanese like their wives virgin on the wedding night."

In London a few days later Georgina asked, "doing anything tonight, Maryanne? We're having a few friends to dinner, and Edouard's coming. It would be fun if you were here."

She was alone in their library when the butler ushered in Edouard. He had taken her hand and awkwardly gone down on one knee. Then he had produced the ring, a square cut, 6 carat emerald.

"But Edouard ... "

Before she was able to finish the phrase the door was flung open and George, Georgina, her mother and a group of their friends had burst in crying, "congratulations!"

There had followed the magical moments of her engagement. A month in the Lebanon to meet her fiancé's family which turned out to be a never ending series of parties, picnics in the hills, beach barbecues, dancing at the Casino, or at the St George's Hotel, with a ball at Beit-Eddine, the presidential summer palace, and others in sumptuous villas in the elegant 'Quartier Sursok'. A dreamlike month during which Edouard had been the perfect companion. Too perfect.

One evening they were alone on the terrace of his father's house at Ashrafia, gazing out at sea.

"Its all so marvellous," she had murmured, going very close to him, "I'm so happy. I love you, darling."

"I love you too. So does all Beirut."

"I don't care about the others ... kiss me, darling."

Had she been more experienced, she would have realized that there was little passion on his side, but the thrill of feeling his lips on hers had sent the blood rushing through her veins. Years later she wondered whether she had been dumber than most girls, or had love made her blind to reality.

Someone should have warned her.

They were married at the end of June without the extravagance which had marked her sister's wedding.

The religious ceremony in the village church was followed by a wedding breakfast for 200 on Chilton Hall's south terrace, and by 3.p.m she and Edouard were already on their way to the airport, destination the South of France, where a chartered

157

twin masted schooner was waiting to take them on their honeymoon.

It had all been so exciting and romantic. They had dined on the aft deck watching the lights of the Riviera fade as they headed for Corsica, and she had thought she was the luckiest girl in the world, married to the most charming, intelligent, and attractive man a woman could want. Thoughtful too. That first night he had not tried to make love to her, and she had been grateful, tired as she was.

The next night, after kissing her on the shoulder, he had turned on his side and fallen asleep. But the following afternoon, back from a swim on her own, she had found him lying naked on their bed with his head in the pillows, and desire had swelled in her. She had stripped off her bathing suit and thrown herself next to him. She had caressed his back, fondled his hair and kissed him in the nape. He had not moved. So she had pushed him over and glued her body to his.

He had disengaged himself gently and with a sad, almost distraught look in his eyes, had stammered "I'm sorry, darling, it's that ... oh, God ... be patient ... please..."

"Is something wrong?"

"No ... don't worry ... it can happen to any man ... maybe in a day or two ... "

She had gone up on deck and gazed at the rugged beauty of Corsica's Capo Rosso. Instinctively she knew it, even if she didn't immediately grasp the full implications. The man she had married and chosen to spend her life with was impotent.

George had known it. He had manipulated her as he had her mother and her brother. Only with her he had gone further.

She bit her lip as she remembered that night, thirty years ago, when she was at his London home just before her sister's death. She had kept Georgina company, then gone to bed early with a book since he was dining out. At around midnight she had heard him come back and walk up the two flights of stairs to Georgina's bedroom.

Ten minutes later, he had pushed her door open without knocking. He was in his dressing gown.

She had looked up from her book, surprised.

"Is something wrong?" she had asked.

He had stared at her lustfully, then had sat himself on her bed.

"Has anyone told you how attractive you are, Manne? You've changed a lot. You're almost as beautiful as Georgina was, perhaps more sexy."

She had blushed and instinctively pulled a sheet to her neck.

"Does Georgina need anything ... I mean ... "

"No, she's sleeping. It's I who need something, and I wouldn't be surprised if you didn't also."

"What d'you mean?"

He had not answered, but had taken her book and thrown it on the floor before reaching over and switching off the bedside lamp. The next moment his fingers had been in her nightdress, encircling her breast.

"George, for God's sake ... " she had cried, pushing him from her and retreating to the other side of the bed.

He had grabbed her by the shoulders and pressed his lips on hers, smothering her protests. He had thrown himself on her, pinning her to the mattress, and torn her nightdress open.

"Stop it ... no ... no ... "

She had struggled while her mind had fought to stifle a sudden desire which flamed in her. Then, as she felt the full nakedness of his body, her resistance had turned to abandon.

When he finally thrust himself into her, she had wanted to scream from the pleasure he was giving her.

"I'm the first, aren't I? You're mine now, Manne," he had whispered arrogantly.

He was still in her, and once again she had felt the heat in her belly set fire to her blood, and her mind and body fuse in a shattering consciousness of what his flesh was doing to her.

He had switched on the light, let his eyes wander over her body, then laughed.

"Who'd have thought young Maryanne could fuck like a whore!"

She had drawn the bedclothes over her. The god of her pleasure had become the brute of a moment's physical passion. The man she knew him to be. She hated him for those words which transformed something beautiful into an act of shame. She had hidden her face in the pillows. How could she have let him? How could she have given herself so easily and allowed her body to dominate her so completely.

"I'm hungry," he had said suddenly. "What about you?" She had shaken her head. "Sure? Then I'll get us something to drink."

She had heard him open the door and go off along the corridor, whistling.

She had brought her knees up to her chin and pulled another pillow under her cheek. What had she done! Why had she let him, she kept repeating to herself. Yet she knew why. In a physical way he had always attracted her, and the very first time she had seen him she had felt that some kind of a bond existed between them, even if she had never really liked him.

She had broken into sobs. If only Edouard had been a real husband! If only Georgina had not had that accident! God! She had made love with her brother-in-law in her sister's home, while she was asleep only a few feet away. It was as if she had committed incest.

October, 1959

Maryanne stared at the doctor. "I suppose there's no doubt about it?"

"None, I'm happy to say. And you're in excellent health. I simply suggest you cut down on smoking and drink. A glass of wine, yes, but keep off liquors."

She nodded absently. Pregnant! The news came as a shock, but she wasn't surprised. Neither she nor George had taken any precautions.

Out in Harley Street, she hailed a taxi and told the driver to take her to Eton Square. George was expecting her at the Ritz but she could not face him immediately. She needed to be alone to decide what to do. Whether to keep the baby or have an abortion. She had always imagined she would bear the child of a man she loved and respected, with whom she would want to share her life. George was not that man.

She needed to confide in someone, in someone who would be sympathetic to her problem. She wondered whether she should tell her mother. She was the obvious person to turn to, but would she understand about gut gripping sex with a man one did not love? Could she help decide what to do with an unwanted baby?

The phone rang. It was George.

"Pack a few things, Manne, we're off to New York this evening. I'll send the car to collect you in an hour, O.K.?"

She fought with herself. "I can't George, not today."

"Why not? What's the matter?"

"I just can't. I'm ... I'm not feeling very well ... "

"Anything serious?"

"No ... I just don't feel up to travelling."

"Come off it, darling. If you're tired you can sleep on the plane, and if you still don't feel up to scratch when we arrive, I'll call a doctor. What you probably need is a change of air. So do as I tell you, pack those bags and be ready in an hour. Also, there's something important I want to discuss with you."

"What?"

"Not over the phone. Remember, one hour, no more. See you at the airport."

"George, honestly I ... ," but he had hung up.

She lit a cigarette as a sudden panic seized her. If George learnt she was pregnant he would force her to have the baby and he would have a grip on her she would never be able to shake off. With time her physical attraction would abate and she would be free of him, but if she bore his child she would be enslaved for ever.

She reached for the phone and asked the operator to get her Chilton Hall. The butler answered.

"Hello Briggs, is my mother there?"

"Morning, Mrs Maryanne. No, her Ladyship has gone to Canterbury for lunch and won't be back till late this afternoon."

"Then tell her ... no, I'll be there before then. Is anyone staying for the moment?"

"No. His Lordship left yesterday, and is not returning till next week. I believe Mr and Mrs Richardson are expected for the weekend."

"Thanks Briggs ... just tell Cook I'll be dining with Mummy and will be there for a few days."

"Certainly, Mrs Maryanne. Will Mr Edward be coming too?"

"No, just me."

Cecily placed a hand on her daughter's arm.

"What's worrying you, darling?" She was sitting on the sofa next to her and had just finished pouring the after dinner coffee. "And don't say, 'nothing' ... I can see there's something. You're an open book for me, not like Georgina ... " She sighed, then smiled wanly. "I could always tell with you when something wasn't right. It's your mouth that gives you away. Can't I help? I am your mother, after all.

Maryanne took the cup her mother offered her and nodded.

"You're right. There is a problem. I'm pregnant."

Cecily's eyes sparkled. "Oh, I'm so glad. But there's nothing to worry about. Happens to the best of us. Just a bit of a bore for the figure, but otherwise it's no problem, believe me. And when's the great day to be?

"A long way off ... I'm only six weeks gone."

Cecily frowned slightly. "Six weeks? Are you sure, darling I mean ... "

"Positive. I saw Ewan Moncrieff this morning. I know what you're thinking, and you're right. It isn't Edouard's baby. Are you terribly shocked, mummy?"

Cecily shook her head slowly. "A little astonished ... but it takes more than that to shock me."

"Then what d'you think I should do?"

"Do? Why nothing, for the moment. I mean ... well, need Edouard know it's not his? He'll probably be delighted when you tell him. Men aren't very clued up on dates, and there's no reason ... or is there?"

"Believe me, there is. That's the problem. There's no way he could think he was the father and, in any case, I wouldn't want to fool him on such a serious matter."

As if reading her mother's thoughts she added, "you haven't asked me who the father is. Perhaps it's just as well if I don't tell you till I've decided whether to keep the baby, or not."

Cecily's hand flew to her hairline in a gesture which, once theatrical, had become second nature to her.

"Darling whatever you decide, don't do it in a rush. Please promise me that. It's an awfully difficult decision to take ... I know how you feel ... but ... "

"Mummy, you can't possibly know what I feel. All I can tell you is that I can't and don't want to marry the father, and I can't foist a child on Edouard. I don't think you can remotely begin to put yourself in my shoes."

Cecily stood up abruptly and went over to the fireplace. She stooped and prodded the logs, then turned to face her daughter.

"You're wrong. I too was once faced with a situation like yours."

Maryanne stared at her, incredulous. "Are you trying to tell me you had an affair with another man while Daddy was alive, and were pregnant by him? I don't believe it. What did you do? Sorry, that's a silly question. Obviously I'd have had another brother or sister."

"It was a very pertinent question, under the circumstances. If you want to know, I didn't have an abortion."

Maryanne blinked as she took in the significance of her reply.

"So I'm the cuckoo in the nest," she said slowly. "Did Daddy ... I mean, well you know what I mean ... did he know too?"

"I'm not certain, though ... yes, I think he guessed. There

was no reason why he should have, really; the whole affair only lasted six days. It happened unexpectedly while he was away in Europe and was beautiful, with nothing remotely sordid or shameful about it. I was swept off my feet by something stronger than me. And I think James understood that. He never questioned me or hinted in any way that he knew. He was like that ... which maybe was why it happened. The person in question was very different from James."

Cecily came back and sat close to Maryanne. "I swore to myself that I would not tell you till the moment was right. Perhaps I might never have, if you hadn't told me what you just have. But I didn't want you to feel guilty or that you couldn't turn to me ... nor that I wouldn't or couldn't understand what you're experiencing ... "

"I'm glad you did," Maryanne said softly. Then added, "is he still alive? Do I know him?" She stubbed out her cigarette and rested her arm on the back of the sofa.

"Yes. He's alive and you've met him, although I've only set eyes on him three times since that fateful week."

"Then I think I know who he is, and I'm glad. Were you very much in love?"

Cecily nodded.

"Then why, after the war, didn't you get together again? Didn't he want to marry you when it was possible?"

"I never gave him the chance ... " Cecily said wistfully, "but I don't think that really affected things. Ours was never meant to be a lasting relationship."

"Now that I know, I think I'd like to see him again, talk to him and perhaps get his advice ... do you mind, mummy?"

Cecily shook her head. Tears were filling her eyes, tears of relief but of emotion too.

"I need a brandy. In a silly way I think this calls for a drink," she said suddenly. "Like one too, Maryanne?"

George glanced impatiently at his watch. 5.26. In four minutes they were due to embark on the New York bound plane, and if Maryanne did not turn up by then she would miss the flight

He strode over to a phone booth and dialled the number of her apartment. There was no answer. Hell, she must have got delayed in the traffic, he thought. He went over to the flight information desk.

"Is there a later flight to New York?" he asked.

"No, sir. The next one is tomorrow at 15.15 hours."

"What about via some other airport. Paris or Geneva?"

The woman consulted the flight timetables. "The only possibility is Lisbon, sir. But it's cutting it pretty fine. If there were the slightest delay in the BEA flight, you'd miss the connection."

"Thanks," he said curtly. There was no question of missing his connection. He'd have to go without Maryanne, and get her to take tomorrow's flight; but to Chicago, not New York. He went back to the phone and rang his secretary.

"Jocelyn? I'm at the airport and my flight has just been called. Mrs Horemi has been somehow delayed, and will most certainly phone you when she finds I've gone. I want you to book her on the first flight to Chicago tomorrow, and telex me to the Waldorf what time she'll arrive. I'll have someone there to meet her if I can't make it myself. Oh, and tell her I'm disappointed she didn't make it this afternoon. Very disappointed."

Eight hours later he walked into the hotel suite in New York and was handed a handful of messages, letters and telegrams. One was from his secretary.

'Unable to contact Mrs Horemi. She is not at her home and Fellows tells me she was not there when he went to fetch her yesterday. Have reserved seat on flight TWA 214 arriving Chicago 18.00 hours but need instructions as to where to contact her.'

What the devil could that mean? Where could she have disappeared to and why? Maybe her mother would know. He got the operator to put him through to Chilton. It was 2 a.m. there.

"Hello Cecily. George here. Do you know where Maryanne is? Yes I know what time it is, but it's important ... dammit, she was supposed to come to New York with me and now she's mucked up my plans. She knew I wanted her with me when I clinch the Vanderwest deal ... listen Cecily I must speak to her ... I'm not giving you orders! Christ! won't you realize how damned important the deal is to me ... well will you at least tell her she's booked on the flight to Chicago tomorrow, and make sure she rings my secretary. She hasn't got to do anything else. Is that clear?"

He slammed down the receiver and cursed his mother-in-law. What the hell was she playing at refusing to call Maryanne to the phone. O.K. she was asleep, but so what? Could she possibly have guessed about him and Maryanne? Even if she had, though, it was none of her business.

He went to the bathroom and turned on the shower, stripped and stepped under it. Soaping himself, he wondered why Maryanne had suddenly changed her mind. Had she been ill, Cecily would have said so. Frightened of what people might say? Hardly, she was too infatuated with him to let that kind of consideration come between them. Yet something must have happened.

He ought to have told her he intended to marry her. That would have reassured her.

He began towelling himself. The stupid bitch, he thought, she should have been there waiting for him on the bed next door. He felt like sex, and with her, not with some whore he would have to have the hall porter send up.

He frictioned his hair with Eau de Cologne, and switched his thoughts to the final meeting he was about to have with Olaf Vanderwest. The old boy was pretending to hesitate still, probably for sentimental reasons. The meat packaging firm had been in the family for three generations, and the thought that control would now pass to an outsider went against the grain with the 'General', as he was known to the company's 2000 employees. But he would convince him.

He looked in the mirror and grinned at his reflection.

The old boy's only heir was a granddaughter. That would be his trump card. Persuade him that the merger would be in her interest. What was the girl's name ... ?

As he drove away from the Vanderwest mansion three hours later, a tingling excitement crept up his spine. Over brandy and cigars the General had capitulated. It had been a gentlemanly battle with no one the worse for it; in a way it had seemed as if the old man had almost welcomed George's victory.

"You're clever, Mr Christofides, and if a man of my experience says so, it means something. There are not many men in this world I would have sold out to ... oh, I know you like to call it a merger ... but lets face facts; the day I die control passes unequivocally to you. And now that we've agreed it I'm glad. I'm glad because I know that you'll carry on the tradition my grandfather started back in 1862. And for us, tradition counts. It may not for those bright-eyed boys on Wall Street who wanted me to sell the whole bag of tricks to the public, but it does for me. Yessir, and I don't like the idea of a lot of unknown jerks running the outfit when I'm gone. That's why I haven't sold out before."

"You aren't 'selling out', Mr Vanderwest."

"Rubbish, young man, I know what I'm doing even if you've been at pains to conceal it ... but I like that. And I like the way you set about convincing me. I know, too, that you won't try to gyp Isabel of what will be due to her ... and don't tell me you couldn't. Of course you could, and I don't need to tell you how. Shares are only bits of paper, and in a company like ours they can be manipulated till they're worth peanuts. And I don't want that for Isabel. She's my only granddaughter and a great little lady. Good looking too, like her grandmother ... Now Mr Christofides ... difficult name that, do you mind if I call you George? Good, and you call me General ... I'm not one, but that's the way my close circle calls me ... I think its time we joined the ladies. Care for another cigar?"

The ladies in question had been the General's 75 year old sister, and Isabel.

George had not expected to find a twenty year old beauty at that dinner. He had not expected anything but a crusty old millionaire whom he was determined to win over. And he had. He had sensed that from the beginning. He had also sensed that the heiress to the man's huge fortune was also ready to be won over; and this was an added perk he had not anticipated. The meat packaging concern was worth a minimum of 55 million dollars, but the man's fortune was estimated at twice that amount. If nothing else, she would be useful to have on his side.

Later, as the lights of Manhattan began dancing before him, the idea of another merger crossed his mind.

The next day he flew to Chicago.

His secretary cabled that a seat had been reserved for Maryanne, but that she still had not been in contact. This news dampened the excitement of the previous evening. For a reason he couldn't explain, he wanted Maryanne more than he had any other woman. He didn't love her as he had her sister, he just longed for her sexually, and no amount whoring could get her out of his system. He had tried that night with a dextrous redhead, but had woken with Maryanne haunting him, defying him almost.

He left for Chicago not knowing whether or not she would be on the plane. As he half expected, she wasn't. So he cut his visit short and was back in New York within forty-eight hours.

There he got her letter. A few lines hurriedly written telling him that he wouldn't be seeing her for a long time, and asking him not to attempt to contact her. Furious, he crumpled the letter and threw it in the wastepaper basket. Who did she think she was! If she imagined she could dictate how he should behave, she was in for a shock. No one had tried that and got away with it since his schooldays.

He paced the room then went to the phone.

"Hello ... I'd like to speak to Miss Vanderwest ... Mr Christofides."

George's marriage to Isabel Vanderwest lasted three years. It started, like his first, in a blaze of publicity and ended in a spectacular divorce six months after the General's death.

He had sensed, the first time he had met her, that her act of the shy and ingenuous girl of good breeding was a sham. And their encounter the day after he had phoned her confirmed it.

He suggested dinner with the idea of taking her back to his hotel suite later, but she immediately opted for the other way round.

"If you like I can come to your hotel and meet you there," she had said.

"Excellent idea. Would 7.30 be O.K.? I'm busy till seven, then will be back for a quick shower and change ... I'll be down in the foyer waiting for you."

At ten past seven, as he was soaping himself under the shower, there was a knock on his bedroom door. Expecting a dossier of papers he called out, "leave it on the table by the window." He heard the door close and a few minutes later, a towel slung around his hips, he walked out of the bathroom.

Isabel was sitting on the table, naked save for a transparent strip of lacy underwear. George stopped in his tracks, then grinned. If that was what she wanted, he was game all right. He went over to her and, without a word, cupped her breasts in his hands. He saw her eyes glance down as her fingers caress his stiffness. Then she looked him straight in the eyes.

"The size'll fit O.K. But let's see how long you can keep it that way. No, not here, over on that chair."

Although he didn't immediately realize it, George had met his mate. Sexually she was the most demanding and perverse woman he had ever experienced. She was wilful and totally devoid of scruples, with an ambition which almost outstripped his.

"You're going to marry me," she said that same evening. "I want a man who'll go places, who's rich and ambitious and will trample on everyone to get where I want him to. Who's a good-looker, sexy, but more important, knows how to fuck. You seem to fit the bill, so I say let's get married. Don't tell me the thought hasn't crossed your mind!"

"O.K., it's a deal," was his form of proposal, and it seemed a good one. Isabel was the General's sole heiress. She was an orphan with no brothers or sisters to share the spoil, beautiful and with a stunning figure. Clever too, with a remarkable memory for numbers, and anything which had to do with money.

Olaf Vanderwest was delighted at the idea of having George as his grandson-in-law.

"I was half hoping you two would fall for each other," he said when they told him of their engagement, "with the new company arrangements it fits in so neatly. Now I needn't worry any more about Isabel; the inheritance will be safe with you keeping an eye on it. I was afraid she might get tangled up with some con man after my money. With you I know it's not the case; you're rich in your own right, and clever enough not to need an heiress to make you a millionaire. She needs someone to protect her, little Isabel does."

Little Isabel had smiled demurely and kissed her grandfather on the cheek.

"You're the most adorable grandpa a girl could dream of. Do you mind if George and I go for a stroll to the stables? I want to show him the horse you bought me."

"Good idea, but don't be too long, dinner's in twenty minutes."

She led George out into the garden to behind a rhododendron bush.

"O.K., no one can see us here," she said raising her skirt "and in case he asks you about the horse, it's a grey yearling, and has one hardly any bigger than yours ..."

There was one aspect of her double personality which troubled him, however

He soon discovered that not only was she a inveterate liar, but a kleptomaniac. Generally, she limited herself to pinching small bibelots from friend's houses, or money from their bags which, as often as not, she would later put back, with no one the wiser. But a real problem arose when she began shoplifting in expensive department stores.

The first time she was caught, George was furious. Not with her, but with the manager and floor detective. He had been waiting for her in their Cadillac outside the store when he saw Isabel appear at the main entrance with a couple of men. She was gesticulating and obviously angry.

"Go and see what's wrong," he threw at the chauffeur who, moments later, was back saying that it was best if George went to the store as there appeared to be a spot of trouble.

Confronted with an accusation that his wife had pocketed a hundred dollar fountain pen and walked out without paying for it, he let fly his temper.

"How dare you insinuate such a thing? Do you know who I am? I'm George Christofides and I could buy this whole bloody store if I wanted, as could my wife. I'll sue you for defamation of character. I'll have you and this fucking creep kicked out of the place. I'll phone the owner right now ... get out of my way, or I'll sue you for assault too."

He seized the pen, flung it at the manager, then marched out of the place pulling Isabel with him.

Once in the car, she burst out laughing.

"God, what a scream! I wouldn't have missed it for anything. You were fabulous ... must try it again."

"You must what?"

"Don't worry, not there again, though it would be rather fun to see if they would dare stop me."

"Are you trying to tell me that you really pinched that pen? You must be out of your mind."

She got angry suddenly. "No, of course not, I was pulling your leg. But for a moment you believed me! Thanks. Shows the opinion you have of me." She pressed the button which operated the glass partition, then leant over towards the chauffeur.

"Stop at that corner, I want to get out."

"Get out; why?" George exclaimed, "we're expected at the Dorvilles."

"I'm getting out because you make me sick. Because you're mean enough to think I could steal a miserable fountain pen! The day I want to steal, it will be something worthwhile..."

"Stop acting like a stupid cunt and shut up."

"O.K. mister big man. If that's the way you want it, I will. But you'll be sorry."

For the following three days she didn't speak to him, nor did she allow him to approach her physically. On the morning of the fourth, when they were due to fly to London, he found a message scrawled on the bathroom mirror. 'Have fun, see you when you're back.'

George was furious, yet there was nothing he could do. The plane was due to leave two hours later and he couldn't put off the trip.

He began to wonder what sort of a woman he had tied himself to. He knew that while the old General was alive she would behave herself, but when he disappeared, what then? She was totally unpredictable, and afraid of no one, except her grandfather. And it wasn't the man she feared, but the possible loss of a huge fortune. Once legally hers, anything could happen. Also, there was something else which worried him. She showed a very definite dislike for his son and daughter.

"I don't want those brats around my house," she said the day after she arrived at his Paris apartment, "they don't like me and I can't stand them."

"Don't be ridiculous, of course they like you. And you'll see, you'll get on fine with them. Just show a little interest. In any case, they're there whether you like it or not, so you'll have to find a solution," he added testily.

She did. She moved into a suite at the George V Hotel.

"Kids give me the jitters. You can't stuff me under the same roof as them and expect that everything will be fine. And that nanny, she's not a woman, she's the abominable snowman's mate, only she hasn't had the works. I wouldn't have her even if she came straight from the White House. Ugh! The very thought of her makes me frigid. You don't want that, do you? No way am I going to that apartment while she's about. In any case, it's more fun here, and we don't have to check that she or one of the little monsters aren't at the keyhole. Hey, what's wrong? Don't tell me you're kaput!"

That was when he first hit her savagely, a prelude to sixteen months of physical and sexual assaults which punctuated their marriage from then on. But he didn't get her to return to the apartment. In Paris she decided she would play the part of a mistress, not of a wife. She refused any of the conventional responsibilities of marriage, like entertaining his friends or business acquaintances, and he found himself having to plead with her to appear at a dinner or a reception with him; threats or bullying got him nowhere.

Infuriated though he was by her behaviour, a part of him was strangely stimulated. He saw it as a challenge to his masculinity, and was determined to come out the winner, as always. Every now and then she cleverly gave him the illusion that he was succeeding. Like when he got back to New York from a ten day trip in Europe, and found her waiting for him in their Waldorf suite.

She was in high spirits, provocative and even affectionate. For at least a week he was deluded by an impression that theirs might turn out to be a marriage in the real sense of the term, not just an amalgam of sex, money and violence. She told him that she was expecting a baby and that made him feel that he was almost in love with her; until she laughed in his face two weeks later and said that it had been just a joke to see what his reaction would be.

He beat her up properly that time, dazing her first with a punch on the jaw, then flaying her with a belt as she sprawled on the bed. He gave her a good eight lashes before she managed to kick him in the testicles and rush to the safety of the bathroom. Unleashing his brutality to that extent, however, proved a mistake. It produced telltale bruises and cuts which she showed her doctor and had documented.

By then George had realized that a divorce was the only solution, but he didn't want one until her grandfather was dead, and she went along with this line of thought, afraid of the old man's reaction if he got to know what sort of a person she really was. So they continued living together linked by an unabated sexual attraction and the lure of the General's millions, while sharpening their weapons for the battle which would take place once he died.

George too now began collecting evidence against her. He had her trailed by a detective, and what he was told made him madder than ever. Isabel had refused to entertain certain of his business acquaintances with him, but she had no such reserves when on her own. It appeared that she was having affairs with at least six of the men he was negotiating deals with, and even went to bed with their chauffeur.

Then, on a frosty November morning, 'General' Vanderwest caught pneumonia and three days later died. The battle between George and Isabel began in earnest.

The day after the funeral the lawyers of both sides instituted divorce proceedings, and for several weeks the public was fed with salacious details of the couple's private lives. Isabel accused George of sexual brutality, mental and physical cruelty, intent to defraud, and unethical business methods. She claimed that he had hoodwinked her grandfather into ceding him control of the Vanderwest Meat and Packaging Corporation, and that he was misappropriating her own inheritance. She sued for 60 million dollars, and alimony of 750,000$ per annum.

He charged her with multiple adultery, of insanity, and hence of being totally incapable of judgement where business interests were concerned, and sued for her to be locked up in a home for mentally deranged and her inheritance left under his control. This to ensure the smooth running of the Vanderwest companies, of which he was now chief executive and largest single shareholder.

The case dragged on for months, giving the couple a notoriety which neither expected nor wanted. George especially. He revelled in publicity, but not when it covered him in ridicule and referred to him as Mr Wanderlusty (she was Itchy Izzy), as well as casting doubts on his business ethics.

Finally a compromise was reached. In exchange for her dropping the accusations of fraud and double-dealing, he agreed to alimony of 400,000 dollars a year. He also withdrew his demand that she be committed to a mental hospital and, in return, was given the right to administer their joint interests in the Vanderwest inheritance for five years. At the end of that period, the 60 million dollars reverted to Isabel completely and the alimony ceased. She was also given the right to appoint a man of confidence on the Board of the Meat and Packaging conglomerate.

From a financial point of view the arrangement was not a bad one for George, no worse than if he had never met and married Isabel and simply gone ahead with the share takeover as negotiated with the General. But it meant that he had to be extremely vigilant, since Isabel's nominee on the Board was a declared enemy, and with at least four of the ten directors hostile to his takeover, he risked having to battle for every major policy decision. From an image boosting angle, however, the divorce and the publicity were a calamity.

Until then, the press had been nearly always favourable to him. He was depicted as the dashing and clever young business genius who had been romantically married to a lovely, but ill-fated first wife, and to a glittering and beautiful second. When it came out that beneath his fascinating exterior lurked a sadist, a megalomaniac, and a shark whose business ethics left a lot to be desired, his reputation was tarnished, and certain influential businessmen refused to deal with him. And it was this which hurt him most. He was a tough and implacable opportunist but he was not a crook, he reckoned, and he smarted from the inferences that he had made his money unethically.

Once the terms of the settlement between him and Isabel had been agreed, he flew to the Bahamas for a few days of rest. Away from the onslaught of lawyers, reporters and cameramen, he was able to reflect and plan for the future. He decided that he would retrench to Europe for a while and let ride the American market until he was in a position of absolute strength. Then he would come back and show the bastards what sort of a man George Christofides was.

Six months later he sold his share in the Vanderwest Meat and Packaging Corporation to a client which his bankers in Geneva produced. Though the name was not mentioned, George had every reason to believe that the client in question was Julius Caspar.

The Crédit Méditerranéen et d'Outremer was situated on the third floor of a modern building in Geneva giving onto the Place du Rhône, one of the city's central squares.

Julius Caspar's office was a corner room with a view which took in the stretch of hotels and apartment blocks along the northern shore of the lake and beyond to the distant mountains of the Jura. It was sparsely furnished with two suede sofas in one corner and a long, mahogany topped desk across another. The colours were subdued, mostly beige and brown but enhanced by a magnificent Ouchak rug where strong reds and blues were interwoven in asymmetric patterns. On one of the walls was a large, abstract painting with a white background and criss-crossing lines of brown, yellow and pale blue by the English painter, Ben Nicholson. It was a room which, in a way, reflected Julius's personality.

At 49 he was a handsome man, his dark hair and beard tinged with silver, framing a face which reflected both strength and intelligence. There was also an element of suffering in the network of lines around the brown eyes, as there was in his limp, which forced him to make use of a cane when the razor like pains in his left leg became too frequent. He never complained of these, nor of the migraines which at times tortured him. He had endured them for seventeen years — ever since his accident — and had learnt to live with and dominate them. Even when his temples ached and his skull felt as if it was about to explode, he was able to discuss projects and formulate policies, listening, suggesting, imposing his will, and even laughing.

To the world he appeared cool, with an aloofness bordering on arrogance. Yet there was another side to him which only the four women who had counted in his life knew of; the man capable of passion and tenderness, loyal devoted and even humble. Maza, Cecily, Marguerite and his mother Anna had known this other Julius — Antor as he was in his Alexandrian days — and now a fifth was to discover the wealth of understanding and love locked away in him.

"Mrs Horemi, sir," his secretary announced.

He stood up and went to greet Maryanne. "How nice of you to come and see me," he said, taking her hand in his. Then he steered her to a sofa near the window.

"Shall we sit here, and how about some coffee, or would you like something stronger?"

"No, coffee would be lovely, if it's not too much trouble."

He gave instructions to the secretary, then sat down next to her.

"You're looking wonderful. If I may say so, marriage seems to suit you."

He was not just flattering her. With her hair swept up and away from the neck, her features were at once accentuated and lightened, gaining a sensuality absent in the bride he had watched walk up the Chilton village church aisle, a still shy adolescent swathed in silks and lace.

He had not seen her since then.

She looked him straight in the eye and smiled slightly.

"Thank you. But ... " She hesitated. "When we first met I asked you if you would be my friend and you said yes."

It was his turn to smile. "Of course, I remember very well."

"Well ... Mummy and I had a sort of heart to heart talk the other day and she told me something which perhaps I should have known a long time ago ... that I wish I had known ... "

She was facing him again and there was a plea in her eyes. An apprehension gripped him, but was followed instantly by a sense of relief as she added, "mummy told me you were very much in love with each other."

They were interrupted as a woman appeared with coffee. When she had gone he said, "why don't you start by telling me all about yourself. There's so much I would like to know."

She hesitated. "Do you mind if first I ask you one or two personal questions?"

"Of course not, Marianna." He pronounced the name with an Italian inflection, caressing the last two syllables. They reminded him of his mother.

She took a sip of coffee. "Are you, well ... married?"

He smiled and shook his head.

"Was mummy the love of your life, I mean the only real love?"

He glanced away. "There was a person before her, when I was very young. I wanted to marry her, but shall we say destiny decided otherwise."

"And now?"

"Now there's a person with whom I am very close, and who means a lot to me. I would like you to meet her. She's not well at the moment and has to follow treatment. But as soon as she comes out of the clinic, will you come and see her?"

"If you'd like me to. Does she know about me, I mean about you and me?"

He smiled. "She knows everything about my life and the people concerned with it."

"And are there any other ... I mean, was I your only child?"

"You're my only, daughter."

"So I have a brother, or rather a half brother. Maybe more than one?"

"I have a son, yes, but I have no real rapport with him."

"Why?" she asked, fixing her large eyes in his.

"I'd prefer to tell you another time. One day, when the moment is right, you'll know all about him."

Suddenly she stood up and went to the window. She looked at the huge jet of water rising from the lake, then faced him again.

"I'm expecting a baby," she blurted out almost defiantly.

"That's wonderful news. I'm so pleased." He saw her frown and bite her lip. "Is there something wrong? You've seen a doctor of course?"

There was a note of urgency in his voice. The memory of Marguerite, dead through giving birth to George, flashed through his mind.

"Oh yes, and everything's fine." She went and sat next to him again. "The problem is that Edouard isn't the father and I don't know what to do. That's one of the reasons I came to see you. I need advice ... Oh Lord, I shouldn't have come, I shouldn't be troubling you with my problems."

He took her hand in his.

"I'm glad you came, you have no idea how glad. Does your husband know?" How mercilessly history repeats itself, he thought. Had Roger Christofides ever known that Marguerite's baby wasn't his.

"No."

"And you're going to tell him?"

"I can't do otherwise."

"Why? Have you decided to leave him? Are you in love with the other man?"

She sighed. "It's not as simple as that. I don't love him. I think I must have been attracted physically, because with Edouard that side never worked. Perhaps had Edouard been a man in the full sense, it wouldn't have happened. At least I wouldn't have let it happen. As it was ... well, he has never really been a husband to me. He's a sweet person, and in his own way I believe he loves me. That's why I don't know what to do about the baby. I think he'd accept to pretend it was his as a kind of cover up for a reality he doesn't want to admit. But if I ask that of him, it means I remain married to someone who's only my husband in name. And that wouldn't be right, either for him or me. Then there's another fact. I'm a bit afraid of how the other man will react when he finds out that I'm pregnant. He'll know the baby is his, and could force me to do something I didn't want to."

Julius said firmly. "Don't worry about him. He can't force you to do anything. Relax now, and later we'll decide between us what you should do."

He changed the conversation and got her to talk of her childhood, of her life at Chilton, at school, and of holidays in Scotland, the South of France and Switzerland. A happy and protected childhood, yet a curiously lonely one. That loneliness was in her as if right from the beginning she had felt a stranger in her family.

He took her to lunch at a hotel up in the mountains, and from their table they had a panoramic view of the lake, with the Alps behind and the city of Geneva down to the right.

Maryanne gazed around in silence, the fears which had beset her gone. Then she looked at Julius while he told the waiter what they wanted, and was struck by something in the shape of his head which reminded her of George. A fleeting impression, which vanished when he turned to her, but which thrust back on her the problem of her pregnancy.

"Do you think I should have an abortion?" she asked bluntly.

It was not his habit to give advice without reflection, but this time Julius did.

"No, not if you have any doubts. It's a drastic measure, and one a woman should take only if she's absolutely certain it's the right one."

"Yes, but ... "

"Let me finish what I wanted to say, please, and then we'll have a look at those 'buts'," he said firmly. "There are several solutions and I suggest we examine them one by one. Are you separated from your husband?"

"Not legally, but he's in Beirut and I'm in London, where I'm continuing with courses at the University."

He poured her a glass of wine. "Have you thought of getting divorced?"

"No, there's been no reason to. It isn't as if either of us wants our freedom to start with someone else. Mind you, I don't think he'd make any difficulties."

"And does the idea of bringing up a kid without a proper father frighten you?"

"Frighten, no. But I'm not sure it would be fair to the baby. I had no father really, and I sort of felt it was unfair ... please don't misunderstand me ... also there's the practical side. I couldn't bring up a child and go on with my studies. I'd have to have someone to look after it, and that costs. I wouldn't dream of asking Edouard for money, if we got divorced."

"You wouldn't need to. You may not know it, but there's a Trust I set up for you which will provide you with quite a substantial income once you're 21. That's in a few months isn't it?"

Her cheeks went crimson.

"You didn't have to ... I mean," she stuttered, "it's wonderful of you, but why? There's no reason why you should have ... simply because you and Mummy were in love and I just happened. I don't want to feel a responsibility for you ... I can get a job and earn a living like anyone else ... "

"Marianna, I am a rich man, and had I married your mother — had she accepted to marry me — you would be an heiress. Through my fault, in a way, you suffered as a child. I want to make up for that. As I see it, the Trust funds are yours by right, no, I mean it, and as for being a liability, put it from your mind. It is I who must be thanking you for coming to me and asking my advice. You can't imagine what it means to me. So let's not talk about financial problems. Given they don't exist, what else could stop you bringing up a child on your own?"

He realized suddenly that he was instinctively persuading her to keep the baby, and that he was even glad if it had no father, because he could then act as one. Yes, his own children he had neglected, but this one he would protect and form into the man or woman his position and aptitudes would allow. It would be his child. His heir.

Antor James Caspar was born in Geneva on March 22nd. 1960. It was a difficult breech birth, and the doctor who attended Maryanne admitted later that the baby had risked being born asphyxiated.

A.J., as he was immediately called, weighed 2.8 kilos and wailed incessantly, yet there was an underlying robustness in him which became evident at feeding hours. He was so voracious that his mother's milk, though rich and plentiful, never satisfied him, and within half an hour of attacking her breasts he was howling for extra nourishment.

Julius, who adopted the baby and gave him his name, had installed Maryanne in a small villa at Coligny, the residential suburb on the southern bank of the Lake, and whenever he was in Geneva he would spend hours there with her and the baby.

During the months which had preceded the birth, a deep and involving rapport had developed between him and his daughter. He found affinities in this 21 year old girl which had little to do with the sentimental fact that she was the fruit of his short, but very real, passion for her mother. He discovered in her qualities he had admired in Cecily; that moral courage and disarming rectitude which he valued too in Don Francesco. There was a basic innocence in Maryanne which in no way impaired the lively and pragmatic intelligence he had noted when speaking of his businesses.

One afternoon, a few weeks after she had moved into the villa, he asked her whether she had ever thought of going into banking.

"Has anyone told you you've got a businessman's mind, or rather a financier's?"

She laughed shyly and blushed. "Only George, my brother-in-law. In a way that's why I went to the London School of Economics instead of to a finishing school. He was the one who decided me."

"Have you thought of continuing your studies?"

"Not really. But I suppose I could once the baby is born."

"I think you should. And why wait for months? You could start immediately, if you like. There's a man I know who could help you. He's a first class economist, and you could also spend some time at the bank getting practical experience. Think about it and, if the idea appeals to you, we could work out a programme."

She took up the idea with enthusiasm. Twice a week a graduate from the Massachusetts Institute of Technology came to the villa, and on other days she would go to the Crédit Méditerranéen et d'Outremer for two or three hours, where Madame Helde, Julius's personal assistant, went through correspondence with her and explained the bank's role in numerous transactions in which he was involved. And she spent hours in the autumn afternoons in her garden reading books on world economics, from Adam Smith's 'Enquiry into the Nature and Causes of the Wealth of Nations' (1776) to the up-to-date theories of economists such as Kaldor and C.L. Allen, whose 'Foreign Trade and Finance' Julius brought her from New York.

She found herself enjoying Geneva. An influx of foreigners fleeing revolutions and tax inspectors had brought a touch of fantasy to the parochialism of Calvin's home town. It was a far cry from London or Beirut, but thanks to friends and acquaintance's of Julius and her mother, invitations to dinners, weekends in the mountains, concerts, and the occasional play by the English Speaking Theatre Group, never lacked. They helped her get over the physical yearning for George, and the sense of loneliness brought on by her divorce from Edouard.

She spent the last month of her pregnancy away from Geneva's *bise grise*, the icy east wind, up in the sunshine at Gstaad. Maza had taken to her immediately, and Maryanne admired the older woman's Byzantine elegance and worldly know-how. She would sit for hours in the chalet's glassed-in veranda, listening to stories of her life as a child in Constantinople before Turkey became a republic; questioning her on the rigid etiquette of court life in the Sultan's entourage and in the Harem, and then of her adolescence in Cairo as the daughter of a Turkish prince, and relative of Egypt's king.

But what she enjoyed most was when Maza spoke about Julius. She felt very close to her then, as if she had always known her, and that the bond which had developed between them had somehow always existed. She confided in Maza more than she had in her own mother. She was the only person she told about George.

Her world changed with the birth of A.J. She was no longer alone. The funny little being who would gaze at her with a mixture of defiance and curiosity, then smile or burst into howls, became the focal point of her existence. Though Nanny was there to look after him, it was she who washed and dressed him whenever she could, hummed him to sleep, and played with him. The moments she loved most were when she stretched out on the grass in the garden, and her son crawled around and over her. Her world would contract to the few square metres of ground around her, the fir tree immediately above, and to A.J., and she was happier than she had ever been.

In the autumn she began going to the bank regularly. Julius gave her a desk in his own office and the responsibility of checking all the documents of a complicated barter deal.

"It's the only way to learn what trade and banking is about. Once you've got the hang of this one," he said, "you'll see that it isn't so difficult to put together. You just have to be very careful about interest and exchange rates. If you get them wrong by even a fraction of a percent, you can find yourself in real trouble. That's what makes or breaks the whole operation."

He had her sit in on meetings with clients and policy reunions, and when he saw how fast she grasped the basic tenets of his financial and commercial transactions, he started taking her on trips to Frankfurt, London and New York, discussing all the aspects of his businesses with her, often asking and taking her advice.

For a twenty-three year old who, until eighteen months before, had known nothing about international commerce, she had developed an uncanny shrewdness. Whether through flair or acumen, she was rapidly able to select the proposals which would be money makers. As Raymond Zekla said to Julius, "Give her a few years, and you and I can retire. I've never seen a person, let alone a young lady, have such an innate grasp of our business."

Julius had full confidence in her and, at the end of 1962, he made her a partner in his bank's New York subsidiary, the Mediterranean and Overseas Credit Bank. The appointment meant leaving Geneva. Maryanne was sorry, as she liked her home there and the simplicity of life in the compact Swiss city where everything, from the electric trolley busses to the lakeside hotels, from the Jet d'Eau to the elephantine League of Nations building, now housing the United Nations, was run with invariable efficiency. It had suited her temperament, but the challenge of an exciting career was like a siren's song.

As she confided to Maza the last time she saw her, "New York scares me but it also fascinates me; like the Big Dips at Luna Parks which terrified me yet I couldn't resist them."

She left Switzerland in March, six months before her confidante died.

Julius had been warned that Maza's end was near, and for her last weeks he stayed constantly with her. The early September days at Gstaad were warm and tinged with unreality, as if time had come to a subdued halt. The fields were sprinkled with crocuses, and the vineyards heavy with grapes, while in the cool of the low lying forests where autumn had not yet begun to gild the rich green of the chestnut trees, the smell of moss was wistfully pungent. It was the season of voluptuous stillness when nature seemed to doze briefly before the outburst of late harvesting and grape picking.

Curiously, Maza had seemed better, defying the prognosis of her doctors. She got out of bed and, leaning on Julius's arm, went for walks to the forest. There she would rest, her back against a tree trunk and her fingers caressing the wild flowers.

"How beautiful it is here, Antor," she said one afternoon — she never called him Julius when they were alone. "Who would have thought when we met twenty years ago, that we would one day be sitting on a Swiss alp, side by side, just the two of us."

She laid her head on his shoulder. "You know, despite all the difficulties and the suffering I've gone through, I've been an extraordinarily lucky woman. Lucky to have been by the pool at Gezira when you did your high dive, lucky to have known and loved you, and lucky to have found you again when the odds were that I'd waste away in a little pension above St Moritz. Lucky also to die with you near me ... "

"Maza," he put in, taking her hand in his.

"No, don't say anything ... we both know that it's only a question of weeks, maybe days. I'm not sad. Sadness went when I found you again; and I'm not just putting on a brave show either. I feel that life has given me a full share of experiences and emotions, and I don't really want any more. If my heart could just stop right now I'd be the happiest of women. It would be wonderful for both of us, and don't think I'm being melodramatic. Selfish perhaps, though I don't mean it egoistically ... "

He was with her when she went, sitting on the edge of the bed and holding her hand. Her lips had parted as if to say something, then the light in her eyes had faded.

Curiously, the terrible feeling of loneliness he had feared did not grip him. Her strength and Maryanne's devotion were responsible for that.

Five days after the funeral Julius received a letter from a notary in Lausanne informing him that Maza had left a will in his favour.

"It appears that the Comtesse de la Marlière owned property in Benghazi, Libya, that's in North Africa, next to Egypt ..."

"I know where Benghazi is, I've been there."

"Oh really?" The notaire looked surprised but went on, "this property was sequestrated during the war, but given back to the Comtesse in 1952 when the Emir Idris of Cyrenaica was acknowledged King of Libya. By the terms of her will she leaves it to you, to do whatever you wish with. She informed me that it once belonged to a cousin of the King who could be interested in buying it back, or coming to an arrangement by which it could be exchanged for other land belonging to the royal family which might be useful to you, or so she seemed to think."

Julius nodded. On several occasions Maza had asked him whether he was interested in prospecting for oil in Libya, hinting that if he were, she could be of help.

"The property in question consists of a villa and some 20 hectares on the outskirts of the city. There are some Roman ruins on it which are also of interest to the King. There's a gardener living on the property who acts as caretaker, and the general administration of the estate is in the hands of lawyer called Pereira, who pays the wages etc."

"And who pays him?" Julius queried.

"I understood from my late client that there was money in

a bank there, compensation in some form for war damage, and he was empowered to draw from that."

"Was, you say?"

"I gather that it was not a large amount, and that there is next to nothing left. But, of course, this Avvocato Pereira will be able to give you all the details. If you like I can write to him."

"No," Julius cut in, "just give me his address and I will deal with the matter."

An hour later, back at his bank in Geneva, he walked into Emile Zekla's office.

"Do you happen to know who is the representative of the Libyan government here?" he asked.

The former Cairo banker shook his head. "Not off-hand, but I can easily find out. Why do you want to know?"

"I need information about a lawyer in Benghazi, and I want to meet King Idris."

"No problem. Leave both matters to me. The head of the Arab Trading Bank there is a friend of mine, so I'll get him to make enquiries about the lawyer. As for meeting King Idris, he comes to Lausanne quite often. I used to know him in Cairo, and I'll arrange for you to see him next time he's in Switzerland. Otherwise, you could go and meet him at his villa on the Côte d'Azur."

That was where Julius was received by the 72 year old Mohammed Idris el Mahdi es-Senussi.

Emile Zekla had told him that the Emir had been in exile in Egypt ever since 1923, when Fascism had taken power in Italy, and had only officially gone across the border again when the British had recognized him as suzerain of Cyrenaica in 1947.

"He spent a lot of time in Egypt, and was a client of our bank. You must have come across him. He was an Emir of the old stamp; autocratic but courteous, with the traditions of the desert in his veins."

Though Julius didn't remember having met the King — at the time he was simply ruler of a stretch of desert and a few lost-to-the-world-oases — he found they had quite a few acquaintances in common. Also Mohammed Idris es-Senussi had been a friend of Prince Zulficar, Maza's father, and he had reason to remember her when she was a young girl.

"I'm sad to hear of her death; she was a lovely woman. Did you know that there was question once that I should marry her? But I was an exile then, and only the nominal ruler of a stretch of desert near the Egyptian border, with the oases of Kufra, Jahbub, Jalo, and the town of Jedabia, a hundred miles from Benghazi. Not a very eligible young man! The prince, in his wisdom, preferred the wealthy Count de la Marlière, who had large interests in Tunisia. I knew him well. He owned a villa which was once the property of a cousin of mine, Ahmed es-Cherif, with interesting ruins of the ancient town of Berenice. Do you know Libya, Mr Caspar? My country is not rich, but it is full of history, especially of the Greek, Ptolemaic and Roman cultures. Come and see me. There is oil under our deserts, and you are an oil man, if I am not mistaken."

"Your Majesty is very kind, and I am flattered by your invitation. My company, Pharos Petroleum, could well be interested in prospecting. Also there is that question of the property which belonged to the Comtesse de la Marlière. You may know that she bequeathed it to me, but I understand that it has a certain sentimental value for you, Sire. I am certain we could reach some agreement by which it returns to your family."

Nine months later, after Julius had made two trips to Benghazi and technicians of the Pharos Petroleum Corporation had spent six months doing geophysical surveys to ascertain which of the royal lands was the most likely to produce oil, an agreement was reached with the King by which Julius's company would prospect, on a joint venture basis, a stretch of desert in the Jahbub area. As a gesture of goodwill, or so it was to appear, Julius made a gift to the monarch of the villa and the 20 hectares. Maza's bequest had proven a remarkably useful leaver to obtain a valuable concession.

New York, 1963

After Maza's death, Julius gave up the lease of the chalet in Gstaad and bought a house on Long Island, near Manhasset.

It was a grey stone mansion surrounded by 4 hectares of lawns and flowerbeds, and equipped with a swimming pool, two tennis courts and a sauna. Julius jokingly said that the reason he had chosen it was a kid's bicycle left in the garages, exactly the right size for A.J.

A hankering to have a place he could consider a home had prompted him to give up his suite at the Pierre Hotel, and Longhaven became as near to one as he had ever had, when at Easter and Thanksgiving he gathered around him there the members of his 'family'; Maryanne and A.J., Pietro and Joan Salvini, with their teenage son Laurrie, his godson, and Clara and Theo Strapakis with their daughter Paola, his goddaughter. The huge house would come alive with the shouts of the youngsters and the cheerful cries coming from the swimming-pool and tennis courts, or from the games room with its ping-pong and billiard tables. And in the evenings, sometimes, the walls would echo with arias from Puccini, Verdi and Bizet when, to please Julius, Clara would sing.

It also became his central office and on Fridays, if he were not in Europe or the Middle East, board meetings were held in the dining room.

One of the first took place a month after Julius had moved there. Five men and a woman sat round the long Sheraton table, and he glanced at each of them before speaking.

Pietro Salvini was the first on his left. He was vice president of AJC Holdings, which owned or controlled all Julius's interests in the USA. But he was much more than a top executive, like the four other men. He was 'my young brother' as the Alexandrian would call him. He was also one of the vice-presidents of the Pharos Petroleum Corporation.

Next to him was Roland Aschenberger, the nephew of Robert, the Swiss partner in the Crédit Méditerranéen et d'Outremer, and chief executive in the New York based

Mediterranean and Overseas Credit Bank. Julius wasn't sure that he liked him, but he respected his business acumen.

His eyes travelled to Jack Leigh, the lawyer. He was the man who, back in 1956, had brought him the land on which the oil wells had been drilled. He had said there would be oil and he had been right. Only it had proved an expensive and difficult job. Despite an initial indication that a pool of oil existed some 1000 metres below, drilling had gone through strata after strata and core samples analysed with negative results, until, on a morning of April 1958, a telegram had reached Julius. 101 years after the world's first oil well was drilled in Rumania, and exactly 99 after Edwin Drake's in Pennsylvania, the newly formed Pharos Petroleum Company struck, at 5000 metres down, one of the richest deposits in southern USA.

He caught the eye of Grant Warner, the director responsible for the company's growing production. It was he who had sent the cable saying: 'Struck lucky at Well 3 this afternoon 16.05 hours. Yahoo!' which had brought Julius from Geneva to Albuquerque in a record 22 hours. A man dead serious in his work but who took life for what he reckoned it was worth, a laugh. With a twinkle in his eye and a ready grin, Warner was one of the shrewdest technicians in the industry, and Julius had got him not so much because of the money he offered, but because of the challenge. At 58 he had wanted to get his teeth into something exciting, as he put it. With Pharos Petroleum he was able to bite deep and firmly.

Next to him was David Mayer, the youngest of the team. Jack Leigh had been responsible for him.

"He's the blue eyed boy at Exxon, but I can get him with us, if you agree," he had said six weeks earlier.

"Why?" Julius had asked, always suspicious of men who could change camp too readily.

"For personal reasons. Let's say there's a personality clash between him and the president — question of background, religion and the boss's daughter."

Was it because it was the old story all over again, the penniless immigrant, clever and on the 'up and ups' versus the well entrenched 'establishment', that Julius was instinctively warmed to the man? No, if he had taken him on, it was for the qualities he recognized immediately in the young Jew from Frankfurt, who had lost his mother and two sisters in Nazi gas chambers and his father three months after getting to New York, and had worked 16 hours a day for ten long years to get where he was now.

He smiled at Maryanne on his right then said, "today we are entering the fifth year of production and if I have convened this meeting it is for two reasons. First, I want to congratulate you and thank you for the remarkable results you have achieved."

He glanced at the papers in front of him. "Last year we were responsible for one third of the entire production of New Mexico — 19 million barrels, and this year's will be up by 30 per cent. The new storage tanks will be completed in three months, and the alkylation plant becomes operative in September. Excellent! But this is only a beginning. The next five years must change Pharos Petroleum from an unknown newcomer into a household name. As I have discussed with David and Jack, we are not going to limit ourselves to producing and refining, we're going to sell direct to the American customer. By the end of the decade I want us to be as familiar to the public as Standard Oil and Exxon. And we can do it. Pharos gasoline stations will be mushrooming in all the southern States within a couple of years, and then they will spread northwards. It's estimated there are 24,000 stations in America, and I plan that 5 per cent of these will be floating our flag in the years to come. That may sound modest, but I'll be happy if 1200 are selling our gasoline by 1969."

He paused and took a sip of water. "And now I come to the other important and exciting matter. I have just been informed that as a result of talks and negotiations with the government of Libya, and as a direct consequence of discussions I have had with King Idris, Pharos Petroleum has obtained the right to prospect for oil on a concession belonging to the royal family. An agreement was reached the day before yesterday, and I am flying to Benghazi on Monday to ratify it."

Julius had driven out into the Libyan desert with a handful of men to inspect the area where Pharos Petroleum was to prospect for oil, and as the sun was setting he asked David Mayer to take him over to a high dune which dominated the landscape. It was mid March, and the afternoon breeze was a welcome caress after the icy winds of Long Island.

The jeep came to a standstill, and for a while he remained silent, gazing across the sands to a distant cluster of huts around a few palm trees.

"Is that the oasis?" he asked.

"No, it's some 10 kilometres further on. What you see is a kind of village with a well, which is apparently fed from the oasis. To begin with we'll get our water from there."

"Is there enough for the inhabitants' and our needs?"

"Sure, while we're prospecting. Only 14 people live there, and from the tests we've made there's enough water for 250. There's an underground stream from the oasis which keeps the level constant, even when we're pumping."

Julius nodded. Water was the prime factor in the lives of these desert dwellers, the bedouins, and more precious to them than all the oil in the world.

He got out of the vehicle and walked a few yards in the sand. Two thousand years earlier water had been plentiful, and on that very spot would have been fruit trees and crops, and lush green vegetable patches, like in the Nile valley. And from the geologists' reports, it was still there, hidden under the layers of sand which the millenia had piled over it. There to be tapped now by modern man, who could give it back to those dusty hovels and change the lives of their weatherbeaten occupants.

He was modern man. He, with his black gold which came from much deeper in the earth's bowels, would provide them with it.

Suddenly the realization of this power to alter the destiny of men made him curiously afraid. Afraid that he might use the immense resources at his disposal for the wrong purposes.

That was when he made up his mind.

He threw his head back and looked up at the darkening sky, breathing in the pure desert air. He needed guidance, and there was only one man in the world who could give it him. The only man he knew with the true sense of a mission.

A shadow of a smile crossed his lips. He would go to him, this friend who had remained so close even if distance and time had separated them. He would not have changed, though a quarter of a century had passed since he had last embraced him at Turin station. He knew he was still the same Francesco of the Don Bosco days in Alexandria, full of faith and enthusiasm and love. Full of the mystic dynamism of saints, and of down to earth pragmatism where help for the needy was concerned.

He turned and walked slowly back to the Jeep. He would fly to see him the next day.

The drive from the airport at Asmara to the mission took over two hours, as an unusual cloudburst had turned the last twenty kilometres of dirt roads into slithery mud tracks. Twice the rented Land Rover got bogged down and had to be pushed, but finally the driver was able to point to lights flickering at the base of a rugged hill.

"Father Salvini mission," he said in broken Italian with a broad grin. "Great man, Father Salvini. Much respected. He done much for poor people."

"You know him?" Julius asked.

"Everybody know Father Salvini. He help everybody, specially poor people. Many poor people in Eritrea. Many sick and hungry people. Father Salvini help all. Not like other priests, he help Copts and Muslims and people who believe in other gods. He help lepers too. I have cousin leper, and he now helped by Father Salvini. I have other cousin who work at Mission for two years, and she make me meet him. Very nice man, Father Salvini. All nice people at mission."

"You're right," Julius answered softly, "he's a wonderful man."

"You know him too, signore?" The man turned his large brown eyes on Julius for a moment, who nodded.

"Oh yes I know him. I've known him since I was a boy. Since he was a boy also. So you see I've known him a very long time."

"Then you very lucky man. I only know him once, but that made me love him. Everyone love him who meets him. I nearly become Christian like my cousin because of him. But he say 'a good Moslem is a good man too. Put faith in God and do your best, and you be like your Christian cousin.' Very wise man, Father Salvini."

Night had settled when they arrived, obscuring the buildings and trees, but a huge moon was already at the horizon, and within a few moments a diffused light spread over the mission. Julius caught sight of Francesco striding in

191

his direction, a tall figure with a white habit billowing in the breeze. There was no mistaking the gait. It was the same as when he hurried across the quad at Don Bosco, arms swinging as if to beat the air around, and the torso bent forward with the shoulders squared. It was the stride of a fighter, but without aggression, a champion of hope. He almost ran the last few metres and, without a word, threw his arms around Julius. They hugged each other, dispelling with that embrace two and a half decades of absence.

"Come Antor, you must be tired and hungry," he said, taking his friend by the arm, "that road is murder when it rains. It doesn't happen often here but when it does, it's with a vengeance. I was thinking of sending the truck out to help, reckoning that you'd probably get stuck. But you chose a good driver, I know him. His cousin was with us for a while."

He went on talking as if they had parted only a few days earlier, brushing aside all that had happened to both of them for over a quarter of a century, and led Julius to a small bungalow, immediately to the left of a chapel. Outside, on a neat lawn, was a table and two chairs.

"That's where we'll dine," Francesco said, "but first I'll show you your room. It's the guest bungalow, and I hope you'll be comfortable." He opened the door and ushered his friend in, switching on the light. Julius glanced quickly around then turned to face him. He smiled and gripped his arm.

"Let me have a look at you. No you haven't changed much … God, it's good to see you again."

Francesco nodded, his eyes twinkling, yet searching. "It's more than good, it's just short of a miracle that the two of us should be together here. You, you've changed. And it's not just the beard … but I still recognize the youngster I knew in Alex. God bless you Antor." He made the sign of the cross then added, "shall we meet outside in ten minutes? If you need anything, just ring that handbell or lean out of the door and call!"

Julius watched him jog across the lawn and disappear into the chapel. He stood in the doorway and looked around. From the cluster of buildings at the other side came voices and occasional laughter. A dog barked and a night bird croaked from a nearby branch, while bats swooped and zigzagged like monstrous butterflies in the equatorial sky. He felt curiously fresh despite the rigours of the drive, and the migraine which had gripped his skull for more than three hours had vanished. He remained for several minutes drinking in the atmosphere until an adolescent appeared with his suitcase. When he had pointed to where he wanted it and the youngster had gone, he went back into the bungalow. Ten minutes later there was a knock on the door. It was Francesco. He had a bottle of wine and two glasses in his hands.

"It's not champagne, but it's fizzy and cold and, to my palate, very pleasant. Let's have some before they bring the dinner. I'm afraid we have no aperitifs or whisky ... "

They sat at the table outside, and to begin with talked about Pietro and Clara. Mostly, it was Francesco who asked the questions, while Julius sketched him a picture of their lives and families, and told him of Clara's successes as a singer, and Pietro's as a businessman.

"Of course I get news regularly from both of them, but it's different hearing it from you. When you tell me, it's as if they were here with us. You're part of their world, and they of yours, so you must forgive me for pestering you with all these questions when I should be telling you about the mission, and the things we've been able to achieve, thanks to your generosity. But I thought I'd show you it all tomorrow, and there's a great deal to see," Francesco said.

"I don't need to see it to know that you've worked miracles here. And it wasn't really for that reason that I came, though I'm eager to see what you've done. It was you I came to see. You, Francesco, who are my best and dearest friend. And after dinner I'll explain why I needed to see you, suddenly like this." He was silent while he sipped, his wine, then continued, "were you very surprised when you got the message that I was arriving out of the blue? You know, I only decided to come yesterday afternoon."

"Of course I was surprised, but only for a moment. Life has taught me to accept the unexpected as part of one's daily routine. A surprise is no longer one when it fits into the pattern of things. And your coming unexpectedly after all these years fits very neatly into a particular pattern. If it didn't surprise me for long, though, it gave me infinite joy. Each one of us needs our friends, and especially ones like you."

They were interrupted by the arrival of three young girls carrying trays with plates of food.

"It's a simple fare, but Sister Angelica is a good cook, and her stuffed pancakes are first class. What are they of, this time?" he asked one of the girls.

"Spinach and goat cheese, Father, but there are also marrow fritters and aubergines filled with rice and tomatoes with chopped onions."

"And what did you have for dinner?"

"Pancakes with spinach, Father, they're what I like best. And a little fish in our rice. Sister Angelica is preparing that for after."

"Is she now! Then we shall need more wine. Is this one all right for you, Antor, or do you prefer to switch to red? An Italian firm here has just made us a present of some bottles of Chianti, and I wouldn't mind an excuse to try it."

"I'm very happy with this. Perhaps we could try the Chianti tomorrow."

It was when they had finished eating and were sipping a mild coffee that Francesco asked, "what's the trouble Antor, or should I call you Julius?"

"Please don't; it's me and not me, if you get what I mean. Julius Caspar is a very different man to the Antor Caspardian you once knew ... "

"Once? I know one man, the one in front of me. He can call himself Antor or Julius, it makes no difference to me. You have changed, yes, but basically you're the same boy, the same youngster that I was proud to have as my friend in Alexandria."

"Perhaps you're right ... at this moment I don't feel very different from the Antor you knew, but I believe that that is due to you and not me. It's because you are immutable in your faith, in your view of life, in your conception of your role as an adult and responsible being. In the eyes of the world I may appear stronger and more powerful, but both of us know that you are the one who is basically unshakable. I risk being that giant with feet of clay Don Michele warned us about. You have let your heart guide you as he urged us. I believe I have used my mind and only my mind ... "

"And what of all this and the millions of dollars you have given without a thought. Don't tell me your heart didn't prompt you there."

Julius shook his head. "If I am to be really honest with you and myself, I must confess that my heart had very little to do with it. I am not an altruist. You know better than anyone that from a certain moment in my life I stifled my emotions and was motivated only by the desire to make money. A lot of it and quickly. Had it not been for you, it would not have even crossed my mind to give the way I have."

"But you did. And had you not done it through or for me, it would have been because of another friend."

Julius sighed. "You always over-estimated my qualities even if you never under-estimated my capacities. There is nothing very exalting about a rich man who gives some of his money for a worthy cause. What does it cost me to write a check this very moment for a hundred thousand dollars? There are men and women working in various parts of the world to make me richer by the hour, so I don't even have to trouble myself with that. I've got caught up in my own game. I wanted money and I've got it. I wanted power and I have that too. And now that I have them, I don't really know what to do next. I realized this suddenly last night as I was standing on a sand dune in the middle of the Libyan desert, gazing across land which will bring me more millions, to a cluster of mud brick hovels where ten dollars would feed all the inhabitants for a week. And the absurdity of my situation was brought home to me. Do you follow me, Francesco?"

The priest nodded and brushed away a mosquito.

"The world is made of contradictions, and most of them are the result of our own misinterpretation of basic realities. You won't be offended, I hope, when I tell you that you are a little out of touch with some of them ... realities, I mean. I too am not aware of certain and, in a way, you and I stand at the opposite poles of a single yet not always manifest truth. What I mean is, though we may strive to achieve certain goals and appear to be successful, we are only so if they remain a challenge. And I'm lucky as I've chosen an easier path than you. My mission is to do with people, while yours is only indirectly so, for the moment. Last night you probably felt confused because you were brought face to face with a human reality which contrasted absurdly with a material counterpart, of which you are more familiar. And because you have a rare quality in a successful and powerful businessman — the respect of your fellow human beings — you were shocked;

shocked that two realities so totally different could exist side by side. Yet they do the whole time, and our job is to adjust ourselves to them and them to us. At least we should try to."

He paused for a moment and smiled. "You will say, as I remember you once said before, that means I condone compromise. In business it's probably a mistake, I wouldn't know, but where human relations are concerned, it is primordial. I have spent all the years here adjusting my ways to those of the people I try to help, and trying to adjust theirs to mine. Call it respect, call it love, call it understanding, but without it, without this give and take of opinions, beliefs, convictions with which everyone of us is filled, life is a tragedy. With all your generosity, with all the good which your wealth is reaping for others, you have lost the human touch, Antor. You have become the rich and powerful Julius Caspar who has no one to challenge him. Return to being Antor Caspardian for a while. Give yourself a fresh goal. Your oil wells will go on pumping the millions you will want to give away, but that is not sufficient for you. You need a new cause for which to battle and pit your wits. Ouf, I talk too much. Let me fill your glass ... "

Julius woke the following morning as the sun was firing the horizon. From his bed he could see out, across the fields, to the distant mountains of Ethiopia. Along the road a donkey with a man walking in front and a small boy trotting behind passed like shadows against the magnificent backdrop of the African scenery.

He thought back to what Francesco had said only a few hours previously; a goal, a fresh goal against which to pit his wits. How well he knew him, that friend of his who dealt with persons and their souls and aspirations, as opposed to goods and money and stock exchange values. He too had his bank, his personal empire, only his success was measured in terms of human joy, of smiles, of gratitude from famished children, maimed lepers and quietly desperate men and women. He fought with and amongst them in a battle which gave him his vigour and from which he would go on drawing strength until he died in it.

Francesco was right. He was reaching his watershed. Soon, money would lose its significance in terms of achievement, and it would not suffice to go on making it and giving it away.

He threw the sheet from him and got out of bed, then went

196

over to the window and peered out. The mission was already bustling with movement, and over the lawn floated voices raised in chant. The chapel door was open and he could see a row of backs with heads bent and the soles of sandals protruding from under the kneeling habits. He felt an urge to go down on his knees too and ask for guidance. It would be so much simpler to let Him decide and point the way. But he couldn't. Ever since he had been a boy he had made his own decisions, convinced that man was master of his own destiny. It would be an act of weakness, of hypocrisy almost, to pray for himself. His fingers touched the cross on his chest, and a moment later he saw Francesco come out of the chapel and look in his direction. He waved to him.

"Ready for breakfast?" Francesco called.

Julius smiled. "Give me ten minutes and I'll be with you."

He watched his friend stride off towards the clutter of neat huts nestling amongst the flowering bushes, then glanced up at the paling sky. A flock of ibis flew by followed by five hoopoes. The uncertainty of the past 24 hours winged away with them and he felt at peace with himself suddenly.

New York, 1965

Maryanne's apartment was on the 18th floor and overlooked Central Park. It was not large, but it had a spacious drawing room and a terrace, part of which was transformed into a winter garden.

She loved it. It was the first home she could consider her own, in which she had been able to choose the colours, the materials and furnishings down to the last detail. She had spent a year browsing around antique dealers and auction halls, buying only pieces she really liked.

It was during a furniture auction that she met Michael. They were bidding for the same American Chippendale bureau, small and elegant, which Maryanne had decided would go perfectly in the alcove in her sitting room. She had outbid him, and when she had gone to pay for it, had found him next to her.

"You got a bargain there. It's a rare piece. I envy you."

"Why didn't you go higher then?" she asked, "I was at my limit."

"I reckoned it suited you more than me. Also that you wanted it badly, so there was no point in just pushing up the price."

She had taken to him immediately, but that day they had exchanged a few more words then gone their own ways.

A month later she bumped into him a cocktail party, and he had asked her out to dinner.

She discovered he was a congressman, divorced, that he loved opera and lived in Washington. On a second outing a week later, that he played tennis, liked garlic and had fallen in love with her the first time they had met.

A further dinner and she found that she too wasn't indifferent to his charm, and that she was attracted to him both with her mind and her senses. Yet it wasn't until a month later, when she invited him out to Longhaven, that she went to bed with him.

They had played a game of tennis, then swum, and after

a barbecue on the terrace she had put on records and they had danced. They were alone, and as he held her in his arms and their bodies had moved together, she had felt a growing desire to be made love to.

He took her gently and with a savoir faire far removed from George's basic and brazen love-making. And the orgasms his virility provoked in her, those slow crescendos of fulfilled pleasure, were very different to the swift, if shattering, convulsions she had experienced before.

Since he lived in Washington, they only saw each other on weekends, which suited her as her days were fully occupied with business and looking after A.J. But Michael was not happy with the situation. He wanted to marry her, and hardly a month passed without his pressing her to become his wife.

Occasionally he would fly up to New York to spend the evening with her before catching a morning plane back to the capital. On one such visit they were finishing breakfast when he brought up the subject again. She reached across the table and took his hand.

"Of course I love you, darling," she said. "It's that I don't feel up to getting married. I'm just not ready for it. And it's not as if either of us want another child. What's wrong with going on like this, it's so wonderful... "

He shook his head and interrupted her gently. "I know you had a bad experience with your first marriage, but there's no reason why our's shouldn't be a wonderful success. I ... well, I feel that just living together occasionally when I can get to New York and you are not on one of your trips, makes our relationship kind of untidy."

"Untidy?" She raised an eyebrow.

He smiled. "Well ... unfinished, if you prefer. All couples who really love each other should get married."

"Who says so? Convention? Is that what's worrying you, what people might think or say?"

"Of course not. Only we do live in a society where certain taboos still exist, and quite apart from the fact that I want you at my side for the rest of my life, I don't see why we should flaunt conventions when we could conform so simply. I want to be able to say to people 'this is my wife,' not 'this is my friend, Maryanne'. I want to be able to say it because it would be right and logical, and because I want to share everything with you."

"I know," she said with a mischievous twinkle in her eye, "but the real reason you want to marry me is political. Senator Michael Lauber needs to be married to the woman acknowledged as his mistress if the scandalmongers of Washington aren't to throw spanners in the works. But that's where you might be making a big mistake. I could do you more harm than good. I'd make a rotten politician's wife ... I'm much too outspoken and in any case I have my own convictions where politics are concerned, which I'm not sure are the same as yours."

"That's unfair, Maryanne. I'm not asking you to marry me to further my career. I simply want you to be with me and to help me. I need your help as I need your love. I don't want us to be always separated, leading compartmentalized lives. It's such a waste ... "

"Shh." She placed a finger on his lips, then took his hand and rested it on her cheek. It was a fine, sensitive hand, with chiselled fingers and a soft and sensual palm. She caressed it while she scanned his features; the broad forehead beneath the shock of dark hair, the thick eyebrows above dark blue eyes, the strong nose and well formed mouth. An attractive face, if not exactly handsome.

"Give me time," she murmured, "maybe in a little while, when the pressure of work eases ... maybe I could then see myself as the wife of an ambitious politician."

He cupped her face with his free hand and smiled. She adored that smile of his.

"I prefer the term 'dedicated'," he said before kissing her. "But don't keep me waiting too long, darling, I can't stand it."

When he had gone she leant back in her chair and closed her eyes. She knew it was egoistic on her part, but she did not want to change her life for the moment. She had an exciting and stimulating career which she would have to give up if she married Michael, and while she was deeply attached to him she was not sufficiently in love to let that happen. Perhaps the day would come when the thrill of concluding a carefully prepared deal wore thin, and the sense of power which being one of Julius' top collaborators gave her, lost its glamour. But until then, she didn't want to think about marriage.

The phone rang. She walked quickly over to her desk and picked up the receiver.

"Hello, yes ... oh good morning, Julius. No, I haven't yet ... I was just finishing breakfast ... of course I'll look into it ... no, Roland should have that ready by about noon. Certainly, the meeting is this afternoon and I'll call you as soon as it's over. A.J.? He went off to school half an hour ago ... sure ... why not this week end? I'll send him out to you on Friday ... no, I can't manage it, but I'd love to come on Sunday ... wonderful, yes, and I'll see if I can get Michael to come so we can have a foursome. All right, I'll ring you back in an hour when I've got that information on the demurrage charges at Lagos ... they could kill the deal."

She went to her dressing room, slipped on a pale green linen dress, then sat at her make-up table and quickly applied mascara to her eyes. She wondered whether she should organize for another kid to be with A.J. so that he was not in his grandfather's hair. Maybe she had better take him with her for Sunday only; a whole weekend with the boy might be a bit too much for Julius.

Not that he didn't get on with his grandson. On the contrary, every time he came to New York he made a point of having the boy with him, and there had developed between them a complicity which was touching. There were moments when it as almost as if Julius and A.J. were father and son, they were so close. But then something would happen and the boy would look at his grandfather as if he were an enemy.

She frowned. Though she hated to admit it, there was a vicious streak in her son which worried her at times, and when it got the upper hand, there was no way of reasoning with him.

The last time, she remembered, had been after a week end at Longhaven. A.J. was playing with a kite on the lawn when she had called to him that it was time to leave. He had taken no notice. So Julius had gone over and caught him by the wrist.

"Mummy's calling you, little man. You mustn't keep her waiting. Come on now," he had said.

The boy had glared at him, then had started struggling. "Let go of me," he had screamed, trying to hit out at his grandfather.

"That's enough," Julius had said, sternly. "Give me the kite or you'll lose it, and you won't get another."

But A.J. had thrown himself to the ground and had gone on screaming. Julius had picked him up and carried him, head downwards to the car. He had ordered the chauffeur to open the boot, and had dropped his grandson into it.

"Now either you shut up and behave yourself or you travel back home in there." The voice was still stern, but there was a suspicion of a smile on his lips.

Taken aback, A.J. had stopped shouting and had stared ferociously at him. Then, very quietly, he had said, "I hate you," and had clambered out of the boot.

Maryanne had been shaken by the intensity of the look her son had thrown at his grandfather; it really had something akin to hate in it.

"Say goodbye and thank you to Uncle Julius," she had said, but he had crouched back in his seat and screwed his eyes shut, refusing to look or talk.

"Don't worry. He'll get over it," Julius had said good-humouredly, "boys have funny notions going through their heads at his age. Bring him back next time I'm here and we'll have another session with the kite."

Back at their apartment, A.J. had behaved as if he had completely forgotten the incident. He chatted away about the weekend, of the swims he had had, the bedtime story Julius had told him and even about the kite he had been given.

"You like your Uncle Julius, don't you?" she had asked, relieved.

He had not answered immediately, but had gone on playing with a toy revolver he had received for Christmas

"Yeah, but not always. When I'm big I want a real one of these ... bang, bang, bang, ... this couldn't kill anyone even if it did have real bullets ... or could it, mummy?"

George had first met Roland Aschenberger, the chief executive at the New York branch of the Mediterranean and Overseas Credit Bank, while negotiating the purchase of the Vanderwest Meat and Packaging Corporation.

The contact had been purely professional but when, two years later, the banker became involved in the sale of George's shareholding, their relationship developed into a social one as well. They lunched together on several occasions and, learning of George's passion for racehorses, Roland invited him to watch the one he owned running. They both bet and won, and the following day George had the banker round to a party in his hotel suite. That was when, sensing the gambler in the man, he suggested a poker session.

George exploited Aschenberger's penchant for gambling for a specific reason. He wanted to find out all he could about Julius Caspar.

He knew, of course, that he controlled the Crédit Méditerranéen and its New York offshoot, and that he was mixed up in certain deals in which he, George, was also involved. But to what extent, or why, he was not sure. So, since Roland's father was a director of the Geneva bank where his Trust also was, he reckoned that through him he might be able to discover more about it, especially who had been responsible for setting it up fifteen years earlier. Neither Emile Zekla nor Raoul Kharami had been prepared to tell him, and the bank employees he had approached with a promise of bribes had remained infuriatingly discreet. But he reckoned that Roland Aschenberger might have his arm twisted if properly manipulated; a question of getting him into a position where he owed him a favour or, better still, money.

The man's extravagant life-style did the trick. For a loan of $50,000, Aschenberger gave him quite a bit of information about the Mediterranean and Overseas Credit Bank and its Geneva counterpart. Not only who were their principal clients, but also where Julius Caspar had other holdings, the extent of these, and on a couple of occasions, even the details of deals he was about to conclude. He also told him that if the bank had supported George so fully it was because of precise instructions from the chairman, and that it was he who had bought George's shareholding in the Vanderwest Meat Company. Why, George asked himself? Was it possible that

Julius Caspar was the other mysterious Trustee? But if so, why had he placed a million Swiss Francs for his benefit when he was a youngster of sixteen? Or had he acted as a nominee for someone else? George was determined to find out.

Through a series of takeovers and mergers in France and England, George had, in the five years from 1964 to 1969, established his reputation as one of Europe's leading young businessmen.

Finance houses on both sides of the Channel which, until then, had regarded him with a certain suspicion, convinced that sooner or later he would outstretch himself, began courting him. And shortly before the end of 1966, he reckoned that he was strong enough to launch into the American market once more. But this time he would not use the services of his usual bankers; he would get the backing of a powerful and very active Parisian one.

The bank in question had become more and more involved in his affairs as his Laboratoires Dinard S.A. grew into a mammoth holding company with assets of over £200 million, controlling pharmaceutical, food, electrical and property concerns. Ten per cent of breakfasts eaten in Britain's homes, the cereals, sausages, milk, bread, tea, and marmalade, came from companies owned or controlled by George, as did 6 per cent of the vanishing and night creams on dressing tables, and 4 per cent of soaps in bathrooms. In France, he had cornered 14 per cent of the animal food market, and produced more toothpastes, sun lotions, contraceptive pills and pain killing suppositories than any of his competitors. He owned, through Laboratoires Dinard Holdings, £30 million worth of real estate in the UK, while in France the group valued its factories, laboratories, shops and land at over £40 million. It was from this commercial bastion that he decided to reach out and grasp a chunk of the US market.

He began by dealing with American conglomerates interested in obtaining a foothold in Europe. To them he sold a number of factories and shops, following a carefully prepared plan to divest his holding company of realty and to produce liquidity for his acquisitions in the USA. Though the market was ebullient in Great Britain, certain enterprising businessmen were already moving across the Atlantic, and

George had no intention of getting on the scene when the best of the pickings had gone.

His first move was to make contact with Westflax, one of the largest supermarket chains on the West Coast of the USA, and sell them his group of rapidly expanding delicatessen shops in the UK. It was an outright sale which netted him £4.3 million. Disposing of real estate and factories in France and England brought in another £12 million and freed him of assets which, he predicted, would lose 50 per cent of their value when the current 'bull' property market turned 'bear'.

Having stealthily prepared his ground, he pounced in May 1967 and gobbled up the very supermarket chain to which he had sold his delicatessen shops only 16 months earlier. It cost his new holding company, G.C. Investments, 11 million dollars, the balance of 43 million being put up by the powerful Parisian merchant bank. He later joked that Westflax had really financed its own takeover.

He had reason to be pleased. Westflax had 300 supermarkets and sales which topped the billion dollar mark. To have gained control of it singlehanded was a real coup and financial papers across the country hailed it as such. Also, the bid had been made by G.C. Investments and not by his Laboratoires Dinard Holdings. It had nothing to do with the Crédit Méditerranéen et d'Outremer either, nor with his Trust. He had carried it off under the noses of two of the largest food conglomerates in the USA, and without one particular interested party aware of what was happening. Julius Caspar owned 4 per cent of the supermarket chain.

Maryanne put down the newspaper and lit a cigarette. She was sitting with Julius on the terrace of his home on Long Island.

George was back on the scene again. On her scene. Though she had watched his business escalation in Europe, and was well aware of the prolific spread of his interests, she had been convinced that he would not cross the Atlantic for a while, content with being a king-pin in the booming European markets.

"What do you think of the way he's brought off this Westlake take-over?" Julius asked.

"Very clever. But I don't like it. Why didn't he discuss it first with the Crédit Méditerranéen? After all they are his main bankers, and have been for years. And you own a sizeable share of his assets ... or the bank does."

He shrugged his shoulders.

"I knew that sooner or later he'd break away, but to be honest I hadn't expected it so soon, nor with a company in which I own quite a considerable shareholding. I take my hat off to him!"

"You sound as if you're almost pleased!"

"I am in a way. Fifteen years ago I had a hunch that he was a young man who would go places, and I wasn't wrong. I backed him, with the result that he's made me a considerable amount of money ... I wonder what his next move will be? Maybe you should have a word with him and sound him out."

"Me?" she exclaimed, "I haven't seen him in years. What makes you think he might tell me, of all people?"

So it was Julius who contacted George.

"I'm ringing to congratulate you on the Westflax deal. Very neat," he said when he phoned him that evening.

"Thanks Mr Caspar, I appreciate that. Kind of you to phone."

"I also wanted to know if you'd care to meet me for lunch or dinner while you're over here."

"I'd be delighted to. Let me see ... I just need to check ... tomorrow would be fine. Only could we make it here at the Waldorf? I've a fairly tight schedule as you can imagine and need to be available. Fine, then shall we say 12.45?"

George received him in his hotel suite.

For a while they talked about France's blocking of England's entrance into the Common Market, and the army's bloodless coup d'état in Greece. Then, when they sat down for lunch, Julius asked point blank, "why did you go elsewhere for the finance for Westflax and not to the Crédit Méditerranéen? Of course don't answer if you don't want to ... "

George laughed. "I knew you'd ask that sooner or later. For an obvious reason; you own a chunk of Westflax equity. You also more or less own the Crédit Méditerranéen and the bank here. So it would hardly have been politic to ask you to finance a deal which would put me in control of a company which possibly you might have wanted for yourself. I must say, I was surprised that you didn't gobble it up when those other two 'big boys' started sniffing around it."

It was Julius' turn to laugh. "Obviously you haven't followed the pattern of my business activities with as much interest as I have yours, or you wouldn't have been surprised. I'm basically a trader; as a true Levantine it's commerce which interests me. Commerce, and a spot of banking which go hand in glove. After all, banks are traders too only their wares are money as opposed to cotton, rice or coal. Yes, I'm a trader and as such the buying and selling of companies, mergers or takeovers etc. are not of prime interest to me. Sure, like every successful businessman, I do control certain companies, and I have interests in a whole series of them. But not for the same reasons as you. You are essentially a post-war phenomenon, at least as far as Europe is concerned. A stock marketeer whose prime and almost sole activity is buying and then selling the shares of a company and making a profit through revaluing its assets, or its trading potential. A more sophisticated method than mine for making money. No, the control of Westflax was of no interest to me. I happen to own some 4 per cent of its stock, more by accident than stratagem. It was the result of a somewhat complicated piece of trading with a former shareholder. And incidentally, if you are interested in purchasing it, I'll gladly sell to you. Only it'll cost you more than what you paid per share. You've pushed up the stock value by some 12 per cent!"

"Maybe I'll take you up on that one. But I'm not completely in agreement when you define yourself as basically a trader. What about Pharos Petroleum?"

"Ah, that! To tell you the truth I never expected it to become what it has. It began as a sideline activity to satisfy a whim. Ever since I traded and refined oil back in the late '40s, when I owned a refinery in Italy, I have had an almost schoolboy urge to own a well. Possibly I was fascinated by the story of the legendary Gulbenkian, Mr Five Percent, or by Rockerfeller and Getty. I didn't plan to buy an oil well — the land was offered me out of the blue, and a hunch told me there was a fortune under it. A long way down, mind you, but there."

"Yet now it's your principal interest and the source of those colossal revenues the newspapers sometimes refer to. Why don't we do a deal with Pharos rather than Westflax. I'd be very happy to buy a share of it."

Julius was immediately alert.

"Why?" he asked when he had finished his mouthful. "Oil

is hardly your line, and I'm sure you know that I wouldn't cede control for any reason."

George stared at him with a surprising intensity, then his lips pretended to smile. "It was simply an idea. After all, we already are indirectly associated through the bank, if I'm not mistaken? But if you change your mind, let me know. It would remain in the family as it were. A spot more wine?"

Julius wondered whether George could possibly suspect anything. He certainly appeared to be aware that the Crédit Méditerranéen's interest in his affairs went beyond simple bank backing. Indirectly, he obviously linked the Trust with the bank, and the bank with its principal shareholder.

He nodded. "Just half a glass. Thank you."

George replaced the bottle in the ice bucket, then leaned forward and fixed him again with his pale green eyes.

"Talking of family," he said, "there is a personal matter I wanted to have a word with you about. Of course, nothing is stopping me going ahead without consulting you, but I feel it's correct to let you know. I intend to get Maryanne to work for me. I need someone who is competent and whom I can trust. She fits the bill. I always reckoned she had a first class business brain which, properly trained, could be a match for any man. And I bet you'd be the first to agree with me there or you wouldn't have given her the responsibilities she has. Also, in a way she's still part of my family, even if she isn't really my sister-in-law anymore, and that means she'll be loyal. I know you'll say the same applies to you too, but not to the same extent. For you Maryanne is an able assistant, competent in the running of your affairs. All right, she's the daughter of an old friend of yours, but a family link doesn't come into it. I could find you half a dozen women to take her place ... "

Julius stifled a mounting anger.

"You're wrong in thinking that Maryanne is just another capable assistant for me," he said calmly. "She's more, much more. But if you want to ask her, do so by all means. And if she wants to go and work with you, I certainly won't try to dissuade her. In any case, I doubt that my raising objections would stop you!"

George grinned suddenly and Julius was aware that he could turn on considerable charm when he wanted.

"You're a great person, Mr Caspar. I admire you. I'm only

sorry I didn't get to know you better earlier ... I can't help thinking that the two of us should get together. Linked in business we could make an unbeatable team. What do you say? Please help yourself to the Stilton. I hope you won't mind if I smoke?" He was leaning back in his corner of the sofa and had lit a cigarette.

"Have you anything specific in mind, apart from Pharos, of course?"

George threw his head back and blew a perfect smoke ring.

"Not at this moment. But one never knows. Let me think it over and come back to you."

Curious how he made it sound as if he were doing him a favour, Julius thought.

Maryanne was in bed, studying a file, when the phone rang. She reached for the receiver and glanced at the clock. 11.08 p.m.

"Hello Maryanne, I don't suppose I'm disturbing you?"

The voice was familiar, but she couldn't immediately place it.

"Who's speaking, please?"

"Come off it, Manne, don't tell me you don't know who I am!"

It was George, of course.

"I didn't recognize you. How are you, George?"

"Are you alone?"

"Yes." Strange how his voice provoked no emotion in her now. She wasn't even irritated by his immediate lack of discretion.

"Good. Then what would you say to our having a drink together?"

"Fine by me. Let's see ... tomorrow's out I'm afraid ..."

"Who talked about tomorrow? I mean now."

"Now? I'm in bed! It's past eleven and I'm working."

"Big mistake. Bed's not for work, unless you're in the profession. Shall we make it in say half an hour?"

He hadn't changed. Overbearing as ever, and convinced that everyone was ready to gratify his slightest wish at the snap of his fingers.

"The answer's no, George. I'd love to see you again, but not tonight. You know, you do have a certain nerve ringing me up like this, out of the blue, and presuming that I'd be here at your beck and call. Hadn't it occurred to you that I mightn't be free, or alone, for that matter?"

"Of course. That's why I asked you. Why all the fuss? Old friends have the privilege of turning up unexpectedly, and at odd hours, otherwise what's the point of having any. I hope you still consider me a friend. But joking apart, I want to see you to discuss something too ... "

"What?" she asked flatly.

"It's a business matter. I never discuss business over the phone."

"And I don't at midnight. What are you doing tomorrow morning?"

"Flying to Chicago. Why?"

"At what time?"

"Around ten o'clock. But I don't see ... "

"Then we can have breakfast together. I have it prepared at 8 o'clock, and I shan't be leaving till 9.15. If you care to come, you're very welcome."

"You're not serious!"

"Dead serious. It's either breakfast tomorrow or we leave it till you get back. Sorry George, tonight's out."

There was a moment's silence while she heard him take a deep breath.

"O.K. I'll see if I can make it, though I don't think it's very nice of you to treat an old friend this way."

"Full English or Continental? I'm talking of the breakfast?"

"Don't you remember?

"No George, and in any case you could well have changed your eating habits in eight years."

"Is it really that long?"

"I think so, though I haven't bothered to count. See you tomorrow ... maybe. And George... "

"Yes?"

"Thanks for ringing, even if it is a bit late in the day."

What exactly did she mean by that, he wondered as he put the receiver down.

The initial rebuff in no way lessened his determination to get his own with her. He reckoned he knew women, and her particularly. Once before she had attempted to resist him, only to give herself to him with a vengeance. He was the first man to have brought on a complete orgasm in her, and her body was hardly likely to have forgotten that, even if her mind tried to.

He had the porter announce him and, as the clock was striking eight, he was being whisked up to her apartment. The front door was opened by a maid who showed him into a closed part of the terrace where a table was laid for breakfast.

"Madam will be here in a moment," the woman said, "will you be taking coffee or tea?"

"Tea, strong and with milk."

"Very good sir." Then, looking around the room she added, "A.J., get up from behind the table there and finish your breakfast. The school bus won't wait for you again. Hurry up now ... "

She turned and disappeared through the doorway.

George stared at the head which had suddenly popped up the other side of the table. It had a shock of dark hair, unusually crinkly, a couple of hostile, almost black eyes and half a nose, the rest of the face being concealed by a napkin tied at the nape. A pistol appeared and was aimed at him. A muffled "bang, bang, bang" escaped from the hidden mouth, followed by "you're dead." George pulled a chair to him and sat down.

"Bang, bang, bang," the boy went on, "I've killed you real and proper."

George was tempted to ignore him, but at such close quarters it was difficult. He didn't care much for kids, they were too unpredictable. Also they were totally disrespectful on the whole, and this annoyed him. As a child, he had been taught to be polite and never rude to grown-ups. Even when, aged 15, he had finally defied their authority, he had done so politely and he saw no reason why all children should not behave in the same way. How old could the boy be, he wondered?

"How old are you?" he asked abruptly.

"Seven and two months."

"Then you're old enough to behave properly. Hasn't your mother told you that little boys should stand up and say hello politely when a grown-up comes into the room?"

The black eyes glared at him. "I killed you. Who were you?"

George noted the logical use of the past tense, logical since he was supposed to be dead. If nothing else, the boy seemed intelligent. Stubborn, fanciful and certainly quick. Who could the father be?

The napkin slipped down to the neck revealing a strong nose and largish mouth. Whoever it was, he wasn't Anglo-Saxon. That was the face of a southern Mediterranean kid. Sicilian or Turkish, very like the pale skinned Arabs he used to see in Alexandria. The eyes held his, defiant and questioning. George realized with a slight shock that the features were familiar. They were strangely like those of his grandfather Wirsa. Not the nose, that was more Maryanne's, nor the expression in the eyes. There was something powerful in that little head which had nothing to do with the indolence of George Wirsa. He had seen that sideways look before, with the forehead tilted slightly forward. But where?

"If you can't be polite, you'd better be useful," he said, attempting a wry smile, "go and tell you're mother your uncle George is here."

"O.K." the boy said unexpectedly and ran off through the open door to the terrace. George heard him shout "Mummy" a couple of times before there was a movement behind him and Maryanne appeared.

"Hello George," she said easily as he stood up, "where on earth has A.J. disappeared to?"

He took her hand and brought it to his lips. "To look for you ... motherhood suits you, you're really beautiful."

"Thanks ... you're not looking too bad yourself. Come on, let's have some breakfast. I'm famished ... oh, Graziella," she said to the maid who had just appeared, "bring us some coffee will you. What have you got there?"

"Tea Madam. The gentleman asked for it."

"All right, forget about coffee, I'll have tea also. Just leave it next to me. Care for eggs George, or yoghurt? No? Then just the usual toast and croissants."

She poured out the tea and handed him a cup.

"No you haven't really changed. Perhaps a little more weight and more serious looking. A successful business man like you has to look powerful ... sugar? ... milk? ... congratulations, incidentally, on the Westflax deal, you must be extremely pleased. I suppose it's the first of a series of spectacular takeover bids in America?"

George was aware that the woman facing him was a very

different person from the one he had known eight years earlier. Then she had been shy and vulnerable, an easy game for a man with the right personality and physique. He had been that man. But this Maryanne was brimming with confidence and conscious of her capabilities; a woman with a strong character, needing no one to steer her through life. Who had been responsible for this metamorphosis? Her current lover, that Jewish senator she had been with for three years? Or Julius Caspar? She had been close to him for a long time. He was her friend and employer. Maybe he had been more since it was rumoured that she had lived with him for a while. Perhaps the boy was the fruit of a relationship between them. Yes, he had something of the Alexandrian; that was where he had seen that sideways look before!

"Possibly," he answered, reaching for the cup. "But let's not talk about me and business just yet ... I didn't come round for that, you know."

She smiled. "For what then, George? Sorry, that sounds rude and I didn't mean it to be. Only last night you said ... "

"Never mind what I said last night. I came round to say hello and see how you were getting on ... "

"At 8. a.m.? I'd like to believe you ... but anyway, I'm flattered. It was sweet of you to find the time, whatever the motive."

"For you, Maryanne, I will always find time." He leant forward in his chair. "Why did you run out on me? Why did you ditch me without a word? What had I done to deserve that treatment? You must have known that I was in love with you and wanted to marry you." His voice had become almost guttural with intensity.

She closed her eyes and drew a deep breath.

"George, what's the point? I'm sorry if I acted the way I did. Yes, it was wrong of me. I should have had the strength to face you and tell you the truth. But I was young and frightened. You frightened me. I wasn't in love with you, just as you weren't with me. We were simply very attracted physically. I believe I even hated you in a way; I felt what we did that night with Georgina dying in a bedroom only a floor above was terrible. And I blamed you for it. No you didn't love me George, so don't pretend you did. Georgina, yes. You probably got as near to love as you ever will with her. I was just an outlet for your pent-up emotions, and after her death you somehow convinced yourself that I could slip into her shoes."

"You don't know what you're saying. Of course I loved Georgina, but what I felt for you was different. It was also love, only of another kind. You have more passion in you than Georgina had, and a brain that commands respect. I've always said so, and I haven't been proved wrong. But now you're more than a clever and passionate woman, you're beautiful. I don't want to loose you again ... "

She interrupted him with a laugh. "What is this, a proposition? If so George, it's the wrong hour, the wrong place, and the wrong woman. Come clean. You wouldn't have waited all these years, then rung me out of the blue just to say you love me. You'd have swamped me with roses, pillaged Tiffany's for the largest diamond you could find, and made sure the press were at my front door. Instead, you prosaically come to breakfast and flatter me with a series of clichés which aren't at all your style. Why?"

There was an ironical twinkle in her eyes which made him change tactics abruptly.

"All right, I want you to leave Caspar and work for me. I'll pay you twice what he does and, if you'll have me, I'll marry you too. I need someone I can trust to help me in my business and I know that you, at least, are 100 per cent honest. You're honest with others but more important, with yourself. It's your brains I want, your cleverness and your integrity, even more than your body. There are few businessmen who are both clever and honest, few in whom I can put my trust, and you're one of them. Note that I said businessmen, not women. The respect I have for your capacities make me place you amongst the very clever men I deal with; above them, as you have a moral integrity which is lacking in most. Come and work with me, Maryanne. Caspar doesn't need you as I do. He hasn't loved or known you the way I have, nor wanted to marry you. He's a man I admire and he's done a lot for you, fair enough. But if he's really fond of you, he won't mind your leaving him. He'll be glad to see you at the side of a man who'll soon be as big as him, probably bigger."

She was shaking her head, and when finally he stopped talking she said: "It's no use, George. You've just said some very nice things and I appreciate them. But nothing you can say will change the fact that I could never work for, let alone live with or marry you. Don't ask me to give reasons ... let's say that I'm very happy as it is, and have no wish or intention to change things. I have a man in my life whom I respect and get on with very well, and as far as Julius Caspar is concerned, I wouldn't leave him unless he specifically asked me to go. Quite apart from business, we're very close. I can't explain it, and don't want to, but he means an awful lot to me. Even A.J. ... "

"Is that the real reason," he said fiercely, "is the boy the link between you?"

"What do you mean?"

"I always knew you had a crush on him, ever since you saw him at my wedding. What has he to offer more than me? He's old enough to be your father and he's had an affair with your mother. What has he got so special to attract first Cecily, then you? Admit it, he was your lover too ... "

"Shut up George. I won't have you ... "

"And the father of that little bastard I've just seen. Deny it, if you can!"

She jumped to her feet sending her cup and saucer crashing to the floor. She was white with rage.

"Get out, and don't dare ever try to get in touch with me again. As far as I'm concerned you're dead. Do you hear? Dead."

He gripped the edge of the table as an animal urge to humiliate her gripped him. He wanted to tear off her clothes and rape her; reduce her to a powerless sexual mass dependant on his body. Her words echoed in his ears as he struggled for control of himself.

Suddenly the boy appeared in the doorway. He looked at his mother and then at George. Bang, bang, bang, clicked the toy pistol.

"He's dead, Mummy, I shot him."

Without even a glance at George she ran over to her son and put an arm around him. Then she led him away down the corridor.

"Did you see him?" Julius asked her later in the day when they were alone.

She gave a small laugh.

"I suppose you're referring to George. Yes, he came round to my apartment this morning. He made me various propositions one of which was marriage."

Julius swung round. "What!"

"Uh-huh. And when he saw that it was no game, he asked me to leave you and work for him ... "

"I suspected he would, but marriage! He must be out of his mind! I mean, simply because he was the husband of your sister doesn't give him a right over you ... How did you get rid of him?"

"By throwing him out. He made a remark or two which I didn't like, so I told him to go. I also said that I had no intention of seeing him again."

"I'm sorry. It must have been very unpleasant. In a way it's my fault. I should have told him where he got off when I had lunch with him."

"Believe me, Julius, it was bound to happen sooner or later. We had a rather strained relationship after Georgina died. He behaved... well, curiously. I think he believed I was his property ... all the Langtons were once he had married into the family, and because I was very young he reckoned he could do with me what he wanted. He just couldn't understand that I had a life of my own and a will to live it my way. If I hadn't been married at the time, I'm sure he'd have asked me to become his wife. Or rather forced me to. He's like that, you know, very overbearing with people near him. Remember, he had a row too with Mummy. I suppose it has something to do with his being an orphan. Anyway, as far as I'm concerned, it's over and done with. I doubt that he'll try again with me."

"Are you sure?" he asked gently. "Would you like me to have a word with him?"

"No ... please, the best thing we can do is forget about him as a person. Inevitably we'll come up against him in business, you more than me, and I'd rather any relationship were totally impersonal."

"As you wish, Maryanne. Only I think I must warn you he's not the sort of man to forgive and forget easily. He has a monumental pride, and one of these days he'll try to make you pay. Me too, probably. We'll have to keep our eyes skinned where he's concerned."

When she had gone, he stood watching the rain fall into an ornamental pond on the terrace. He thought of Maryanne and George, his daughter and son who, by a quirk of destiny, had become brother and sister in the eyes of the law. Who might even have become wife and husband! He shuddered. To think that A.J. could have been the fruit of such a union ...

But it could never have happened. Instinctively Maryanne was repulsed by her brother. Nature and Providence had been kind. He wondered whether now was the time to tell her of their relationship. No, he decided. First the waters had to calm between them.

Julius was not a womanizer — only for a brief period in his life had he been sexually promiscuous — yet for a man who exuded a strong sexual magnetism he had had surprisingly few affairs. If he was capable of passion, as his love for Marguerite and Cecily had proved, he was also of sexual abstinence. He had never been to a brothel and had never paid for sex; he had never needed to. And at 60 he was still as physically attractive as the young man Renée Maggiar had made her lover, with the physique of an athlete and a greying of the temples and beard which softened his features and gave him an almost romantic look. And there was a way he had of smiling, that began with the eyes and then involved the whole of the face, which few could resist.

But that particular smile, with its boyish warmth, was reserved for only his family and a handful of friends, for those he really cared for. He never knowingly used his charm, and people only saw the other side of him, the courteous but distant man of influence, immeasurably ambitious and infinitely self cantered. It was a mask he only cast off on rare occasions.

Until he found Maza again, gossip columnists were at a loss what to say about him and women. Certain, in their frustration, had hinted that he was a eunuch, castrated by an accident during the war, and the few women who could testify to the contrary felt that their friendship with him counted more than the kudos of being labelled as his mistress. The affairs Julius had with them were brief and discreet, seldom lasting more than a few weeks, and invariably involved persons who reminded him in some way of Marguerite, Cecily or Maza.

After Maza had died, Julius channelled his tenderness towards Maryanne, and inevitably Cecily began to play a part again in his existence. He was conscious, with the passing of the years, and on the few occasions when they met, that she represented more than a poignant memory, and that the love which had exploded with such passion thirty years earlier was still latent in him, waiting to be kindled.

The occasion arose when she suggested he come to Chilton for the marriage of her son, Julian, early in June 1970.

She was over 60 by then, yet her looks and figure were those of a woman ten years younger. As beautiful as ever, she captivated Julius again through a femininity which was both maternal and provocative.

He arrived the day before the wedding, and she came to greet him as he stepped from the car.

"Come," she said, "let's steal a few minutes on our own."

She slipped her arm through his and walked him to the Hall's long south terrace overlooking the park. It was a warm June afternoon and a light breeze toyed with her cotton dress, now moulding it to her body, now billowing it to reveal her well shaped legs.

"Aren't the gardens beautiful! I don't think they've been so full of colour for years. And what do you think of the lake? I had the woods thinned, so one can see it now from here. In the evening, when the sun's rays slant through the trees, it takes on a really magical look. We'll walk down there later and you'll see what I mean. But the herbaceous borders are the showpiece this year. I don't think there are any to rival them in the whole of southern England, not even Sissinghurst's. With luck they should draw crowds."

Julius smiled. "It must be wonderful to live surrounded by so much beauty, so much traditional beauty. Tell me, for how many centuries have the owners of Chilton and their friends strolled along this terrace then rested in the shade of that huge oak tree, or gone to have tea in that little building by the lake ... what do you call it?"

"A gazebo. That actually was a recent addition. I believe it was built around 1860, whereas the house dates from 1690. But the gardens, in their present form, were laid out by

Capability Brown in the middle of the 18th century. We still have some of his sketches in the library."

"It's amazing to think that someone actually sat down and designed it all. Apart from the steps, it looks as if nature produced it just as it is. And what about the famous borders?"

"They're brand new, comparatively. James' mother had them planted, but I take some of the credit, along with Ogden, the head gardener. Herbaceous borders are my hobby; I've even written a book about them."

"Which you never told me about."

She gave a little laugh. "My dear, there are hundreds of things about me you don't know, and half as many again that I don't know about you. We're modest, that's all." She squeezed his arm lightly. "You know, I'm so glad you were able to come, and for more than just half an hour. Maybe we'll have time to get to know each other a little better."

They strolled past the sunken rose garden, and on to the lawn on the west side of the house where three children were playing croquet. One of them, Julius noted, was A.J.

"Who are the two with him?" he asked.

"Nelson and Jemima. The boys are pages at the wedding, and Jemima's the principal bridesmaid. They're nice children and on the whole well behaved. And I love having them, especially Jemima. She's a darling and very pretty. Oh there's young A.J. getting into one of his tantrums again. It's funny, he can be sweet and docile till all of a sudden bang, to use one of his favourite words, and it's hate with a capital H. I think we'd better go and try and calm him."

"Leave him to me, I know how to handle him."

He walked hurriedly towards A.J. who was threatening the other two with his mallet. The little girl had run to her brother for protection, who was shouting at his cousin to stop it.

Suddenly Maryanne's son tripped and fell. Julius ran and pinned him to the ground.

"Hello young man," he said, "up to your tricks again?"

A.J. lay panting on the grass and stared defiantly at his grandfather.

"You didn't expect me here did you?" Julius went on, "now either you get up quietly and go on with the game properly, or I'll sit on you all afternoon. I'm quite prepared to if necessary."

"He's crazy," Nelson cried, "we don't want to play with a

nutcase like him. He's always cheating or trying to hurt us in some way."

Julius looked at the boy. He was tall with curly, chestnut hair. He had his mother's eyes and mouth, and there was something of his uncle Julian about him. A good-looking youngster.

"Say how do you do properly to Mr Caspar," Cecily said, "and then tell me what all this is about." She put her arms around the girl.

"How do you do, sir." Nelson bowed slightly to Julius. "It wasn't our fault, grandma. He wanted to play out of turn, so I only told him to wait till Jemima had played, and he began shouting that he wasn't taking orders from anyone, and tried to barge Jemima away."

Cecily was only half listening. She brushed the girl's hair back with her hand and knelt by her. "This is my little Jemima," she said to Julius. "Say hello to the gentleman, darling."

Jemima bobbed a slight courtesy. "Hello, Mr ... " she glanced questioningly at her grandmother who whispered Julius' name in her ear. "Mr Caspar."

Julius couldn't take his eye's off her. She was dark haired with a pale skin and features so familiar that he almost gaped. She was Marguerite in miniature.

"Hello, Jemima," he said softly as he let go of A.J. and crouched down in front of her. "Will you give me a kiss?"

She smiled, Marguerite's smile, and put her arms around his neck. Then her lips touched his cheek.

"Will you call me 'uncle Julius'," he went on, hugging her.

He looked at Cecily. "You never told me she was like this." He stood up and took Jemima's hand in his.

"I want you to be very sweet to this young lady," he said to A.J. who was eyeing him angrily. "Come on, kids, I'll stay while you finish the game. I might even try to play myself. You don't mind, do you Cecily?"

She laughed. "Of course not. There are one or two things I must do, in any case. Will you join me for tea in half an hour or so? Behave yourselves children, and no more fighting."

He watched her walk off towards the house and an emotion which he had not felt for years gripped him. It was as if suddenly the past and the present had blended and the essence of his youth was surging in his veins again. For an instant he was with a real family, with a son and a daughter and the children of his children.

The moment passed, but a touch of it lingered on. He smiled. He was alone with his three grandchildren and only he knew it. Alone with them in this beautiful garden, watching a woman very dear to him walk away, while the hand of Marguerite's granddaughter nestled in his.

He turned to find the three children looking at him fixedly. Nelson with curiosity, Jemima with affection and A.J. with hate.

Later in the evening, he and Cecily found themselves alone in the library. The children had gone off to have an early dinner and the house guests were in their rooms changing.

"Will you pour me a sherry, Antor, and yourself whatever you'd like."

He went over to the tray with the drinks. As he was filling her glass, she asked, "what did you mean, this afternoon, when you said about Jemima 'you never told me she was like this'?"

"Was that what I said?"

"Yes. Like what, Antor?"

"I had a curious sensation when I saw her," he said, pouring himself a whisky, "well ... that little girl is the image of a person I knew a long time ago. You remember that earlier I told you I once wanted to marry and raise a family, and that I had remained faithful to a memory. It was to the memory of an 18 year old girl who came from one of the best families in Alexandria. I was a modest bank clerk with no money and no social position, so a nobody as far as her parents were concerned. We fell in love, and though two years later I was in a position to give her the sort of home and life she was accustomed to, her father and mother — her mother especially — had other plans for her. We tried to keep our love secret but they found out, rushed her off to Europe, and forced her to marry one of Alexandria's eligible young men, the son of Anglo-Greek friends of theirs."

He paused, staring into the middle distance, then added: "He was called Roger Christofides, and Marguerite died giving birth to a son, George."

"Oh dear, I had no idea," she said putting aside her glass and laying a hand on his. "It must have been terrible for you.

I just don't know what to say … yet how marvellous, and extraordinary in a way, that her son should have married my daughter and become Maryanne's brother-in-law. It means there's a kind of link between your Marguerite's granddaughter and you … it makes Jemima a sort of grandniece of yours." She leaned over and kissed him gently on the cheek. "And what's more, it makes you and I that much closer. I'm so glad you told me, I can't wait to tell Maryanne."

He frowned slightly. "I'd rather we kept it to ourselves for the time being, if you don't mind."

"Why, for heaven's sake?"

"It's a secret I've lived with for a long time — I mean about Marguerite — and I'd like it to remain that way."

Cecily nodded slowly. "Of course, Antor. Forgive me, it was egoistic and unfeeling of me to want to shout it around the place."

"You could never be that. It's just that for the moment I wouldn't want George to find out that his mother and I were in love. He could tarnish something that was pure and beautiful. Also, he might try to stop me seeing Jemima again, and I'd rather that didn't happen. She's such a lovely little girl."

She smiled and reached for her glass of sherry. "I saw how you took to her, and she to you. Don't worry about George, I'll see that that never happens. And I won't even be jealous if you choose to come here when she's with me … "

He looked at her with a tinge of reproach in his eyes. "You know the reason why I never came in all these years … "

"Forgive me Antor, I was only joking. What I meant was you can count on me to have Jemima here every summer, and that I want you to feel free to come to Chilton whenever you like. Consider it a second home."

He took her hand and kissed it. "You're wonderful, Cecily. Thank you." Then he added, "will you come to London on Friday and have lunch with me?"

"Why not stay on here instead of rushing off to Town? The guests will have gone so, apart from the children, we'll have the place to ourselves."

"I'd like to do something special … please come."

"All right, I accept with pleasure."

Julius arranged for a car to collect Cecily at Waterloo Station. He had wanted to send it down to Chilton, but she would not hear of it.

"There's a perfectly good train, which I always take, so why make a poor chauffeur drive all the way here?"

Since the most convenient one got in an hour before she was due to meet Julius, she had arranged to call in on her doctor first rather than the following week, as planned. He had said he would have the results of the tests.

Seated in his consulting room, she looked him straight in the eye. He was an old friend as well as her personal doctor, and she had complete faith in him. Only two days earlier he had been down at Chilton for the wedding, drinking to the newly weds, and cheerfully toasting her too, all the while knowing what he did.

Curiously, at that moment she felt herself feeling much more sorry for him than for herself. Poor Ewan, what it must be costing him to tell her.

"I want you to be perfectly honest with me, Ewan. How long have I got?"

He looked at his fingers. "It's difficult to tell ... if you go in for treatment immediately, it could be a year, even two. If not, well ... a matter of months, four or five ... but one can never really tell. There have been cases where doctors have been completely wrong, and the patient has gone on for years ... "

"You don't have to sweeten the pill for me. I can face death; it doesn't frighten me. I just hate uncertainty. I suppose there's no doubt about it?"

He shook his head, as she knew he would. Ewan Moncrief was not the sort of man to tell a patient she was doomed if he felt there were a possibility of a reprieve.

She took a deep breath, as she used to before going on stage, and threw back her head. "I won't go in for treatment, I don't see the point if all it will do is drag out an existence which normally should terminate. But as I'm a bit of a coward physically, I'll ask you to give me the necessary painkillers when the time comes."

He took her hand in his. "I promise you, you won't suffer at all, and I'll do everything to make the next months as comfortable as possible."

There were tears in his eyes, so she leant forward and gave him a kiss on the cheek.

"Don't be sad for me," she said, "I've had a wonderful life, far better and more privileged than most. All I ask you is not to tell the family. I want to live these last months I have fully, and if they're moping around it would make things much more difficult." She stood up. "Remember, I was an actress, and in a way it'll be a challenge to play a part again. And it'll have to be my best, as I shan't get another chance!"

When she walked out of the doctor's house into the sunshine she felt curiously elated. She looked up into the sky, shielding her eyes, and thought what a beautiful day it was, and how wonderful it was to be alive.

Why wasn't she shocked or terrified by what Ewan had told her, she wondered? Was she punch drunk by the news, and would the anguish come later when she fell off her little cloud and back into reality?

She smiled at the chauffeur who held the car door open for her.

"Is everything all right, m'lady?"

"Yes thank you. Would you take me to Claridges now?"

She opened her handbag and took out a pocket mirror. She touched her hair and examined her lips. Then she looked at her eyes. There was a twinkle in them. That was the way it should be, and that was how she would keep them. The act was on now.

The chauffeur was saying something.

"An autograph? With pleasure. It's years since anyone has asked me for one ... makes me feel as if I'm on stage again."

Julius was there to greet her as she came into the hotel.

"How do you manage it? You look more radiant each time I see you. Would you like a cocktail first or shall we go straight to the restaurant?" he asked, taking her hand in his.

"To the restaurant please, I'm famished!"

As the maître d'hotel led them to their table she exclaimed, "I think it's the same one we had when we last lunched here ... yes I'm sure it is."

"That's why I chose it," he answered simply. And no sooner

224

were they seated than the sommelier brought them a bottle of Dom Perignon.

"Did you have a pleasant journey up?" Julius asked as their glasses were being filled.

"Perfect. I got in early enough for me to change an afternoon appointment into a morning one and get it over with. Like that I'm free."

"I'm glad. I've done the same. I want you to show me London after lunch. You know, whenever I come here it's generally for a few hours, the time to get from the airport to a meeting and back there again. I've done that Western Avenue and Cromwell Road so many times, I know them backwards. But that's all, and the inside of a few hotels. I'd like you to take me to see the real London, your London. I know an afternoon isn't much, but it would be a beginning."

"What a marvellous idea. Let me think. Have you ever been to the House of Lords? No? Then we'll start there. We can also have a look inside the Abbey. I haven't been there since the coronation ... I'll show you where I sat, more or less. Then I'll see if a friend is around so that we can go and have tea on the Lord's terrace, overlooking the river ... "

Julius was smiling. "Whatever you decide is fine with me. But first let's choose lunch. How about caviar to begin with and then some fresh salmon. The maître d'hotel assured me it's delicious. O.K., you've got that?" he asked the waiter. Then reverting to Cecily, "so we do the Houses of Parliament today, and what tomorrow?"

"Tomorrow? But I must go back to Chilton this evening," she exclaimed.

"Why?"

"Well, I've got things to do. All the aftermath of the wedding. Also I've nothing to wear, even if I could stay on."

"That's no problem. Either the car takes you there tonight and brings you back tomorrow morning, or you stay and it goes to collect whatever you need for a week to ten days. That's if you'll put up with me for that long."

"Oh Antor ... you're confusing me now. I ... I can't ... "

"Of course you can, Cecily. What's really stopping you? All you have to do is relax and let me look after you, so that we can get to know each other again," he pleaded.

She blinked back the tears she felt were creeping into her eyes and forced the actress in her to take over again. Whatever she did, she must not let him guess the sudden feeling of emptiness which was threatening to engulf her.

She sipped the champagne and said, "you're right. Do you know, except for those few days we spent together, I have only seen you for a maximum of twenty-four hours. And never, apart from that lunch here and yesterday afternoon, alone. What fools we humans are sometimes ... and that applies to both of us! I'll go back to Chilton tonight, collect some things, then come and spend a few days with you here in London. I have my club ... I'll stay there. It's not far from here."

He gave her one of his special smiles. "And while you're on your way you'll plan what we'll do. Is that a deal?"

She laughed softly. "Its a deal, Antor."

First she took him to visit the House of Commons and explained the role of the Speaker, question time, and where the members of the Government and the Opposition sat. Then they went to the Lords' Chamber, with its royal blue carpet, the Woolsack, the Throne, and the pews for the peers of the realm.

Pointing to one, she said, "that was where James made his maiden speech. It was before the war, and had something to do with sanctions against Italy when Mussolini invaded Abyssinia ... do you remember? Julian hasn't made his yet, but I hope he will now that he's settling down."

Julius had the impression of stepping through a looking-glass into a world once removed from modern reality, and he marvelled at the grace with which Cecily moved in this labyrinth of pageant and tradition. Was it the actress in her which enabled her to, or was she an integral part of it?

They walked to the Abbey and half way up the great nave she stopped and pointed to a spot. "Yes, it must have been about here where James and I were ... I'm talking about King George VI's coronation back in 1937 ... I didn't make the Queen's, as stupidly I broke my ankle two days before. Julian came with Georgina instead ... I was glad in a way as I saw it all much better, and very comfortably, on television."

Later they went for tea on the terrace of the House of Lords with a friend of hers, a banker whose father had amassed a fortune in South Africa and got himself a peerage.

"I suppose you Americans think all this tradition is a bit of a waste of time ... and in a way you could be right," the man said.

"Nothing was further from my thoughts," Julius put in rapidly.

"But we British are born sentimentalists and we like to hark back to customs and people of the past. Our traditions give us a sense of security ... d'you understand what I mean?"

"Sure, as well as a sense of values, which is rapidly disappearing in many societies," Julius answered. "Let me assure you, Americans have a great respect for your traditions, and I in particular. I was born of a family whose ancestors also lived their traditions. Not the great ones which you English have, but valid and respectable ones all the same. We lost most of them when we were forced to flee our homeland, and the only traditions my parents were able to pass on to me were humble and personal. Maybe that's why I admire yours so much."

They watched the barges moving down the Thames and Julius told them of the graceful *feluccas* which had sailed the Nile and in his youth, transporting the great bales of cotton.

"They are still there, though barges now do most of the heavy work." He turned to Cecily. "One day you must come out to Egypt. The cities have changed but not the river, and to sail it is an experience you musn't miss."

Her mouth stretched in a smile but her eyes clouded with momentary sadness. "I'd love to," was all she said.

Around six o'clock they wandered back through the Houses of Parliament and out onto Wellington Square, where the car was waiting. They drove the short distance to the Savoy Hotel and, as Julius was about to get out, Cecily asked, "are you sure you won't come to Chilton for the night?"

He took her hand and brought it to his lips. "I'd love to but I can't. There's a spot of business I have to deal with and I want to clear it before tomorrow. Can you make it in the morning?"

"Of course. I'll leave early and be here at ten. Is that all right?"

For the next five days Cecily guided Julius around the London she loved, mixing visits to the Tate Gallery, the Wallace Collection, the British Museum and the 'V and A.' with strolls through the rose garden at Regent's Park and by the Serpentine. She even took him to see the Inns of Court.

"I never imagined my solicitors worked in surroundings like

these," he said, gazing at the four storeyed 18th century buildings clustered elegantly around lawns and courtyards. "It all seems so quiet and remote. More like a college campus than the background to tough legal battles and criminal proceedings."

They went to a ballet at Sadler's Wells and an Opera at Covent Garden, but not to any plays. Julius wanted to remain with the memory of the first time he had seen Cecily. He had no wish to watch another woman, a stranger, steal her former limelight. His mind and senses were concentrated on Cecily in a softer and fuller way than when he had first met her. He slid gently and knowingly into love again, conscious that her presence was now essential to him.

On the Wednesday morning she told him that she would have to go back to Chilton for a day or two.

"Why don't you come for the weekend? London isn't the only part of England I want to show you. There's Canterbury and we could do Glyndebourne ... "

"It's kind of you, but if you have to go back, I'll slip over to Geneva for the day, then we can be together again on Friday. The car will take you there and when you've done whatever you have to, it'll bring you back."

They lunched at Simpson's and afterwards, as he helped her into the hired Daimler, he said to the chauffeur, "drive carefully, you have a very precious passenger. And don't forget my instructions."

An hour later, as the car neared the Maidenhead bypass, the chauffeur slowed and said, "Mr Caspar asked me to give you this, m'lady." He handed her a cellophane packet containing a beautiful orchid with a small silk pouch attached to its stem. Intrigued, she opened and into her hand fell a magnificent ruby ring.

She was so taken aback that she gasped. For a moment she wondered if there were not a mistake, and that the flower and ring weren't meant for someone else. But then she saw the four words and the signature on the card. They read, 'Will you marry me? Antor-Julius'.

The strength ebbed from her and the actress gave way to the woman. 'Oh God,' she moaned and convulsed with silent sobs.

Kent, 1971

Julius walked over to the flower covered grave.

The little cemetery was empty now and he was alone with her. He put down his stick and leant on one knee, fingering inside his shirt for the cross while he murmured her name. The late autumn wind was blowing leaves into a small heap by a wall, and a gust swirled a few up and away to the woods beyond. He stood up slowly and let memories engulf him. They came haphazardly and in no logical order, like dragonflies zigzagging across the lawns of time. She would be leaning across the table on the terrace of the House of Lords, then slipping her arm through his as they strolled through the gardens she had loved so much. Thirty-four years flashed back and her Venetian gold hair was swathed in a towel as her eyes smiled the recognition of their sudden love in the dressing room of a theatre. How briefly yet immeasurably their passion had flowered, how deeply it had fashioned their lives.

He began to walk slowly to the gate, wending his way between the time-weathered tombstones. What a consummate actress she had been. Not for one moment, during those days in London together, had he guessed she was playing a role, her last and most difficult.

The evening she had been driven off to Chilton, she had phoned him. All she had said was, "I'm afraid I can't come to town tomorrow, but it's terribly important I see you. Can you come down here? And Antor, the ring ... it's so beautiful, I don't know what to say ... "

"Don't say anything," he had put in hurriedly, "of course I'll come. You're not feeling ill?"

No, she had replied, she was feeling quite all right, only she wanted to talk to him and not in the impersonal atmosphere of a restaurant or a hotel lounge.

When he got there she took him to the gazebo near the lake and they sat silently for a while, her hand on his. He remembered how the ruby looked magnificent against the pallor of her skin. She had glanced at him and her eyes had followed his gaze.

"It's the most beautiful ring I've ever seen," she said softly, "but I must give it back to you, Antor. I ... I can't marry you, and not for any reason you might think. You don't know how marvellously happy I am that you should have asked me, and to know that you love me enough to want me as your wife. But I can't ... "

"Why, for heaven's sake? But before you answer, I want you to know that I'd like you to wear the ring whether you'll marry me or not. And if you really can't for some reason, I'll understand ... "

Her eyes had gone moist and with a flutter of her hand she had brushed away a tear. Then she had thrown back her head with a movement for which she had become famous, and had calmly told him.

He had pleaded with her to fight what was perhaps not irremediable, to let him take her to specialists in America and get the best treatment money could buy. But she had remained adamant.

"There are decisions one has to take which are hard, even terrifying at the time. Yet once one's mind is made up, then somehow a sense of peace comes. I have that inner peace now, and you have contributed to it with your love and understanding. Don't try to talk me out of my decision, please Antor. No amount of treatment or operations will change the fact that I have a terminal illness, and I don't want to spend the days that are left me in consulting rooms and clinics. I want to live them fully, these Indian summer days of mine."

She had stood up and taken a few steps towards the lake, and he had filmed her in his mind.

"Will you share them a little with me?" she had asked.

"Of course, my darling." He went over to her and took her in his arms.

"And will you promise we will never mention my illness between us or to anyone?"

"Not even to Maryanne or Julian?"

"To no one. It would only cause useless anguish and I don't want that. I'd like the next few weeks to be happy and carefree. I think I'd like to travel a bit; could we do that? And in say September we could come back here ... Do you know it'll be

40 years this November since I came to Chilton for the first time. I wasn't married then, I came to a ball for James' 25th birthday, and I can remember it as if it were yesterday." She laughed suddenly. "I stepped out of the car into the largest puddle I could find, squelched my way across the hall to where James' mother was receiving the guests, and had to dance barefoot for most of the evening. You should have seen old Lady Brentwick's eyebrows. They shot up to her hairline in disapproval. But she was quite nice to me when James and I got engaged, even if I wasn't the girl she had hoped for as a daughter-in-law."

He smiled, concealing his anguish. "I can't imagine any woman not wanting you for her son. My mother would have worshipped you. But what you've told me isn't a valid reason for not marrying me. And apart from anything else, if we're to travel together, we should be husband and wife. What might people say otherwise!" He had tried to make a joke so as not to seem too persistent and she had taken the cue and replied, "they'll be shocked and quite rightly. But somehow we'll live through it."

Had she realized the irony of her words?

He took her to Italy, first to Stresa on Lago Maggiore with its cool waters reflecting the nostalgia of a bygone age, then to Siena, the jewel city of Tuscany, where the evening sky is sumptuously dark yet lit by the sparkle of the brightest stars. And from there through the Chianti hills, where cypresses and vineyards reproduce the paintings of old masters, down to historic Florence, an oasis of art and beauty shimmering in the mid-August heat. Two days later they were at Livorno boarding the yacht Julius had bought the year before.

They sailed to Elba, Sardinia, Capri and through the straits of Messina to Crete, then for a month around the Greek isles, and up the Turkish coast, until they reached Istanbul, where East meets West in a supreme mixture of cultures, creeds and races; where beauty and brash ugliness walk hand in hand, and one-time churches sprout minarets to Allah.

As they glided up the Bosphorus, Cecily gazed in rapture.

"It's fabulous darling, it's the most magic place I've ever been to."

"That's because you haven't set foot in the city. Wait till we go ashore; some of the glamour disappears with the noise and the flies and ... "

"Shhh, don't spoil it for me, leave me my illusions…"

She remained with them. That evening she had felt tired suddenly, and the next day had stayed in her cabin. Julius phoned her doctor who recommended she be brought home. So they drove straight from the yacht to the airport and seven hours later she was being helped into bed by Tessa. Yet the illness which was then making itself felt did not mark her physique or alter her morale. The pain-killing drugs subdued her vitality but not her determination to live her life to the full. She was out of bed within 48 hours, helping her daughter-in-law with the running of the house, discussing with the gardener new plants to be added to the herbaceous borders and suggesting to Julian how best to deal with the first influx of visitors. It seemed as if those moments were the most carefree and happy of her existence.

Then had come the news, just two days after he had seen her for the last time, waving to him from the front door.

His eyes smarted and he reached for a pocket handkerchief. Cecily, Maza, Marguerite, they had all gone leaving him with only memories.

And yet they were part of him, integral elements of his cosmic experience, and as such they would live on in him. Only when he too shut his eyes for the last time would they disappear finally from this Earth.

He pushed open the churchyard gate and crossed the village green. For a moment he walked towards the Hall, but turned and took a lane which gave onto the stables. From there he could reach the lake and the gazebo without anyone spotting him. He wanted to be alone with her for a while longer; alone along those flower borders she had helped create and which, in this late autumn, had faded away as she had.

He stopped walking and gazed at the great manor house, then across at the terraced gardens. With her gone, he felt a stranger there again, like he had the first time she had brought him to her home. He shivered as the cold wind blew around him. There was no more warmth at Chilton.

A.J.

Crete, Summer, 1972

A yacht was cruising the waters of the Mediterranean that summer, and on July 31st it anchored in a bay on the southern shore of the island of Crete.

The site was spectacular, with mountains climbing straight out of the sea to peaks two thousand feet up and a small fishermen's village perched precariously on a ridge with a series of steps carved in the rock, leading down to a wooden jetty, to which were moored a few fishing boats.

"What do you think of the place?" Julius Caspar asked the man sitting next to him on the deck. "I come here every year if I can. There's a kind of dynamic tranquillity between those mountains and the water which both exhilarates and relaxes. You'll see."

Edgar Monahue gazed about him and nodded slowly. "It's breathtaking. Makes one realize what ants we are and that all our battling for wealth and power means so damn little."

"I'm not sure I agree with you," Julius said after a moment's reflection, "this place doesn't make me feel small. On the contrary, it elates me."

"That's because you're a remarkable man, Mr Caspar. Which brings me to what I've been wanting to speak to you about. I don't know whether you're aware of it, but the President holds you in high esteem, as does the Secretary of State and one or two others close to the President." Edgar Monahue paused and glanced at his host who was staring at a seagull perched on the boat's funnel.

"It's kind of you to say so, Senator." The brown eyes swooped down and held his.

"They have asked me to approach you and ... well, to see if you could be persuaded to devote some of your time and energy, as well as your considerable influence, to a cause which we are sure is close to your heart."

He leant forward in his seat. "The Republican Party needs your help, Mr Caspar. Not for the coming elections, though your backing would be very helpful, but for the advice you could give and for the opportunity of using your expertise of Middle Eastern affairs in a practical way. There have been serious mistakes made by previous Administrations, even Republican ones, I have to admit. As you know Foster Dulles made an enemy out of Nasser when we could have had him as a friend. Nasser is dead and we don't want the same mistake with his successor. We want Anwar El Sadat to be and to remain our friend, and the President reckons this is of vital importance. Egypt is the most important country in the Middle East and we don't want it veering again into the Russian camp. So far relations with the Egyptian President are good, and we want them to stay that way. But above all we want peace in the whole of the Middle East. If there's a way to prevail upon Egypt and Israel to put down their arms and live like civilized peoples — which they are, or should be — we want to back it. You were born and bred in Egypt and you know the Middle East like the palm of your hand. What's more, you have large interests and friends in high places in the Lebanon, Syria, Jordan, Libya, as well as in Israel ... "

Julius nodded. "Yes, I do have a few friends there ... in Israel. You know, I admire the Jewish people and I have always understood their need for a homeland, especially where their roots are."

"Exactly, and that's why the President and the Senate's Foreign Relations Committee would welcome your aid. You have a foot in both camps and you have no axe to grind, so you'd be impartial. Also, you're an American ... "

"All this is very flattering, Senator, but I am not really a political animal ... "

"You don't have to be when you're serving the cause of humanity," Monahue replied quietly.

There was a moment's pause while the Senator stared up at the high cliffs and thought what a curious man this Julius Caspar was. Anyone else would have grabbed at the chance of being in cohorts with the White House and advising on the foreign policy of the most powerful state in the western world. He just didn't seem interested in using his immense influence for himself, at least not for political aspirations; his last words had made that clear.

"What has the President in mind I should do?" his host asked suddenly.

"To be a special envoy, an ambassador extraordinary of goodwill. The man who would constantly feel the pulse of the Middle East situation and tell Washington what action it should take, and why. Who, knowing the people in power and aware of the needs and aspirations both financial and political of these changing leaders, can guide the State Department through what otherwise is a morass of social, ethnic and political contradictions. Does that give you a picture?"

Julius nodded. "It does."

"And may I refer back to the President that he can count on your support?"

"Give me a few days to think it over. It's not that I don't want to, on the contrary, I'd be glad to be of service to humanity, as you put it. And to America, obviously. I have a moral debt to my adoptive country, and I would like to be of help to the President, if it is within my capacities. He was Vice-President when I was naturalized, so in a way I feel I owe it personally to him. No, it's simply that I want to be sure in my own mind that I can effectively be of assistance in the way you have just explained. Let's say I'll give you my answer when I get back to New York in nine days' time."

"I appreciate that, Mr Caspar. But believe me, you can help, and how."

"I hope so." Julius said, then changed the subject. "Do you like fishing? There's some great tuna fish swimming in these waters, and the chef would welcome not having to go to the market for our dinner!"

"That's one hell of a good idea. Deep sea fishing used to be a passion of mine, but these last years have been too packed with politics to leave me much time for it. Are you a keen fisherman too?"

Julius shook his head. "No, but I know someone who is. Young A.J. will jump at the opportunity. He's only twelve but he's a devil with the harpoon gun. Don't worry though, he won't go for your tunas, his objectives are squid. I'll get hold of him and have the motor boat ready in say half an hour. Is that O.K. by you? I'll also see whether any of the others want to go, but I doubt it. They're none too keen on exertion.

They'll manage the ladder down to the water, but that's about all. Ah, here's Maryanne. She'll organize A.J."

A.J. was down in the engine room watching the engineer fix a faulty gasket. It was his favourite spot on board, and when he was not swimming, or out with his harpoon searching for squid, one was sure to find him there.

On this particular cruise there were no other kids, and he was glad. It meant he didn't have to play with them. He was a loner. He had no real friend, nor anyone with whom he was close. It was in his nature not to need one, and he felt happier on his own or with complete strangers, preferably grown-ups, who didn't demand any emotional link. He was allergic to affection.

Only from his mother did he accept love. A love he distilled and returned in a form of devotion in which sentiment had little play. She was the only person he respected and from whom he took orders without a spirit of rebellion. Whoever else imposed obedience became an object of hate. And hate came with furious ease to A.J., accompanied by a will to destroy. In his imagination he had killed most of the beings who formed part of his young world; schoolmasters, the family doctor, door attendants, the dentist, as well as a horde of older boys, taxi drivers and hotel employees.

Few men or boys ever realized the murderous hate they provoked in him, since he seldom exteriorized his emotions. He would simply glare and say nothing. But sometimes he got relief by killing a guinea pig or a kitten, even his mother's canaries. He would do it cleverly so that no one would guess that the corpses were his responsibility. There were moments when he wondered if one day he could do the same to a person. The thought both fascinated him and scared him.

He heard his mother call him.

"Ah, there you are." She was peering from the door above, "do you want to go fishing with Senator Monahue?"

"You bet Mum. When's he wanting to go?" He was already scrambling up the steps. It wasn't often he got the opportunity to go out in the motor boat and swim around with his harpoon, and not constantly be told to mind what he was doing. Mostly the boat was used for water-skiing, and he wasn't wanted then.

"In about twenty minutes, so don't keep him waiting. And

whatever you do, don't start going for the fish he's after as you did with that other friend of uncle Julius, or you won't be asked again. Keep to squid and leave the tuna to the Senator. And remember, I prefer it to tuna."

He grinned. "O.K. Mum, I'll get you a whopper ... "

He ran along the deck and down to his cabin. He stripped, got into his bathing trunks and put on his goggles. Looking like a tadpole with his rubber fins already on his feet, he made his way to the rear deck where he kept his harpoon gun. Nearby two sailors were about to lower the motorboat into the sea.

"Hey, wait till I get in it," he shouted, climbing over the deck rail and jumping onto the boat's cushions.

"Stupid little bastard," one of the sailors muttered loudly, "he almost ripped the seat with his bloody harpoon!"

"So what!" the other answered, "start worrying when he gets it up his arse. If he slips while playing silly bugger, the shit's on us. The old man dotes on that brat."

They were speaking in French, thinking he couldn't understand. He did though, and a sudden rage mounted in him. He felt like shooting the harpoon right through the two of them. He grit his teeth and clenched his fists, swearing that he'd have his own back somehow.

One of the two deckhands lowered the gangway while the other, the redhead who had called him a brat, ran down it and hopped onto the motorboat.

"Move your bum, kid," he said as he stepped over to the driving seat and gave A.J. a slight shove with the palm of his hand.

"*Ta gueule toi!*" A.J. threw back at him.

"So you understand when I talk to you."

"You bet I do, every bloody word."

The redhead grinned unpleasantly. "Then make yourself useful and grab that rope. Don't let go of it till I tell you. Get a move on there!"

A.J. gave him a look of fury but did what he was told.

Edgar Monahue now appeared, followed by the other sailor who was carrying rods, fish-hooks and a canvas bag containing the rest of the fishing equipment. He smiled at A.J.

"Hello young man, coming fishing with me?"

A.J. nodded. "Yes, Senator." It was the way everyone seemed

to address the man, so he reckoned he would too. He reached for the bag he was holding.

"Thanks. Be careful with it, it's got bottles so we've got something to drink when the sun gets too hot. Put it under the bench in the shade."

The Senator sank into one of the seats and nodded to the deckhand that he was ready to go.

"I guess this should be good fun," he said to A.J., "I've been told you're pretty good with the harpoon ... let me have a look at it ... hmmm, a Grampion ... very neat, and bad news for your squid."

"I don't only go for them, but it's fun when they give out all that ink when they're hit. Kind of like you shot them in the heart. That gives me a kick. But I also go for ordinary fish if they come my way."

"As long as you keep away from whatever I get on the line, it's O.K. by me. Wow, here we go!"

The boat roared off towards the open sea, veered to the left past a slight promontory, and on to a vast bay where the coastline was softer and the mountains receded to leave space for low, gently sloping hills. Roughly two thirds of the way across the sailor slowed the boat, then brought it to a halt. He let it drift for a few minutes before throwing the anchor overboard.

He turned to A.J. "Tell him this is the best place to start at. The tuna come in shoals around here."

A.J. repeated what he had said and jumped into the water with his harpoon. The sailor watched him and shouted, "stay away from the boat. I don't want you scaring the fish away for the Senator."

A.J. pretended not to hear, but his blood was boiling. He adjusted his snorkel and swam off.

The sea wasn't deep and he could see the sandy bottom quite clearly.

Kicking the water gently with his fins, he floated around, searching for a prey. He wanted to shoot something special to show that bastard of a redhead that he wasn't the stupid kid he thought he was. Not just any old fish, not even a squid unless it was a giant one, the sort that could kill a man.

Suddenly a shoal of tuna shot past him and he pointed the gun in their direction. A dark shadow appeared a little to the left but he was too absorbed with his prey to notice it. And then, just before he actually pressed the trigger, there was a face in the place of the fish. A face he knew and loathed. His finger closed and the spear shot off. He saw the arms spread out as the body convulsed and a thick ribbon of redness curled through the water.

As he watched, a feeling of awe mixed with elation filled him. He took a deep breath and ducked low in the water, swimming rapidly to retrieve the harpoon. Just before he got to the man, he surfaced and looked about him. The boat was some fifteen metres away and the Senator was sitting with his back to him, immobile with a fishing rod between his knees. He dived and went right up to the dead sailor. The harpoon had transpierced the throat. He pulled at the long metal rod but the spear stuck, so he put his feet against the torso and tugged for all his worth. Still he couldn't free it. He knew then that he would have to use his knife.

He reached for it and started hacking at the neck. Blood now billowed out, enveloping the dead man in a gruesome opaqueness. And suddenly he was afraid, not for what he had done, but because he knew the blood would draw the sharks, and if he didn't get away, they would attack him too.

With a final slash he managed to cut through the muscle and free the harpoon. He swam as fast as he could to the boat, clambered up onto it, then looked back. The telltale fin of a shark was cutting the waters towards the dark patch a little way off.

Edgar Monahue glanced round. "Oh, it's you. Catch anything interesting?"

A.J. shook his head. "Thought I saw a shark's fin, so I came straight back. They can be dangerous. I ... I once saw what they did to a man ... ," he shivered, "tore him to pieces ... almost ripped off his head."

"You've been seeing too many T.V. horror films. Didn't you know that sharks only attack if they smell blood? Hey, something's bitten ... must be big from the way it's pulling ... give me a hand while I get properly into position ... I don't want it to give me the slip."

A.J. climbed over the seat to where Edgar Monahue was straining against the cushions.

"Here, hold the rod while I get the belt fastened," the senator said, "and whatever you do, don't let go of it ... grip it tight ... O.K., you can give it back to me ... it's a real fighter, this one … it'll lead us one hell of a dance … see if you can spot the sailor, I'll need him to help bring this baby aboard when I've reeled it in."

A.J. pretended to look around the water's surface. "Can't see him anywhere. Maybe he's diving for something." He sat down and began to tremble.

The senator glanced at him. "What's wrong kid? Don't tell me you're cold! Throw that towel over you."

A.J. didn't move but went on shivering. "It's those sharks, they really scare me. I hope … well that sailor doesn't get caught by them … "

"Jesus, it means business, this one. O.K. let's give it a bit of play before reeling it in good and proper. There now, that's about enough … trouble with you son, is that you fantasize too much. They were probably dolphins … I saw a couple just before you got back. Ah, I've got you now, mister, and you can fight as much as you like but I'm bringing you in. Get the hook ready, it's there under the seat. Hell, we'll have to manage on our own! O.K. now you hold yourself ready and when I've got it within striking distance shove the hook into it, just behind the gill."

Still trembling, A.J. reached for the fish hook. He climbed back over the seat and heard a slight thud as if something had bumped into the boat. He scrambled to the fore and stared into the water just below. The dead man's snorkel was tapping against the hull. And some ten metres out was floating a body, almost unrecognizable, with part of an arm missing and the head only attached to it by a piece of muscle.

"Senator," he cried in a hoarse whisper, "over there, look over there."

Edgar Monahue took no notice. "What are you up to? It's here that I need you, on this side. Quick, I've nearly got it!"

But as he saw that A.J. didn't move, he looked to where he was pointing. He tried to stand, but the belt held him. So he hurriedly fixed the fishing rod in the grip on the floor and clambered over next to A.J. He shielded his eyes from the glare, then gave a gasp.

"Oh God, no!" He put an arm round him as if to protect him, and drew him rapidly to the back of the boat.

"Cut the line," he said, slipping into the driving seat. He switched on the engine and then realized that the anchor was still down. So he went up fore again and began tugging it up.

The rope came, bringing the boat nearer the corpse as he pulled it in. Suddenly it stuck. He swore, gave three sharp jerks and nearly fell into the water. The body was almost within reaching distance and, stifling an urge to vomit, he shouted to A.J. to pass him a knife. He cut the anchor rope and the next instant was slamming the engine into reverse. Then they sped away, the throttle fully out, and raced across the bay.

Five minutes later they rounded the promontory and the yacht came into sight. As they approached it, Edgar Monahue slowed the boat.

"Can I leave you to tell them what has happened while I go back there with help?" he asked.

"Do you have to go back?"

"Of course I have to. You can't leave a man like that!"

"But he's dead. What's the point?"

The Senator stared at him and was about to answer, but shook his head.

"Forget it, kid. Just tell them what has happened. Can you manage that?"

"Sure," he replied, leaning over to catch the gangway. Then he jumped onto the lowest step and climbed up to the main deck.

"There's been an accident," shouted Monahue. "I need help. You two, come down here."

A couple of deckhands hurried down to the motorboat and a moment later it was speeding off again. A.J. watched them go and turned as a hand was laid on his shoulder.

"What's happened, for chrissake?" It was the skipper who had come out of the wheelhouse. "Where's Jean-Pierre?"

"If he's the bloke who came with us, he's dead. The sharks got at him."

The man gripped him by the arm. "What the hell d'you mean. If this is one of your stupid jokes ... "

"Let go of me," A.J. shouted. "They got him while the Senator was fishing."

"What the bloody hell was he doing in the water?"

"Let go of me, damn you. Why should I know? He was in it, that's all. I've got to tell uncle Julius, the Senator asked me to."

He slipped from the man's grasp and ran to the sitting room. It was empty. So he trotted along the passage to his grandfather's study, and was about to knock on the door when it was opened by one of the secretaries.

"Hello, A.J. what do you want?"

"I've got to speak to uncle Julius. It's terribly important, it's a message from the Senator."

"But you know he can't be disturbed when he's in here ..."

"What is it, Sheila?" Julius called.

"It's A.J., Mr Caspar. Says he has an important message for you from Senator Monahue."

A. J. pushed past the secretary and ran over to his grandfather.

"That sailor, uncle Julius, he got killed by a shark."

When he woke the next morning after an eleven hour dreamless sleep, A.J. didn't get up immediately, but stared through the porthole at the nearby cliffs. He curled on his side, thinking back to what had happened the day before, and smirked. He would mark it as a red letter day in his diary. August 15th. 1972. And red was for blood. He had actually done what he had so often daydreamed; killed a man he hated.

How many of his age could boast of that? Not that he was going to boast or even hint it to anyone, he wasn't crazy. It was his secret, and that was how it would stay. He wondered suddenly what it would be like to kill someone he didn't hate, in cold blood as it were. Would it give the same kick?

He threw the sheet off him and stared at his toes. It had been fun, all that coming and going of people from the mainland; it made the whole business seem terribly important. Only he wished he had been there when the body had been brought on board. He would have liked to see how much the sharks had eaten.

He swung his legs over the edge of the bed, stood up and stretched. It was great to think that only he knew what had really happened. It made him feel cleverer than all of them, more so even than uncle Julius, who was supposed to be terribly smart.

He ambled along to the bathroom and looked in the mirror. He grinned at his reflection. Jesus, was he hungry! He would have the lot for breakfast, cornflakes, eggs, bacon and sausages, masses of rolls with honey and marmalade ...

Forty eight hours later, after the police doctor had attested the accidental death, the next of kin had been informed, and arrangements made for the repatriation of the body by air to Nice, Julius ordered the skipper to head straight back to the South of France as he wanted personally to be present at the funeral.

Shortly after the yacht had steamed out of the bay, he took Maryanne and Edgar Monahue on deck, and pointed to an island silhouetted against the horizon.

"That's a place I'd like to own," he said, handing the Senator a pair of binoculars. "Do you see the outline of a building? It's the remains of a monastery. No one lives there now, but before the war it was inhabited by monks who left in 1941 and never went back."

"Why don't you buy it?" Maryanne asked.

"Because by Greek law no foreigner may own land on the coast."

"And there's no way round that?"

"Sure. I could get a Greek national to buy it for me. But I'd never do so. Far too risky. Instead, I'm negotiating with both the Government and the priests who own it to see if I could be allowed a long lease, say 25 years."

"Will you take us to visit it? It must be lovely."

"Lovely no, but there's something about the place which attracts me. Originally, way back in the 14th century, certain warrior priests apparently lived there, and maybe that explains the curious atmosphere."

"Don't tell me it's haunted!" she exclaimed.

Julius smiled. "Not in the way you mean. It's as if there's something impregnated in the soil, not hovering around. Maybe that's why the Franciscan monks who went there later didn't stay long. They probably didn't feel in harmony with the place."

"And you do, Julius?"

"Yes. Mind you, I'm not trying to say that I have anything in common with those pious warriors of six centuries ago, but I wouldn't mind absorbing a little of the strength they left behind, buried in the earth like a hidden treasure."

Senator Monahue chuckled

"Mr Caspar, the picture of you searching around for strength just doesn't convince me. Say rather that you want to realize a schoolboy dream and become a modern Count of Monte Cristo."

It was Julius turn to smile. "Maybe ... It's called Krinos, but you know what? It too was once known as the Island of Christos!"

Nelson and Jemima

George's children had been brought up in Paris under the supervision of their governess, Elizabeth von Wilder, hardly aware that the rather frightening man who appeared every now and then was their father.

Nelson grew into a good looking boy with his mother's features and his father's build. He was tall with fair hair, dark blue eyes and a sensitive mouth which tended to pout rather than smile. His character was neither George's nor Georgina's. Perhaps because he had lost his mother so young and seldom saw his father, he was often withdrawn as if scared of people. Only when he was with Elizabeth or other members of the household would the warm side of his nature appear.

Nelson adored Jemima and when she was a baby he was happy to play with her for hours.

Jemima loved Nelson too, but in a different way. He was her possession, like the woolly giraffe she went to sleep with or Bouboule, the giant panda almost as big as her, which suffered all kinds of torments when she dragged it about the apartment, gouged out its eyes, or unwound its arms. Only Nelson was better than a toy. He was her protector too. He was always there, ready to stand between her and a world which both fascinated and frightened her. People especially. Not Elizabeth, she was on her side like Nelson, as were Adèle the cook, and Janine the maid. But the person she called Papa, that huge man she sometimes bumped into when she rushed along the corridor frightened her, as did his friends.

Often she would have nightmares in which Papa was an ogre, a sort of bear with elephant tusks and the roar of a lion, and when that happened she would call out, and Nelson would come to her bed and take her in his arms. She always felt safe nestling against him.

Neither of them had any real friends. Sometimes, during the holidays in a rented villa or aboard a yacht there would be the children of their father's business associates who would appear for a week or two, then not be seen again. Nor were there relations of their ages, only their cousin A.J. whom they saw once a year at their grandmother's house in England. But they didn't like him much, and while they went to parties and had a few of the boys and girls from school back home from time to time, they never got close to any.

The only person Nelson loved outside the home circle was a fifty year old piano teacher, Stanislas Chav- chavetski, who could have known a brilliant career had he not had a weakness for vodka.

One afternoon he did not turn up for the lesson. It was not the first time, and Nelson reckoned he must have had a few too many again. Then came the phone call which gave him his first emotional shock. Stanislas had been knocked over by a car and had died on the way to a hospital.

It took two years for the affective void left by Stanislas to be filled, but this time it was by a youngster with no musical aptitudes and only three years older than him. Bruno, the cook's son, entered his and Jemima's lives.

Bruno Ragonetti was seventeen, and both physically and morally the opposite of Nelson. He was short and muscular and brimming with energy, with dark curly hair, cheeky eyes and a full mouth. The nose was slightly upturned and he had a large dimple in his chin. He wasn't good looking but was full of southern charm, and when he spoke, it was with the sing-song lilt of the Midi. Their friendship was immediate.

Bruno turned up one Saturday in July 1971 at the villa George had rented at Cap d'Antibes. His mother, Adèle, had suggested to Elizabeth that he could be useful taking Nelson and Jemima fishing and sailing since he had worked on a schooner and knew about boats. Elizabeth thought it an excellent idea and was delighted to see how quickly the two boys took to each other. Jemima also liked Bruno, and the three of them spent most of the summer there sailing, swimming and fishing together. Sometimes Elizabeth would join them and they would picnic on one of the islands in front of Cannes in the shade of the castle where the 'man in the iron mask' was supposed to have been imprisoned, or the boat would tack eastwards and sail past Nice to the bay of Villefranche where they would lunch at a restaurant in the picturesque port.

For two years, until Bruno went off to do his military

service, there was hardly a weekend when Nelson and he were not together. After the summer in the South of France, he turned up in Paris and made himself useful doing odd jobs around the apartment. Also Elizabeth used him as a chauffeur as soon as he had passed his driving licence, and sent him to do shopping or had him drive her around in the car at her disposal.

Sometimes he would take Nelson and Jemima to school, if the official chauffeur was otherwise employed, and return to collect them in the afternoon before having tea with them in the pantry. And as often as not, once Nelson had finished his homework and done his two hours of piano practice, the boys would have dinner in the kitchen and watch television, or listen to records in the box room which had been turned into a bedroom for Bruno who had become an integral part of the family.

Though not an athlete, Nelson was a reasonably good skier and every year he and Jemima spent their Christmas holidays at a French or Swiss skiing resort.

That year they went to Megève, and for once it was his turn to show Bruno what to do. Now 1m. 82, and looking a good two years more than his sixteen years, the psychological age gap between the two youngsters was gone. Also, slender and romantic looking, it was Nelson who now attracted more than a passing interest in the girls on the ski slopes.

Bruno teased him continually about it, but although he laughed and pretended to spur his friend into a first affair, giving him details of how to set about it and what to do once he had got the girl into bed, there was an element of jealousy in his attitude, as if he feared that he might lose some of his influence over Nelson.

The two of them shared a room at the hotel. One evening, while Nelson was soaking in a bath, Bruno stripped and got into it with him. It was the first time they had shared a bath but Nelson took it as quite natural. He wasn't even surprised when he felt his friend's foot press gently into his groin then his hand caress the inside of his thigh; only abashed that the intimacy was suddenly arousing him. To hide his confusion he made to get out of the bath but Bruno laughingly pushed him back.

"You'll do O.K. with your first lay if you know how to go about it. Want me to show you?"

247

Nelson closed his eyes as the tingling excitement between his legs became a burning. He felt his friend's body slither onto his and fingers encircle him. Then came the tearing pleasure which convulsed him with shudders as Bruno bit deep into his shoulder and grunted with gratification. Instinctively Nelson began moving against him again.

That night they slept in the same bed, and for the rest of his life Nelson was to be attracted to young men who reminded him of Bruno.

Jemima too fell for Bruno the moment she saw him. She loved his good humour and the way he was always inventing games for her and Nelson. Then, with puberty, her body changed and with it her feelings for him. She wanted to touch him and have his arm around her waist when she leant her head against his shoulder. Next came the desire to have her leg against his and his lips brush hers rather than her cheeks. That was when she began to dream about him and grow jealous if he and Nelson went off without her. The Christmas in Megève, when they spent so many evenings locked in their hotel bedroom, had been agony for her. She had felt unwanted by the two beings she loved most. So she had tried to separate them by telling Nelson that Bruno had been beastly to her, and Bruno that Nelson thought him a creep and only put up with him because there was no one else. But they had taken no notice, so she decided to wrench them apart by pulling Bruno to her. A girl at school had told her how.

"He's sexy, that chap who comes to collect you. What is he, the chauffeur?"

"No, he's a friend, a very good friend. He often stays at home and helps out by driving the car sometimes."

"Is he your boy friend? Do you go to bed with him?"

"No. He's Nelson's best friend."

"What's that got to do with it? If he slept at my house I can tell you it would be in my bed. What are you waiting for? He looks the sort who would be good at it. You're not still a virgin are you?"

Jemima hadn't answered.

"I suppose you are. You've got to start sometime, so why not with him? How old are you, sixteen?"

Jemima lied by fourteen months with a nod. Then she asked:

"But how do you get him to do it, I mean, if he doesn't want to?"

"Don't be stupid. No man 'doesn't want to'. They think about nothing else. Give yours a chance and he'll jump on you."

For three weeks Jemima waited for the opportunity to be alone with Bruno, and it came when Nelson caught a serious bout of bronchitis. That evening she went down to the room where he sometimes slept and let herself in. It was empty so she got into the bed and waited. Then she fell asleep.

Suddenly she woke to find Bruno staring down at her. He hadn't switched on the light, but the little room was lit from a lamp in the corridor.

"What are you doing here?" he whispered.

She was tempted to rush away but she remembered what the girl at school had told her. "Don't panic. Just take his hand and put it on your tit and you'll see, you won't have to speak or do anything more."

From a sexual point of view that first experience was a success. Bruno had an epidermic charisma and a sensuality above the average male, and the instinct and experience to make his partner enjoy his body to the full. Jemima was no exception, and before going back to her room she had knelt by him while he fell asleep, and laid her lips on the back of his neck. She was happy not so much because of the pleasure he had given her and would do so every night, but because he was hers now, more fully and completely than he could ever be with Nelson.

She got up, unlocked the door and silently let herself out. A few moments later she was stretching in a steaming hot bath. She had a wonderful feeling of sensual well-being. It had been as that girl had said, fantastic, and the thought that it could happen every night sent thrills of anticipation through her. But when Nelson got better, what then, she wondered? Perhaps she would tell him, or Bruno would. The shock came three nights later.

"You haven't any other girl, have you?" she asked as he lay on his back smoking. "You don't do this with anyone else, do you?"

"Not with another girl, no."

She turned on her tummy and looked into his eyes. "And what's that supposed to mean. That you have an older woman?" She giggled. "It's not Elizabeth, is it? Tell me, is it her? Honestly, I won't mind if it is. Go on, tell me."

"It's not Elizabeth and it's not any other woman."

"Then why insinuate that there is."

"I didn't insinuate anything. You just got it wrong."

"O.K. then you're mine and only mine. I don't share you with anyone."

He glanced up at the ceiling. "There's always Nelson."

"Yes, but that's different. You don't do what we do with him."

He didn't answer but stubbed out his cigarette and rolled on top of her. "And supposing we did, would it worry you?"

"Don't be silly."

"I'm not. It happens between boys, or didn't you know?"

"Yes, but they're different."

Later, when they lay in the dark side by side, she asked, "did you mean that about Nelson? Have you really ... really made love together?"

"Yes."

"Often?

"Uh-uh."

"Why? I mean, you're not queer, so why? Have you been with other boys?"

"Sure."

"And you like it as much as with a girl? As with me?"

He didn't answer immediately but reached for a packet of cigarettes and lit himself one. "It isn't a question of liking it more or less. I just get pleasure from screwing. Lots of youngsters masturbate, I don't. I need a body, and it doesn't really matter what sex, as long as I like the person, and feel that he or she likes me. I won't do it with anyone. There has to be an attraction of some sort. I've been to bed with strangers, but only if I feel there's a basic sympathy. I love you and I love Nelson. You're my best friends. It's natural that we should be attracted physically to each other. I suppose it happened first with Nelson because he's older. We didn't start till he was a man and could enjoy it properly. He told me that when I went away for military service he went with a woman, a girl friend of your father's on the yacht ... but I think he preferred me to her ... if you had been older, probably it would have been the other way round ... "

"You … you mean that you'll go on with him when he's better!"

"Probably. But don't worry, it won't change anything between us."

She had broken into sobs. Bruno wasn't hers as she had hoped, he was Nelson's too.

He took her in his arms and wiped her tears with the edge of a sheet. "What are you crying about? I promise you I won't even look at another girl while we're together. What more do you want?"

"I want you to promise that you won't, well, that you won't with Nelson."

He grinned. "I can't promise that, and I don't want to. What's bitten you? I thought you loved him. I thought you wanted to share everything with him. What difference does it make what he and I do. Don't you understand? The fact that you and I go to bed together doesn't make any difference to what I feel for Nelson or what he and I do. Now I come to think of it, he too will probably start making a song and dance about it when I tell him."

"But you're not going to, are you?" For some reason she couldn't explain to herself, she didn't want Nelson to know.

"Why not? But if you don't want me to, I won't. Does that make you happier?"

"Swear you won't. On your mother's head, swear you'll never tell him."

Suddenly the door was thrown open and her brother appeared.

"Hey Bruno … " he began, then his voice froze and, after what seemed an eternity, he turned and rushed away.

Bruno leapt off the bed and pulled on his jeans.

"Don't worry, I'll take care of him. Throw me my shirt, will you," and he raced after Nelson.

Jemima lay on the bed and stared at the ceiling. Oh God, she thought, what had she done … what would Nelson think…?

She got up slowly, went over to the washbasin and put her face under the cold water tap. She dried it, combed her hair and left the room. There was no one in the kitchen, but as she emerged into the hall above she came face to face with Elizabeth.

"Ah, there you are Jemima. Has Nelson told you?"

"No, what?" she answered absently.

"About your father, of course! He's getting married and he wants you here at 8 o'clock so that he can tell you on the phone himself."

She stared at Elizabeth. She didn't care what her father was up to, it was Nelson who mattered.

"Is he here, with you?" She ran to the sitting room and peered into it.

"Of course not. He's in New York ... "

She shook her head impatiently. "Nelson, I mean. Haven't you seen him?"

Elizabeth raised her eyebrows in surprise. "Yes, but then I think I heard him run out a few minutes ago. Is something wrong, Jemima?"

She didn't answer but hurried off to her bedroom. For a reason she couldn't explain, she was suddenly afraid. She threw herself on the bed and buried her face in the pillows. Oh God, she wished, let nothing happen to him. Then she turned on her side and drew her knees right up to her chest. Deep inside her she knew that her life would be different from then on.

New York, 1976

One day, when George was lunching at the Colony Restaurant with Roland Aschenberger, two women came in and sat at a table near theirs.

The banker got up and went over to greet them. The elder woman had a face which was vaguely familiar to George.

"Who are they?" he asked when Aschenberger returned.

"Clara Strapakis, the opera singer, and her daughter Paola. As you probably know, Clara is Peter Salvini's sister."

Of course, George thought, and he had heard her at the Festival Hall in London some five months earlier when she had given a charity recital.

"How does she fit into the Salvini outfit, financially I mean?"

"She doesn't really, she's a wealthy woman in her own right. You know that she's one of the world's top sopranos? She and her husband made a marvellous team; he was a first rate pianist and accompanied her at all her recitals, till he was killed in a car crash about three years ago. She's very close to her brother."

"And the daughter?"

"Paints with a certain success. I don't care much for what she does, but she seems to sell, and one or two critics have hailed her as an up and coming star in the naif movement. But whether that's due to talent or the fact that she's Caspar's goddaughter is debatable."

"Married?"

Aschenberger shook his head. "No."

George downed his glass of Chablis and reached for the bottle. "I'd like to meet them ... no, not now ... get them to come to a party at my house."

"O.K. I'll see what I can arrange. When?"

"Whenever it's suitable for them. Preferably next week ... and I'll ask other people round when I know they're coming. Does she live with her mother?"

"I wouldn't know, but I doubt it. Why?"

George ignored the query. He was observing the two women.

"She's Caspar's goddaughter, you say?"

"Yes. He has always considered Clara a sister, and I believe he provided for her as a kid. Her family was very poor and her elder brother was his best friend, or so the story goes. And as he had no family of his own, he kind of adopted the Salvini youngsters as soon as he was in a position to do so. That's why Peter Salvini is number two in the Caspar empire. He's one of the few that our friend trusts completely."

A thought crossed George's mind. Peter Salvini and his sister were probably the only two of Julius Caspar's entourage who had known him as a young man. Peter Salvini had worked for him in those early days, Aschenberger had told him, so there was a possibility he might know something of what happened when Antor Caspardian had bought the Christofides Shipping Agency. He, George, could not approach him, but if he played his cards right, he might be able to get Paola or her mother to probe for him.

The idea of using Paola Strapakis for anything more than helping him resolve the riddle of the Trust funds did not occur to George immediately. It was after meeting the young woman a week later that he decided he might cultivate her and develop a rapport which could be more than a passing one.

Paola was half Greek and half Italian. She had an oval face with hazel eyes beneath dark eyebrows, a nose which was a bit too long and a mouth a shade too wide. Her lips were full but needed lipstick to give them colour, and her skin was pale but thick grained. Yet it was a face with a touch of mystery.

She came round for drinks at George's brownstone house in 72nd. Street five days later. Some twenty other guests were sipping cocktails by the indoor swimming pool in the basement decorated like a tropical garden, with banana trees, cascades of red and pink bougainvillaea and yellow and white frangipane bushes.

George offered her a daiquiri and then asked if it would amuse her to see some of his modern paintings.

"Roland tells me you paint and I'd like to have your opinion," he said, taking her by the arm and guiding her up to the sitting room on the first floor. In one corner were stacked five naif paintings by Yugoslav painters which he had ordered his secretary to get for him the day before.

"Why did you buy them?" she asked bluntly. "Don't tell me you like this type of work."

"Believe it or not, I do."

"Then I will show you mine, which even if I say so myself, are incomparably better than those, which are coarse and probably produced by the dozen for the tourists in Dubrovnic."

He slipped an arm around her waist and pulled her to him.

"I'll take you up on that one day. But come upstairs with me. I find you very attractive. I want to make love to you."

It was a straightforward proposition and expressed with unusual civility for him. He had not said "I want to fuck you," which was his usual approach. Yet Paola was shocked.

"You must be out of your mind," she flung at him and left.

George would not have given her another thought, only it was not sex he really wanted from her but something more subtle and involving. So he sent her five dozen roses and a jade bibelot she had admired, and begged her to forgive his unpardonable behaviour.

For a man used to getting his own way with people immediately, he exercised unusual patience with Paola. Over a period of three months, whenever he was in New York, he accompanied her to art galleries, exhibitions and jazz sessions, and took her to lunch on Tuesdays or Fridays, the only days she accepted to eat out. They were her 'safe' days, she explained, when nothing malevolent was supposed to happen, according to a spiritual master she went to see twice a month. In her contrary way of seeing and living life, she added that it was probably all nonsense but one never could tell.

Then, as they were walking out of a private viewing of paintings by Croatian artists, she slipped her arm through his and whispered; "do you still want to make love to me?"

He was taken aback. "Sure, more than ever," he replied squeezing her to him, "let's go to my place."

She giggled. "Oh, I didn't mean now!"

"When then?" There was an edge of exasperation to his voice.

"Soon, when the time is right. I'm seeing my spiritual master tomorrow, and he'll tell me."

He laughed to hide his anger, and swore to himself that one day she'd pay for her stupidity.

She opened her eyes wide. "That wasn't meant to be funny.

Do you love me spiritually too? Sex is important, but if it's to work with me, first my psyche has to experience its orgasm."

She's totally nuts, he thought. "Of course, Paola, you must have realized I do."

"Then you'll marry me."

It was more an affirmation than a query, yet it demanded an answer and George took one of the fastest decisions of his life.

"If you'll have me, darling."

His words were prompted by the sudden perception of what marriage to Julius Caspar's only goddaughter could bring him.

Julius learned who Paola was going to marry while in hospital recovering from an operation for the removal of a tumour wedged between the cerebellum and the top part for his spinal cord. A tricky operation, which took seven hours but which finally rid him of the brain splitting headaches he had suffered for so long.

Maryanne was reading him telegrams from well-wishers when the phone rang. She reached for the receiver, listened for a moment, then placed her hand over the mouthpiece. "Paola's downstairs with her fiancé. She wants to bring him up and introduce him. Do you feel up to it?"

"Sure. I wonder who he is? Have you any idea?"

"None. The last I heard she was with a painter, but I never knew his name, and somehow I don't think it's him."

She stood up. "I'll leave them to you. She won't particularly want me around."

"No, don't go. I know you don't care for each other, but I'd rather you stayed."

She went to the window and looked down at the hospital's parking area while a young nurse came in and changed the flowers. A florist's van pulled into it and she wondered whether it was again delivering bouquets for Julius. She had lost count of how many had been received so far.

She turned as she heard footsteps and voices in the corridor. The next moment the door was pushed open and Paola came in. She ran over to Julius and kissed him.

"Uncle Julius," she cried in her husky voice, "I want you to meet the man I'm going to marry, George Christofides." And beckoning to George she added, "come on in darling, this is my godfather. But I'm sure you know each other."

There was a moment of silence while Julius, stunned, stared at George.

"Hello Mr Caspar, glad to see you're looking well."

Julius gave him a nod and looked at his goddaughter, forcing a smile.

"My very best wishes, Paola, I had no idea … "

"I know. No one had. That's what's so funny. Oh, hello Maryanne, I hadn't seen you. Do you know George?"

George was for a quick civil ceremony but Clara Strapakis had always dreamed of a full church wedding for her daughter. And Paola, mainly because the idea of being a traditional bride amused her, told George that it would be a religious ceremony or none at all. Clara had also hoped that the priest who would marry Paola would be her brother Francesco. So Julius sent his private jet to Eritrea to bring him to New York.

On the eve of the wedding, Julius was alone in the library of his Long Island home with Francesco, and the two men had spent an hour talking about the problems of the Mission and what could be done to help the drought hit inhabitants of the nearby villages, when Julius asked, "what do you think of Paola's fiancé?"

Francesco reflected a moment. "I suppose you mean what do I feel about him. A difficult question. I have never come across a man like him. The world in which I live is closer to nature and the elements than the one I have discovered in these last few days. The people who surround me have their passions, their absence of passion, their qualities and their defects, like all of us. But they are more clear cut. Your friend George is not clear cut, though he is forceful, obviously brilliant, and I would say very single-minded."

"But you don't like him?"

"Shall we say I don't understand him. Possibly, if I had the opportunity of getting to know him better, I would find elements of his character which I admired and liked … "

Julius nodded. "To put it bluntly, you don't approve of him as a husband for Paola."

"It isn't a question of approving. I just find it difficult to understand why he should want to marry Paola. Don't you?"

"Yes. By the way, why did you call him 'my friend' George? I hardly know him. He was once married to Maryanne's sister, but I have probably only come across him half a dozen times in my life. I had absolutely no idea that he even knew Paola till they came to the hospital to announce their engagement."

"I said it because I sensed that there was some kind of a link between you. Maybe it's the fact that he too comes from Alexandria, originally. Or am I mistaken?"

"Only in a certain sense. As you know he is Marguerite's son ... you remember that she married Roger Christofides ..."

"I remember well. It was a very difficult moment for you. Yet in the long run it proved a blessing for a lot of starving people, if that can be of comfort to you. Had you married Marguerite you wouldn't have been the man you are today. You would have made an excellent husband and father to the children you would have had, and your world would have been limited to them and your few friends. It's the fact that you had no family which made you the remarkable businessman you are, and allowed you to dedicate your fortune and your energies to other people. If you had had a son ... "

"I have one," Julius said quietly, "and a daughter, and grandchildren. Does that surprise or shock you?"

Francesco smiled. "No." He stared at the ceiling for a moment then stood up and went over to the fireplace and spread his hands out as if to gather the warmth in them. "If you've mentioned them to me I presume you would like to talk about them. It must be difficult, and a little sad, to have a family yet have to conceal the fact. Or is it a shared secret? If it is, it must be between you and your children. Pietro and Clara have never hinted to me over all these years that you had a family. Maybe it's a matter you have kept all to yourself. Yet something tells me that Maryanne knows you are her father."

Julius looked at him with surprise. "How did you guess?"

"She has your mother's eyes, Antor. I remember your mother very well, a wonderful woman. And, of course, she has a Caspardian streak in the forehead and shape of the mouth. Then, there is an intimacy and understanding between the two of you which jumps to the eye immediately. You are fortunate in having a daughter like her. She is strong, as your mother was, but in a different way."

Julius smiled, then stood up and went to the drinks tray. "A little more sherry?"

The priest accepted. "You know my weaknesses. But I will

have to be careful with the wine later on, or my liver will start making a nuisance of itself."

Julius filled their two glasses and walked over to his friend.

"There is something about George I want you to know. Something I have confided only to one person, who now is dead. It is a secret I have lived with for over forty years, but I want you to know it, for should I die I don't think it should die with me." He slipped his hand into the pocket of his jacket and brought out a piece of paper which he unfolded and handed to Francesco. "Read it, please," he said.

The priest took it and, putting on his glasses, read rapidly. When he had finished he sighed and a wan smile appeared on his lips.

"I suppose he has no knowledge of this?"

"None. No one has. Possibly his stepmother did, the girl Roger Christofides married a year or two after Marguerite's death. She was in Luxor that day when we became lovers and she was a good friend of hers. But she saw very little of George who was brought up by his grandmother."

"You never tried to see him when he was a child?"

"No. Helen Wirsa wouldn't have let me, and would have denied any paternity claim by me. Also, I must have rejected him subconsciously as being responsible for Marguerite's death. I wanted nothing to do with him emotionally. Your family took the place of the one I should have had. I only began to take an interest in him when I saw him, quite by chance one day, at the Alexandria Sporting Club. That was fifteen years later, and he was off to Europe the same day. As you know I was quite a rich man by then, and I decided to set up a Trust for him in Switzerland so that when he came of age he could be independent of his grandmother. It was the only gesture of parental responsibility I made towards him, but thanks to it he was able to develop into one of Europe's most successful businessmen. It's curious to think that, had I not received Marguerite's letter, he probably wouldn't have become the man he is today, and you and I would not be here talking to each other. You know, I didn't set eyes on him after that time at the Club till the day he married Georgina, Maryanne's sister. So you can imagine what I felt knowing that, by an incredible twist of fate, he had become his own sister's brother-in-law."

"It wasn't a twist of fate, as you put it, it was part of a

pattern. Like the fact that he is now to marry Paola. But we must pray that this pattern will not lead to tragedy."

"Why should it?"

Francesco ignored the question. "You were never a great one for prayer so I will do it for both of us. Only don't you think the time has come to tell George?"

"I don't know. There are moments when I feel I should, and then I say to myself that it has no sense now. Had I wanted to I should have a long time ago, and I'm not at all sure that it would please him. It could even make him bitter towards me. Also there's Maryanne to consider. She doesn't like him and remember, her son has been adopted by me. There is very little I could bring George now, I mean in the sense of a father. I think I will only tell him if something drastic happens; otherwise I'll leave it to you, once I'm dead. And in the meantime we'll pray, as you say, that this wedding will be a successful one. I would like to say happy but maybe that's asking too much. I'm thankful, though, that you're here to bless it. Somehow I feel it stands a better chance."

The marriage was celebrated at St. Mary Magdalene's, and although the two persons most concerned considered the whole affair a kind of charade, the ceremony was moving for Julius.

While he escorted Paola up the aisle, he thought back thirty years to that morning in Alexandria when he had given Clara to her husband, and he marvelled at the circumstances which had led him to be handing her daughter in marriage to his son with his dearest friend uniting them in wedlock. Certainly the ways of the Lord, as his mother would have said, were unexpected.

He stepped into the pew next to Clara as George took his place beside Paola, and looked at Jemima. She was one of the three bridesmaids. How like Marguerite she was with her chestnut hair and pale skin, and the blue velvet dress. It was a blue that the girl he had loved often wore. He glanced around the people near him. Everyone who had counted in his life, except Maza, was present either in person or through a child or grandchild. And though only he knew it, they were his family, and he would cherish and protect them. Even George. For Marguerite's sake he would try to get nearer him. And those children of his, from now on he would consider them as his own flesh and blood. Jemima especially. Maybe he could get A.J.

and them to become friends. They could be a happy and united family, his family, the one he had been cheated of, but which had grown and multiplied and was there to be loved if he wished.

As Francesco blessed the couple he closed his eyes and touched the cross beneath his shirt. He thought of his mother. How happy and proud she would have been if she could have seen them.

The wedding made Maryanne feel that shades of the past were catching up with her.

"It's as if he's broken his way into another family circle of mine," she confided to Michael Lauber. "I don't like it and I suspect his motives for marrying Paola."

"What does Julius think?"

"I don't really know. He was terribly taken aback to begin with, but now ... I suppose he's just accepted the situation. We haven't talked about it very much on the rare occasions we've been on our own. The curious thing is that Paola, who never saw much of her godfather, is constantly going out to Longhaven when he's there, and dragging George with her."

"You need a change Maryanne. It's not just George and his marriage which is bothering you, it's the whole set up. Get away from them all. Come with me to Mexico. I've got to go there on a mixture of business and pleasure next month, and if you came it would be all pleasure ... "

"Sounds lovely, but you know how busy I am," she murmured.

"Darling, in business no one is indispensable. Ask Julius. He'll tell you."

She did, and Julius said exactly what Michael had.

"He's right. You should take time off. Six months, a year. Forget about business, about me too. Go with Michael, he's good for you. And Maryanne, if I may say so, gentlemen are few and far between these days, and he's one."

"Then you think I should marry him?" It was not the first time they had discussed the subject, and his reply was always the same.

She went to Mexico for two weeks but it took her another three months to make up her mind.

It was not an easy decision. Apart from her business and philanthropic responsibilities centered in New York and Geneva, there was the problem of A.J. He didn't like Michael or his two sons, and when she told him she was thinking of getting married, he went into one of his icy furies and refused to speak to her for days.

And there were other factors involved. Michael was Jewish with a background culture very different from hers and certain political beliefs she found hard to accept. Also he was a Zionist, and while she had a great respect for Israel and sympathy for its peoples, she shared Julius' conviction that a rapprochement with the Palestinians and with its Arab neighbours was essential if some form of durable peace were to be established in the Middle East. That meant concessions, a word Michael would not tolerate.

Yet she realized that she had reached a moment in her life when she needed what until then she had never had, that constant love and presence of a husband and the warmth of a family nucleus. So on May 3rd 1976 she married Michael, quietly, in Washington. Only Julius and the bridegroom's sons were present. A.J. was away at school in Switzerland.

A.J. was 15 when he went to Le Rosay, the international college frequented by the sons of wealthy and famous parents of the so-called jet set.

He was not unhappy there, just bored. He made no friends the first year and showed little interest in studies or games.

Then Jean Horemi — 'Jeannot' to his intimates — appeared.

He was Lebanese, and the son of a cousin of Edouard, Maryanne's first husband. His father had been Minister of Agriculture and his brother was a militant in one of the Christian phalanges.

He fascinated A.J. with accounts of the civil war which had just broken out in the Lebanon, and he became his first and only friend.

That summer Jeannot invited A.J. to the Lebanon.

"Tell your mother she needn't worry, we'll be staying at our house on the beach at Saadyat, it's perfectly safe there. The trouble is only in Beirut. And we're well protected with Amin around. He makes sure there's an armed guard wherever we go."

Maryanne said no. She did not want her son in a country in the throes of a civil war, however well protected. But the following Easter Jeannot got his father to convince her that at Saadyat they ran no risk, and A.J. spent three weeks there and met two persons who were to alter his life. Amin, Jeannot's elder brother, and a young Druse girl called Najla, whose father managed the Horemi estate.

In Amin, A.J. discovered an idol, and in Najla, his first love. He only met her once when they toured the citrus plantation and then had tea together, but the way she had smiled at him made him want to return to the Lebanon as soon as he could.

Amin saw in him a possible recruit for his militia, and A.J. was thrilled by the thought of fighting alongside the 1 metre 80 mass of muscle who boasted of the men he had killed with his bare hands.

"If you want to fight for a cause and give the Palestinian bastards what they deserve, come and join us. Only get into shape. Turn these ribbons into muscles," he said gripping A.J.'s forearm, "we've no use for weaklings. No drinking or whoring either ... "

A.J. knew nothing about the various political and religious factions which were to reduce the paradise of the Mediterranean into a hell of death and rubble. He was not interested in the rights of the ones and the aspirations of the others. He saw only that Beirut was a city seething with violence, where a gun was a licence to kill. He couldn't wait to get back there.

To the gym master's surprise he took to jogging, doing press-ups and body building exercises, and spent hours at the rifle range. He even gave up the odd cigarette, and refused the customary glass of white wine at the local café. Milk became his staple drink.

"Don't tell me you're taking what Amin said seriously?" Jeannot asked. "He's nuts. He tries to talk all our friends into joining his outfit. I'd stay clear of him. I mean it, even if he is my brother."

A.J. said nothing. He was determined to get back to Beirut the day school broke up, and not only for the fighting. Amin would take him to the family plantation where he had met Najla. The Druse girl with her frank, hazel eyes was haunting his dreams.

He was now 18, but did not look the part of the commando he dreamed of being. He was of medium height with narrow shoulders and little muscle, despite his body building. Only his legs were well shaped and in curious contrast with the rest of him. He had dark crinkly hair and a nondescript face in which sloping eyebrows gave him a perpetually worried look. The mixture of Armenian, Greek, Italian, Copt and English blood had not resulted in a harmonious or striking physique. He had a face and body which seemed to belong to no particular race, and had somehow taken form in defiance of hereditary norms. He could have been mistaken for a native of any Mediterranean country, southern European or Arab, Israel included.

It was not until eighteen months later that he was able to get back to Beirut. Maryanne had taken him to New York with the idea of getting him into one of the Universities, but he managed to talk her into giving him a ticket to Eritrea so that he could spend a few months at Father Francesco's Mission where Jemima was. Then he simply changed the booking and flew to the Lebanon.

When he got there Amin Horemi was abroad buying arms for his militia, so he stayed for a few days with Jeannot in the family's apartment, awaiting his return. He wanted to go to their country estate to see Najla, but his friend told him she had left.

"Where's she gone?" he asked.

"Don't know. They're Druses, kind of Moslems, and I think pressure was put on them by the Palestinians to stop working for a family like ours ever since Amin took part in an attack on a bus full of them at Ain El Roumani a couple of years ago. It was one of the reasons my father sent me to a school abroad. He reckoned Beirut was getting dangerous for anyone who had connections with the Phalanges."

"But there doesn't seem to be any fighting for the moment.

I haven't heard a gun shot in three days." A certain disappointment was in A.J.'s voice.

"Don't worry, it won't be like this for long. Fighting can break out any moment, and when it does make sure you don't wander into the Moslem area."

"Why the hell did it all happen?" Antor asked. "I thought there'd been Christians and Moslems living happily side by side for years."

"Sure, but the problem came with the Palestinians. They started settling here when Palestine was handed over to the Jews. Then, when Israel defeated Egypt, Jordan and Syria, and took over the West Bank of the river Jordan, a whole lot more came. The last lot fled here when Arafat and his men were thrown out of Jordania by King Hussein after they'd tried to take over that country for themselves. Nobody really likes them as they're always causing trouble. If they hadn't come, Lebanon probably wouldn't be in the mess it's in."

"I get it," A.J. said, "and I see why Amin can't stand their guts. I'd feel the same. Jesus, if I was a Lebanese I'd want to eliminate the lot of them!"

"Come off it, you sound just like Amin. Father says only a handful are the real trouble makers. The rest are simply refugees without homes. But the net result is that the Moslems and the Christians now hate each other and so do even some of the rival Christian factions. It's a hell of a complicated problem, and getting rid of the Palestinians won't automatically put an end to the fighting."

"What d'you mean?"

"Ask Amin. He was ambushed and almost killed by rival Christians not long ago. It's pure luck he's still alive ... that, and the fact that his reflexes were quicker than theirs."

Amin Horemi arrived back ten days later, and A.J. immediately told him he wanted to join his militia and fight whoever he was ordered to.

"I don't care who they are. If they're your enemies they'll be mine."

"O.K. But what about your mother? She's not going to love us if she gets to know you're caught up in the war here."

"Why should she know? I'm not telling her."

"You've got to, or it's no deal, and you're on the first plane out."

A.J. thought fast. He could placate her with a lie, but it would have to be one Amin would go along with.

"Look, why don't you take me to a training camp for a few weeks like that I won't be mixed up in the fighting, and we can tell her I'm not in a danger zone. Please Amin, and I promise to leave whenever you say so."

Reluctantly, Amin agreed, and sent Maryanne a telegram saying that her son was with him in the country, and would be going back to America at the beginning of September.

For a month A.J. was put through intensive training at a camp in Southern Lebanon, fifty kilometres from Saadyat. The discipline was tough, but he endured it with masochistic fervour. The more his muscles ached and his pride was trampled on as he sweated in the July heat, the sweeter was the thought that soon he would be shattering the brains out of an enemy's skull. Also, his hands learnt how to kill with a quick blow on the neck, and his fingers to manipulate explosives and concoct bombs which could blast cars into twisted metal and tear the occupants apart as if they were putty.

During the third week of August, Amin Horemi suddenly called to collect him.

"Time you got out," he said tersely. "The Palestinians have moved into a village only seven kilometres away, so the Israelis will be bombing the area any moment. Get your things together; we leave in half an hour."

"Where are we going?" A.J. asked.

"I'm taking you to Saadyat."

A.J. stared at the man as he sprinted off towards a nearby hut. Saadyat meant being out of the action and confined to a well guarded house and a thirty metre stretch of beach. Some might consider that a slice of precarious paradise, but for him it spelt purgatory. He had no intention of being done out of the fighting for which he had trained so hard and which he reckoned Amin had promised him. Hell, he'd have to find a way to get him to take him to Beirut, or to somewhere other than the villa at Saadyat. Why not to the family plantation?

"Because in a week's time you and Jeannot are off to Europe, and I've promised my father to bring you back to him safe and sound," Amin replied as they sped away in his Jeep.

"But you promised me ... "

"I promised you nothing. You asked me a favour and,

because I needed my head examined, I agreed to let you train in one of our camps. You've had your fling at soldier playing, and now you're going back to school. I'm not getting landed with the responsibility of what happens to you. I couldn't care less what you do as long as I'm not involved."

A cold rage took hold of A.J.

"Let me get out," he said, " and then go to hell. You're not my keeper."

Amin took no notice and kept his eyes on the road. He accelerated instead of replying.

"Stop the bloody car, I want to get out." Antor's voice had risen to a shout.

"Shut up, you stupid shit. I've a good mind to take you straight to the airport and shove you on the first plane. And I will if you don't stop breaking my balls."

The admiration he had had for Amin was replaced by a murderous hate. He leant back in his seat, pretended to reach for something behind him and, as Amin slowed the Jeep to take a turning, gave him a vicious blow on the neck.

He grabbed hold of the steering wheel and wrenched back the handbrake, then flung open the driver's door and shoved Amin out.

He did not know whether he had killed him or knocked him unconscious, and did not care. He slipped into his seat, trod on the accelerator and sped off in the direction of Beirut.

Suddenly, he braked and reversed until he was level with the body on the roadside. He hopped out, rummaged through its pockets, found a wallet and pistol, then climbed back into the Jeep.

When he got to the outskirts of the capital, he abandoned the vehicle and walked to a bus stop. He decided to go to the American University in the Western section and then see what to do next. Someone would tell him of a pension, or a cheap hotel where to stay.

He opened the wallet and found it bursting with banknotes. It also had Amin's identity card, driving licence, and various credit cards. He grinned. Luck was with him, and something in his bones told him it was there to stay.

He slipped his hand inside the canvas bag resting on his knees and let his fingers caress the cold metal of the revolver. It would be his constant companion from then on.

Maryanne was at Chilton when she received the telegram.

Regret to inform you that your son has disappeared. I have contacted the American Embassy and every effort is being made to find him. He was last seen with my son Amin two days ago on his way to our house at Saadyat. Should he contact you kindly let me know through the Embassy if you cannot telephone Beirut. I will cable you as soon as I have news of him.
Michel Horemi.

Shocked, she lost no time in telexing Julius and phoning her husband in Washington. She knew that both of them would do everything to find A.J., Julius through his connections in the Middle East, and Michael with the C.I.A. and his friends in Israel. She wasn't as much worried as angry, after she had got over the initial shock. Angry with her son for having gone to Beirut, and with the Horemis for having welcomed him.

The next day Julius phoned her. He hadn't as yet any news of A.J. but he would be found, he assured her. Then he told her that Amin Horemi had been discovered lying in a coma on the side of a road, and his Jeep abandoned in the outskirts of Beirut.

"I'm afraid it looks as if A.J. has been taken as a hostage by a group of Palestinians. Which means that he's alive and not involved in an accident. I have been personally in touch with Arafat's right-hand man, and he has given me his word that if any of his men have the boy, he'll get him released and immediately flown to Geneva. We'll know more when Amin Horemi is able to talk; he'll certainly know who's responsible for it all, and once he tells us it won't be difficult to negotiate A.J.'s return."

He was through again to her a few hours later. "I have news at last. Amin Horemi regained consciousness two hours ago. A.J. hasn't been captured or kidnapped by the Palestinians."

"By whom then?"

"By no one. He knocked Amin unconscious and left him on the side of the road, and went off to Beirut with his Jeep which he abandoned on the outskirts of the city."

"You mean ... you mean A.J. did that! Attacked Amin, then disappeared without telling anyone?" she stuttered, torn between the joy of knowing that her son was alive, and the horror that he could have done such a thing.

"I'm afraid so. I've also discovered that for the last six weeks he's been at one of the Christian militia training camps."

"Doing what, for heaven's sake?"

"Being taught how to be a guerilla. That was Amin Horemi's responsibility, and he paid heavily for taking A.J. there. He's lucky not to be dead."

"But where's A.J. now?"

"We don't know yet. The main thing is that he's not in danger, and sooner or later one of our contacts will find him. Unfortunately, he probably has quite a bit of money with him. Amin Horemi's wallet was gone too and it was full of dollars and different currencies, which means he could go into hiding for some time, if he wants to."

"But, for heaven's sake, why should he do that?"

"Apparently he wanted to fight with the Christians. It was when young Horemi threatened to put him on the first plane to Geneva that he knocked him unconscious. We're hoping now that he'll try to contact the Phalangists, in which case they'll tell us immediately. Only he's no fool, even if he gets the craziest ideas. He knows that Horemi and his clique will give him the thrashing of his life when they get hold of him, so he'll probably keep clear of them. He could join one of the other factions — the Gemayels or the Chamouns who have little love for each other — anyone's guess is good. But we'll very quickly make contact with him, I promise you."

Contact was made, but not in the way expected. That same evening, while Michael and she were having a drink before dinner, she was called to the phone.

"Is that Mrs Langton, Mrs Maryanne Langton?"

"Yes ... only I'm Mrs Lauber now."

Whoever was calling ignored that. "I have a message for you, Mrs Langton. Your son wants you to know he's well, and that there's no reason for you to be concerned. Also, that you mustn't try to contact him. If you do, it could cause him trouble ... "

"Who are you?" Maryanne demanded. "Where is my son?"

"I'm a friend and I am only transmitting a message. Your son will contact you regularly, but he will not be going back to Switzerland. You must not worry, Mrs Langton ... "

"Listen to me. I've got to know where he is. If you won't tell me, I'll go to the Lebanon myself and stay there till I find him. And I have powerful connections who will make sure my son is found, wherever he is."

"We know that Mr Caspar is a very influential man, but that will make no difference. Nor will the efforts of the man you have married, Mrs Langton, even if he is in the pay of the Zionists."

The line went dead. She replaced the receiver slowly and stared at the portrait of the 4th Viscount Brentwick hanging above the phone in the hall. Then she sat down and burst into tears. God! she cried to herself, what had got hold of her son?

She felt an arm around her shoulders. "Maryanne, darling, what's the matter. What was the phone call about?"

Michael guided her back to the library and put a glass of whisky in her hand. "Drink it and then tell me what upset you."

When she had given him the gist of the conversation, he was pensive for a moment. "Didn't he make any other remarks which might have given a clue to his identity. He was Lebanese, I presume?"

"I suppose so. He did say something which was odd though. He said you were in the pay of the Zionists. Why?"

"You're quite certain that was what he said?"

"Absolutely."

"Then A.J. is in with a group of Palestinians and not Christian Lebanese. Only one of them would make that sort of remark."

A.J.'s eyes never left Najla's face. She was so beautiful, he thought, with her hair drawn back in a short pigtail, her moss coloured eyes flashing with intelligence, her small nostrils flaring occasionally as her lips enveloped words he couldn't understand.

She was leaning forward in her chair and talking with three men. He knew that he was the subject of the discussion, as every now and then she would nod in his direction and one or other of them would glance at him. He wasn't worried about the outcome of the meeting; Najla had told him that she would convince them to accept him in their group, and he sensed that she was succeeding. Their attitude towards him wasn't hostile anymore, and one of them even chuckled as his name was mentioned.

270

"It won't be easy," she said, the day after she had taken him to visit the Palestinian refugees at Sabra. "They are suspicious of everyone, and rightly. The entire world has betrayed them. Also you are an American, and the Americans are the friends of Israel and the enemies of the Palestinian people. You are a friend of the Horemis and your mother is the wife of a Jew. Amin Horemi has killed many Palestinians, but I know that you are not like them, and they will believe me."

By an extraordinary stroke of luck he had bumped into her in Ras Beirut near the University.

She had recognized him but, as she admitted later, had tried not to show it immediately.

"I didn't expect to see you there and we hardly knew each other. Also you were a friend of the Horemis and that meant you were hostile to our cause."

"I thought you were all good friends. Hadn't your father worked for the family for years? Jeannot told me that you had all grown up together, and Amin ... "

She frowned and her eyes darkened with sudden anger. "Don't mention his name to me. He's the reason we had to leave the Horemis' estate. Don't you know that he has personally killed dozens of helpless people? Women and children too ... "

"What would you say if you heard he was dead, murdered."

"I'd pray to Allah that it were true, and I'd kiss the man who killed him."

They were sitting at a table on the terrace of a tea-room sipping lemonades. He ran his finger around the rim of his glass and, without looking at her, said, "I did yesterday ... kill him. I'm telling you because I trust you, Najla. You won't give me away to the police or anyone?"

"You're not joking?" She was leaning forward and there was a sudden urgency in her voice. He looked up and saw that her eyes were wide open and shining now, while her lips were parted, ready to stretch into an excited smile.

"No, I swear to you it's true."

When he had told her how it had happened and that he was now looking for somewhere to hide, she stood up suddenly. "Wait for me, I must phone. Perhaps I can help you."

She was back in a few moments. "You have some money?" she asked.

He nodded.

"Then there's a pension you can stay at for a few days where no questions will be asked, while I speak to some friends and see whether they'll accept you with them. But first I want you to come with me. There is something I want to show you ... "

She hailed a taxi and told the driver to take them to Sabra. "Where are we going?" he asked.

"I want you to see with your own eyes and feel with the pores of your being the tragedy of a people without a homeland. They have the right like every human to a country and a home. No one can realize the hell they have suffered since they were deprived of what was historically and rightfully theirs. Israel and the Imperialist powers are responsible for what you are going to see, and the cause which I and my friends fight for is the cause of the just, the cause of a people forgotten and disinherited ... "

Antor wasn't listening to her. He was conscious only that this wonderful girl was at his side, her knee at times touching his, and the warmth of her breath occasionally caressing his neck when she leant towards him. And the admiration in her eyes made him feel great.

She took him to meet people at the 'camp', mostly women surrounded by toddlers and old men. One or two of them spoke a smattering of English learnt when Palestine was under British mandate, but on the whole they answered her in Arabic, and she translated their fears and laments and occasional cries of vengeance in her quietly precise French.

Later, she went with him to the pension and told the owner to serve him dinner in his room.

"It's better you don't go out to a restaurant," she warned, "the police might be looking for you. I'll come here at ten tomorrow morning, and I'll tell you what I've been able to arrange with my friends." Then she smiled and her fingers went up to his cheek. "Let the beard grow, it will suit you, and make it more difficult for anyone to recognize you ... "

Suddenly, she leant forward and kissed him lightly on the lips.

"That's for killing Amin," she whispered and left.

Now she turned away from the three men and said, "Amin isn't dead. An army patrol found him and took him to a hospital. He's in a coma but they expect him to live. Which means that when he regains consciousness everyone will know that it was you who attacked him. I have told my friends here that you weren't his friend and you tried to kill him because you despised him for what he has done to the Palestinians. I have convinced them that you want to fight for their cause. That is so, isn't it?"

He grinned and nodded. "I'll do whatever you want, Najla."

He was excited again. These men were extremists and trained to kill. He didn't care about what motivated their activities, or whether their cause was a valid or criminal one. He wasn't interested in the political, religious or ethnic squabbles which had resulted in the savage tearing apart of this once peaceful country. What he wanted was to have his finger press a trigger and know that he had the power to quench the life out of a man as easily as he could squash a mosquito. That, and to keep Najla's eyes shining with admiration.

Paris, 1977

On the first day of Spring 1977, Jemima celebrated her 18th. birthday. Yet in spite of the presents she had received which included a Triumph roadster and one of her father's racehorses, she wasn't excited or happy.

She awoke and a feeling of jadedness gripped her as she remembered that it was the day a ball was being thrown for her. How she wished she could have been left in peace and not forced to face crowds of well-wishers she didn't give a damn about. But her father was like that. He wanted to parade and exhibit her to his connections. And she had no illusions. It was not for love of her that he was splashing all that money on the dinner and dance at the Ritz Hotel. It was to impress the 300 carefully chosen guests with his bloody wealth. That was all that counted for him, she thought bitterly, and any occasion was good.

There was a knock on the door and a maid appeared with a breakfast tray.

"Good morning Mademoiselle, and happy birthday. Madame said I was to wake you and serve you breakfast in bed today."

"Thanks, Anne, but I don't want any. You can take it away."

"Not even a cup of coffee? Anyway, I believe there's a present under the cover."

She placed the tray on a bedside table and then went to draw the curtains.

"No, for God's sake don't open them," Jemima cried, "I've a hell of a head. What time is it?"

"Just after nine. Do you want me to pour you the coffee?"

"Please. But prepare me a bath, will you, and make it hot, I'm freezing."

She reached to the tray and looked to see what was under the silver cover. A pearl necklace with card. 'Many happy returns of the day, with love. Paola'.

Stupid sort of present, she thought, she'd never wear it. Well, perhaps just for the ball. After that she could flog it and give Nelson the money.

Poor Nelson. Their father had been terrible with him. Kicked him out and virtually disinherited him just because he had pinched some of Paola's jewels to pay for the drugs he couldn't do without. And because he was gay. When George had found out that he was having an affair with a Portuguese waiter at the nightclub where he played the piano, he had gone into a rage, and told him never to show his face at home again.

Jemima shuddered. It had been terrible, and she had felt guilty in a way, as Nelson had taken to drugs after discovering that Bruno and she were going to bed together. And Bruno had put him on to them.

What a bastard he had turned out to be, trading on their love and friendship. Yet God, how she missed him...

The maid put her head round the door. "Your bath is ready, Mademoiselle."

She gulped down her coffee and slipped out of bed. She would have to hurry if she wanted to see Nelson. At 12.30 the lunch guests would start arriving and she had to be back for them. Also, she would have to wheedle some money out of her father to take to him. At least that should not be too difficult today, she thought.

She was in luck. She got two cheques. One from Julius Caspar, which came with a huge bouquet of 60 pink roses and a note which said "Forgive the lack of originality, but like this you can get yourself something you really want," and another from her father.

She threw her arms around him and kissed him, something she had not done for a very long time.

"Thanks Papa, you're great!" But the kiss and thanks were not really for him.

She went straight to the bank, paid in the two cheques and drew out cash. Then she hailed a taxi and went to an old building near the Gare de l'Est. She climbed to the fifth landing and rang a doorbell.

"How is he?" she asked the man who opened the door.

"Quiet for the moment, but in a couple of hours he'll need a shot. Have you got any, or some money? I'm sorry, I've none left."

She nodded and handed him the envelope with the banknotes.

"Try to make it last a week ... I'll bring more, of course..."
She did not like him, but at least he was devoted to Nelson.

She ran across to the bedroom which was cold with stains of dampness on the walls. Her brother was lying on the bed, fully dressed and wrapped in a duffle coat. He had three days beard and dark circles under his eyes and he was so thin his cheeks had caved in.

"Hello," he murmured, attempting to smile. "I was hoping you'd come. Many happy returns and all that..."

"Oh, shut up. It's a day I hope will never return. The only good thing about it is that from now on I'll be getting a decent allowance, so I'll be able to help you more."

"What would I do without my little sister? But at times I wish ... well ... that I had the strength to finish with it all. At least you wouldn't have to bother about me any more ... "

"Oh don't start on that again," she pleaded.

He looked away and asked, "what's happening today? The usual family lunch with heaps of guests and presents? Sorry, I didn't get you one ... what have you had so far?"

She told him, and chatted until Rodriguez got back, then she leant over and kissed him. He smelt of stale sweat. "I must go now."

"Have fun tonight. I should have got myself taken on as a pianist with the orchestra ... no one would have recognized me," he said as she walked from the room. She forced a grin, waved to his friend in the kitchen and let herself out. She drew her coat tightly around her and ran quickly down the stairs.

God! she thought. Was it really possible that her brother, the son of one of Europe's richest men, could be lying like that in a miserable little flat, with hardly any money and only a overworked waiter to help him and keep him company. She had to do something about it. She couldn't let him waste away like that. But who could she turn to without her father knowing?

Then she had an idea. Yes, he certainly would help, only she would have to see him and explain it all; phoning wouldn't be enough. With luck he might be in Geneva where Paola had said he owned a bank. If so she could catch a train and be there in a matter of hours. She could even go tomorrow.

That day she had little opportunity to think about Julius Caspar. Back at the apartment she had just time to change before a series of guests started arriving for lunch.

In his usual manner, George had decided to make his daughter's 18th birthday one of the most talked about social events of the Paris season. Forty leading industrialists, politicians and bankers with their wives toasted her on the terrace overlooking the Invalides and speculated on who amongst the eligible young men would be lucky enough to marry the beautiful young heiress. And no sooner had they gone than she had to get ready for the ball at the Ritz Hotel where three hundred guests, including the Presidential couple, Princess Margaret, members of the European royal families, famous actors and film producers, and leading socialites from London, Paris, New York and Madrid would dance until the early hours of the morning.

Jemima hated every moment of it; the people, the music, the ambience and the blue Guy Laroche dress specially designed for her. She hated her father too that evening for the way he had treated Nelson. She even hated herself for being there and not having the courage to yell to everyone what a heartless bastard he was. She spent a lot of time hiding in a lavatory and pretending not to feel well, and the rest looking petulant and refusing to dance. Nelson's emaciated features kept appearing on each of the faces around her.

Julius stared at Jemima. He was only half listening to what she was saying, while his eyes focused this memory which had somehow become incarnate. She had Marguerite's features, the same hair and colouring, and her identical figure. Only the expression in her eyes was different, and the way she moved; the voice too, he realized, when he began to be conscious of it. It was lower pitched than Marguerite's, and her French was Parisian, and not Alexandrian.

Then he came to grips with what she was saying.

"He needs help, and what I can do isn't enough. Papa doesn't want to hear about him and he won't give a penny, and Paola can't do much either, he won't let her. But he'll die if something isn't done, I know he will. That's why I thought of you. Please, do you think you could ... I mean, perhaps you might be able to talk to Papa, or do something so that Nelson isn't left like that … " The voice trailed off and he saw that her hands were nervously twisting a silk scarf she had pulled from around her neck while she was talking.

He leant forward and took them in his. For a moment he said nothing but smiled gently at her. At the intensity of his gaze she looked away, almost as if she were suddenly trapped and sought a way of escape.

"Don't you think you'd better tell me the whole story? What's wrong with Nelson and why won't your father help? And then I'll decide what should be done. But don't worry, I'm your friend … you were right to come to me."

She told him in fragmented phrases, and when she had finished she began to cry. He let her, slipping his arm around her shoulders until the sobbing ceased. Then he handed her his handkerchief and went over to the window and looked out at the tranquil waters of the lake.

What had gone wrong, he wondered? What had pushed this other grandson of his to despair and self-destruction? It was absurd. While he spent millions helping total strangers, his own flesh and blood was reduced to abject misery without him even knowing it. Nelson a junkie, existing only for the twice daily shots of a vicious and deadly drug!

A flood of impotent rage surged through him. He flung open the window and breathed in deeply the chilly afternoon air. His eyes travelled to the distant snowy peaks, and slowly the fury ebbed as her words echoed in his ears.

"He needs help … I give him what I can but it's not enough … he's so thin and ill … it's terrible … I don't know what to do … no one really understands. It's more than a year now … please, can you do something … I don't know who else to turn to … Aunt Maryanne's the only other person, but she never comes to Paris and I don't know how to contact her."

"You were right to come to me. I only wish you had sooner," he said softly. "Tomorrow you and I will go to Paris and you'll take me to Nelson. I will make sure that he is properly looked after, I promise you. You and he are part of my family now. I consider you like grandchildren, Jemima. I want you to trust and confide in me as you would a grandfather, a friend too. Do you promise to do that?"

She nodded through her tears.

How fragile she was, he thought. How like Marguerite.

Thank God that at least she had not fallen prey to the drugs which were destroying her brother. He would protect her. Nothing and no one would harm her. Who else had he to cherish and care for now?

Krinos, 1977

Julius had secured a 25 year lease on the island of Krinos in 1975, but due to the fact that everything had to be brought over from the mainland, work had taken longer than expected. So it was not until the spring of 1977 that he was able to spend five days there with Maryanne and her husband Michael.

He had entrusted the restoration to a Greek architect, who had done an excellent job, respecting the Venetian and Turkish influences which marked many of the buildings on the mainland. Julius was delighted.

"I never expected it to turn out as well as it has," he confided to Maryanne. "There's something about it which makes me want to spend time here and forget about the rest of the world. Or do you think it's old age creeping on? Come for a walk, and I'll show you what I'm thinking of doing with the monastery itself."

They crossed a large, stone flagged terrace in front of the house, walked past a magnificently gnarled old olive tree, and down to a small vineyard.

"It was in total abandon, but I'm assured that next year we'll have a hundred or so bottles of what'll probably be undrinkable wine. Apparently the vines stretched quite a way beyond over to the left there, but the broom got the better of them. Isn't it beautiful!"

Maryanne breathed in the fragrance of the yellow broom which was in early flower.

"Do you remember that when I said the island must be beautiful, the first time I saw it from the yacht, you said 'no it isn't, but there's something which attracts me' ... "

"Uh-huh. Only then a whole team of people hadn't been working to make it into what you see now. There was hardly a tree and most of the wild cypresses — one could see the stubs of their trunks over on that slope — had been cut down for firewood by men from the mainland or from Gavdhos, that's the island on the horizon. So I had a hundred replanted, together with the chestnut trees and pines. When I first came it was barren with only shrub oak, yellow broom, old olive trees and a fig tree here and there. There were wild roses which we had to pull up, but I've had a proper rose garden planted where the monks grew vegetables in front of the monastery. I'll take you there now."

Work was well under way on the long, one storey building.

The crumbling walls and gaping floors had been repaired and the chapel, which for some reason had remained intact, was almost terminated. Inside it, on a ladder near the altar, was a man putting finishing touches to a fresco.

"This is Domenicos Theotocopulos who comes from the same family as his famous predecessor, El Greco, and has almost as much talent. Isn't it magnificent, Maryanne?"

She gazed at the Madonna and Child in wonder. "Did you paint it?"

"I have only restored what some genius once painted, Madame."

"Stop trying to be modest, Domenicos, it's not like you. There was virtually nothing left of the original frescos, and what there was had to be removed as it was too badly damaged by dampness and hardly worth keeping. Regrettably, El Greco didn't come to practice his brushwork here before going off to Venice."

"I hadn't realized he was Cretan," Maryanne said, "I thought he came from Greece."

"He was born at Irakklion, Madame, or Candia as it was known, at a time when Crete was a Venetian possession, which was fortunate for him as he was able to go to the Serenissima and study under Titian, and learn from Tintoretto and the younger Bassano. He didn't move to Spain till he was thirty ... "

Domenicos went on giving details of his namesake's life coupled with an outline of Cretan history. "It is probably the island which has known more conquerors and internal strife than any in the history of the Mediterranean. And to think that once it was a formidable power which rivalled ancient Egypt and Greece in civilization and splendour! But in the last two thousand years it has changed hands ten times — eleven if one counts the German occupation during the last war — and religion has anchored a bitter enmity between its own people. Now it seems quiet and peaceful, and yet the distrust for the Moslems still lingers on."

"Curiously this island remained in the hands of the monks even when Crete fell under Turkish dominion in the middle of the 17th century," Julius told Maryanne as they emerged from the chapel, "and perhaps that explains the feeling of serenity and strength there is about the place. Yet life can't have been a bed of roses for whoever lived here. You see that well," he said, pointing to a corner of the building, "it gives onto a large underground cistern which collected the rainwater from off the roofs. That was the only source of water, and if it didn't rain and it dried up, they couldn't wash or even water the vegetables."

"You mean the island hasn't any fresh water at all?" Michael asked.

"None, until we drilled an artesian well. Had to go down forty metres below sea level to get a good supply. Otherwise, it meant bringing it by boat, and that was a non-starter. I got the well dug even before I signed the contract for the place. But come and have a look at the monastery itself. I've told Dimitri to restore it exactly as it was. The only concession to modern living is that a few of the cells have been turned into bathrooms. I don't know whether one can see much for the moment, but at least you'll get an idea of what it was like once."

They wandered around the ground floor which housed the huge refectory, the kitchen and storerooms.

"It's enormous," Maryanne exclaimed. "What are you going to do with it once it's ready?"

"I haven't made up my mind yet ... "

Julius was to do so only a week later when he stopped in Geneva on his way to New York. What Jemima told him about Nelson decided him. He would turn it into a home where drug addicts would have the chance to get over their problems, well away from the peddlers and other junkies; where they could learn to live again and get the strength to face the world.

That same day he flew to Paris with her, and got her to take him straight to Nelson.

He was shocked by his grandson's condition, but didn't let

it show. He sat on the edge of Nelson's bed and put a hand on his shoulder.

"Jemima told me you weren't well, and that's why I'm here. You're going to let me take you to see a doctor ..."

"I don't want to see anyone. There's nothing wrong with me. And why should you care? Leave me alone for Chrissake. Why the hell did you bring him here, Jemima?"

The petulance of his early years had returned.

"It's natural I should care. I was a close friend of your grandmother, and your aunt Maryanne is like a daughter for me. Also, I heard you playing the piano at Chilton. I'm no musician, but I can detect talent when it's there. You've got a great gift and you've no right to neglect it." Julius was speaking quietly, but his voice had a note of command in it. "So you're going to do what I tell you. I know what's wrong with you. It won't be easy to get well but you'll manage it. Now you're going to get up and follow me. I'm taking you to a clinic where they'll know how to look after you and make you healthy again."

"I can't just walk out like that," Nelson tried to object, "there's my friend to consider ... "

"He'll be O.K., I'll see to that. And if he's a real friend, he'll be glad to know you're in proper hands."

Nelson gave up the struggle. He had never been a fighter, and there was something more in the man's attitude than just authority. In the eyes which held his was the understanding and affection he had never had from his father.

Nelson spent three months in a clinic near Lausanne, and when he had got over the worst, Julius had him flown to Krinos. There, with the quiet and the sun, the swimming and the walks, he rapidly regained health. He put on weight and got a tan, and his good looks returned. But there was a despondency which nothing seemed to get rid of. Julius had a grand piano shipped over so that he could find himself again through his music, but Nelson refused even to open the keyboard. One day he wandered into the chapel and stayed a while, watching the painter at work.

"It's beautiful," he said, "I wish I could paint like you."

"If you want, I'll try to teach you. But from what I hear, you would do better to stick to piano playing."

"I've finished with that. It's part of the past ... "

"The past? Sounds funny to hear a young man like you speak of his past. I'm sixty-two and I don't really feel I've had a past yet ... but if you want, I'll teach you what I can."

So, for a month Nelson spent three or four hours a day watching Domenicos paint, helping him mix the colours, and even trying to sketch him.

One evening he asked the painter to the house for dinner. When they had finished eating, Domenicos took a glass of wine, sat himself in an armchair and lit a thin cigar.

"That was a very pleasant dinner, my young friend. Thank you, it is a long time since I have enjoyed myself so much. But to make this evening really perfect, may I ask you one great favour?"

"Of course, Domenicos. Anything you like."

"Then play something for me. I long for some music."

Nelson's face clouded. He shook his head slightly. "Don't ask me that ... if you want some music I'll put on a cassette; there are a whole lot of them ... "

"I don't want to hear other people's playing," Domenicos answered leaning forward in his chair, and pointing his cigar at Nelson, "I want to hear you. It's not asking much, and you promised ... "

"Oh, O.K.," Nelson said shrugging his shoulders, "but you'll be disappointed. I haven't touched a piano for months ... I wish you wouldn't insist, I really don't feel like it." But he was moving over to the piano. He opened the keyboard and let his fingers run silently over the notes.

"Have you any preference?" he asked, sitting on the stool, "Chopin, Mozart, Debussy?"

"Chopin, I'd love that."

He reflected a moment, tested the piano with part of a Lizst étude, then plunged into a nocturne. Half way through it he stopped suddenly and stared at his hands. "God, that was terrible ... "

"I thought it was wonderful," the painter said quietly, his eyes shining with admiration, "go on, don't stop like that."

"I massacred it ... a beginner would have played better ... it's my fingers ... somehow they won't do what I want them to." But he began playing again, this time a Polonaise.

When he had finished he fished in a pocket for a handkerchief and mopped his brow. He glanced at Domenicos.

"That was a bit better, admittedly it was a piece I used to play a lot ... let's try a spot of Schumann."

After that there was no stopping him. He went on for four hours, and the following morning he didn't go round to the chapel until almost midday.

"I'm sorry, I'm late. I've been practising a bit, trying to get the rust out of the joints. I thought of sketching you at work today, what do you think? Won't be easy but ... "

"Listen to me, Nelson. Just stick to your piano. You'll be a great pianist, but you're the lousiest painter I've come across. You've got a rare gift in those fingers of yours, so get them working again and show the world what you can do. I'll miss not having you around, but it would be a crime to keep you from that keyboard. In any case, I'll have finished here in a week and will be going back home, so what do you say to a swim now and a glass of wine afterwards with some white cheese and olives before we both get down to work again?"

When Julius arrived a week later he had the piano transferred to one of the rooms at the monastery. Nelson was practising eight hours a day and was so totally absorbed by his music that a servant had to call him to the house for meals, or he would have forgotten to eat. The ravages which the drugtaking had wreaked on his body had gone, and even psychologically he appeared to have overcome the ordeal. Yet Julius didn't want him to leave the island.

"You've a couple of years to catch up on, and this is the best place to do it. I've been on to the Academy of Music in Athens, and they have a first class teacher who is prepared to come here every weekend and coach you. Oh, and he has a daughter who's a flute player. She'll be coming with him, like that you'll have a spot of young company."

Julius was well aware that Nelson wasn't much interested in girls, but he hoped that the appearance of an attractive and gifted one at a moment when the young man was ripe for an affair both physically and sentimentally, might have the desired effect. He had seen the girl and sensed a strong yet harnessed sensuality in her. If she were attracted by Nelson she could well make him her lover. He needed a woman to help him forget what he had been through.

Nelson was happy to stay on. Krinos had become his home and he felt at peace with himself there. Gone were the fears and complexes which had pushed him onto drugs, as were the depressions which had followed his disintoxication. The piano had seen to that. Julius found himself becoming fond of him and the affection was reciprocated. Nelson discovered in this enigmatic friend of the family the father he felt he had never had.

Work on the monastery was terminated in September and immediately the first patients began arriving. Nelson helped by organizing concerts for them on Saturday evenings, when Sophia and her father — who played the violin — were there.

Sophia fell for Nelson the moment she set eyes on him. Yet it was not until a month later that she felt he too was attracted.

Early one Sunday morning, she went to his bedroom and slipped under the sheets with him. He was still asleep, but at the feel of her body his latent sexuality awoke suddenly.

Later, when she fell asleep for a while, he propped his head on his elbow and gazed at her. A mass of dark hair lay loosely on the pillow framing her neck and profile. An arm covered her breasts and the rest of the body was veiled by the voluminous nightdress. Her features were curiously familiar to him now that the eyes were closed. The hairline, the almost straight eyebrows meeting just above a nose a shade too long to be beautiful, the full lips parted for breathing, and even the position she had taken were Jemima's. A surge of tenderness swept through him. Was it because she was so like the sister he had loved and protected that he was so drawn to her, he wondered?

The following weekend she didn't return to Athens with her father on the Sunday evening. Julius had invited her to stay on; he had noted the looks she and Nelson exchanged and reckoned it wasn't the moment for them to be separated. Discretely he left them on their own at the villa.

Three weeks later Sophia told Nelson she was pregnant. It was an eventuality which had never crossed his mind.

"Are you sure?" he asked, bewildered.

She nodded, then threw her arms around him and held him tightly.

"Isn't it wonderful!" She felt the reticence in him. "Don't worry," she said softly, "if you want I'll get rid of it and no one will know. Is that what you want?"

A feeling of claustrophobia gripped him and he disengaged

himself. He didn't know what he wanted or how to cope with the situation.

"Oh God, I'm sorry," he mumbled, "but we'll find a solution, I promise you." He stared out of the window and added, "do you hate me?"

"Hate you? Why? Because you've given me something wonderful which I can't keep? No, Nelson, I love you. I'm just a little sad. It might have been all so beautiful, but it's not your fault."

There were tears in her eyes.

"Don't cry, please. I ... why don't we get married?" he blurted, not fully conscious of what he was saying.

"Do you really mean it? Oh Nelson, it would be so marvellous. Quite apart from the baby, we'd have such a wonderful time together. And you've no idea how much I love you."

She gave him no time to change his mind. She ran downstairs and out to her father who was breakfasting on the terrace.

"Nelson and I are going to get married," she cried. "Oh Daddy, I'm so happy."

They were married at the Town Hall in Iraklion as soon as Julius was able to get there. Maryanne and Jemima came with him, and the only other witnesses to the ceremony were the parents of the bride, two aunts, her best friend, and Domenicos.

The same evening Julius' yacht took them off for a month's honeymoon cruise up the coast of Italy, along the South of France to the Balearic Islands and down to Gibraltar. From there they caught a plane to Rome and the train to Florence. Julius had chosen the Tuscan city as the best place for Nelson in which to get accustomed to urban life again. Also because there was a professor who coached such pianists as Pollini and Campanella, and who could prepare him for his first concert.

Julius had also rented a flat for the young couple up in the hills of Fiesole, determined that nothing should trouble the marriage of his eldest grandson, especially now that A.J. was causing him and Maryanne a lot of worry.

London, 1981

Possibly it was resentment to Julius' ever increasing fame and acclaim as one of the world's leading businessmen and philanthropists which prompted George to negotiate a title for himself. At least it was a distinction which the Alexandrian could never receive.

He had counted on a life peerage after a series of hefty political donations, but had to be content with a knighthood in the New Year's Honours list of 1981.

On April 14th he was preparing to go to Buckingham Palace with Paola and Jemima for the investiture when he was told that his daughter was nowhere to be found.

"In that case we'll go without her," he spat angrily at Paola. "Why the bloody hell didn't you make sure she was punctual for once. Christ! Do I have to think of every damned thing in this family!"

Ten minutes later they were being driven to the Palace. Jemima was not with them.

That evening there was a party in his hotel suite and he forgot about her until it was time to fly to Paris in his private jet.

"Then she can go by public transport like anyone else," was his only comment when she still had not turned up.

The following day, while on his way to catch a plane to New York, he said to Paola, "I've a good mind to cut her allowance. She'd show a little more respect if she were short of cash. She's too bloody spoilt, and don't start taking her defence just to contradict me."

"I'm not. I simply wanted to point out that something might have happened to her."

"Like what? There exists a machine called a telephone. She was probably getting herself screwed rather too well for once, that's what happened to her."

It turned out he was not far off the mark.

Two days earlier a photo of him, Paola and Jemima arriving at their hotel had appeared in the Evening News, and at around 7 p.m. a call had been put through to Jemima. At the sound of the voice on the line she had gasped.

"Bruno it isn't true! Where are you ... in London, but that's fantastic. When can we see each other? ... no, this evening I can't. I've got to go to the theatre with Papa and then on to a dinner ... no, there's no way I can get out of it. Tell you what, we could meet afterwards ... well, around midnight. Yes, of course I know the Carlton Towers ... what's your room number? I'll be there as fast as I can, Bruno. Christ am I glad to see you again, I missed you ... Nelson? no ... I'll tell you all about him when I'm with you ... "

That phone call was to change Jemima's life.

She was trembling when she put the receiver down.

In a few hours she would be with him again, she thought, and her body began to yearn for his. He would be sensual and tender and make love to her as only he knew how to.

She got back to the hotel with her father and Paola just before midnight, pretended to go up to her room, then walked out and caught a taxi.

"To the Carlton Towers, please," she said.

Once there, she went straight to the lifts and took one up to the 4th floor. Room 401 was along to the right. She was about to knock when the door opened and a man appeared. He was not Bruno.

"Oh, I'm sorry," she murmured, "I thought ... "

"Bruno's inside, if you're looking for him."

He gave her an unpleasant leer then closed the door behind her.

Bruno was by the window, looking down at the gardens of Cadogan Place. A towel was slung around his hips and his black hair was still wet from the shower he had just taken. He did not see her immediately as he turned, and there was a scowl on his face which took her aback. Then he caught sight of her and the familiar grin was back while he gazed her up and down.

"Ce que t'es belle," he said coming over to her, "and what a figure. You're a real stunner. Is your old Bruno allowed to give you a kiss?"

He slipped an arm around her waist and drew her gently to him. He caressed her cheek then slowly pressed his lips against hers.

The yearning for his body became fierce as with a movement of his hips the towel fell to the floor and her hands ran over his naked body.

Yet curiously when he whispered the words of love she had longed to hear, she felt an undercurrent of unease. What had changed in him, she wondered, or was it she who no longer needed them?

Even so, when later he got up and went over to the fridge, and she watched him uncork a bottle of champagne while she stretched voluptuously on the bed, she thought he was still the man she preferred to make love with.

He came back to the bed with two full glasses and handed her one.

"To us," he said kneeling in front of her. Her eyes travelled over his torso and she noted a scar below the rib cage. She dipped a finger in the champagne and passed it along the thin red line.

"How did you get that?" she asked.

"*Oh, ce n'est rien.* An accident on a boat. Drink up, there's plenty more in the bottle."

Then she felt her head begin to spin and seconds later she was asleep.

Jemima's was a kidnapping with a twist. She had been lured to a hotel and into the bed of a lover, then drugged and taken to a hide-out where she was administered regular doses of heroin, but she wasn't locked in a room with her eyes bandaged or chained to a pipe in a cellar with no idea who her ravishers were. Had she wanted to, she could have walked out of the place, hailed a taxi and been driven to wherever she wished. But she did not, since she was in no state either physically or mentally to do so. The man who had masterminded her disappearance had seen to that.

Five days after she had gone to the Carlton Towers, Lou Mendosa called Bruno to his office.

"It's time you contacted the family. But remember, no threats or demands for payment. Just let them know that you're aware of where she is, and that she's there of her own will. No one's forcing her to stay. You're afraid she might fall into bad company, that's all. Have you got the brother's phone number?"

"Yeah, but I'm not sure he's the right person. The father has more or less disinherited him and from what Jemima told me they haven't seen each other for a couple of years."

Mendosa stared at Bruno with unblinking eyes. "Don't try to play silly bugger with me. You're soft on her still, aren't you." He leant forward and pointed a fat finger at him. "I don't care how much you fuck her and, once someone's paid up, you can do it till you're blue in the arse. But if you want to clear that little debt of yours, you do exactly what I tell you. You know what happens otherwise."

Bruno paled and looked down at his feet. "O.K., O.K. Whatever you say, I was only trying to be helpful."

"Who asked you to? Get in touch with that brother. Now." He pushed the phone over to him.

Nelson was in Florence, rehearsing for a concert when Bruno phoned. At first he refused to believe that Jemima had succumbed to drugs.

"It can't be true. There must be a mistake. She'd have told me if she was in trouble. And she hated the stuff ... she saw what it did to me."

"I can only tell you what I know, Nelson. Believe me, she's in bad way. And she needs someone of her family to help her. You must get in touch with your father or someone who can take care of her."

"Why don't you do something, Bruno? Dammit you owe it to her ... "

"I haven't seen her in years ... no, she needs someone of her family, someone she trusts completely. It's urgent..."

Nelson turned to the only person he knew would help, but it took him 24 hours to get through to him.

Julius was about to leave for Washington to meet with the Secretary of State and the Foreign Ministers of Egypt and Israel. It was a meeting of utmost importance, and not one he could afford to miss. Yet for once his loyalties were torn. Jemima was his only granddaughter, and had become very precious to him. From what Nelson had told him it seemed that she was now in grave danger. Supposing something drastic happened which left her handicapped for life or even killed her?

What was more important, he asked himself, the life of Marguerite's grandchild or political tugs of war and intrigues, where the destinies of whole peoples might be involved?

He decided that as long as someone he could trust to do everything in his power to help Jemima was with her, his actual presence was not essential. He toyed with the idea of telling George, then dismissed it. He would only make the situation worse.

The man he chose to send to London was Laurrie Salvini. Lorenzo was Pietro Salvini's son. He was 26 and, until Julius had taken him on to look after his personal security, had been in the US armed forces. Trained as a Seal Team commando and promoted to the rank of major at the age of 25 for his exceptional leadership qualities, he was tough, dependable and efficient. Discreet too, and Julius knew that in a delicate emergency he could be relied on completely.

He had him come to the airport on his arrival at Washington, and as soon as he had outlined the problem, sent him straight off to London. The instructions were clear. Laurrie was to contact Jemima and, if she was in a state to travel, fly her to the clinic in Switzerland where Nelson had been looked after.

"I'm afraid it's a question of heroin and her condition could be desperate. There's a room reserved for you at the Piccadilly Hotel, and there a certain Bruno will get in touch with you to tell you where Jemima is. You'll have to play it by ear, and I give you carte blanche. If there is a question of payment, go to Mr Mitchell at the Midland Bank at Piccadilly Circus. He has my authority to give you whatever may be required … that Bruno, I have my doubts about him. A few years ago he was a close friend of both Jemima and her brother but something tells me he was a bad influence, and I'm sure he's not being helpful for the sake of friendship. If it's money he wants, and it'll help find the girl, give it him. But also make enquiries about him. I don't want him hanging around her if he's undesirable."

"Don't worry, *padrino*, I'll make sure she's looked after and in good hands. May I have your authority to deal with whoever put her onto the stuff. It's not right they should get away with it."

Julius put his hand on the man's arm and gave it a slight squeeze.

"I leave it to you. But remember, my prime concern is Jemima and her well-being. Once you've got her to the clinic, you can do what you like with whoever is responsible ... within limits."

The moment Laurrie set eyes on Bruno he sensed that the man was a crook. There was something about the way he dressed and spoke, a mixture of arrogance and subservience which put him on his guard.

They had arranged to meet in the hotel's coffee room, and after they had shaken hands and ordered coffee, Laurrie came straight to the point.

"I want to see Jemima immediately and arrange for her to be hospitalized. I gather she's in pretty poor shape. So let me have the address where she is ... "

"*Un moment,* mister ... first we talk. Who are you? Friend of family, doctor, lawyer?"

"Does it matter?" Laurrie said testily. "As far as you or anyone else is concerned, I am here to help her, at the request of the family."

"You know that she not want to be found. That she hiding from family and friends? Even from Bruno?"

"What do you mean?"

"*Elle veut qu'on lui foute la paix* ... you understand ... only I think it not right. Someone must help."

"That's big of you," Laurrie muttered between his teeth, staring coldly at him. "Why didn't you do something if you're such a friend?"

"I am not able. The man who tells me her address wants ... " he rubbed his forefinger and thumb together, "money."

So that was the game. "How much?"

"Many dollars ... too many."

Laurrie said nothing but took a sip of his coffee.

"Too many for me or you, but not for her father, who is very rich man ... multi-millionaire."

"I asked how much?"

"He say half million dollars."

It took a lot of self control on Laurrie Salvini's part not to knock the table over, seize Bruno by the throat, and squeeze until he choked out of him where Jemima was being kept. There was no doubt now that she had been kidnapped and would only be released against payment.

"He's out of his mind. Unless she's been kidnapped. Tell me, Ragonetti, is that what has happened?"

"*Bon Dieu,* no. Why you think that? She is free to do what she want. You will see, she is not prisoner. She is O.K ... "

"She'd better be. If anything happens to Jemima you'll answer personally to me, and I can assure you that won't be a joy ride."

"What you mean? I love Jemima. One time she my girl friend, and maybe I marry her when she is found. You don't threaten me. *Merde, alors,* I try to help and I get insulted." He was working himself into a fury.

The old ploy, Laurrie thought. "O.K., don't get all worked up. I simply want to get things straight between us. Who wants the money, and how?"

"Then you pay?" The sudden eagerness would have been comic in other circumstances.

"I didn't say that. It doesn't depend on me. I'll have to contact the family. They'll pay something, sure, but not half a million bucks."

"You ask them. You tell them it essential. If you like we can make arrangement, you and me, you understand?"

"I understand only one thing, you're the lousiest little bastard to crawl this side of the Atlantic. You're going to put me in touch with your so-called contact and he's going to tell me where I can find Jemima now, or I'll break every bone in your body. Get me?"

To his surprise Bruno grinned. "*Bien sûr.* Only you hurt me and you never get address. But I take you to the man if you want, now. See? I try to be good friend to Jemima. Waitress, the bill."

"Separate checks please. I want to pay for my own," Laurrie said acidly.

They got into a taxi and Bruno told the driver to take them to Soho Square. There they got out and walked to a building in Dean Street where they climbed a flight of stairs and the Frenchman rang a bell at a door on the landing. It clicked open and he signalled to Laurrie to follow him. Then he ushered him into an office at the end of a corridor.

"You wait me here," he said.

Laurrie looked around. The room was comfortably furnished in a modern style, and could have been the office of a successful businessman. A lot of brass and mahogany, low leather sofas and wall to wall carpeting. Only there was no clue as to the business carried on. No reference books or files or samples. He lit himself a cigarette and strolled over to the window, wondering what sort of person normally sat behind the desk. He didn't have to wait long to find out.

The door was pushed open and a small, plump man in his middle fifties rolled in. He was expensively dressed in a dark grey pinstriped suit and smelled of 'Eau Sauvage'. He seemed at first sight to be made of soft sinews, fat, and pink skin, with no bones or muscles, but a glance at his eyes showed that there was steel at the core, unbendable and unflinching. The smile too was metallic.

"Mr Salvini? Please take a seat and tell me how I can help you. My name is Louis Mendosa and may I ask you to extinguish your cigarette, I am allergic to smoke." His voice was soft, and though he was southern European, he spoke English fluently. Laurrie decided to use the same kind of language as his. He extinguished his cigarette without a word and went to sit at the furthest end of a sofa.

"And I am allergic to wool, the sort that certain people try to pull over other's eyes. You know very well why I'm here, Mr Mendosa." He crossed his legs and leaned back, and returned the fat man's stare.

The seconds ticked by, then Mendosa put his elbows on the desk and joined the tips of his fingers.

"I gather Bruno has told you my conditions?"

"I don't think so. He mentioned the question of a payment which I didn't take seriously ... "

"A mistake. But before we go any further, would you be good enough to hand Gaetano your gun, or whatever the metal object you have on you. It was signalled to us as you walked through that door."

Laurrie smiled despite himself. The clever bastard! He reached into his jacket and took out his revolver and offered it to a man who had appeared in the doorway.

"It will be returned to you, of course, as soon as you leave. To revert to the conditions, if you or anyone else wishes to know where to find the unfortunate Miss Christofides, it will cost 500,000 dollars. How and where they are to be paid I will tell you once you have the authorization to do so. I say 'unfortunate' Miss Christofides as she is far from well, and if she were my daughter I would waste no time in getting her proper medical treatment. But then I am not her father. You, though, are the cousin of Lady Christofides, her stepmother, if I am not mistaken, so you can refer to her and Sir George my concern for their daughter. My advice is not to waste time."

"You realize that you are committing a criminal offence. Kidnapping and extortion are punishable by death in certain States of the USA, and in this country they could get you a life sentence."

"I realize nothing of the sort. I have not kidnapped Miss Christofides and nor am I attempting to extort a cent from you or anyone. I wish simply to be paid for certain information I have. It is a straightforward business proposition which you are free to accept or reject. And if you have in mind going to the police, I would suggest you think twice about it. I doubt whether the young lady's family would care to read in all the newspapers that their daughter is a heroin addict who, to find the money for her twice daily shots, prostitutes herself at £25 a go. No use getting angry, Mr Salvini, you'll need your sang-froid to convince Sir George to pay me half a million dollars. From what I hear he is not an easy man, but I suppose for his only daughter he will make the effort. And now I will have to ask you to excuse me as I am busy, unless you have any queries."

For the second time that morning Laurrie controlled his rage, but he swore to himself that he would make Mendosa pay one day.

"When do I see her?"

"As soon as you have the money Bruno will take you to her. But I think it fair to warn you that I am being paid only for information. I can't guarantee that you'll get her to go with you once you've found her. She has taken a certain aversion to men, and only Bruno can convince her to do things. You'll have to be patient and extra nice with him."

"Don't worry, I will," he said grimly.

"I don't worry, Mr Salvini. How you treat the young man once I have the money is of no concern to me. I was simply giving you advice."

He stood up to mark that the meeting was finished and called to the man behind the door. "Gaetano, show the gentleman out and don't forget to give him back his revolver."

"One moment. How do I contact you?"

"When do you expect to be ready? This afternoon, tomorrow?"

"I'll give you our answer this evening."

"Then I will phone you at your hotel at 10 p.m. Good day, Mr Salvini."

Laurrie walked back to his hotel. He needed the exercise to get the hate out of his system. He had seldom felt such a strong dislike for a person yet he knew that for the moment he would have to overcome his aversion. He had to be in total command of himself if he were to complete his mission successfully, and it was turning out to be much more delicate and dangerous than he had anticipated.

Quite apart from the money angle, it could prove very tricky to persuade Jemima to leave wherever she was and have medical treatment, and he wasn't certain that he was the right person to do it. A woman would be necessary. Someone Jemima would trust and confide in, and who could get her away from the influence of Bruno Ragonetti, always supposing that what Mendosa had said was true.

Back in his room he put a call through to the number Julius Caspar had given him in Washington. He glanced at his watch. It was 7.15 there and, with luck, the Alexandrian would still be in his hotel bedroom. A secretary answered and a moment later he was put through to him. Briefly he explained the situation, neither dramatizing nor attempting to sound optimistic. Nor did he offer advice. If his *padrino* wanted any, he would ask it.

"The money will be available to you in a matter of hours," Julius said. "You can collect it before the bank shuts this afternoon, otherwise it'll be for first thing tomorrow morning. If there's a chance of recuperating it somehow, fine, otherwise forget about it. What's important is finding and saving Jemima. That comes above all else. Have you any recommendations?"

"Yes. I feel that a woman should be with her immediately, someone she knows and trusts."

"Very well, I'll see if her aunt will come. It's a question of contacting her. As soon as I have arranged something, I will phone you. And Laurrie, thanks."

Maryanne caught a Concorde and was in London 6 hours later.

Laurrie Salvini was waiting for her in the foyer of her hotel.

"Sorry I didn't come to meet you at the airport but I had to finalize certain details," he said kissing her on the cheek.

"There was no reason why you should have, Laurrie. Give me, a few minutes to get myself together and then I'll be ready to go to her."

"Don't rush. I have to go and meet the contact who'll take us to her. When everything is ready I'll ring you and give you the address to come to. The car will bring you there."

Ten minutes later he was walking up the stairs to Mendosa's office. He rang the bell, and when the door clicked open he pushed it and went straight to the room at the end of the corridor. He stood in the doorway for an instant staring at the fat man who hadn't bothered to look up. One of these days I'll beat the supercilious shit out of you, he promised silently, then strode into the room.

Mendosa glanced at his watch, then over at him.

"You have it, I presume?"

"Sure." He raised the briefcase he was carrying.

"Gaetano, call me Bruno."

There was silence until the Frenchman appeared.

Then Mendosa stood up. "Bruno will take you to her and you will hand the case — I presume it contains the money — to Gaetano. That is all Mr Salvini. Oh, perhaps we had better check it first. I would hate there to be a mistake and my man or Bruno blamed. Not that I doubt your integrity, but business is business."

Laurrie handed the case to Gaetano who placed it on the desk in front of Mendosa. Two minutes later it was shut again and handed back to Laurrie.

"Thank you, Mr Salvini. I need keep you no longer. It has been a pleasure to deal with you."

Had he not been revolted by what the man stood for, he might have admired the effrontery with which he had handled the whole transaction. He was a very smart operator, with the nerves and flair of a successful gambler. He had not made one false move and had placed the stakes at exactly the right amount. $500,000 was the sort of money an immensely rich father would pay to find his daughter; pay without calling in the police or trying to devise some method for getting it back. And he had not tried to threaten or blackmail. He had managed to place himself in the position of someone helping and not obstructing the girl's family. Only, helping for a price. A business transaction, as he had said, which he might have got away with if it had concerned any other girl and any other family. In this particular instance it had involved him, Laurrie Salvini, and the next time he and Mendosa met, business or other ethics would not come into play.

Maryanne held Jemima's hand in hers. She glanced sideways at the girl and then whispered across to Laurrie, "I think she's asleep, thank God. How long do you reckon before she needs another shot?"

"Five or six hours. With luck we should have her at the clinic by then."

She was about to ask what would happen if there were a delay, but thought better of it. There just must not be any delay, and there was no reason why there should be. They'd be at Gatwick in an hour, and over to Geneva by three o'clock. That would leave a couple of hours to get her to Lausanne before the withdrawal symptoms started again. She shuddered. She didn't think she could face that once more. It had been a horrifying experience, far worse than she had expected. The sight of Jemima howling like a beast, offering herself to that Frenchman and even to Laurrie while she begged for the only possible remedy to her suffering, was something she would never forget. How, she kept repeating to herself, could a healthy, sweet girl have been reduced to such a state? How many others must be going through the same agony, but with no friends or family to come to their rescue?

Laurrie offered her a cigarette.

"Thanks, I think I will." She leant forward for him to light it and after she had inhaled deeply, she asked, "will you be coming to Switzerland with us?"

"Not unless you really want me to. There's a qualified nurse waiting on the plane, so she can cope with Jemima if she needs anything."

Maryanne nodded. "I suppose you're going straight back to Washington?"

"More or less. There's a spot of unfinished business I must attend to in London, and then I'll be off."

"Do you have to tell Julius everything? I mean, he's very fond of Jemima, and if he knew what she had really been through, it would pain him terribly. He considers her almost a granddaughter. She reminds him of a person who meant a great deal to him ... "

"Don't worry. He won't learn anything from me. But somehow he'll know all the same. You can't hide much from him."

Suddenly Maryanne thought of George and what he would do when he discovered what had happened. The last thing Jemima needed was an insensitive parent throwing his weight around. Somehow the truth would have to be kept from him.

"I don't think George should know what happened, not for the moment," she said to Laurrie while her niece was being helped onto the plane. "He can be told she's gone on a trip with me, or better still, that she's decided to lend a hand at Krinos. It won't be far from the truth. And do tell Julius not to worry, I'll look after her. Poor darling, she'll need someone close she can trust and confide in if she's to get over this awful experience. I'll do my best to be that mum she never had ... "

Once back at his hotel, Laurrie Salvini rang Washington. He was put through to Julius immediately.

"Everything's O.K." he said, they'll be landing in Geneva in a few minutes and ... "

"How is she, Laurrie? I want the truth."

"She's in a bad way; heroin does that and I'd say they gave her a packet of it. But with treatment she should be all right. How long it will take I don't know, but she'll pull through."

"And psychologically?"

"She's pretty shaken, but I reckon Maryanne knows how to cope ... it's a question of time, *padrino*." What else could he say? He fingered the flat matchbox Bruno Ragonetti had thrown into an ashtray in the bedroom he had taken them to, and noted the name of a nightclub on it. He'd make the bloody little bastard pay for what he'd done to Jemima, if it was the last thing he did.

"I guess you're right, Laurrie." There was a moment of silence, then: "As you're over in Europe, take a few days off and relax. London can be fun at this time of the year. If you like I'll phone someone to show you around and introduce you to the right people. Or go down to the South of France; for a young man like you it can be pretty good."

"Thanks, but I'd prefer to get back. Can't say I care much for this city. Maybe it's just the people I've come across ... I want to get straight with a couple of them and catch the first plane out."

"Fair enough, Laurrie. I suppose I should try to stop you, but you wouldn't listen to me even if I did. Only take care of yourself."

Laurrie put the phone down and stretched on the bed. Then he called the Hall Porter's desk. "Ring me at 9 p.m. please and I don't want to be disturbed till then."

He kicked off his shoes and loosened his tie and fell instantly asleep.

Three hours later the phone rang. He showered, dressed and walked out into the bustle of Piccadilly. Turning left, he skirted the Circus and strode up Shaftesbury Avenue then into Soho. The hunt for Bruno would begin at the nightclub.

He got back to the hotel at 3.a.m. His knuckles were swollen and there were stains of blood on his shirt sleeves. He wondered when someone would discover the broken mass of bones and bruised flesh, sprawled on a heap of garbage. Then he thought about Lou Mendoza. He would have to use different methods where he was concerned, and first there was the question of getting back the money. He glanced through a pocket diary. Yes, he reckoned he knew who could put the screws on him.

Before getting into bed he sank to his knees in prayer and asked forgiveness. Not for what he had done to Bruno, but for the pleasure he had got from it.

Maryanne was true to her word. She was at her niece's side constantly during the three weeks at the Swiss clinic as well as for the first two months on Krinos. And it was largely thanks to her that Jemima got over the suicidal depression which gripped her the moment she came face to face with the reality of her ordeal.

"What's the point of going on. Nobody cares about me; no one ever has or ever will. And when they know what happened ..."

"Shh. There are a quite a few people who care a lot about you, me to begin with. Uncle Julius, Nelson, your father."

"He doesn't care a fig about anyone, least of all his children."

"That isn't so, honestly. It's just that he doesn't know how to express his affection. But I assure, you he has always talked about you in a way only a father who loves his daughter would."

"Even if that were so, I don't give a damn now about what he feels. I don't want to see him ever again. I don't want to see anyone, not after all this. I hate myself now."

"Jemima, darling, you musn't. What happened was no fault of yours ... "

"Yes it was. I was the one who went to Bruno when he whistled for me ... like a bitch on heat ... it would never have happened otherwise ... "

"I'm afraid it would have somehow or other," Maryanne said softly laying a hand on her's. "Bruno was only an instrument with which to get hold of you. Those criminals were determined to kidnap you, so it really had very little to do with your going to that hotel room. If you hadn't gone, they'd have used some other means. It's not fair to blame yourself in any way. You were a victim and in no way responsible for what happened. Life can be very hard on one sometimes, and at a given moment we all can be, and often are, victims of circumstances. The one you've just been through was particularly cruel, but I know that with time you'll come to accept it not just as a horrible moment in your life, but one which can and must bring out certain qualities you never thought you had."

"Like what?"

"Like courage in adversity; like caring for those who are a lot worse off than you and I; like knowing yourself and making the best of whatever gifts you have. Believe me, darling, there's a great potential in you for helping others, and it would be a crime to waste that. There's so much you can do with your life, so don't let what happened in London spoil that. I won't say try to forget it. There's no way you could, and you shouldn't. But accept it as you might an accident or a bad illness."

"That's all very well, but even if I manage to, what can I do? I'm not trained for anything except to be the wife of some millionaire goof papa had in mind, and that's decidedly out now. You're right," she said with a hard little laugh, "there's at least that of positive. They won't be queuing at the altar for me any more. And I wouldn't touch a man with a bargepole now. I hate them all. So you tell me what I can do!"

Maryanne did, though not immediately. It was after she had settled Jemima at Krinos and given her time to adjust herself psychologically to an ambience very different to the one she had been used to, and where no one knew who she was or from what background she came, that she suggested she do a course in nursing and then go out to Eritrea to help at Don Francesco's Mission.

August 1st, 1990

Jemima and Christian were travelling by train from Cairo to Alexandria.

They could have done the journey with Maryanne and Michael, Peter Salvini and his wife, Clara and Paola in Julius' plane. But after working for three months in the slums of Cairo with Soeur Emmanuelle, the remarkable nun who had spent more than half her life bringing comfort, help and hygiene to thousands of urchins living in appalling conditions among the city's refuse dumps, to have stepped from such misery into the flagrant opulence of a multi-millionaire's private jet, was too stark a contrast.

"I need time to adjust myself," Jemima had said the night before, "let's go by train."

They had climbed into a second class wagon and found two seats near a window. The compartment was stifling.

She closed her eyes and leaned her head against Christian's shoulder, trying to obliterate the present in sleep. But it would not come. Not because of the noise and discomfort, but because of a gnawing fear which crept over her.

She reached for her husband's hand. "God, I wish we weren't going there. Do we have to? I'm scared. Don't ask me why, I just am. Can't we get out at the next stop? Uncle Julius wouldn't mind. He probably wouldn't even notice if we're there or not. And I'm sure he'd understand. If you want to know, it's because of my father. I can't face him. I know it's childish, but the idea of actually seeing him again gives me the jitters."

Christian squeezed her fingers gently. "It's as you like, chérie. But your father can't bite you. He can't do anything now ... "

"You don't understand. I've never liked him. Even as a little girl he frightened me. And when I think of the way he treated Nelson ... his death was partly his fault."

"I know. But that's all over with. And I think you owe it to Julius Caspar to be there for this occasion. In a way he saved your life, from what you told me. Also, I'd like to meet him and thank him for what he did for the Mission, and for the aid he is sending now. I am sure he'd be hurt if you didn't show up, whatever you may think. I would be." He gave her hand another squeeze. "Just relax. It'll all work out O.K."

The train sped through the Egyptian Delta and she gazed in silence at the fields of *birseem* and cotton, at the orange and mango groves and at the black skinned buffalos treading never ending circles around the water mills. A sense of peace gradually enveloped her, brushing away the panic. Christian was right. There was nothing her father could do now. He couldn't hurt her any more. He belonged to a part of her life which was finished. She smiled wanly.

"Don't worry, I'm all right now ... it was also the thought of all the rigmarole this evening. I love uncle Julius and I wouldn't miss his 80th birthday for anything. But I wish it were just a family affair and not the state event it's going to be."

An hour later a taxi took them from Alexandria's main station to the Eastern Harbour waterfront. "My God," Jemima gasped as the huge white yacht came into sight, "it can't be that!"

"It certainly can," Christian murmured, "must say, it's magnificent."

"It's awful. I don't want to go on it. There's something terrible about it."

"It's just very, very big, colossal for a private yacht. Think of it as a small liner which we're going on for a week's cruise. Forget it has anything to do with Julius Caspar or your father."

"I can't."

She went on staring at it though her mind had closed on itself. She was back to her childhood, to those summers spent on chartered boats around the Greek Isles or along the French or Italian Rivieras; lonely weeks with Nelson, and only the occasional company of a son or daughter of a business acquaintance her father wanted to please. How she had hated holidays on yachts.

Why had uncle Julius got himself one like this, she wondered when the taxi was halted by a policeman on the quay. And while Christian got out to show their passports at a police block at Quoit Bey fort and explain who they were to an officer sitting at a makeshift desk, she thought back to the last time she had seen the Alexandrian in Paris, in that sordid attic of Nelson's in 1979. How kind and patient he had been, caring for her and Nelson as if they were his own children. How she wished she could have had a father like him. He was so different to what others made out. Or was he really the ruthless business tycoon, a megalomaniac like her father, who cared for no one and was solely interested in his personal aggrandizement? Maybe, but not where she and Nelson had been concerned. Not for Don Francesco nor for Soeur Emmanuelle either. Through his charity he had saved men, women and children from starvation; through his caring he had saved her from that terrible ordeal, and Nelson from drugs. Why then did this floating palace of his chill the blood in her veins? Why the apprehension causing goose pimples on her arms?

The taxi was allowed to proceed through the fort's gates and stopped some 50 metres further on, beside the stairs leading to the boat's second deck. There were more policemen, identity checks and body frisking before they were allowed to set foot on the rolling staircase.

As they were being carried up, Jemima spotted a familiar face on the lower deck. It was Laurrie Salvini's. She waved and called "hello there." Laurrie smiled and waved back. Then she noticed the surly youngster who was standing next to him and staring at her. But that was A.J.! There was no mistaking the sloping eyebrows, the prominent nose and his curious way of looking at one from the corner of his eyes with his face turned partially away. What on earth was he doing there? Wasn't he a terrorist wanted by Interpol?

She gripped Christian's arm. "My God, did you see who's there?" she whispered, "my cousin A.J. I'm sure it was him. Why is he on board?"

Christian threw an arm around her waist and smiled.

"Ask your uncle Julius. If it really was him, there's bound to be a good reason."

She nodded and took a deep breath. Christian was right. He always was, somehow. She gazed up at him, and with a surge of tenderness thought back to the day she had first seen him at the Mission.

The Mission hospital was like hundreds of others scattered throughout equatorial Africa. It consisted of a central, prefabricated operating theatre and two whitewashed, brick and thatch-roofed wards, one for men and the other for women and children. The men's ward was a little smaller than the women's and had fewer beds, 10 instead of 16. Four nurses, two of them nuns, and a doctor cared for the sick, and they had had their hands full in the last few days with a bunch of guerilla casualties from the renewed fighting twenty kilometres from Asmara.

Don Francesco walked slowly between the beds, stopping to give a word of comfort or a smile as his fingers touched an arm or rested on a forehead. The young doctor from *Médecins sans Frontières* accompanied him, explaining the condition of each patient. He was dark skinned with a frank look, and came from Martinique. Now and then he simply shook his head and the priest would say a few words or whisper a prayer, and the anguish on a face would disappear.

Christian Gautier noted that Don Francesco did not always make the sign of the cross or administer last rites to all the dying, and when they walked out of the ward into the blazing sunshine he asked why.

"Most of them are Muslims," Francesco said. "It would be discourteous to wave the 'infidel's' cross in front of them the moment they need most the succour of their religion. You know, Islam has much in common with Christianity. I have learnt by heart parts of the Koran and I recite it to them. What counts is the faith a man has in God and after-life more than the outward manifestations of a belief, which is what religions are. I try to give every man the comfort he needs to help him meet his Creator, and it's not because this hospital is run by Catholics that we have to force our beliefs down everyone's throats. Don't you agree?"

"Of course, Father," the young doctor replied, shading his eyes from the glare, "but it's not always the case."

"Maybe not, but here we try to make it so."

There was a moment's silence as they crossed the 25 metres of beaten earth to the second ward.

"Doesn't the fact that those men are mostly guerillas make things awkward with the authorities? They could accuse you of aiding and abetting the enemy."

"They could, but so far they haven't. And while they reckon we're being useful in some way, they won't. Mind you, they've threatened several times to kick us out of here if we go on helping the wounded, but basically they know that someone has to do it. Also, only the worse cases are brought here, the ones that probably won't be able to do any more fighting. The others get their wounds patched up in their own camps and don't come to us. Of course, I'm supposed to report every man that's brought here and have him taken away to a prison camp as soon as he's well. Needless to say I don't. I tell them if someone has died, but I don't think they care really. The guerillas are a problem they've been coping with for a quarter of a century, and slowly they are wearing down their resistance. It's heartbreaking, but these men are fighting a lost cause."

Don Francesco shook his head. "Whichever way, they are doomed. Either they fight and get killed, or they let themselves be herded off to some other part of the country where there will be even less for them to eat than here. We're witnessing a genocide, only unlike Biafra, the slaughter isn't immediate, and a lot of it is left to the elements. These last few years have been more terrible than anyone can remember. No rain, no crops and the earth cracking like the parched lips of these unfortunate people. Don't judge by what you see around here. We have wells, so water isn't a real problem. But go beyond that low ridge of hills over there and you'll see why so many have so little to hope for. And the tragedy is that it needn't be like this. Man can harness nature if he sets his mind to it. In our own small way we have here, and it could be the same everywhere in this country."

"Then why isn't it, Father?"

"Because man has forgotten that he was created in the image of God, and apes the devil. Come, though, we mustn't keep the patients waiting."

He lifted the fly net which curtained the opening to the second ward, and went over to the nearest bed where a little boy was lying, emaciated, with beads of perspiration trickling from his forehead into two huge brown eyes. A victim of malnutrition and dysentery, he had only a few hours to live. The priest sat on his bed and with a handkerchief wiped the sweat from his face. Then he smiled and began talking in Tigrina, the local dialect.

Christian saw a faint sparkle appear in the lifeless eyes and a suspicion of a grin on the child's lips. He glanced across the ward to where a nurse was changing the bandages on a small girl's arm, and walked over to them.

"Ciao," he said, squatting by the bed, aware that most Eritreans knew a smattering of Italian. "*Stai meglio oggi?*"

He turned to the nurse and, nodding at the bandages, asked, "is it healing all right?"

"Not as well as it should," she murmured, "but there's so little resistance left in her that it'll be a miracle if it ever does."

He examined the chart hung on the bed, stood up and watched her for moment. "I wouldn't say there's much resistance left in you either," he said. "You need some rest, and to eat a little more."

She shot him a look of reproval. "You're not suggesting I stuff myself while the whole country is crying out for a morsel of food. And as for rest, I get it like the others."

She moved over to the next bed and drew the sheet back, revealing the sagging bosoms of a mother who had endured too many maternities. Then she reached for a syringe in a metallic basin, held it to the light, and squirted a little liquid from it.

"If you let yourself get as weak as her, you won't be much help to anyone," he answered as she rubbed the woman's arm with disinfectant and pushed the needle in. "You're heading for a breakdown if you go on like this. I've watched you at mealtimes the last few days and you've eaten next to nothing. What's the matter? Have you a problem? You can tell me ... "

"A problem?" she muttered as she put the syringe back in the bowl. "Are you trying to be funny?"

She turned and faced him, her eyes darkening with anger. "Isn't what's happening to these poor wretches, and to millions of others in Africa, enough of a problem for you? What more do you want? Does their suffering leave you totally indifferent? Don't you care about them at all?"

"Hey, steady on. I wouldn't be here if I didn't care. I just try not to let the tragic situation get the better of me. If I crack, who the devil is going to look after them? And that applies to both of us. We have a responsibility towards these poor people, and we have to face it."

She didn't answer but bit her lip nervously. Then, avoiding his gaze, murmured, "you're right. Sorry, I didn't really mean what I said."

"Forget it. I'm sorry too if I seemed aggressive. But promise me you'll eat properly at dinner and get a good night's sleep."

She forced a slight smile. "I'll try."

He studied her while she turned to an old woman in the next bed.

She was really quite pretty, he thought, with the fragility and resilience of a bird. Yes, she reminded him of a kingfisher he'd had as a kid, but with the colourings of a black headed gull. He'd been attracted to her the moment Don Francesco had introduced them a few days earlier.

"Jemima, this is Christian, our new doctor," the priest had said, adding "Jemima is in charge of the women's and children's ward, and is a great favourite with everyone. Been here ... how long is it now, *cara*?"

It was the look in his eyes which had struck her. They had a gentleness absent in those of other doctors who had come for a few months at a time to the Mission. But her attraction, which had nothing physical about it, was tempered by fright. He was a male, and she had a pathological distrust, bordering on terror for men. But when she found that he did not try to make advances and wanted to be her friend, little by little she began to relax. She found that with him she could laugh again, and the agony that had been in her since her kidnapping eased.

The change was not wholly beneficial for it developed in her a new sensitivity to the suffering of those around. Until then, she had thrown herself into that sea of distress with an almost suicidal desire to drown. She now came to grips with the terrifying reality and found it difficult to live with. At moments, especially when she was washing the emaciated body of a famine victim, she would be seized by uncontrollable fits of sobbing, and she began to wonder whether she could live much longer among so much despair.

Christian asked her to marry him after one such moment. He was in the ward and, looking up from a patient, saw her huddled in a corner, shaking. He went over to her, put an arm around her shoulders and took her outside to sit in the shade of a jacaranda tree. He said nothing but handed her a

Kleenex with which to dry her tears. Then he began talking about the five year old boy he had just examined.

"He's coming on fine, you know. The boils are beginning to disappear. He's got a real soft spot for you, as they all have. You should see the way he watches you move around the ward."

"You're sweet, Christian ... but I'm such a mess. I don't think I can take it much more. Sometimes I wonder what I'm doing here and what's the use of it all. It's like trying to empty an ocean with a bucket."

"Shhh. You're overdoing it, that's all. You need a change. Tell you what, this evening I'll take you to Asmara. We can go to a cinema and have dinner in a restaurant. I bet you haven't been out of here for months."

"Years. Not since I arrived. No one ever asked me to, and anyway, I wouldn't have gone, even if they had."

"Why?"

"Because ... well, I just didn't feel like it. With you it's different, I feel you're a real friend. You don't know how much I need one ... "

He removed his arm from around her and started playing with a ring on his little finger.

"I do," he said softly. "Maybe because I need one too. I was very lonely till I came here. But you've changed that. I'll always be your friend if you want."

He paused and swallowed to relieve the parchness in his throat.

"Will you marry me, Jemima. I mean, I want you to know I'd like to be near you always and to be able to help you when necessary ... "

He was staring at the distant hills and struggling to keep himself from throwing his arms around her and smothering her with kisses.

"I can't," she said, "one day, if we remain friends, I'll tell you the reason, but not now."

"Is it because I'm coloured?" he asked with an urgency which made her eyes open wide. "If you're really my friend, you must tell me."

She shook her head slowly. "Oh, Christian, how could you think that ... "

"Then why? I've got to know."

She turned and faced him. There were no tears in those eyes which had become dry, opaque pebbles.

"All right, I'll tell you, and let's see if you're still a friend when you know what sort of girl I was; if you still want to marry me and not just take me to bed."

She spared him no details, the words erupting like bile through her tight lips, echoing her pent-up fears and obsessions.

"I hate men," she cried at the end, "I don't want to hate you too ... "

He turned and gripped her by the shoulders.

"I don't care about the past, except that I want to help you forget it. I love you, Jemima, can't you understand that? I want to be your husband, friend, lover, your brother too ... I'll never hurt you, I swear. You need me almost as much as I need you, but if for the moment you only want a friend, I'll be happy to be that and no more. Let me marry you so that I can protect you ... don't throw away a happiness which is there for both of us."

He let go of her, took her hand and brought it to his lips. Then he stood up abruptly.

"I guess we'd better get back in there," he said, mastering his emotion and nodding in the direction of the ward. He reached down and helped her to her feet. "First though I want to know if you're game for a film and dinner this evening. And you'd better be or I'll make it a doctor's order!"

She gave him a wan smile and murmured, "thanks." Then she leant over and placed a kiss on his cheek. "Maybe I will," she added.

Only afterwards it occurred to him that she was perhaps answering another question with that phrase.

They were married a month later in the Mission chapel, yet Jemima only became Christian's wife in name. He didn't attempt to make love to her during the week's honeymoon on the shore of the Red Sea, sensing that she hadn't got over her phobia of a man's body and sex. And back at the Mission he had a second bed put in their room, and made a point of never appearing naked or showing the excitement her body provoked in him.

One night she knelt by his bed and laid her head on the

pillow. She caressed his hair then his cheek, and let her lips brush his.

"Be patient a little longer ... you know something? You're really quite good looking!" she whispered. She kissed his eyes and then went back to her bed. A few days later she slipped under his sheets and let him caress her shoulders and run his fingers down her back to her waist. But when he tried to fondle her breasts, she moved away. "Next time, darling, I promise you."

She kept that promise. She reached out to him very early one morning and took his hand in hers. She kissed its palm and whispered, "come next to me." Half asleep he climbed out of his bed and got into hers. It was she who now caressed him, kissing the sleep from his eyes and rousing the passion forcibly latent in him for so long.

"I love you, Christian," she said at last as her body moved fully against his and she gazed deep into his eyes. "God, you've no idea how much I love you. Forgive me for making you suffer ... "

He didn't take her immediately but went on caressing and kissing her until it was she who demanded it. Gently he went into her whispering his love. Though his orgasm burst from him within seconds, a wave of immense tenderness engulfed her. It was not a climax, but that would come later, she knew. Her eyes filled with tears. How wonderful it was now that love was involved.

The spectre of Bruno had vanished at last.

Crete, 1984

On July 20th 1984 Julius went to see how his new project was getting on at Krinos, the island off the coast of Crete.

Tension in the Middle East had increased alarmingly with the exile of Iran's Shah Reza Pahlevi and the arrival on the political scene of Ayatollah Khomeini and his Shiite followers, the traditional opponents of Moslems who did not recognize Ali, the Prophet's cousin and son-in-law, and his descendants as the true Caliphs. Rapidly a certain fanaticism made itself felt. Attempts were made on the lives of other Moslem heads of states, war broke out between Iran and Iraq, and another religious faction began fighting in the Lebanese civil war.

Terrorism seemed to become an accepted way of life throughout the Middle East, Europe and the whole of the Mediterranean basin, and nine months earlier Julius had decided it was a scourge that had to be eliminated.

For over ten years he had devoted most of his time and energy to fostering peace without great success, he admitted, and the idea of doing something personally to combat terrorism had been germinating in him for quite a while. In May 1981, when an attempt was made on the life of Pope John Paul II, he decided the time had come to act. Though not a religious man, the fact that Christ's Vicar could be a political target shocked him. As he said to Laurrie Salvini, "someone should set about getting at these terrorists before they're able to act. I want to see the root of the problem attacked, and by that I mean capturing and, if need be, eliminating those basically responsible for international terrorism, or at least, rendering them innocuous."

"That also means putting the screw on men like Ghedaffi who not only encourage terrorism but finance it." Laurrie observed.

"Exactly. As I see it, there should be a special squad trained specifically for that, but independent of Governments, or it would be a non-starter. There will always be some reason trumped up why political pressure should not be put on a

Ghedaffi, a Hafez Assad or a Khomeini at a particular moment by one or another nation. But a private organisation would be free to act as it reckons right. And that's how I want it. A commando unit trained to strike at the nerve points of terrorism. It would work hand in hand with police forces and secret services, but not be under their control. It could do things which governments might want to do but for political or economic reasons can't or don't dare to. You're going to set one up for me, and you'll have Krinos as your base. The youngsters who are in the monastery at the moment can be transported over to a villa on Crete. My island will be unique for training purposes as no one need ever know what's happening, and secrecy in such an operation is 90 per cent of the game. Also look how strategically situated it is. Barely 250 kms from Libya, 800 from Beirut, hardly more than 700 from Istanbul … "

The idea became rapidly a reality. A quarter of a billion dollars went into financing a squad of 24 highly specialized commandos, and transforming Krinos into an island fortress with patrol boats, military helicopters, rocket launching pads and training grounds, and on January 2nd the major, as Laurrie was now called, had told him that the unit was ready for inspection. The whole operation had been carried out in total secrecy. No one, apart from he and Laurrie, knew the purpose for which the men were being trained or the reason for the new constructions. Visitors were forbidden on the island, and anyone trying to photograph it from out at sea was kept several kilometres away by armed guards on patrol boats.

Julius had finished his tour of inspection and was walking over to the helicopter which was to fly him to the airport on the Cretan mainland where his private jet was waiting, when a secretary ran out from the villa and told him that there was a call for him from New York.

He signalled to Laurrie Salvini sitting in the pilot's seat that he was going indoors again and would be a few minutes.

Laurrie switched off the engine, jumped to the ground and sprinted towards the old monastery. Four minutes later came the explosion.

As the helicopter disintegrated in flames and black smoke, he raced to the villa, shouting to the men who were now running to the scene to get back into the monastery, and in the entrance almost collided into Julius. He pushed him into the hall.

"Stay indoors please! I'll have the other one ready as fast as possible."

It was respectfully said, but an order, and accepted as such. Julius nodded and without a word went back to the library from where he had taken the phone call. To the secretary and servants he said quietly, "there's nothing to worry about. It's an accident, and no one has been hurt. As you saw, Major Salvini is O.K. and so am I. I'll be leaving as soon as the other helicopter is ready."

He had no illusions though; it had not been an accident. Someone wanted him dead. He sank into an armchair and reached for a cigar. Who could it be this time, he wondered? The problem was that his enemies were a legion, a faceless multitude who reproached him his wealth and influence and hated him not for what he was, but what they thought he stood for. Even his philanthropy was misinterpreted as a means to an end. He was both the implacable capitalist, the ally of imperialism, and the dangerous radical, depending from which political shore he was viewed.

Certain Congressmen regarded his past friendships with such leaders as Tito and Nasser and the Italian communist Berlinguer as proof of his real allegiance, while Arafat, Ghedaffi and the Ethiopian Mengistu denounced him as in the pay of Zionists and an arch enemy of socialism and Islam.

He frowned. The instigators of this new attempt on his life were probably to be found among his Islamic political detractors. Yet the leader of the O.L.P. and his henchmen were fully aware that he was no more a Zionist than Hammer a communist, and the others, Ghedaffi and Mengistu, knew that he had no political axe to grind, even if he had not hidden his views about the Libyan leader's support of international terrorism, or the Ethiopian's treatment of starving Eritreans. But those were hardly motives enough to have him eliminated.

He stood up and went to the window. A trail of smoke was spiralling into the sky behind the old fig tree, forming a question mark as a light breeze wafted the upper part towards the mainland. Whoever was responsible had got uncomfortably close this time, and that preoccupied him. Not the fact that he could die any moment, but that a fifth columnist could be there on his island, inside his own home.

Enemies and their hate he could deal with, but betrayal unnerved him.

All of a sudden, what Maryanne had said on the phone came back to him. Israeli Intelligence had just informed her husband that A.J. now formed part of Abu Nidal's organization, the terrorist group responsible for some of the most lethal highjackings and explosions in the previous decade, culminating in the shooting at the Viennese synagogue only eight months previously. The implications of what she had said became unpleasantly clear. A.J. himself might be involved in what had just happened. His own grandson could be behind what could easily have resulted in his death.

He shook his head. No, that was unlikely. He was an irresponsible hothead who had espoused a just cause but the wrong way and with the wrong people. One day he would come to his senses and realize how criminally useless terrorism was, and when that happened he would come to him for advice and even protection.

There was a knock on the door and Laurrie appeared.

"Everything's ready, sir, the second 'copter can leave when you want."

Julius nodded then asked, "it wasn't an accident, was it?"

"We haven't had time to establish the cause but ... " he bit his lower lip, "well, I reckon it was a bomb. How the hell they managed it, I don't know. Probably someone at the airport did it when it was there this morning. A bad slip up, but I prefer that than to think someone here could have been responsible."

"How can you be certain it wasn't an inside job?"

"I can't, only I know every one of my men, and there's no way any of the staff could have got to the aircraft here without being spotted. Also they've been with you for years ... Christ, *padrino,* I'm responsible for your security and yet this happened! I'll never forgive myself."

Julius smiled wryly and put an arm around his shoulders. "Don't take it that badly, we're none of us infallible. O.K, it was a near shave, but we're both here. Only we're warned, so you and your men will have to keep your eyes really skinned, even here and on the yacht. Remember, they nearly got you too, and if they had, I wouldn't have forgiven myself either. Come on, let's get over to the airport."

"If you don't mind, I think I'd better stay here to find out exactly what happened. I've told Mercier to take you there."

Julius nodded. "By the way," he said as they walked out of the villa, "it was a terrorist organization which indirectly saved both our skins. That call I got was from Maryanne to tell me that A.J. is now with the Abu Nidal outfit. It would be ironic if they were the ones who planted the bomb!"

June 1984

George was beaming. For two years he had been after Betty Schafferman's 48 per cent shareholding in her late husband's Trans-Oil Corporation. Two years of planning and subtle negotiating during which he and his lawyers had tried to convince the 'black widow' and her advisors that $102 per share was a highly advantageous offer. Also, that the merger with his Black Star Oil of Virginia would make her vice president of the eighth largest oil company in the USA; not a position offered to many women.

The dream had suddenly become a reality. Betty Schafferman had decided to accept his offer and her lawyer, Joseph Sebag, had just phoned to confirm it.

"If you agree, Sir George, we will draw up a memorandum which the parties can sign, after which an announcement can be made to the press."

"By all means," George had answered, "only I'd prefer it were made public once the official contract is signed. Let the others wait for the good news, it won't do any harm. We can celebrate the matter privately. Why don't you and Mrs Schafferman call round at my house, say tomorrow evening, and we could toast the occasion while we have that memo signed. May I leave it to you to see if that's all right for the lady?"

When he had flicked off the phone he leant back in his seat and lit a cigar. As president of the new company he would be bigger and more powerful than Julius Caspar, and from this position of superior strength he would finally be able to get the better of him.

His marriage to Paola had not dampened his determination to have his revenge on the man he was now convinced had somehow robbed him of his heritage; it had simply made him realize that only by outsmarting him in business would he find the way to crush him. Trying to gain control of Pharos Petroleum by laying his hands on a large percentage of its equity was impossible because of the way the Alexandrian had structured the Corporation, and the influence he had over the banks and other institutions who owned chunks of its shareholding. But now the situation could change. If he made a really attractive bid from the position of power which the merger with Trans-Oil would put him in, those other shareholders would have to consider his offer, and when that happened Julius Caspar would find himself in an awkward position.

He drew on his cigar. Bless Betty Schafferman. He could kiss the old trout!

Twelve hours later he raised a glass of champagne to her.

"To us, Madam, and to the memory of a remarkable man, your husband, Jerome Walter Schafferman, who would have rejoiced at the wise decision you have taken."

"That was very nicely said, Sir George. I too am certain that the late Mr Schafferman has helped me make up my mind. It was not an easy decision but I am sure it was the right one. I hope it will mean that you and I will become good friends as well as good business associates. And now I believe you and I should initial that document, isn't that so, Mr Sebag?"

George smiled to himself as he reached for the memo and laid it out on the table in front of her. She had played coy for two years but now couldn't wait to sign up. The thought crossed his mind that he might have obtained her shareholding for less, but he didn't care. It was money well spent as it secured him what he had set out to get. He'd make Julius Caspar pay for the extra dollars per share he had had to offer her.

As she scratched her initials at the bottom of each page, he wondered why the Alexandrian's henchmen had not managed to tempt her into their camp. Rumours had it that an offer had been made, but that she had turned it down. Caspar of course hadn't dealt with the matter personally, he was too tied up with Middle Eastern politics to give much time to business, and that was his weakness now. He was out of touch with what was going on and the men who worked for him hadn't his flair or charisma. Even Maryanne had dropped out of the game, and she was the only other person who could have handled a negotiation like this.

He reached for his own pen and in turn initialled the

document. Then he handed it to the lawyer who said, "thank you, Sir George. I will ask the vice-president of Trans-Oil to do likewise for the Corporation and then I will let you have a copy."

"Send it to Michael Webster and liaise with him over the actual agreement. I'll be in Europe for three weeks and when I get back we'll be able to complete. Needless to say he'll be in constant touch with me, so if there are any points you have to discuss for some reason or other ... "

"I don't see why there should be any. The basic ones are agreed, Sir George."

George left for London the following afternoon. He had been asked to address the Institute of Directors and a dinner had been arranged two days later at 10 Downing Street where his advice was to be sought on the question of the denationalization of some government controlled industries. He knew that the Prime Minister had it in mind to set up a commission to study how best to hand these back to private enterprise, and his name had been put forward to head the commission. And that could mean a life peerage and a position of power in the country's affairs in the area which interested him most. Also there was to be a meeting the following week in Paris of the Trilateral Commission, an event he did not want to miss. As one of Europe's leading industrialists, he had been asked to address its members, an honour he was especially looking forward to since he had been told that Julius Caspar was to be present.

The five days in London proved a series of personal successes. His speech at the Institute of Directors was widely and approvingly commentated in the press, and two days later the Prime Minister's Secretary phoned him to say that he would be receiving the official offer to head the commission as soon as he had indicated that he would accept it. To cap it all, his horse won at Epsom, beating the Aga Khan's favourite against all provisions.

After the weekend at a friend's country house where he won £40,000 at poker, he flew over to Paris and on the Monday afternoon rang Michael Webster.

"You haven't yet received the memo from Sebag? Then what are you waiting for to get on to him? It should have been with you on Wednesday. Phone him now and ring me straight back."

Webster did. "Nothing to worry about. It's simply that the Trans-Oil vice-president who has to initial the document for the Company wasn't available. He'll be back in a couple of days, and Sebag has promised to see to it personally that he signs, and have it round to us immediately. In the meantime, we are getting on with the agreement so that everything will be ready when you return."

George put the matter from his mind and went to address the Trilateral Commission. He was vexed not to find the Alexandrian among those present but an invitation to lunch at the Elysée Palace with his friend Giscard d'Estaing, followed by a ceremony during which he was invested with the *Légion d'Honneur*, made up for it.

Back at his apartment he received a phone call from Michael Webster. "We've got that agreement drawn up. Shall I send it round to Sebag for comments or would you like to see it first?"

"What comments? You've drawn it up together, haven't you?"

"Well, yes and no. We saw each other on Friday, after you phoned, and drafted it in principle, and it was agreed that I would get it into proper shape while he was away. He's due back tomorrow and I was going to arrange a meeting so that we could go through it together ... "

"Have you received the memo yet?"

"No, but as the vice-president has been away and so has Sebag ... "

A sudden rage gripped George. What the hell was that bloody little lawyer of Betty Schafferman playing at? He had no right to delay matters simply because it suited him. And as for the vice-president of Trans-Oil, he would be out unless he had a very plausible reason for not having been on the spot when needed.

"I don't care a fuck where they are," he shouted. "If the memo isn't with you by noon tomorrow, I want you to phone that Schafferwoman and tell her that the two of them are taking us both for a ride. Christ! Who do the little buggers think they are dealing with!"

"I assure you, Sir George ... "

"You bloody well assure me you've got that memo, that's

all. If I have to take a plane back because you haven't got it tomorrow, there'll be hell to pay."

George's anger was partly due to the fact that he was not complete master of the situation. He was not in a position to bluff, as he had so often in the past, because this was a deal which involved much more than a remarkably good piece of business, and the apex of his career. Through it he would finally be in the position to fulfil his fundamental ambition of vengeance. To topple and trample on Julius Caspar.

It was a deal he could not afford to lose.

Aboard his yacht anchored outside the bay of Monte Carlo, Julius contemplated the twinkling lights of the French Riviera. Indoors some thirty guests were listening to a piano recital by Nelson, a foretaste of the concert he was to give the next evening at the Opera House.

Julius had slipped out onto the deck for a few minutes to take a decision. It was an important one, for it had to do with George, and it was the first time that a question of sentiment was entering into play with his business.

For several months he had been aware that his son had set his sights on Trans-Oil, but he had not been particularly concerned as he knew that whatever decision Betty Schafferman might take, the vice-president was totally against a merger with George's Black Star Oil.

However, matters had suddenly come to a head when, a few hours earlier, he had received a phone call from Jack Leigh.

"I have just learned from a colleague that Mrs Schafferman has agreed to do a deal with Sir George Christofides at $102 a share. Steve Carradis, the vice-president, is as sore as hell but reckons there's little he can do if he wants to retain his job. He's stalling, but at a given moment he'll have to ratify a memo setting out the terms of the agreement, unless someone comes forward with a better proposition."

"Meaning?"

"Betty Schafferman isn't married to Sir George, yet. Only engaged as it were. And, according to Carradis, she'll swap fiancé if the price is upped."

"What does it work out per share?"

"112."

"Give me a few hours and I'll come back with my decision."

"If you decide to go ahead I suggest you get straight through to Joseph Sebag, her attorney. I'll give you his number."

Julius turned and looked into the room where Nelson was playing one of Brahms' rhapsodies. His gaze travelled over several faces until it came to rest on Paola's. Through her, he reflected, he and George should have become closer, yet none of the overtures he had made had led to anything. George had persistently, almost defiantly, given him the cold shoulder. His absence today was just one example. He had preferred to miss Nelson's concert rather than accept his hospitality.

The rhapsody came to an end and the guests clapped enthusiastically. Julius was shaken out of his reverie. There was no option. His personal rapport with his son must not influence his decision. He could not let pass a business opportunity in the hopes that, by so doing, relationships with George might improve.

They never could. George was an adversary who could become dangerously powerful if he got control of Trans-Oil. The fact that he was his son and married to his goddaughter, had nothing to do with it. He did not trust him. He could not trust him.

He walked slowly to his study, switched on the 'Do not disturb' sign and went to sit at his desk. He remained for a long while gazing at the portrait of Marguerite. Then he leaned forward and called the radio operator over the intercom.

"Get the following number in New York and say I want to speak personally to Mr Joseph Sebag."

George got the news on the Tuesday afternoon. Michael Webster phoned him to say that there had been a slight hitch as Sebag had been delayed out of New York, but that they would get together by the end of the week. George slammed down the telephone and caught the first Concorde to the USA.

He was certain now that more than a last minute hitch was responsible for the breakdown of the negotiations. It wasn't just a move by Betty Schafferman to squeeze a few dollars more per share, nor an internal fight between her and the other shareholders of Trans-Oil. Something much more serious and fundamental had taken place, and he cursed himself for not having sensed it nine days previously when the promised memo hadn't been immediately signed by the company's vice-president, and sent round to Michael Webster.

There could only be one answer, he thought grimly as his plane taxied along the runway; someone else had made a bid for the 'Black Widow's' shares, a better one than his, and she was in the process of tying up the deal. But she would not get away with it. If she tried to, he would slap an injunction on her and stop her coming to an agreement with anyone. He'd sue her to her last dollar, the bloody bitch of a woman. But who could have come up with a last minute bid, or had she been playing a double game for months? He speculated on a few financial giants who might be behind the coup, but discarded them one by one. Curiously it never even crossed his mind that Julius Caspar could have done it. For him the Alexandrian was out of the money power game; he was to be the victim and not the victor of the Trans-Oil merger.

He arrived at his house at 3 a.m. As usual the morning's newspapers were already on the table next to his bed. He picked up the first and glanced at the various headlines. His eye rested on a caption towards the bottom left hand corner. 'Oil companies in $8 billion deal'. There it was in black and white. Trans-Oil had just announced that they were being merged with Pharos Petroleum which had made a $8.3 billion offer for its stock. Principal shareholder, Mrs J. Walter Schafferman, commented that the offer was unexpected but that it was one neither she nor the company could turn down. It represented $112 per share.

George felt the blood drain from him and a strange sensation of timelessness grip him. A spectator at his own impotence, he saw himself reach out to the table to keep his balance, slip and fall to the floor. He watched a decanter of whisky hurtle down next to his cheek and smash on the foot of the bed. He passed out as the amber liquid splashed over his face.

The noise brought his Portuguese manservant hurrying into the room, and when George came to, he was being heaved up onto the bed.

"Are you hurt, sir?"

Suddenly his blood rushed back to his brain, and his fury broke forth.

"Bloody shit," he yelled at the man, sending his fist in his face. "What the fucking hell do you think you're doing. How dare you ... " He stopped half way through the phrase and glared wildly around the room.

The valet retreated to the door. "Sir, it wasn't my fault. You must have fallen … I came and you were on the floor."

George looked balefully at him. "What the hell's wrong with you? I'm the one who fell, not you." He had absolutely no recollection of having hit him. "Christ! I'm soaked in whisky. Help me get these clothes off. Come on, man, what the devil are you waiting for?"

Then he caught sight of the newspaper and he remembered what he had read. He struggled out of his jacket and loosened his tie. Kicking off his shoes, he stripped and threw clothes at Enriques. His mind was icily clear again. He would sue the 'Black Widow', Trans-Oil and Pharos for the heftiest damages in corporation history. As for Julius Caspar, he would use every weapon in his power to crush him.

"I'll kill the bloody bugger," he yelled suddenly, smashing his fist down on a table top.

For a second time he was seized by a moment's giddiness. He steadied himself, and when it had passed he made his way slowly to the bed. He glanced at his watch. 3.40 a.m. He had given instructions to be woken at 7.15, so he tried to get some sleep. He managed 35 minutes and the rest of the time he stared into the darkness formulating a plan of action.

He would engage Joseph Jamail, the personal liability specialist who was the USA's most spectacularly successful lawyer in this type of litigation. He would call a press conference and expose the Alexandrian as one of the most unethical wheeler-dealers of the international business world, and he would make sure that no member of his family had any further dealings with him. If Paola as much as addressed the man a nod, he would divorce her on the spot, and Nelson would be told never to have anything to do with him again. Jemima would be ordered home; Don Francesco was Caspar's closest friend and as such an enemy from now on.

The decisions brought him respite, but the frustration of having been outwitted by the man he had planned to humble — and on the specific deal which would have given the power finally to triumph — took much of the zest out of the game.

Eritrea, 1984

During the last two months of 1984 an event took place which most of the world either ignored or knew nothing about. Several thousand Falashas, the Jews of Ethiopia, were secretly transported by air from neighbouring Sudan to Israel. The airlift of these persecuted people was known as Operation Moses.

The Falashas had been a respected minority until the Marxist military government deposed the ageing Emperor Haile Selasse, and instituted a policy of discrimination against the Jewish elements of the population. These were grouped mostly in the northern areas, those adjoining and forming part of the Tigre and Eritrean provinces.

Tradition has it that the Queen of Sheba — Sheevah for the Ethiopians — had a son by King Solomon, and that this son grew up to be the first Emperor Menelik. His tomb is at Aksoum, considered by many a holy town, and by the Falashas a second Jerusalem.

Aksoum was 80 kms from Don Francesco's Mission, and inevitably he had come in contact with the Jewish minority who had lived in dignified co-existence with the rest of the population for over thirty centuries.

The nearest Falasha village, situated between Aksoum and Dukambia, was only some 30 kms to the south-west, and on several occasions Don Francesco had visited it and had talks with the Rabbi. He was fully aware of the growing anti-Semitism encouraged by the military junta, and when it came to aiding a number of Falashas cross into the Sudan, he immediately offered to help.

Jemima and Christian assisted by accompanying refugees over the border and making sure they reached the camps in the Sudan safely, a tricky operation as it was imperative that the Sudanese did not suspect they were Jewish and different from the other fugitives from Ethiopia. The Sudan was predominantly Moslem and had recently adopted Islamic law. The ruler, General Nimeyri, was a friend of Egypt's but a firm opposer of the Camp David agreements between Israel and his northern neighbour. Jews, even if refugees from a hostile country, were persona non grata. The Ethiopian ruling junta considered the exodus as dangerous to national security and imprisoned, or put to death, anyone caught helping the Falashas or suspected of being involved in their leaving the country. And, there was the danger of being denounced by an informer, as often or not a relation or someone close to a refugee, who hoped to ingratiate himself with the local governor.

Don Francesco was already looked upon with suspicion for his medical help to the guerillas, and the man in charge of crushing them, a colonel at the Asmara army headquarters, was waiting for an opportunity to get rid of this enemy of Islam in the pay of imperialists, as he called him. It came with a tip-off about the priest's involvement in Operation Moses.

In the night of December 8th, while he was celebrating Mass for the Feast of the Immaculate Conception, two lorry-loads of soldiers armed with kalachnikovs roared up to the mission. Three strode into the chapel with their leader, a young captain, and seized him, while others broke into the Missions' wards and living quarters. They arrested a doctor and a male nurse, as well as three nuns and then turned their guns on the beds of the men's ward. With the excuse that they were executing rebel traitors, they murdered 11 men who had nothing to do with the Tigre Liberation Front but were simply victims of chronic malnutrition.

When Don Francesco attempted to intervene he was knocked unconscious with a blow from a rifle butt, and dumped in a truck. No one was allowed to tend his fractured jaw, or nurse his head as they bumped along the dirt road to Asmara. He lost consciousness and was still in a coma when the trucks entered the barracks on the outskirts of the city.

Christian and Jemima had left with a convoy of refugees two days before, and it was only when they tried to return into Abyssinia that they learned what had happened. Not the full implications, only that Don Francesco had been arrested and that they themselves were not allowed back into the country. The frontier guard had been replaced, and their offer of money was brusquely brushed aside. So they decided to get back to the nearest town and phone Julius.

Five days passed before Jemima was able to contact him and still no one knew exactly what had happened to the priest. But Julius had few illusions as to how his 77 year old friend would be treated. Political prisoners in certain African countries were often worse off than thieves or murderers.

He threw all his prestige into getting Francesco freed, even offering a huge some of money for his release. But Mengistu, the country's dictator, was away in Moscow and no one in the junta was prepared to take a decision. He tried to have pressure brought through the US Embassy and even had his contacts in the Kremlin intercede, but with no result.

On December 16th Julius phoned Laurrie Salvini in Krinos.

"Your uncle has been thrown into prison. With the sort of treatment he'll get, and given his age and health, he could die if he's not freed immediately. I've tried every method to secure his release, but with no result. So we have no alternative but to take the matter into our own hands. In a few hours I hope to have details of where he and the others are being held. When we know that, you have my blessing to act as you think best. Remember, Don Francesco is the man closest to my heart. I don't want to lose him."

"You won't, *padrino*," Laurrie answered. It was a statement of fact not just a promise.

Forty-eight hours later the M.Y. Marguerite was cruising at maximum speed out of the Gulf of Suez and into the Red Sea. On board were 12 of Julius' special force, trained to make attacks on terrorist strongholds and to release hostages. They had already managed one such successful exploit in the outskirts of Beirut, and the prospect of freeing the uncle of their own leader from the clutches of military thugs gave them an added motivation.

The plan of action was simple and daring. The yacht would sail to within a few miles of Massawa. From there a helicopter was to fly them straight to the military camp outside Asmara. A lightning attack in the middle of the night would surprise the men guarding the priest and other members of the Mission. They would free whoever they could and, with luck, would be away again before the guards became aware of what was happening. Julius had been able to get details of the camp from a business acquaintance in Asmara who was a friend of the Governor, and who had been allowed to speak to the officer in command, and see the sheds where the prisoners were kept. They were in good health, he had been assured, even if Don Francesco was recovering from a 'slight accident' and had to stay in bed.

The raid was successful to a point of vengeance. Five guards were killed; and the man who had smashed the priest's jaw mortally wounded in a four minute bloody skirmish, during which the six captives were freed and whisked away by helicopter before the rest of the garrison had woken to what was happening.

Yet the price paid by those for whom Don Francesco had toiled a lifetime to help was terrible.

While the yacht was heading back towards the Gulf of Suez, a lorryload of soldiers was on its way to the Mission. This time the machine guns spared no one. Seven women and nine children were shot to death in their beds and the wards were burnt to the ground. Two nearby villages were also razed, and their inhabitants brutalized before being led off to desert camps.

There was immeasurable sadness in Francesco's eyes when Julius visited him in the yacht's infirmary.

"Bless you Antor, it's good to see you," he murmured through his bandages, "but how I wish it were in different circumstances. You should have left me there, I'd have been all right ... all that violence, that shooting and killing ... it was wrong ... "

"I know, Francesco, but it was necessary. I tried every other way but they wouldn't listen. And we couldn't leave you there, you'd have died. I couldn't let that happen, you know that."

A faint smile appeared on his friend's lips. "Do you reckon you're powerful enough to challenge death too? I'm an old man, older than you, remember. But my days are counted by He who gave them to me. Oh, my friend, don't think I do not appreciate what you and Lorenzo have done, and all those brave men with him. Especially, I am glad for those you managed to bring away with me. But what will happen to the people at the Mission? My place is with them, not here, even if I'm glad to be with you. As soon as I am well you must arrange for me to go back. Promise me that, Antor."

330

Julius took his hand in his. "I'll see what can be done, that I promise you. But first you must get better. Those savages ... "

"No, don't call them that. They are misguided. Their lives are so difficult it is not easy for them to discern what is right and wrong, just or unjust. Violence can only be overcome by love. You know that or you wouldn't have helped me with my work for nearly half a century. Nor would you have devoted so much of your time and energy, of your wealth too, to furthering peace in the world. There can be no peace without understanding, and no understanding without love. Get me back there quickly, Antor ... "

Don Francesco was not taken off the yacht when it arrived back at Krinos. The shock of his imprisonment and the blows he had received — his body showed marks of kicks and beatings — had weakened his resistance to a point that doctors reckoned he had only a few days to live. Julius moved into the cabin adjoining his and stayed constantly with him.

On Christmas Eve the Salvini clan — Pietro and his wife, Clara Strapakis and Paola — arrived from New York to celebrate Mass with him. And the next day they gathered around the man who had been more than a brother, an uncle, a friend, knowing that his smile and blessing would be the last they would receive.

Shortly after midday Francesco's bed was brought to the glassed-in foredeck and from there he was able to scan the horizon beyond which stretched his beloved Africa.

"Get me back there soon," were his last words.

Julius knelt by the bed on which Francesco's body was resting.

A feeling of tragic loneliness seized him. He closed his eyes and gripping tightly the cross on his chest, prayed. Not to God, but to the friend who was no longer with him.

"Help me be the man you wanted me to be and not the one I am. Help me walk the path you did; help me love and understand people."

Yet how could he, he cried within himself as his heart ached with grief and bitterness? Love meant justice and there never could be justice while men of violence were allowed to perpetrate acts of terror. Peace, understanding, love, those words which, in the mouth of Francesco had had a profound and ultimate significance, were meaningless in a world ruled by treachery and indifference to human dignity.

He could not love those men. He could only fight them.

Rome, 1987

A.J. stared at the massive, gates of the American Embassy in Rome. He then glanced at his watch. In a couple of minutes the guard plate would be lowered and the Ambassador's limousine would come out into Via Veneto, turn left into Via Bissolati and disappear down Via XX Settembre towards the Quirinale.

He watched the traffic move slowly, pretending to wait until he could cross to the other pavement. When the lights went red he glanced again at his watch. A minute late, he reckoned. He decided to cross, dodged between the two rows of oncoming cars, and was pausing in the middle of the street when a policeman strode out and halted the traffic. The Embassy gates swung open, the guard plates lowered, and a black Cadillac, followed by a police car sped out, passing within two metres of where A.J. was standing.

He had a good view of the man sitting in the back, and for a second he caught the eye of his victim designate. A faint smile flickered on his lips. In forty eight hours the Ambassador would be his prisoner, or dead.

"Remember, we want him alive. So keep your finger away from the trigger. You're only to kill if things go wrong and there's no other solution," had been the orders.

The decision to kidnap the Ambassador had been taken after one of President Reagan's forthright denunciations of Libya's Colonel Ghedaffi as the man behind international terrorism, and his threat to take effective action against him. The diplomat had been chosen because he was both American and Jewish, and as such incarnated the enemy of certain Islamic extremists. Also, Rome was the rallying point of anarchists, and the group with which A.J. worked could be sure of help. A base was needed, as were arms, false identity cards, transport and contacts, and in Italy these were all available.

He had arrived clandestinely two days earlier. A sailing yacht had picked him up in Malta and disembarked him on the island of Ponza. From there he had caught the ferry to Terracina and a local train to Rome. He travelled with a Swiss passport under the name of Antoine Basche, in which his profession was stated as bank employee.

Once in the Italian capital, he walked to Via Firenze, five minutes from the station, and went to a pension where a room had been reserved for him. There he met up with Najla, who took him to an apartment a little beyond San Giovanni in Laterano in Via Taranto. They walked up to the third floor, where she knocked and then tapped with her nails on a door. It was opened by a man A.J. did not know, who welcomed them with the particular salute which the members of the group used between each other. In a room off a corridor he found two of the men who had been his companions in most of the terrorist activities in which he had taken part. Immediately, they sat around a table and explained the plan of action.

Two hours later he left with Najla and dined in a *pizzeria* near the pension. Then they went off to bed, each in his own room.

A.J. wondered whether Najla would come to him that night. Sometimes she did, especially before a dangerous and important coup. The first time had been three years earlier when he had been sent into Israel to blow up a bus of Jewish American tourists visiting Jerusalem. It had been a disaster, as abortive as the terrorist action. But Najla had not taken it badly.

"Don't worry," she had whispered, "it can happen to the best of men. And it's your first time, isn't it?"

He had risen to the second occasion, but only just. It wasn't that she didn't attract him, but when it came to the act, somehow the physical excitement lessened and he wasn't always able to consummate it. If the thrill of a killing or of a successful terrorist action was still with him then, yes, he could make love, even several times running.

That evening, thinking of the violence he'd shortly be involved in, the sexual urge began to make itself felt. But he didn't go to her room. He had never taken the initiative, leaving her to decide when she wanted him, just as he let her choose which missions he should be sent on and when. He was so much under her sway that he could have even killed himself had she had demanded it.

Other than for his mother, his feelings for Najla represented the only form of love of which he was capable. Curiously passion and tenderness had nothing to do with it, nor even shared political ideals. She represented a force which was absent in him, yet vital, and his infatuation was a form of adolescent hero worship, dominant if tenuous. An undisciplined loner, A.J. yearned for authority. Through her and the terrorist group, this subconscious need was fulfilled.

Lying naked on his bed, he grinned in the darkness. That Ambassador, he remembered suddenly, was a friend of his uncle Julius. What would the old bastard think when he learned that it was he who had carried out the coup? He reached for a packet of cigarettes and lit one. He wondered if he already knew that he was now with a terrorist group. Sure, the man always knew everything. A monster, was what Najla had called him. And when he had told her that he was the Alexandrian's adopted son, she had left him on his own in his hide-out after shouting that if he were related to that man he could drop dead as far as she was concerned.

But she had come back and no mention again had been made of Julius Caspar.

"We've decided you need a *nom de bataille* and not keep the one you have," was the only indirect reference she had made to his past. And from then on he was known as Assad, [the lion]. "You're not much like one, but it'll do. At least I don't think you lack courage."

It wasn't courage which made him undertake dangerous and daring tasks. It was a complete absence of responsibility, and the killer urge in him. Also an almost desperate desire to shine in the eyes of the one person he loved in his warped way.

The cigarette finished, he stubbed it out and turned on his side, his face to the wall. She wouldn't come, he knew it now. Perhaps tomorrow night, before the planned action for the following morning. He went over in his mind what had been said that afternoon.

"He's expected at the F.A.O [Food and Agriculture Organization] building at 10.30 a.m. Normally he has a motorcycle escort as well as his bodyguard in the car. If all goes according to plan, he'll leave the Embassy at 10.10 and take this route. The place we must strike at is here. It's a short cut to bypass Piazza Venezia, and his chauffeur nearly always takes it."

Someone had interposed "and supposing he doesn't'".

"We'll make sure he does by creating an accident in Via IV Novembre, so he'll have to. Then the car following him will be cut off by a van which'll hurtle out of this side street the moment his car has gone by. After which, just before he reaches the Via dei Fori Imperiali — that's the large avenue leading to the Colosseum — a car will come out and ram the front motorcyclist. We'll deal with the other while you and Najla attack the Cadillac. How you do that is your lookout. Only remember, the Ambassador's car is bulletproof and there'll be a man inside armed to the teeth. The success of the operation depends on speed. A similar attack was carried out successfully a few years back when the head of the Christian Democrats here was kidnapped, so there's no reason why this one shouldn't work if each one does his job properly. We have the weapons and you can choose what you want. We've also organized where to hide the man and how to get him out of Italy. Fortunately we're not alone in our fight against American and Israeli imperialism."

A.J. brushed a mosquito away. If only the plan had been to kill and not kidnap, he thought. Had he been allowed to shoot him or blow him up, it would have been so much simpler. He and Najla could have arranged that on their own without having to rely for help from other terrorist organizations. One could never tell if they would really do what they had promised, or be certain that one of them wasn't an informer. Also a shock killing of an important US Ambassador would have a profound effect on public opinion. Execute five or six of them, and Reagan would lose his bombast as well as the support of the average American. That was what the Organization wanted.

He reached under the pillow and touched the butt of his revolver. The cool steel had an immediate and calming effect on him. Within seconds he was asleep.

The following day he was driven to the spot where the hold-up was to take place. He spent half an hour pacing the street and choosing where he would stand with Najla at the moment of action, discussing with her and the other two men the exact timing of the attack. Then, abruptly, he said that he wanted to visit the Colosseum.

"It's that place over there isn't it? O.K., we can meet up again this afternoon. Najla, coming with me?"

She nodded and the two made their way down the Via dei Fori Imperiali to the great arena some 500 metres away.

Once inside, A.J. gazed around in silence. "Don't you find it terrific here," he murmured. "Jesus, it must have been great to be alive in Roman times. Think of the excitement when slaves fought each other to death, and lions gored Christians. I can just see it all. And the emperor deciding with a turn of a thumb whether a man was to live or not. Hell of a guy that Nero."

"Get your facts right and calm down," she threw at him. "The Colosseum wasn't built when Nero was alive. He had his Golden House here. The place you're thinking about, where he had the Christians killed, was the other side of the Tiber, near the Vatican.

"How the hell do you know?"

"By reading this guide book. But come on, let's have lunch. I'm hungry. Vittorio told me of a place near here which isn't bad."

She led him to a restaurant in Via Claudia, opposite the high walls of the Ninfeo di Nerone, which was full of students and hardly any tourists. After a *pasta all' arrabiata* and an *ossobuco,* washed down with a white wine from the Roman hills, they wandered along the Via San Stefano Rotondo to the Lateran, through the Porta San Giovanni and across to the apartment in Via Taranto. There they remained until dusk, when they caught a taxi back to their pension.

They dined in a *trattoria* near the station, and by 10 p.m were heading back to their rooms when A.J. stopped in his tracks and said suddenly, "I want to go back to the Colosseum. Coming with me? It's full moon and it should be terrific."

She shook her head. "No. I'm going to bed, as you should."

He hesitated, waiting for a hint that she might share that bed with him, but it didn't come.

"I'm not sleepy. I won't be long, not more than an hour. I'll knock on your door when I get back. O.K.?"

He watched her cross the road and turn into Via Firenze, then climbed into a taxi. Five minutes later he was there.

In the moonlight, the huge walls seemed even more impressive. He walked round them, oblivious of the traffic shooting past, trying to find a way to get inside. But all the entries were barred, and this provoked a sense of frustration in him which turned to irritation then apprehension. Earlier it had represented a kind of spiritual home, exciting and vitalizing. Shut out of it, he got the sensation that fortune was somehow against him. The elation turned to anxiety and the muscle in the pit of his stomach began to knot. Instinctively he reached for the gun tucked in his trousers.

He crossed the road and tried to hail a taxi, but several passed before one stopped. He got out of it in Via Nazionale and walked quickly down to the spot where he had left Najla. He was about to cross into Via Firenze, when two police cars skidded past him.

Immediately on the alert, he ran to a nearby café, from where he saw that they had stopped in front of his pension. Thirty seconds later shots were heard.

He didn't panic, and the reflex of self-preservation, developed over six years of training, jumped into action. He went back to the main thoroughfare and made for the station.

He was in luck. There was a train leaving for Pisa ten minutes later. So he ran down to the washrooms and got himself a shower cubicle. He shaved off his ten day stubble of beard and combed his hair with a parting. He then ripped the photograph from his passport, tore it to threads, and threw it down the lavatory. The rest of the document he dumped in a waste bin before boarding his train.

Antoine Basche existed no more. His place was taken by an American student called Tony Holt. If the Italian police, or Interpol, were on the look out for Najla's accomplice, they wouldn't take much notice of a serious looking youngster over in Europe to gather data for his thesis on Renaissance Humanism.

There were two other people in the compartment, a young soldier and a dark haired girl. He made a point of not catching their eyes, and stared out of the window.

With the immediate danger over, he began to wonder what could have happened. A tip-off from a police informer, or had he and Najla been spotted somehow by the special anti-terrorist section of Interpol?

And Najla, was she wounded or had she been killed? The thought that he might never see her again didn't sadden him; he was conscious only that he no longer needed her, and that from then on he would act on his own. He would show his fellow terrorists and the world in general, that 'Assad' could mastermind and carry off alone any exploit, however dangerous. He'd kill the President of America or any Head of State to prove his point. Let them ask him, and they would see. Yes, for his next coup they'd have to choose a really important person. No small fry any more, but someone to measure himself against once and for all.

He rested his head on the seat cushion and closed his eyes. He would have to tread carefully during the next 24 hours, as stations, airports and harbours would be crawling with police, and the rendezvous with the man who was to get him across to Corsica wasn't until the following evening. But that didn't worry him. It wouldn't be the first time he gave Europe's police forces the slip, nor the last.

He reached under his jacket for his revolver. As long as he had that, no one would trap him.

The case brought by Sir George Christofides and his Black Star Oil Company against the Pharos Trans-Oil Corporation, Betty Schafferman and Julius Caspar was due for hearing by the Supreme Court on February 20th 1989.

The conflict between these two giants of the business and finance world was common knowledge, and there were several astute men who sought to draw advantages from it. One of these was the chairman of Mega Petroleum, who was waging a series of takeover battles against some of the best entrenched oil companies, and making the weaker ones scramble to the shelter of a merger before they found themselves swallowed up by this whale devouring piranha.

Admittedly, Mega Petroleum, with its 1988 sales of $385 million, was small fry in comparison to either Black Star Oil [sales $960 million] or Pharos Trans-Oil [$3.7 billion] but George, obsessed by his case against Julius and blind to what was going on around him, had not taken much notice of this dangerous competitor even if his methods to gain control of large corporations were much the same as those George had used to build up his own empire. Julius, however, was very conscious of the peril, and one of the reasons he wanted to come to terms with George as quickly as possible was to make quite sure Mega's chairman did not pounce the moment the case was over. For he was certain that whatever the outcome, either Black Star or Pharos would be the man's next target.

Julius was not concerned for his own firm, but he was for Black Star. The businessman in him rejected the idea that a company which normally should be merged with Pharos should go to an outsider, and the sentimentalist longed to have his own son with him rather than in the clutches of a stranger.

Also, he was aware that the rift between them would become unbridgeable once the case went for its final hearing. Whatever the jury's decision, the sentence could never fully quench George's thirst for vengeance, and risked cementing his bitterness into a stolid wall of hate. Which was why he took the initiative of inviting Mega's chairman to a meeting with him in the New York offices of Pharos Trans-Oil. The proposal he made his potential opponent was straightforward.

"Everyone knows you've set your sights on Black Star, and I wish you luck. But let me tell you this. Make your bid before the Supreme Court hearing and you won't have me interfering with your plans. If you wait until after, either Sir George Christofides will be so full of money that a takeover will be useless even to consider, or I will have won, and you'll have me and my company to contend with."

"Has it occurred to you that yours might be the company I'm interested in and not Black Star?"

"Sure, but I put the thought away, as obviously you did. I respect you too much as a businessman to think that you'd want a company landed with colossal damages to pay in the event — a remote possibility, but one all the same — that we lose the case. And if the ruling is in our favour, as I expect, then we'll be too much of a tough nut to crack even for your sharp teeth. Forgive the metaphor, but it's meant as a compliment."

The boss of Mega Petroleum chuckled. "I take it as such, Mr Caspar. O.K. then, what's the deal? You didn't propose this meeting simply to get me to make a bid for Black Star before February 20th."

"You're right," Julius said, lightly drumming the arm of his chair with his left hand fingers. He was silent for some thirty seconds and then went on: "Gas, that's the deal. You know the stocks we have in reserve. I'll give you an option on a quarter of them at a discount of 20 per cent if you make that bid for Black Star Oil within the next ten days. Work it out for yourself, it's one hell of a present I'm making you."

"I agree. And that's what worries me. You've never been known to make any in business. Let me hear the rest of the deal."

Julius pursed his lips. "An option for me on some of Black Star shares at today's price if you are successful in your bid."

Again the other man smiled. "On how many exactly?"

"I'm open to suggestions, but to give you a guideline, I had in mind Christofides' personal holding."

On February 4th 1985, Mega Petroleum made it's bid for Black Star Oil. The board of directors of George's company were not in agreement on what policy to adopt, certain even welcoming a change of chairmanship.

In a meeting which began at 8.30 a.m. and went on until exactly 12 minutes past four in the afternoon, strategies were suggested, voices raised and loyalties questioned. George stormed out of the room three times. He was determined to beat off the bid whatever the cost, changing the companies bylaws if necessary, or even adopting a poison pill defence action such as to make the takeover so expensively unattractive for Mega that it would withdraw its offer.

Then someone suggested dropping the case against Caspar and doing a merger with Pharos Trans-Oil. That someone was Ron Taggart, who had been primed by Jack Leigh, the man who had set up Pharos Petroleum twenty five years previously.

George jumped to his feet, his eyes blazing, and crashed his fist down on the table.

"How dare you mention that man's name to me," he shouted, "I'll give this company away to Mega rather than see a single share go to him. You bloody bastard, what's he paid you to propose that? Get out of here, I won't have a man on the board who … "

"Sir George, please calm yourself," the director sitting next to him cried as he leant over and placed a restraining hand on his arm.

"Let go of me, damn you, and you Taggart … "

He never finished the sentence. Suddenly he tottered and the next moment fell forwards onto the boardroom table, splitting his head open on a glass of water. His lips went on twitching while his left eye stared blankly at the rivulet of blood seeping its way into the notepad beneath his jaw. Ten minutes later an ambulance was rushing him to a reanimation centre.

Thanks to the skill of one of America's leading brain surgeons George did not die from apoplexy. His life was spared, but he remained completely paralysed, not even able to speak. He could understand what people were saying, but only the expression in his eyes gave a hint of what passed through his mind.

Julius flew to see him as soon as he learnt what had happened. The moment of truth had come, he said to himself as he paused in the doorway of George's hospital room, and measured the hate in the blue eyes beamed on him.

There was a chair by the bed and he went over and sat on it. Then he turned to the nurse and asked if they could be left alone.

He began to speak in French, perhaps because it was the language of his far away youth, of Alexandria and Marguerite, perhaps from discretion. What he had to say was not for the ears of others, not even for the walls around them. He came straight to the point.

"If I'm here it is not simply to say how sorry I am, or to wish you a speedy and full recovery. You wouldn't believe me. It's because there is something you must know about the two of us. Maybe I should have told you it a long time back, but somehow circumstances prevented me. I'm not trying to excuse myself by saying that."

He was silent as he reached inside his jacket and brought out an envelope. He stared at it for a moment then locked his gaze in George's.

"Your mother wrote this letter fifty years ago, and it contains a secret which concerned her, you and me."

He paused again as he drew the letter from the envelope.

"What you must know is that I loved her and, as this letter will tell you, she loved me too. God, how we loved each other! We wanted to marry, but her mother and father wouldn't hear of it. Instead they made her marry the man whose name you bear. And when you were born, they made sure no one knew the truth; a truth I learnt only through this letter."

For a moment his face softened into a smile. "We had promised ourselves to each other, and in the eyes of God we were husband and wife. I was the father of the baby she bore; your father."

Once more a moment of silence. Then: "You grew up an orphan, her family wanted it that way. Yet I was partly to blame, and in all these years I have paid the price for not having claimed you as my son. I feel you hate me, though why I don't exactly know, but perhaps it was right that you should. At least until this moment. But now you and I must be what we should have been from the day you were born, George, friends. I want you to feel that you have someone on whom you can depend entirely as you would on a father ... "

343

The door opened and the nurse came back. "I'm sorry," she whispered, "but the doctor wants me to stay here."

Julius nodded, then went on, "I saw you once when you were a boy. It was at the Sporting Club in Alexandria and you were about to leave for Europe with your grandmother."

The blue eyes were riveted in his. Was the intensity in them still the essence of hate? Suddenly he realized they were Helen Wirsa's eyes.

"If there was one person I ever hated it was her ... what a terrible woman she was. What a terrible mother. It was then that I decided that whatever happened, you had to be free of her when you reached manhood. That was why I set up the Trust for you in Switzerland. Yes, it was I who placed those initial one million francs in it, and it's curious to think that, had I not seen you that day, I might not have done it."

Was he imagining it, or had George's lips moved as if trying to say something? He went on talking, reminiscing about the past, evoking his early days in Alexandria, and then of the interest with which he had followed George's rapid successes. "I backed a winner," he said, with a ring of admiration in his voice, "what a formidable team you and I could have made had we worked together. There was a time, some twenty years ago, when I hoped that would be the case ... "

The light seemed to fade from his son's eyes, and for a terrible moment he thought death had passed between them. He looked anxiously at the nurse.

"You should go now, he's tired and needs sleep." It was a softly spoken order.

Julius nodded and stood up. George's face was strangely calm now that the eyes were closed. The passions no longer tyrannized it and the lips, though distorted by paralysis, gave an impression of contentment.

Three months later George left the hospital. Though his condition had improved slightly — he could grunt and move two of the fingers of his left hand — he needed the constant attention of two male nurses, and had to be fed and carried like a baby. The doctors had warned that it was improbable he would ever regain the use of his limbs or be able to speak.

Julius installed him on his yacht, the 86 metre palatial floating home in which he now lived most of the time. He took to spending hours next to him at the special massage pool he had had built, or walking by his side on the main deck, a hand guiding the electrically controlled wheelchair.

He talked to him of matters concerning George's widespread interests, of decisions he suggested be taken and which he would relay to managers. A court order, obtained with George's consent through his lawyer, had given him the necessary powers. One tap of a finger signified agreement, two, dissent, but seldom were the times George tapped twice. He also talked to him of his youth in Alexandria, of his love for Marguerite, of destiny which had made them foes instead of a devoted father and loving son.

"How different our lives would have been, George, had Helen been a mother who cared for her daughter; had she let her marry me, the man she loved, instead of forcing her to become Roger Christofides' wife for the sake of snobbery. She was responsible for so much unnecessary grief. I can't blame her for Marguerite's death, but I can for depriving you of a father and me of a son. Because of her I never had the family which was rightfully mine … "

As the weeks became months Julius had the feeling that a certain understanding was developing between them, and a curious attachment for the pathetic, mute hulk which was his son grew in him. He found himself wanting him near, as if his physical presence was somehow beneficial, like that of a talisman. And the forging of this link brought back the nostalgic and poignant memories of Marguerite, and their two unforgettable years of love.

One spring evening, while gazing at the portrait of the young Cleopatra painted by Jean-Gabriel Domergue which he had managed to buy at an auction of Helen Wirsa's possessions after her death, he thought back to that ball, given for Marguerite's 18th birthday. Suddenly she was there again in his arms, her eyes bright with love and laughter, her hair swept up in Grecian curls, allowing her temple to rest every now and then against his chin. God, how he had loved her, he cried silently to himself as he blinked back his tears and fought the echoing loneliness which her memory conjured. How many such balls there should have been in fifty six years. How many times should they have danced and loved each other as they had that evening.

That was when the idea came to him. In a few months it would be his 80th birthday, and to mark the occasion he would throw a ball in her honour on the yacht he had named after her. It would take place in Alexandria and the President of Egypt and his wife and all the dignitaries of the country, as well as the representatives of other states would attend it. But it would be more than just a brilliant reception for the elite of a country. It would be a party for the Alexandrians, for the men in the street, for the poor and the forgotten, for the old who hobbled on the pavements where his own father had limped, and for the young who played, full of impossible hope, in the alleys of their forgotten city.

September, 1989

Maryanne put an arm through Sophia's.

"You mustn't worry too much," she said, "it's probably some bug he caught over in Mexico. In any case he'll be out of hospital in a few days won't he? So relax. Honestly, Sophia, there can't be anything terribly wrong with him if they're letting him go home."

The younger woman nodded, then sighed. "I know, I worry too much. But you see, it's not the first time it has happened. A few months ago he had the same symptoms, but they couldn't really tell what it was. That's what's unnerving, not knowing. For him especially. Quite apart from the concert he has had to cancel at the Wigmore Hall which upset him, he's been depressed."

"And who wouldn't be in his place? What he needs is rest and a change of air. He must have been working too hard. He's never been terribly strong, as you know. The year before you met him ... "

"Yes, but he had got over all that. In the first two years after our marriage he didn't even catch a cold, and God knows Florence can be icy in winter. He got some kind of an infection in the lungs about eighteen months ago but otherwise didn't know what illness was. Well, ordinary illness."

"What do you mean?"

They were walking by the lake at Chilton. Sophia had come to stay for a few days, at Maryanne's suggestion, while waiting for Nelson to get out of the Paris clinic where he was having treatment and undergoing tests.

It was a sunny afternoon and her young son, Paul, was throwing pellets of bread to a pair of black swans gliding on the lake's still waters.

"Don't get too near them Paul," Sophia called out, "they could try to bite you."

She spoke to him in Greek, and Maryanne realized that it was the first time she had heard the language used at Chilton. Then Sophia reverted to French. "Sorry," she said, "but if he isn't warned, one of these days they could attack him ... " She lapsed into silence.

"You were telling me about Nelson's illness," Maryanne prompted softly.

"I suppose I shouldn't talk about it, but I need to and you are my friend, aren't you?"

"Of course I am. What's the problem?"

"We don't sleep together any more. He explains that he's tired and under stress from all the concerts, which I can understand. But it's not natural, and I don't think there's another woman ... can a man go without sex for months on end? Can he become impotent so young? Or do you think it is my fault somehow?"

"Certainly, it can happen, but for heaven's sake don't start thinking that you are to blame. I too suffered the same experience with my first husband. Then I knew another man ... do you love him very much?"

"He's my husband and the father of my child; yes, I love him, but not in the way as when we got married. At the beginning it was wonderful ... I could have died, I loved him so much. But after Paul was born he seemed to draw away from me. He was gentle and kind, yet I felt a barrier had somehow come between us. He would come to bed late and get up early, as if he wanted to avoid the contact of my body. I thought it was because before and after childbirth he felt he shouldn't. And to begin with I was grateful. In the two years that followed, I think we made love a dozen times, no more. Then I too lost interest in sex till I met someone who made me feel a woman again. Maybe Nelson knew about that but he never said anything, and it was almost as if he didn't mind. Of course he was away more and more, and then he started getting ill and that drew us further apart. He won't even let me come and see him in hospital, and he won't tell me what's wrong. If it's something serious I want to know ... perhaps you could help. Maybe he would confide it to you. You are his aunt, and I know he likes you ... "

"Of course I'll help if I can. But why don't you just go to his doctor and ask him? Surely he'll tell you."

"No, I couldn't. It would be like reading someone's private correspondence ... it has to come from him, and if you talk to him perhaps he'll understand ... will you go to him, Maryanne? Please, this uncertainty is driving me crazy.

Perhaps it's simply that he doesn't want me any more but hasn't the strength to say so. He must, though. If not for my sake, then for Paul's."

Nelson stared at the ceiling of the hospital room and realized that he was no longer afraid.

Now that his mind was made up everything seemed so clear and uncomplicated. The thought that he would not live to see Sophia and Paul again saddened him, but there was a certain softness in his sorrow which verged on nostalgia. Jemima too, he would have liked to see her. Thank God at least she had come out of the nightmare into which Bruno had dragged them. Yet there was no hate for the friend who had ruined his life, no bitterness either.

He thought back to that day when he had last heard his voice. It had been just before his first concert and Paul's birth. That same evening he had come across Antonio, and the lust in his eyes had excited him the same way as Bruno used to. Antonio, Marco, Jonathan, André, Mike; sexual shadows in a twilight of epidermic stimuli, all reminding him in some way of the young friend who had been his lover. Which of them had signed his death warrant?

He looked down at his hands. While there was strength in them he would go on playing. He would even give that concert scheduled for July 14th, if the illness let him. The doctors had said he would be all right for a while.

Maryanne hadn't seen him for nearly a year, and was shocked to see how thin he had grown. It was almost as if he had fallen prey to drugs again, she thought, remembering how he had been when he had gone to Krinos to recover. Yet there was a determination in his eyes which reassured her. Also, he was out of hospital, so he must have got over whatever had been wrong with him. He was at the Paris apartment now, and they were lunching on the terrace.

"I'm sorry about what happened to him," she said, referring to George, "have you seen him since his stroke?"

He shook his head. "No. Perhaps I should have, but I haven't seen anyone since I got ill. You know he disinherited Jemima and me?"

"Yes, Julius told me. But you know your father, he gets into rages for no reason at all ... I'm sure it could all be sorted out if you saw him. And Nelson, why don't you have Sophia and Paul with you, now that you're out of hospital and getting better ... she's worried, both about your health and ... well, your relationship. I have the feeling she thinks you don't love her any more."

"I can't, Maryanne. I'm a sick man." He drew a deep breath and looked out across the roofs of Paris to the distant church of the Sacred Heart at Montmartre. "I'm glad you came as I needed to confide in someone. I suppose Sophia asked you to."

"In a way. But Julius too was wondering what was happening. Why do you say you're ill? I thought you were cured of whatever it was. Are you sure you're having the right treatment? Who's been looking after you?"

"The best for this type of illness. The problem is that there's no cure and when they do find one, it will be too late. I've got AIDS ... I think you know what that means."

She stared at him in numbed silence, unable to speak in her dismay. It couldn't be, not that, she kept repeating to herself. When words finally came she heard herself stammer: "Oh my God, but are you sure? ... I mean, there couldn't be a terrible mistake could there?"

He met her anguished look and shook his head. "No, and you understand now why I can't have Sophia with me? I don't want her or anyone to know, not because I'm ashamed of what the illness implies, but because of the suffering it would cause her. I want to spare her that. You'll help me, won't you?"

She nodded then reached for a handkerchief. Curiously, her thoughts at that moment were not for the young Greek woman who could soon be a widow, but for Julius. He had an almost paternal affection for Nelson and held great hopes for his future as a musician. This would come as a terrible blow for him. And George? As if guessing what was passing through her mind he said, "they need never know. Promise me you won't tell anyone."

"Of course." She paused, then in a hoarse whisper asked,

"how long before ... ?" but she couldn't bring herself to finish the question.

"Two or three months, perhaps a little more. Gives me time to get ready for my concert on July 14th. Can you come to it? It would be nice to have someone from the family there."

"Of course, Nelson."

When she left him she didn't immediately hail a taxi. She walked along the Quai d'Orsay to the Pont de la Concorde, skirted the Tuileries Gardens and turned into the Rue de Rivoli. A few minutes later she was out of the Place Vendôme into the Ritz Hotel. She went straight to the ladies room and locked herself in a lavatory.

And there she wept, hugging herself and swaying from side to side. She wanted to wail, but suffered her misery in silence. Why had both Georgina's son and hers been marked for tragedy? Was George's seed damned, or did the blood of the Brentwick's carry a curse through their women? It could not be simple chance that a perversion had lurked in both of them, to manifest itself only when they had grown into men. What had generated the destructive energies in the two cousins?

A terrible fear cut short her flow of tears. Would their destinies follow the same pattern? Nelson would die within a matter of weeks, but A.J.? Where was he, that son of hers? When would she see him again? If only Julius could do something to save him from himself before it was too late.

In November 1989 a symposium of international terrorists was held in Libya. Present were leaders of the Irish I.R.A., the Basque E.T.A., the Philippine NOROS, the KANAKs of New Caledonia, as well as extremists from South America, West Germany and from the Palestinian PLO. There were also such top-ranking terror activists as Carlos and Abu Nidal, and it was one of these who was given the task of eliminating Julius Caspar.

Although the raid on the military barracks in Eritrea had been carried as secretly as possible, inevitably news of it, and who was behind it, had come to the ears of certain Middle Eastern power peddlers. Some applauded it but others regarded it an outrage and the Alexandrian's private militia a potential menace to their lives. Also, though he spent most of his money and energy for the cause of peace in the Middle East, there were those who resented what he did and stood for, which was why the helicopter had been blown up.

Somewhat illogically, that had been ordered by the leader of a Lebanese Christian phalange who had not realized that Julius' overtures to the Syrian President were motivated purely by a wish to obtain a permanent ceasefire in Beirut, and had interpreted the substantial economic advantages offered through him by America as a sell out. But now, after several anti-terrorist actions by his commandos, Julius had come to represent more than simply a political nuisance for those who backed terrorism. Hence the directives to the most efficient band of extremists to eliminate him.

It was no easy task. The Alexandrian, as they all knew, was virtually invulnerable while on Krinos or aboard his yacht. Short of using missiles against him, out of the question as it would be tantamount to an act of war against the USA with the MY Marguerite sailing under the American flag, the only solution was to infiltrate someone into the yacht's crew or the staff of the villa on the island. But here again the chances of success were minimal. The men who worked for Julius Caspar were hand-picked, and as carefully vetted as members of a secret service. But early in March, the problem was unexpectedly resolved.

A.J. had never revealed his origins to the organization he worked with. For them he was simply 'Assad'. Najla had been the only one to know who were his mother and adoptive father, and she had died with the secret, and the Horemis, who could have blurted the truth, had fled Beirut after Amin bad been killed in 1984. So it was purely by chance that a leading terrorist discussed with A.J. the assignment he had been given. Normally he formulated his policies in secret, and those who were to carry out an attack were kept in the dark and given their instructions at the last minute.

'Assad' had reported to the man's hideout in Baghdad to get orders regarding a kidnapping of an American diplomat in Beirut. A file was open on the desk and while the terrorist leader was out of the room A.J. glanced at it. Staring up at him was a photograph of his 'uncle' Julius.

"Why are you interested in him?" he asked when the man returned.

"None of your business." A pause then, "do you know who he is?"

"Sure. What's more I know him personally. Don't tell me you want to kidnap him!"

"No. How well do you know him?"

"I just told you. As a kid, very well."

"How come?"

"Tell me first what that photo's doing there."

There was a moment's silence. "Does he know that you're one of us?"

"Of course. Everyone knows that 'Assad' is one of the organization's key men. Hell, I've killed enough people for the cause, haven't I?"

The leader frowned.

"Forget you saw this photo. That's an order."

A.J. stared at the man. If he was planning something around Julius Caspar, he damned well had the right to know it. Christ! if anyone had, it was he. He felt a fury rising in him.

"No way. You owe it to me to tell me what it's doing in that file."

"Owe it to you?" the voice was heavy with a menacing sarcasm. "Who the fucking hell do you think you are to tell me what I owe or don't."

"I'm Julius Caspar's adopted son, that's who I am," he shouted.

The initial plan was to get A.J. onto Krinos and for him to work out, on the spot, the best way of getting rid of his 'uncle'.

He hadn't balked at the idea of killing the man who had adopted him. On the contrary, it gave him a perverse satisfaction. He had always nurtured a curious resentment towards Julius, which at times had bordered on hate. He couldn't explain why, nor had he ever attempted to analyse either the reasons or the feelings themselves. Deep down inside him, he knew that if ever he were able to kill him, it would be the most thrilling moment of his existence. But for years he had ceased even thinking about him. He had cut all links with his boyhood, and only communicated with his mother twice a year. Everyone who had to do with his past had been blotted from his memory. He had a new family for whom Antor James Caspar did not exist, and as far as he was concerned the name of Caspar had lost all significance.

Now suddenly it was claiming him in an exciting and unexpected way, not only offering him the challenge of his lifetime and the chance of fulfilling what he saw as his destiny but also a substantial heritage.

"Who will all those millions go to once he's dead? You? If so, remember they could be damned useful to our cause."

Certain information received from Cairo made for a change of tactics.

"You are not just to eliminate Caspar. We now know that on August 1st he'll be entertaining the Egyptian President and a large number of high government officials and members of the diplomatic corps on his yacht in the harbour of Alexandria. Our orders are to dynamite it with all of them aboard. We have three months to organize that, but remember, you're our only chance. If the coup is to work, one of us has to be aboard. The security arrangements will be such that no one will be able to get anywhere near the boat. So an underwater job's out. The dynamite will have to be smuggled on board — we'll work out how and when later — and it'll be your responsibility to place it where it is sure to blow up the whole of the boat, and everyone on it. I'll count on you to make certain that happens."

The plan was that A.J. would go to Krinos on his own and ask Julius to give him asylum. He was to pretend that he had repented his terrorist activities, and was afraid that the organization would also try to kill him, both for wanting to abandon its cause and because of the danger he presented as a turncoat. To prove that he was ready to sever all connections with it, he was to give the Alexandrian information about an arm's cache and a coup planned for the early autumn to blow up an Israeli airliner. When Julius' commandos attacked the cache, as they were bound to do, they would find not only arms but details of the coup. That would be sufficient to make A.J.'s repentance appear genuine. There was one imponderable factor, however; would Julius Caspar agree to give him refuge, or would he hand him over to the authorities? Interpol was anxious to lay their hands on 'Assad' and there was an international warrant out for his arrest. Which would dictate his decision? Civic sense, or family sentiment?

Late in the morning of April 9th, a rubber dinghy with an outboard motor approached Krinos. When it was within five hundred metres, a speedboat raced out to intercept it. A man called through a loudspeaker to go away while a second pointed a machine gun at it.

"I want to see Mr Caspar," A.J. shouted back.

"Who are you?"

"His son."

He was escorted to the shore, searched, then taken to Laurrie Salvini at the monastery.

"There's a guy here who claims to be Mr Caspar's son and wants to see him," one of the men called through a doorway.

"Bring him in."

Laurrie looked up from his desk and stared at the young man. Jesus! he thought, it's A.J. What the devil was he doing there, and why had he come to Krinos? He hadn't seen him in eight years, but there was no mistaking the features; the sloping eyes full of sullen arrogance, the thin and mean mouth.

"O.K., leave him with me," he said to the man who had brought him. Then, to A.J., "sit down, I'll deal with you in a moment."

Staring at his papers he struggled to hide his surprise. "What are you doing here?" he asked after a moment.

"I've come to see the old man."

"Why?"

"That's my business. Stop being a bloody fascist and tell him I'm here."

Laurrie looked up and stared at him coldly. "You know I

could simply send you to the mainland and have you handed over to the police? It's what I've got a good mind to do."

"And what would he say when he found out that you didn't even let me see him?"

"Nothing. He'd approve. He doesn't like people who murder innocent men, women and children."

Suddenly A.J. was rattled. The man wasn't kidding; he was narrowing his eyes and probably speculating on what action to adopt. If he didn't convince him now to take him to Julius, he would find himself being escorted to the nearest police station. He changed his tone.

"Look Laurrie, be a sport. I've ... well, I've put all that behind me. I know you won't believe me, but I've changed. And I need help. If you take me to the police they'll get me ... I mean the group I was with will. They're out to kill me ... they reckon I know too much ..."

"How come this sudden change?" Laurrie's voice was edged with sarcasm.

"It wasn't sudden. For some time I've kinda realized that what I was doing was wrong ... only I didn't know how to stop. And then I saw what happened to a guy who tried to break away ... "

"So you reckoned that you could hop across here and get us to hide you ... "

"Yeah, and it's natural, isn't it? Wouldn't you have done the same if the old boy was your adoptive father?"

"Christ, you've got a bloody nerve. You think I believe that crap about repenting. You've got no conscience, no gratitude, no morality, no loyalty. You haven't even got a minimal amount of respect for your fellow humans, and you expect me to fall for that bullshit? You're just scared rigid because you've got what you deserve coming to you. And you won't pull wool over his eyes, either. Sure, I'll take you to him, if he agrees to see you. But I swear that if he does help you and you betray his confidence again, I'll kill you with my own hands."

He stood up suddenly and strode to the door. "No, you stay there and don't move till I say so. Mike," he called, "come and keep an eye on this guy."

Julius was in his study, dictating letters, when Laurrie brought A.J. to him.

"All right, Catherine, I'll continue later. Will you leave us," he said calmly to his secretary, then turned to face his grandson.

Two contrasting emotions wrestled within him; a furious urge to beat him until every bone in his body was broken, and a desire to hug to his breast this youngster in whose veins ran his and Cecily's blood. The silence was broken by Laurrie.

"If you'll excuse me, I'll get back on shore ... "

"No Laurrie, I'd rather you stayed. Well A.J.?"

"I ... well, I guess Laurrie here has told you everything ... if you'll have me I'd like to stay with you."

"Is that all you have to say?"

"No, of course not," A.J. stuttered, "it's just that I'm kind of embarrassed. You're looking great, uncle Julius. You haven't changed at all in all these years."

"And how many years has it been?"

He bit his lower lip. "Must be seven, I haven't really counted."

"Have you counted the number of people you either killed or whose lives you made a misery during those seven years? Have you stopped to think of the suffering you caused your mother? Yet now you choose to forget all that, and suddenly come and ask for help from the very man the criminals you associate with are planning to assassinate. Don't try to deny it. We have proof that they have orders to kill me. Maybe that's why you're here!"

"No uncle Julius, I swear it. That was one of the reasons I broke away from them ... I couldn't let them do that. If I'm here it's because you're the only person I can turn to. If you don't help me, I know they'll kill me. Please uncle Julius, I'll do anything you ask; I'll fight for you if you want ... I can give Laurrie a whole lot of information about the organization ... their hideout in Beirut, and about the next El Al plane that's to be blown up ... I'll work on the yacht as a deck hand, or in the engine room ... I'll do anything you want ... anything to make up for what I did and to get you to forgive me some day ... "

Curiously, he found himself believing what he was saying. For an inexplicable reason which had to do with the personality of the Alexandrian, at that moment he really did want to please Julius.

The steely brown eyes were delving deep into the bowels

of his subconscious and he surrendered himself to their grasp. Hypnotized, that forgotten part of him which had once felt an almost filial attraction to a father figure, leapt to the fore. He all but sank to his knees, and for a minute the real purpose of his being there was cancelled from his mind. That moment of transient sincerity tipped the scales in his favour.

"It's not my forgiveness you should want ... " Julius said more softly. Then he got up and went towards his grandson. He stretched out a hand and placed it on his shoulder. It was not a movement of affection but an unconscious desire to touch and claim back a distant part of his own identity.

"I'll keep you here for a while. For the time being you'll do what Laurrie decides, and if he tells me that you've told the truth and that you really mean what you've just said, I'll see what can be done to rehabilitate you in the eyes of others also. Till then I don't want to have any form of communication with you. I will welcome you back into my home when Laurrie tells me that I can do so, and by that I mean that neither I nor those who cared for you will be disappointed."

"You won't be, uncle Julius. I swear it. And thanks ..."

"Don't thank me. Just make sure Laurrie can bring you here again."

"O.K. A.J., let's go," Laurrie said, taking him by the arm and propelling him to the door.

As they were about to disappear Julius added, "and Antor, don't make me wait too long. I'm not eternal and once I've gone no one else will be around to help you. Just pray I live to escape an assassin's bullet ... "

On an afternoon late in May, Nelson struggled out of bed and dragged himself to the bathroom.

He looked into the washbasin mirror and stared at his reflection with a mixture of fear and self-pity. He stood there for a long moment until a desperate need for air had him grope his way through the apartment and out onto the terrace.

He pulled himself over to a chaise-longue and rested, listening with his eyes shut to the muffled roar of the Paris traffic. A fleeting sense of peace enveloped him. He had always loved that terrace. In a curious way he felt sheltered there, as if out of reach of life's tragedies. He gazed at the great cupola of the Invalides. Yet tragedy had not spared his family, he thought, as tears filled his eyes. Neither his mother, nor his father, nor even Jemima. And least of all him, born with a golden spoon which had turned into plated verdigris.

He got up and staggered towards the parapet. He wanted a good look at the world at his feet. He needed to sense and feel part of its throbbing vitality.

He took in the distant Sacré Coeur of Montmartre, the nearby Seine, and the Esplanade des Invalides right below.

A small boy was riding a bicycle there while a woman watched. He shut his eyes tight and rested his forehead on his fist. They could be Paul and Sophia. No, his son and wife had gone from his life, chased away by his desperate urge to hide from them.

"Oh, God," he muttered, "if only they could be with me, just for this moment."

He opened his eyes and gazed at the boy again, and suddenly he was back twenty years to his own childhood. Those had been his happy days, the ones when he too had ridden down there with Jemima.

He leant further over to watch the kid zigzag between the trees and it was as if he were with him, with his youth and purity. With his hopes.

And the agony in him eased.

He knew it was the end, yet it was a beginning again. It was all so simple. So beautifully and wonderfully simple.

A smile lit his face. It remained as he threw himself over the parapet.

August 1st, 1990

Julius jogged ten times round the swimming pool, then dived in.

Despite his eighty years, his body was still that of an athlete. The waist had not thickened nor had the muscles sagged, and the powerful strokes of his crawl cut a quarter of a century off for anyone assessing his age. Only the white of his hair and beard contrasted curiously with the image of perennial youth.

He swam three lengths, turned and floated on his back, closing his eyes as he propelled himself with a gentle kicking of his feet. When his fingers touched the pool's edge he looked up to see a face less than a metre from his. It was A.J.'s.

"Morning, uncle Julius. Laurrie said you wanted to see me ... and, oh, happy birthday."

"Thanks A.J. ... throw me that towel, will you."

He watched his grandson straighten and walk to a deck chair. What was it about the youngster that invariably got his hackles up? An ingrained insolence which showed in the very way he moved? He fought his irritation and tried to be fair. A.J. had behaved perfectly in the weeks he had had him on board, and even Laurrie was satisfied with him. And yet there was something in his attitude which jarred, as if he were playing a part which was fundamentally alien to him.

Julius climbed out of the water and threw the towel across his shoulders. "Had breakfast, or will you join me?" he asked pleasantly.

"We have ours at six ... " The sullen implication was that he was treated like the crew and not as Julius Caspar's adopted son should be.

"O.K., it's as you like. I wanted to have a talk with you and, since today marks a certain point in my life, I reckon it's as good a moment as any. First I want you to know that there's a surprise in store for you." He forced himself to throw an arm round his grandson's shoulders and give him an affectionate hug.

"But I'll let you discover that for yourself a little later. What I wanted to discuss was your future. Obviously you can't stay here for ever, or on Krinos. You've got to take your place in the world ... "

He sat down at a table laid for breakfast and indicated a chair to A.J. Then he dug a spoon into a bowl of yoghurt, covered it with honey, and savoured it slowly.

A.J. watched him whilst glancing now and then at the sweep of the city's sea front. The Corniche was bustling with traffic, and small crowds were gathering on the pavements and gesticulating excitedly while policemen barred the way leading to fort Quoit Bey.

Somewhere in that stretch of apartment blocks and offices, three others of his group ...

"Normally, as my heir, you'd have been trained to take over from me, that's if you'd wanted to, of course. You'd have always been free to do what you wanted with your life, within reason. I say within reason as we are none of us totally free ... you must have realized that by now ..."

... would have a telescope pointed on the yacht waiting for his signal that everything was ready ...

"The problem is your terrorist activities have made you a wanted man by at least six different police forces. I've got a certain influence in one or two countries and could probably arrange with the authorities to have charges against you minimised, if I choose to ... "

... and that in fourteen hours exactly a Head of State, seven ambassadors, six ministers and a number of leading Middle Eastern international businessmen and bankers, would be wiped from the face of the earth ...

"But for that to happen you've got to show that you're a hundred per cent with us in our fight against terrorism. I'm convinced you are — you've already proved yourself with the information you gave Laurrie about the arms cache — and I believe that you really do want to rehabilitate yourself in the eyes of society. If you want your freedom, though, I'm not the one you have to convince ... "

... And he would have been the one to do it on his own with nobody's help. He 'Assad', would show the organization and the world in general that the so-called master minds of terrorism were babes compared to him ...

"Help catch the ringleaders, whoever they are, or get me ir-refutable proof of the people behind them. If you can be in-strumental in establishing without doubt who exactly is promoting and financing international terrorism, I think I can guarantee you a clean slate. It will take time, but it would be worth it for both of us."

What crap this phoney 'uncle' was mumbling. There he is munching complacently, certain of his invincible superiority, while fifty kilos of one of the most powerful explosives ever made are about to blast his arrogance into a heap of torn flesh.

A.J. grinned at the thought.

Julius wiped his lips with a napkin and smiled back. "O.K. we'll talk more about it tomorrow. Keep your eyes skinned today; I wouldn't be surprised if a terrorist action wasn't planned for this evening with the President aboard. They won't get near the boat with arms, the Egyptian secret service will see to that, but one of them might try to slip aboard somehow ... and if you spotted him ... "

A.J. choked back his laughter with a sudden fit of coughing.

"Sure uncle Julius," he managed to croak, "I'll do what I can ... mind if I get some water ..." and he ran off, his eyes wild with a near hysteria.

Julius watched him go and frowned. It wasn't the first time he had had the impression that Maryanne's son was not completely normal. There was a suppressed excitability in him which was worrying at his age. What had he said which he could have found so funny? Maybe there was a streak of insanity which could explain the sudden childhood rages and unaccountable changes of character. A question flashed through his mind. Who could have been his father, or more to the point, his other grandfather? Genes often jumped a generation.

8.30 a.m.. A.J. listened to Laurrie giving orders to the twelve commandos.

"At midday the Egyptian security police will be coming aboard to search the yacht. Before they get here, I want you to inspect every centimetre of it to make quite sure there is nothing unusual. You know the routine; every cabin including Mr Caspar's must be gone over, and anything suspect reported immediately to me. O.K, get cracking; oh, don't disturb Sir George Christofides, I'll check his cabins with A.J."

When they had gone, A.J. said, "we could do it now, I saw him being taken up on deck a few minutes ago. Like that we won't upset him."

Laurrie nodded. George hated anyone prying in his rooms, and the doctors had been adamant about not upsetting him in any way. A sudden increase in blood pressure could be dangerous for him.

They walked down to the lower deck and along to the suite of cabins occupied by George and his male nurse. A maid was changing the sheets in the principal bedroom while a steward dusted and polished the sitting room. An open door led into a second bedroom, next to which was the bathroom. Nodding in it's direction, Laurrie told A.J. to begin there.

"I'll be with you in a sec., the intercom's buzzing."

A.J. walked slowly to the bathroom and began opening drawers and closets and passing the metal detector over the walls and panels of wood. He worked slowly and with what seemed conscientiousness. But a smirk was never far from his lips. The bastards would never find anything, not now that the old geezer was being wheeled around on the decks, he thought. The detonating mechanism was hidden in his chair, and no one was going to put a detector under his arse! Nor would anyone ever guess that the new four metre long plastic table ordered specially for the reception and placed in the glassed-in fore section of the middle deck, would transform itself into fifty kilos of deadly dynamite the moment he decided.

The organization had done a good job. The table had been ordered regularly through the Italian boatyard which had built the yacht. It had been brought on board two weeks earlier when they had stopped at Livorno for an engine overhaul, and no one had thought of checking how it had got to the docks, not even the shipyard's representative dealing with the customs formalities. For all concerned, it was a straightforward table, built to seat 18 people. Even Laurrie hadn't sniffed the danger, the stupid bugger!

1.p.m. A.J. shoved his head through his cabin porthole and watched the helicopter land on the pad. It was them all right, the Salvini contingent. Laurrie's father and mother and cousin arriving to join in on the bandwagon, as they always had.

He glanced at his watch. Christ, how the time passed slowly. Another hour to wait until lunch. Julius wanted him to be present this time for the private birthday celebration with the rest of them.

He went over to the washbasin and grinned at his reflection. What a birthday present he had in store for him!

He frowned. He had better check that George was firmly strapped to that goddam chair of his, and then wheel him up to the lunch himself.

1.45.p.m. Julius raised his glass to the men and women around him.

"I'm very touched that you should all be here with me, not because today is my birthday — at my age one ceases to count them — but because this evening will symbolise a significant moment in my life which I particularly wanted to share with you. Sixty or so years ago I was here in Alexandria, a young man who had just lost father, mother and the girl he loved and wanted to marry. Yet thanks to you I wasn't alone, as I am not alone today. You were and are the family I yearned for but couldn't have. Bless you, and thank you for coming so far to be with me."

"We're the ones who must do the thanking," Pietro Salvini said, "without you where would Clara and I be today? Perhaps still over there in a shabby Alexandrian suburb. And the world can thank you too for Clara's voice. If she's one of the best sopranos, it's because you cared for her and helped her."

Clara stepped over to him and hugged him. " It's true. I'd have never made it if you hadn't been there to look after us as children when Francesco had to go. It was you who made it possible."

When they had all toasted him, he took Maryanne by the arm and led her aside.

"I'm particularly pleased you were able to make it. I have a surprise for you."

"I wouldn't have missed your birthday for anything in the world. And it's so exciting to be in Alexandria at last. I can't wait to visit it. The Governor offered to show me around tomorrow, but I'd much prefer to see it all with you. Discover where you were born, where you and your parents — my grandparents lived. How can I put it? It's as if I'm discovering a whole part of me I knew existed but had somehow never come to grips with. I keep asking myself why I never came here before ... you should have made me ... "

He shook his head. "I had no reason to. The Alexandria you see today has very little in common with the city I was born and grew up in. Even twenty years ago it had changed beyond recognition. Of course, I'll take you to see where we lived; if nothing else it will give you an idea of the poverty my family had to endure to begin with ... I'll show you also the house I still own ... once it was in the most elegant part of Alexandria, now it's surrounded by slums. But see that police car over there on the causeway — yes the one with two men standing by it — that's roughly where I used to swim from when I had an hour off at lunchtime from my first job. It was in an office which faces the main port on the other side of those buildings ... with a company which once belonged to the Christofides family..."

"How is he ... George?" she asked.

He shook his head slowly. "Improved a little but well, you'll see for yourself in a moment. I'm afraid he'll never really recover. All I hope is that he regains his speech. The doctors say that's possible with time."

"I'm sorry. It must be awful for him and for you too."

She had not understood why he had taken such sudden care of George. They had never been friends, and the fact that George had married his goddaughter was hardly sufficient enough a reason.

She changed subject. "You said you had a surprise for me?"

"Yes, and he's coming along with George, over there." She followed his gaze down the deck.

"My God," she cried " ... it can't be! ... but it's A.J.!"

She thrust her glass at Julius and ran towards him.

"A.J., darling ... " She stopped in her tracks abruptly as if a barrier had sprung up between them. Instead of coming towards her as she had expected, her son was staring at her aghast, a look of horror on his face.

"What is it?" she gasped. Then her eyes travelled down to the man in the wheelchair and riveted themselves in his.

"Oh, no!" she groaned. Those eyes were desperately trying

to say something while a pathetic, gut-gripping groan escaped from the distorted lips.

Maryanne felt the strength leave her legs as the sound of gushing water filled her ears. Just before she fainted she saw her son reach out and shout "Mum".

He rushed to her, put his arms around her shoulders and lifted her to a sitting position. "Christ," he cried as Michael Lauber and Christian Gautier dashed to help, "why didn't anyone tell me. Why wasn't I told she would be here. Why didn't you tell me. WHY?" He hurled the last word at Julius as if it were a knife. He felt like killing him right there. What right had the bloody bastard to entice his mother on board this floating bomb, he howled to himself, his eyes wild with reproach.

Maryanne came to almost immediately, and they helped her to a sofa.

"I'm sorry," she stammered, "I don't know what came over me. Must be the heat and the excitement of seeing A.J. and ... but what a marvellous surprise ... no, no, I'm fine now ... perhaps a glass of water ... Stay next to me, A.J. Let me look at you. I can hardly believe it ... it's been such a terribly long time ... "

He let her take his hand and stroke his hair, and for a few seconds the world around him was blotted out while he breathed in her love.

Then a voice shook him back into reality.

"Sure you don't want to rest in your cabin, darling?"

A.J. glared up at Michael Lauber and the stifled hate exploded in him again. The Zionist swine. Thank God he had come too. At least he would be eliminated tonight. But Jesus, what would he do about his mother? The organization could not expect him to murder his own mother!

"Honestly Michael, I'm all right now. I want to stay and enjoy this moment with you all. With A.J. especially. I can rest later."

3.45 p.m. A.J. tapped on the door of George's stateroom and let himself in.

"Mr Caspar would like Sir George to join him on deck," he called to Tom who was resting in his cabin. "But don't worry, I'll take him up."

George eyed him suspiciously and gave an annoyed grunt

when he started wheeling him rapidly along the passage to the lift.

Once up on deck, he pushed him to the covered area where the dinner was to be served, and over to the huge centre table. Making sure there was no one about, he reached under the seat of the wheelchair and removed a small electronic detonating device from a hidden cavity. He had put it and a gun there, while the yacht had berthed at Porto Santo Stefano for twelve hours, three days earlier.

He had persuaded Laurrie to let him take George ashore for a drive around the Monte Argentario peninsula, and had told the driver to take them to the Don Pedro Hotel at Porto Ercole, ostensibly to let George have a drink and go to the lavatory. But when he had brought the invalid back to the car it was not on the same chair. No one had noticed this, though to a critical observer there was a slight difference. The seat was seven centimetres deeper. Back at the yacht, a metal detector was passed over him and George, but not over the wheel chair. The means for blowing up the boat was safely on it.

A.J. set to work quickly. He slithered under the table and found the niche in which the detonator had to be plugged. Then he took the detonating device with the timer, set it for 9.45 p.m. and fitted it into position. He scrambled back onto his feet, and seconds later was guiding George back to his cabin.

No one could suspect that in five hours and twenty four minutes exactly, Alexandria's pleasure harbour would be rocked by the most colossal explosion in its history.

Once he had parked George back in his cabin. A.J. went off to see his mother. He knocked on her door and poked his head in.

"Are you alone, Mum?"

She was. She patted the mattress of the bed where she was resting.

"Come and sit here and let me have a good look at you ... no, you haven't changed all that ... just as skinny as ever ... don't they feed you properly?" She kissed him then took his hand in hers. " Oh A.J., you've no idea how worried I've been all these years, not knowing where you were or what you were up to, only that you had got mixed up with a dangerous bunch of criminals ... didn't you stop to think what I might feel? And to be told that you were a wanted man, that you had killed innocent men and women ... tell me that wasn't true."

"Mum, they aren't criminals and in every war there are victims. But in any case that's all over. Hasn't uncle Julius told you?"

She shook her head slowly. "No ... maybe he wanted you to tell me." She was gazing deep into his eyes. He looked away.

"I've changed. I made a mistake, and I'm trying to make up for it by helping now to track them ... the members of the organization, I mean. But Mum, there's something I want you to do. Promise me you will ..."

"If I can, of course darling." She reached up and passed her fingers through his hair.

"Come with me this evening into the town. I hate these large dos and no one will notice we aren't there..."

She laughed. "You can't be serious! I've come from New York specially ... I can't not be there."

"Well then, just for half an hour, there's something I want to show you."

"Show it to me tomorrow, we're staying two or three days."

"It's urgent you come ... it's tonight or never ... I mean it'll have gone by tomorrow ... Jesus, Mum, you must do this for me, you've got to come, it's vital you do."

She cupped his cheeks with her hands. " A.J., what's the matter with you? I don't understand what's so pressing that I've got to ditch the President and a whole lot of important guests — not to mention Julius — right in the middle of a reception at which I'll be acting as official hostess? Be reasonable, darling. Ask me anything else ... "

For a moment a sense of panic gripped him. "Christ, why won't you ever do what I ask?" he shouted, jumping to his feet. But the instant of rage left him and he fell on his knees next to her. "Sorry Mum, I didn't mean that ... it's just that ... oh hell ... how will I get you off this bloody boat ... " Realizing that perhaps he had said too much he changed tactics again. "I mean, I've been cooped up on it for such ages, it would have been fun to go off for a while with you, perhaps just go to a restaurant the two of us."

"But we will," she said softly. "I promise you that. Now relax and tell me about yourself. Do you realize that it's eight years since we last saw each other and had a chance to talk ... "

"Hell, what's the use of it all," he wailed, blinking back tears of frustration. He'd have to find a way to get her off the bloody yacht; if it came to it, he would even throw her overboard. Turning away from her he added abruptly, "I've got to go," and ran from the cabin before she could say anything.

6.40 p.m. The library doors were thrown open and Maryanne entered followed by her husband. They were in dinner clothes, Michael in a white tuxedo and she in a stunningly beautiful pale blue crêpe-de-chine dress signed Valentino, while a magnificent necklace of diamonds and aquamarines glittered around her neck. Julius thought he had never seen her look so beautiful and told her so, then added, "are you sure you feel up to a whole evening of acting as hostess? Remember, if you feel tired, just disappear and rest. Paola can take over ..."

"Heaven's no, I feel great, and she'll have her hands full with the British, French and American ambassadors ... she knows them all personally, which reminds me, when will the guests start arriving?"

"For security reasons, quite early." He glanced at his watch. "In about 45 minutes. The President and his party are due on board at 8.30 and it will take a good hour for the others to get through the various police controls. A nuisance, but a very necessary measure these days. There are quite a few terrorists who'd give their right eye to get on the yacht and take a shot at the President, and me while they're about it." He saw her frown, "but there's little chance. The security police here are top rate and our own men are pretty good too. So you don't have to worry."

"Oh, I don't. It's only that every time one mentions terrorism I think of A.J. Stupid of me, I know, but I can't help it."

"It's natural you should," he said quietly, "until today you thought he still was one. I didn't want to tell you he was here with me till I was certain he really had changed, and I now believe he has. How did you find him?"

"Different, of course. Yet there's still something very young and vulnerable which I didn't expect after the life he has led."

"Did you manage to talk to him. Or get him to talk to you?"

"Very little. He came to my cabin a couple of hours ago, but only to tell me that he wanted me to go and have dinner with him alone ... he said there was something he wanted to show me on shore, and that he had to get off the yacht for a few hours as it was getting him down, being on board. Obviously I told him this evening was out of the question, and that got him into one of his tantrums. It was curious, as if getting off the boat was the only thing that really mattered to him."

"What did he say?"

"Nothing much. He muttered something like 'what's the use of it all', then disappeared."

"I wouldn't worry," Julius said, "he's a strange young man and probably seeing you suddenly like that, when he didn't expect to, upset him. Also being cooped up in here for weeks on end as he has, must be frustrating. But he can't go ashore tonight or any time, not for the moment. He knows it."

He frowned, then looked towards the door. Sophia had just walked in with her eleven year old son, Paul. The boy glanced around at the various grown-ups and, catching Julius' eye, ran towards him.

"So Mummy's letting you stay up for the party, is she?" he said giving him a kiss on the forehead.

"Yes, uncle Julius, because it's your birthday and because the President's coming. Maman says I can stay till nine, but you'll make her let me stay on a little won't you?"

"Nope, if Mummy says nine, nine it'll be. I'll see whether she'll let you stay for the fireworks, if you behave really well, but remember Paul, your mother's the one who decides, not me."

"When Papa was with us he always let me stay a little later."

A film of sadness misted Julius' eyes.

"I know, Paul, but it's different now," he said gently. Then he looked towards Sophia. She was talking to Laurrie who was listening to her but with an eye on the passageway outside. They formed a handsome couple, Julius thought, and well assorted. Maybe they would get together one day. Laurrie, he knew, was in love with Nelson's young widow and she needed a man with character and strength to help her get over the tragedy she had experienced. And she seemed to like him.

"Will you run over to the major and tell him I'd like to have a word with him," he said to the boy.

"You mean, Laurrie ? O.K. uncle Julius, but don't forget to tell Maman ... " He ran off to the other side of the room.

A moment later his godson was next to him.

"What's A.J. up to this evening?" Julius asked.

"Nothing in particular. He's off duty. I reckoned it was best if he wasn't seen around. I told him to stay in his cabin or on the lower deck."

"O.K., but keep an eye on him every now and then. He told Maryanne he wanted to go ashore and he's quite capable of trying to."

"Don't worry, no one is allowed off without my authority. He can try till he's blue in the face but he won't be able to, and if he attempts to dive overboard he'll get picked up immediately."

7.30 p.m. The guests were beginning to arrive. They got out of their cars and went through a police checkpoint, then walked fifty metres between banks of flame red hibiscus and pink oleanders to a moving companion way which lifted them to the yacht's middle deck. There they passed through a carefully concealed metal detector and an X-ray screen, controlled by security men in dinner jackets, and emerged onto the glassed in area where a seven piece orchestra was playing old musical favourites of the 40s and 50s. They were offered a drink and were announced over a loudspeaker while one of Julius' secretaries guided them towards the right-hand sweep of deck, where he and Maryanne were waiting to welcome them.

They were then accompanied to Paola, standing at the entrance to the huge drawing room, where other members of Julius' entourage were ready to entertain them.

By 8 p.m., when more than half the guests had filed past them, Julius suggested to Maryanne she go and rest. She shook her head and smiled.

"No, honestly, I'm not tired. When they're all here and the President has arrived, maybe then I'll disappear for a few minutes."

8.35 p.m. A.J. stared through the porthole at the crowds gathered along the harbour's waterfront. Suddenly there was a chorus of shouts followed by clapping and he reckoned the country's President Hosni Moubarak had arrived. Minutes later he heard the orchestra strike up the Egyptian national anthem. He glanced at his watch. He had just under half an hour in which to act. At 9.15 the doors to the covered front deck would slide open and Julius would escort the Presidential party to the table of honour. Before that happened, he and his mother had to be off the yacht.

It wouldn't be easy, but with luck and with the help of the gun hidden in George Christofides' wheel-chair he would manage it. He had to.

He slipped on a white shirt and black trousers, a ready-made black tie and a white cotton coat, combed his hair and then left his cabin. He made his way to George's suite.

He told Tom, who was preparing the invalid for the reception, that he would take him up and that he could have the evening off. For three minutes he sat waiting until George was lifted onto the wheelchair, and when Tom left the room, he turned the key in the door's lock then moved towards the cripple. Who did a curious thing; he backed the chair against the wall.

"What the hell are you up to?" A.J. muttered as he made to remove George's fingers from the command button.

With the chair in that position he could neither reach into the cavity to get hold of a pistol hidden there, nor get behind it to guide it towards the door. He caught George's eye and a moment of panic gripped him. The man knew something.

George had regained the use of three of his fingers and had developed a considerable strength in them. They now bolted themselves onto the arm control, and it took A.J. nearly a minute to wrench them away. "I'll kill you if you try that again," he whispered furiously.

The chair moved forwards and he was able to crouch and get hold of the pistol and the back-up remote control detonator apparatus. He slipped this in his pocket and pointed the gun at George's temple.

"And stop that noise," he added menacingly.

George was grunting, his only form of vocal expression. It sounded like an animal in distress, and could easily be heard by anyone passing outside. With the steel of the pistol barrel against his temple he became silent, and A.J. got to the door, unlocked it and drew it open. He was about to guide the chair into the passage when a form suddenly barred the way.

Maryanne was fretting about her son. He had not gone back to see her as he had said he would, nor had he come to the family gathering in the library. She decided that, as soon as she could, she would slip away and go and find him.

So, while Julius and Paola were looking after the Egyptian President and Madame Moubarak, Maryanne excused herself and went to look for Laurrie. She found him at the head of the main stairs leading to the lower deck.

"Do you know where A.J. is?" she asked.

"I'd say in his cabin. If you like, I'll have him brought here."

"No. Just tell me where it is.'"

"If you turn right at the bottom of the stairs, it's the fourth door on the right ... the one before last. But he may be in George's, he's got into the habit of wheeling him about as he did this morning. When you see him, would you mind telling him to come and report to me ... that's if he's not with George."

She found his cabin but it was empty. So she retraced her steps and came across Tom, the male nurse.

"Have you seen A.J. by any chance?"

"Yes, Madam, he's with Sir George."

"Which is his cabin?"

"It's at the end of this corridor. I'll accompany you there."

She shook her head. "That won't be necessary?"

She reached the door and was about to knock on it when it was opened. In front of her was A.J., pistol in hand, and the pistol was pointed at George.

At that moment George roared with the fury and despair of a trapped lion.

Maryanne cried, "for God's sake A.J.!"

But the killer instinct had him press the trigger without his even realizing it.

George's head lolled to one side and blood burst through his shattered skull. Maryanne screamed. A.J. grabbed her by an arm, dragged her into the room and slammed the door, locking it again. Then he turned and stared at his mother. She was whispering words he couldn't understand "You've killed your own father. You've killed him A.J. ... your father.

Do you understand me?" Her eyes were unseeing, turned inwards, as if searching within herself for the reason of her son's horrendous act.

"I had to do it Mum, don't you see, and he'd have died in a few minutes in any case. Everyone here will. That's why you and I have got to get out. The whole boat's going to blow up … "

His words seemed not to get through to her. "You've killed your father," she kept on saying.

He took her by the shoulders and began shaking her. "You've got to follow me and get out before they stop us. The dining room table is dynamite and in half an hour it'll explode. We've got no time to lose … "

There was a banging on the door. It was Laurrie. "Open up, A.J. or I'll break the door down," he shouted. "I know you're in there."

A.J. looked wildly about him, then at his mother.

"Sorry, Mum, it's the only way … " and he stuck the revolver against her waist. "You bet I'm here, you bastard, but so's my mother," he yelled. "Shoot, and you'll hit her."

Turning to Maryanne, he pleaded, "don't be frightened, it'll all be O.K., I swear. It's the only way to get out … "

At that moment, two men the other side threw themselves at the door and it burst open. They almost fell onto the dead George. Behind them Laurrie pointed his gun at A.J.

"Give me that gun before it kills someone else," he said quietly.

"Get out of the way, Laurrie, and tell those other bastards to keep clear. I'm taking my mother ashore, d'you understand!"

"You won't get away with it."

"Drop that gun and tell the others to as well!"

Laurrie looked at Maryanne. She was turning to face her son. Still as if in a trance she was shaking her head slowly. "You've killed him … a helpless invalid … you've killed your own father."

Suddenly the listlessness in her was gone. She straightened, her eyes blazing. "You monster!" she screamed and throwing her hand up, hit him across the face. The gun went off and she sank slowly to her knees.

"Mum, Christ, mum, I didn't mean to … Oh God no … " he cried.

Laurrie took aim and fired. The bullet hit him between the

eyes. He staggered and fell backwards as Laurrie rushed across to Maryanne.

"The table, the dining room table, he said it was dynamite ... do something ... " she murmured. Then she lost consciousness.

"Quick, get Doctor Gautier but don't let anyone know," Laurrie threw at one of his men, and to the male nurse who had come to the room, "take Mrs Lauber to the infirmary, if she can be moved. Otherwise do what you can for her."

He stood up and was about to stride out of the cabin when his eye caught sight of an object which had fallen out of A.J.'s pocket. He picked it up and his jaw muscles tightened. That little toy could detonate a bomb from a radius of two kilometres. What Maryanne had said must be true. And from experience, he knew that a timer would also be set. The remote control system would be used only if the timer went wrong. There was not a second to lose.

He raced to the deck above, calling three of his men to follow and to another to get a motorboat round to the front of the yacht, then rushed to the covered fore deck where dinner was to be served.

"Take everything off that table," he ordered, "and get it overboard and on to the launch." He turned to the surprised stewards, "replace it quick with two trestle ones."

He ran to the radio room and got through to the head of the Egyptian security police, warning him that a motor boat was being loaded with material and mustn't be intercepted when it left the harbour, orders from the President. After which, he went back to the main reception room and made his way over to Julius.

"May I have a word with you?" he asked, drawing him aside. "I'm afraid Maryanne has had to be taken to the infirmary."

"Heavens, it's not serious I hope. I'll go to her immediately." Laurrie laid a restraining hand on his arm. "No, it wouldn't help. Christian is looking after her and has given her something to make her sleep."

Julius must not know in what a critical state Maryanne was, he decided, nor that both George and A.J. were dead. And no one must suspect that the President and the 200 guests had come within minutes of death by the hand of their host's adopted son.

Julius nodded. "Tell Christian I want to know the moment she comes to. It's my fault in a way, I should have realized she wasn't well. Get A.J. to her, she was fretting about him earlier on."

"Sure ... oh, there's one other thing. We've had to change the main table, so don't be surprised when you see a different arrangement."

Julius raised an eyebrow but said nothing.

Laurrie hurried out to the covered foredeck where stewards were covering a makeshift board with an embroidered cloth to hide the trestle legs. Through the window he could see the derrick swinging the huge table across the deck rails. He stepped outside and watched it being lowered onto a launch. Then he called to the sailor aboard it, "take it through the harbour opening and switch on the automatic pilot. Head it out to sea, and as soon as you can, lose it. Dive and swim to the fort."

"You mean I've got to abandon the launch?"

"Exactly that. And hurry, you're sitting on dynamite. Get cracking before you become part of the fireworks display."

He walked back into the glassed in foredeck. All was set, flowers, silver and the exquisite Sèvres dinner service. No one, not even the Alexandrian himself, would suspect that only six minutes earlier the beautiful arrangement, fit for any head of state, concealed one of the most murderous devices the terrorists had dreamed up so far.

At exactly 9.45 a flash lit the distant horizon, but no one on the yacht noticed it. Only the radio operator murmured to an assistant, "curious, there seems to have been an explosion out at sea. Can't have been summer lightning."

The spectacle Julius had reserved for his guests and the whole of Alexandria began at 11 p.m. The yacht left its causeway berth and moved to the middle of the harbour. Suddenly five powerful projectors were beamed on it, swathing it in a magic luminosity.

Against the dark background of the harbour's fort, it stood as a glistening symbol of the Alexandrian's success. Then came the fireworks which, for forty five minutes, held the crowds on the waterfront speechless with enchantment. Never, for as long as they could remember, had such magnificent entertainment been offered them. And it wasn't only their eyes which were filled with wonder; there was food also for their stomachs. One hundred itinerant vendors distributed *foul medammis, kefta* and the flat Egyptian bread free to the 50,000 men, women and children who fought their way to them. There were sweets too for the children, thrown by sackfuls from a helicopter.

On board the yacht, the guests went to the dance floors and moved to the music of two orchestras at each end of the 86 metre deck. Every twenty minutes Laurrie would come to Julius and whisper "not yet, *padrino*, she's still under sedatives."

At a little past midnight the Presidential party left. But before, Julius and the Head of the State of Egypt walked up onto the top deck and surveyed Alexandria and its crowds. The search lights went out and a single one was beamed on the two men. A roar of applause went up from the people nearest the yacht and was caught by the multitude like a tidal wave of rejoicing and thanks. The President was in white, while Julius in midnight blue and the two great men of the occasion appeared like a dual manifestation of the city's ancient Pharaohs.

And for a moment which seemed timeless, Julius was once again an Alexandrian, and nostalgically proud to be one.

He filled his lungs with the intoxicating night air and stretched a hand towards the city of his youth as if to grasp it. But a whiff from the nearby fish market reached him with its gut gripping stench, and the moment of pride vanished.

Midnight. Julius stared down at Maryanne then looked questioningly at Christian Gautier.

"I've managed to stop the haemorrhage and her condition is stationary. But it's still critical, as the bullet damaged the kidney. We couldn't move her so the major organized for the best surgeon to be flown here from Cairo. He's expected in minutes."

"Thanks, Christian, I know you have done your best."

How peacefully she slept, he thought. Curiously he felt no terrible distress at the sight of his daughter stretched in a no man's land between life and death. The reality of the triple tragedy had blasted emotion from him and with it the insidious luxury of despair. He had listened to Laurrie's account of what had happened and then had gone to see

George and A.J. They were stretched side by side on the twin beds in the cabin where the killing had taken place. His son shot dead by his grandson and his grandson shot dead by his godson! And the ghoulish melodrama might include his daughter killed by her son! But still the full implications of the human disaster had not revealed themselves.

Gazing at the two bodies he fought to keep his sanity. There was a moment when he felt the rage and chagrin in him about to explode with a terrifying rending of his psyche. He gripped onto Laurrie and let himself be led to the library, where a soothing numbness froze all feelings.

The minutes ticked into hours and the warm Egyptian dawn stretched leisurely across the city and the sea. A steward brought him the strong sweet tea he had drunk for as long as he could remember. He struggled against the flood of memories, but as he sipped at his cup he let himself slip into one; back to that morning in the distant past when he had sat in George Wirsa's library for the first time.

Suddenly, he stood up and called for Laurrie. "I want to go ashore, and I'd like you to come with me."

Before leaving he went to the infirmary. Maryanne was still asleep, and the surgeon was preparing to operate a second time.

"If we manage to save her, and I believe we will, it will also be due to Doctor Gautier's help and the remarkable equipment you have here, Mr Caspar."

"Make sure she lives and I'll give you the best operating theatre in the Middle East," Julius said, then left.

As he was driven through the still familiar streets towards Moharrem Bey, he turned to Laurrie and asked, "did she realize it was A.J. who shot George? That her son had killed Jemima's father?"

"I'm afraid so. But probably she was too shocked to know what really happened. She repeated several times 'you've killed your own father' before hitting him. That's what must have caused the shooting. It was an accident. I don't think he meant to shoot her. But obviously she wasn't really conscious of what she was saying ... "

Julius closed his eyes. NO NO! A.J. the fruit of incest? It couldn't be. A lead-like weariness hunched his shoulders. How brutal could fate be! Not even this ultimate, outrageous secret had been spared him.

When the car drew up at the iron gates of the mansion he sat for a moment in silence, gazing around at the endless slums which now surrounded it.

"Do you want to go in?" Laurrie asked.

Julius nodded. "For a last time."

The chauffeur rang the gate bell and a form emerged from a door by the garage. It hurried to the gates and, after an exchange of words, flung them open. A woman appeared, wrapped in black, and handed the watchman a key, while the car drove in and parked in front of the main steps and the overhanging glass and wrought iron awning. Julius noted one of the glass panels was cracked. He glanced at the garden. It was still tended, but most of the flowers were dead. Then the front door creaked open and the servant bowed to Julius.

"May Allah be with you and your family, *gnabel howager*," he said reaching to kiss his hand.

Julius removed it quickly and walked past him.

God had forsaken him and had taken his family from him. He was accursed.

He paused in the hall and his eyes followed the great sweep of the stairs up to the landing, wavered, and travelled down them again as if accompanying a presence. Then he walked towards the library while the servant threw open windows and shutters.

"No," he cried, when they reached it, "leave us. I want to be alone." For a moment he hesitated on the threshold.

"Wait for me, will you," he said to Laurrie, "I won't be long."

He went in and closed the door behind him. In the partial darkness lit by strips of light from the shutters, he could make out the contours of the heavy furniture, the empty bookshelves and the brass chandelier, all static symbols of a bygone age and suddenly void of meaning. He felt himself a stranger in a family tomb which was not his and where the air was stale and no longer musty with memories. He shivered and stepped back to the door. An irremediable emptiness was within him and it softened the edges of bitterness. Marguerite was gone, taking with her for ever the fruits of their forbidden love. He had lived too much in the past, too much in the memory of a love which was damned.

He shut the door behind him and without thinking turned

the key in the lock. With that movement, he put a lifetime of emotions from him.

When the car drove through the gates he did not look back; Marguerite, her parents, their villa and the city in which they had lived had to be forgotten if he were to pass his remaining years in a semblance of peace. He would leave Alexandria and turn his eyes only to the future. There was still so much he had to do, so much he had to prepare for those who would come after him.

One day little Paul, his great grandson, would inherit one of the world's largest fortunes, the combined Caspar and Christofides empires. At least in him, the material reconciliation of a senseless family feud would finally take place. Family? No, George had never been his son just as A.J. had never been his grandson. He had no family. Any illusions he might have had, had vanished in George Wirsa's library. Helen had won; she had been right, he could never be one of them. And the tragedies which had struck at her daughter, grandson and greatgrandsons were hers, not his.

He shook his head slowly. No, he couldn't cheat with reality. He might blame Helen for the evil which had been in A.J. but not for the channelling of it into a killer force. Others were the culprits. A rage swept over him, tensing every muscle. Whoever they were, those ugly-souled men who had manipulated the youngster, he would get at them. He would spend his money and the years left to him, fighting them.

The rage gave way to a fleeting weariness. He knew it was the lost cause of a lost man he was setting himself.

Three hours later, the yacht glided out of the harbour like a glistening white swan, beautiful and enigmatic. The crowds watched it in silence, wondering when it would return bringing again a moment of wonder.

On the top deck Julius stood alone, gazing out at sea, his back turned on the place of his birth. A man joined him.

"I wanted you to know that she'll pull through. It was touch and go, but the second operation was a success. She's O.K." Michael Lauber said gripping his arm.

Julius stared up into the heavens and whispered, "thank you."

On his own again, he reached under his shirt for the silver cross and, taking it in both his hands, kissed it. He bent his head, and for the first time in sixty years repeated the Pater Noster.

Slowly he turned to say farewell to Alexandria. His eyes took in the harbour front with its chaotic traffic and bedraggled buildings and followed the great Corniche trailing away like a faded ribbon between beaches and apartment blocks, and he strove to free himself of the subtle spell which the city still cast over him. As he did so, the words of the poet Cavafy came to mind:

'When, at the hour of midnight
an invisible choir is suddenly heard passing
with exquisite music, with voices —
do not lament your fortune that at last subsides,
your life's work that has failed,
your schemes that have proved illusions.
But, like a man prepared, like a brave man,
bid farewell to her, to Alexandria who is departing.
Above all, do not delude yourself, do not say it was a dream,

that your ear was mistaken.
Do not condescend to such empty hopes.
Like a man for long prepared, like a brave man,
like a man who was worthy of such a city,
go to the window firmly and listen with emotion,
but not with the prayers and complaints of the Coward,
                              [Ah supreme rapture!]
listen to the notes, to the exquisite instruments of the mystic choir
 and bid farewell to her, to Alexandria you are losing.'